THE SANDYCOVE SUNSET SWIMMERS

SIÂN O'GORMAN

Boldwood

First published in Great Britain in 2023 by Boldwood Books Ltd.

Cover Design by Head Design Ltd

Cover photography: Shutterstock and iStock

A CIP catalogue record for this book is available from the British Library.

Paperback ISBN 978-1-80426-998-5

Hardback ISBN 978-1-80426-993-0

Large Print ISBN 978-1-80426-994-7

Ebook ISBN 978-1-80426-991-6

Kindle ISBN 978-1-80426-992-3

Audio CD ISBN 978-1-80426-999-2

MP3 CD ISBN 978-1-80426-996-1

Digital audio download ISBN 978-1-80426-990-9

Boldwood Books Ltd
23 Bowerdean Street
London SW6 3TN
www.boldwoodbooks.com

For my dad

It's always ourselves we find in the sea...

e. e. cummings

1

Saying 'yes' to *life* was actually the very last thing I wanted to do, but when I was cornered by Mum's best friend Lorraine at Mum's retirement party, somehow I got roped in to the latest of Lorraine's hare-brained schemes.

Lorraine's front room had been decked out with balloons and streamers for the occasion. There was a bunch of balloons with 'Sorry You're Leaving' and a life-size photograph of Mum in her swimsuit, taken on one of their holidays together. 'Lorraine!' Mum had said, when she'd seen it. 'For God's sake!'

'You look fabulous, Annie,' Lorraine had replied to Mum. 'Like a film star. If you've got it, flaunt it.' Lorraine topped up her own wine glass to the brim. 'And, Annie, your problem is, you hide yourself away. You need to live a bit larger, now you're retired. You've got to say yes more. "No" is not in my vocabulary, which is why I have led such a full life.' Lorraine turned to me. 'You too, Catríona.'

After leaving nursing after forty years, Mum was looking forward to doing nothing, she had said. And I was doing fine, thank you very much, living alone in my lovely house, my best friends Sinéad and Becca close by, and I had an interesting and varied job as a reporter on a little-watched Sunday morning farming television show called *Farming Weekly*. Recently, I'd even had a brief moment of social media fame when a cow had knocked into me while I was trying to interview a farmer. I'd ended up slipping over on some mud and then slaloming through dung, across the farmyard, shrieking, all caught on camera. My producer, Mike, had jettisoned my dignity in favour of entertaining the nation and the clip went viral.

'It will make great television!' he'd said once he'd stopped laughing. 'Just to see you, Catríona Jones, our intrepid roving reporter, falling about... the mud... the cow dung, your face!' And as there weren't many laughs to be had in the world of farming, obsessed as we were with tractors, the climate and EU subsidies, the piece made the final cut. I was hoping to return to interviewing people about serious farming issues and put this behind me, but Mike still couldn't speak to me without laughing. 'I can't...' he would say, already starting to laugh again, 'it was just when you... and then the... and you... arms flapping... screaming...' He would have to take a moment to compose himself.

And so, here we were at Mum's retirement 'do' on a Friday night in July, hosted by Lorraine – who never needed any encouragement for a social gathering – when the 'yes' plan was proposed.

Lorraine lived just around the corner from Mum and Dad, and I lived around another corner from them, in Sandycove, a village, just along the coast from Dublin's thriving cosmopolitan city centre. It was a world away from the traffic, the pollution and all the people. I could never imagine living anywhere else than here, where the sky sparkled with rainbows, where there were four seasons in an hour, a place where people and the sea were entwined, from sailing and paddleboarding to swimming and kayaking. Walking the seafront every evening was an obsession, and at this time of year, the end of July, the weather was warm, the days stretched like elastic, and the whole village was upended as people lived their lives outdoors – unlike in winter when people hurried from shop to shop.

Lorraine – the kind of woman for whom there was no such thing as too many accessories – was often caught up in 'adventures'. Mum and Lorraine were the exact opposites, but Lorraine made Mum laugh, and Mum was the grounding influence that Lorraine desperately needed. She had married a waiter once, after falling in love over a sun-baked week in Kuşadası in Turkey. Another time, she'd chained herself to the railings of Dunnes supermarket when they discontinued their own-brand Prosecco. And there was that day a couple of years ago, when Lorraine was pulled aboard a float at Dublin's Pride festival and spent the next eight hours dancing around to disco classics. Mum had spotted her on the news that night. 'Is that Lorraine?' she'd said, squinting at the TV. 'Janey Mac, it *is* Lorraine!'

'If she's looking for husband number five,' said Dad, 'she's on the wrong lorry.'

Resisting Lorraine was something Mum had never mastered. Mum was the one Lorraine had called from the cell of the Garda station to pick her up once they'd managed to cut off the handcuffs. Mum was the one who had to drive to Belfast when Lorraine had her handbag stolen, and it was Mum who had organised all four of Lorraine's hen nights over the years.

'It's just saying "yes" to everything...' said Lorraine. 'And I'm challenging everyone I know to live large and embrace everything the world has to offer, just by saying "yes". Now, vino? Who's for more vino? Red, white, rosé or sparkling?'

Dad, standing beside me, said quietly in my ear, 'Pity she said "yes" to husband number three. And to carrying that suitcase for that "charming" man to Ibiza that time.'

Dad had been retired for the last five years and had already perfected its subtle art. Never the most gregarious of men, in this post-work life, he took his hobby of fixing old electronics to a whole new level by retreating full-time to his shed and made it an obsession. Every time I called in, there was something electrical and ancient – from radios to old heaters to vintage record players – left in the front porch, ready to be fixed or collected by the owner.

Lorraine pointed a finger at me. 'You, Cat, *you* need to get out more and do more... you do nothing but stay in. You're wasting the best years of your life!'

'Lorraine!' Mum gave her a sharp elbow in the ribs.

'It's true!' As my godmother, Lorraine had always felt able to speak her mind and probably would have preferred a slightly wilder god-daughter to go drinking with and on weekends to Palma Nova, if she'd had the choice. 'We *all* need to be more open to life. You too, Annie.'

'I've just retired from nursing after forty fecking years,' said Mum. 'I want to put my feet up.'

Lorraine gave her a look and I watched Mum's resolve dissolve in front of our very eyes.

'Okay, then,' Mum said. 'I'm in. How long do I have to say "yes" for? And what do I have to say "yes" to?'

'A month,' said Lorraine. 'To everything. You too, Cat.'

Now it was my turn to try to resist her powers.

'But there's nothing I want to say "yes" to,' I countered, as Lorraine poured more wine into our glasses. 'Can I say "maybe"?'

'It's just "yes",' she said, sounding weary. 'Say yes to life. For one month only. That is all. For four short weeks, you both' – she fixed us both with a look – 'just say "yes" to everything.'

'Everything?' quailed Mum.

Lorraine nodded. 'Everything. It has changed my life, it really has.'

I was already shaking my head. 'No' was my go-to answer to

everything and it had never let me down. Maybe I had missed out on a few opportunities over the years, but it had kept me alive. And sane. And there were a few things that I was glad I'd said 'no' to. PJ Doyle, my ex-boyfriend, was one of them. A handsome, successful chef, who was often featured in the Sunday supplements glaring menacingly with a meat cleaver in his hands or in bloodstained chef's whites. Short of stature and, it turned out, he had an even shorter fuse. He would become almost comically hysterical if I accidentally used one of his special knives to chop an onion or mentioned 'veganism'. I'd said a very firm 'no' to him, when, on a weekend away, I'd had enough of his rantings and ravings, and I flew home. And blocked him.

'It's a month,' said Lorraine. 'Are you two so scared of life that you can't do something for a month?'

Mum and I looked at each other. A month didn't sound *that* long. I had a bag of salad in my fridge which had lasted longer. I could, I thought, just say 'yes' to nice things, such as seeing my best friends Becca and Sinéad more, or 'yes' to eating more ice cream, or to lie-ins and long baths, and to early nights, to reading an extra chapter of my book in bed.

'Okay,' I said. 'I will.'

Mum nodded. 'Me too.'

Mum and I smiled at each other.

'I was thinking of saying yes to another glass of wine,' said Mum. 'Maybe...'

Lorraine rolled her eyes. 'The Good Friday Agreement was more easily accepted. Now, Annie, what I'd like you to do, as your first assignment, is a parachute jump. In aid of the hospice.'

Mum gulped. Lorraine knew the hospice was Mum's weak point after Uncle Paul was minded amazingly and lovingly by the staff there.

'And yours...' Lorraine looked at me. 'Yours is...'

'Having an extra glass of wine?' I suggested, hopefully. 'Some more crisps?'

'Yes, you can do that,' said Lorraine, 'but I have just the thing for you.' She had spotted someone. 'Margaret! Margaret!'

A tall woman, in a peach jacket and skirt, with hair that looked as though it had been cut with a blunt scissors, came over. 'Hello, Lorraine... lovely party...'

'This is Margaret,' Lorraine said, 'my next-door neighbour... Margaret swims every day in the Forty Foot. She has a tribe...'

The Forty Foot was our local bathing place in Sandycove. A small, craggy promontory of rock, jutting out to the sea, smoothed by the feet of the thousands of intrepid cold-water explorers. I was not one of them.

'A tribe?' said Margaret, who looked like the last woman on earth who would have a tribe. 'Oh, you mean the Forty Footers? Yes, we've been going to there every evening... winter, summer... for years now.'

Oh no. I could tell by Lorraine's face that this was my challenge.

'Cat is going to join you,' she said to Margaret. 'She wants to try new things and expand her horizons.'

Margaret smiled at me. 'Well, isn't that lovely? And, of course, come down to the Forty Foot and join us. We're a friendly group, I promise. And we're always up for a chat afterwards.'

'I am not sure...' I said.

'She's doing it,' insisted Lorraine. 'It's a month. That's all. Say "yes" and try different things.'

'It's very good for the head,' said Margaret. 'It's helped me, a great deal. We've all lost people... or some of us find solace in the sea for other reasons, or it helps with stress. When you're in the sea, everything drifts away, all your problems, and for those ten minutes or so, it's just you and the waves.'

'Waves?' It sounded terrifying.

Margaret nodded. 'And currents and tides and seaweed... and even seals. That's the joy of it.'

'Seals?' After my experience with the cow, I wanted to be as far from large mammals as possible.

'We're a mixed bunch,' continued Margaret. 'There's Nora, Brenda, Dolores and Malachy. And we just meet every day, as the sun begins to set. Nora was the first – she's swum there for years. And I started going when my mother passed away. Malachy was always there on his own, and we just got chatting to him... Dolores comes for her health...' She gave a nod. 'And Brenda is one of those people who minds herself. We've all had a few knocks in life, and it's become a very important part of our day. A few minutes of total immersion...' She laughed to herself. 'Literally. Total dedication to being out of one's corporeal self.'

'In other words, just swimming,' said Lorraine. She looked at me. 'You agreed, Cat? God, anyone would think I was asking you to join the army or something actually challenging. Sea swimming is no big deal. And didn't you say you wanted to get out of your comfort zone, move your body, feel the cold, face the dangers of the deep...?'

'You said that,' I replied. Surely, Lorraine didn't mean we had to do something we didn't want to. She wouldn't *actually* make Mum do a parachute jump? I didn't *really* have to swim. In the *sea*? With *seals*?

Lorraine looked hurt. 'All I am trying to do is help the two women I love most in the world, you and your mum, just broaden your horizons, help you get more out of life... and at the first hurdle you both let me down...'

I had never been the most confident of people. I mean, I was fine. I didn't exactly suffer from social anxiety. I could make my reports for *Farming Weekly*, but I would never watch them back. In the same way, I would never talk in public or have a social media account. I kept a low profile as much as possible. I wasn't wild or exciting and I didn't like to do anything scary. Lorraine was lucky; she wasn't intimidated by anything.

'We're going to really try,' Mum said, 'aren't we, Cat? But, Lorraine, you know Cat is always cold... and I'm... well, I don't want to fall through the sky, plummeting towards earth...'

Lorraine fixed us with a look. 'Do you want to spend the rest of your lives being afraid, or do you want to grab it by the horns and ride it until it flings you off?'

I excused myself and was in the kitchen searching for crisps when Mum found me.

'Are you okay?' she said.

'Just had to get away from Lorraine,' I replied. 'She's so controlling.'

'Her heart's in the right place,' said Mum. 'And she does have a point. When was the last time either of us did anything out of our comfort zone?'

'But that's the whole point of a comfort zone,' I said. 'It's comfortable. Why would anyone do something that wasn't?'

Mum sighed. 'I know,' she replied, 'but she's right. I mean, is this all there is? I am waking up tomorrow morning and there is literally nothing to do. I mean, I could start decluttering, but am I going to declutter the house for the rest of my life? And yes, I know I said I was looking forward to doing nothing, but I don't really want nothing. I want something. I want to have fun and to meet new people and not fade away while wearing a dressing gown and slippers. I want to be *out* there.'

'But a *parachute* jump?'

'That won't happen,' said Mum, firmly. 'But there are other things I could do... I don't know, like an exercise class or going on an art tour or walking barefoot in the garden.'

'Wow, you're really aiming high,' I said.

Mum laughed. 'I've heard barefoot is very good for you. Grounding. But what about you?' she said. 'You're single...'

'Happily so.' I shuddered when I thought of PJ, glad to have all of that in the past, dead and buried. I loved my single life, the big bed all to myself, not needing to run anything by anyone else, being able to please just one person – me. Living my small life.

I stopped. It *was* a small life. When was the last time I had done anything big? When was the last time I had done something which was exhilarating or exciting?

'But I think...' Mum paused.

'Go on...' I braced myself for some of Mum's advice.

'Well, are you happy?'

'Perfectly.'

'Are you living life to the full?'

'Like Lorraine is?'

'She's living life for four people,' said Mum. 'I mean living enough for you? I mean, are you satisfied? Content? Do you feel that you are grasping every opportunity?'

No, I wasn't. There was that presenting job for a new science series I'd been offered last month to which I'd said 'no' because it was just too scary and I didn't feel as though I had enough experience. And there was the walk over a mountain in Wicklow that one of my colleagues organised that I hadn't gone on because they were all so much fitter than me. And I'd even said 'no' to that weekend away to a posh hotel in County Clare that Becca had arranged because I would be the only single person there. And the trip to Sardinia, with Sinéad and Conor and their three-year-old, Rory. I'd said 'no' to that as well, because I said I had too much work on, but really I had just lost confidence for some reason.

'No,' I admitted to Mum. 'No, I don't. But I don't know how to be out there more. I don't know what to do. And it seems so silly, doesn't it?'

She shook her head. 'Not at all,' she said. 'I feel exactly the same. But we can do it together? Just a month?'

'Yes to everything,' I said. 'For one month only.'

'But not,' she said, 'to a parachute jump. That's a step too far.'

'You mean, a jump too far?'

'Exactly,' she said. 'Now, did you find those crisps?'

THE GIRLS!

Becca: Anyone awake? Haven't slept at all. Need decent coffee. Fancy meeting in the cafe?
Sinéad: Rory and I will be there.
Me: Me too.
Becca: How was your mum's retirement do?
Me: Fine. Bit worse for wear. Have been set a challenge. See you soon.
Becca: In an hour?
Sinéad: Suits me.
Me: Me too xxx

2

The following day was a bright and blue-skied Saturday and I spent the day feeling a little worse for wear after all the wine that Lorraine had plied us with. In the afternoon, I met my best friends, Becca and Sinéad, in Alison's café in Sandycove. Alison's was a small, cool little place, all Scandinavian plywood, a lovely seating nook at the back with benches and large black-and-white photographs of the surrounding coastline on the walls.

They had both already arrived when I got there. There was Sinéad's blonde ponytail bobbing as she wiped down the perfectly clean table with anti-bac wipes, while her three-year-old, Rory, played with some Lego. Sinéad had given up work three years earlier, her maternity leave stretching endlessly on, and ever since she'd had Rory, her perfectionism had gone into overdrive. There she was, scouring Rory's chair with the wipes and anything else he might potentially touch, including the small vase of roses on the table.

She and Rory were always both immaculately turned out: Rory in T-shirt and shorts and socks and sandals; Sinéad permanently dressed in designer leggings and hoodie. She'd always been the most academically conscientious out of the three of us, sailing from college straight into a big accountancy firm and heading towards being made a partner. No one had expected her to take motherhood so seriously, but her life began and ended with Rory. 'I'm a mother now,' she'd told us in the maternity hospital, in an oxytocin-fuelled fug, clutching her precious newborn to her breast. 'I will never work again,' she'd vowed. 'I am going to stay at home forever, just me and Rory.'

Becca, on the other hand, was never interested in having a child and had always taken school and college work far less seriously than Sinéad, except when she'd discovered events management after a part-time job in the first year of university. She'd switched courses to marketing and even before she'd graduated she had set up her own company, Ignite, which had started with planning small launches and had grown to be one of the most successful boutique events planners in the country. She wouldn't have been caught dead in athleisure, however, and was never out of expensive jeans, cool trainers and artfully faded T-shirts. Her hair which, growing up, had been a halo of frizzy, dark waves, was now laboriously and daily straightened to a sleek, glossy mane. She always wore red lipstick and little other make-up.

She was eyeing Sinéad's meticulous and liberal sanitising.

'You've missed a bit, Sinéad,' Becca said. 'You haven't done the ceiling.'

Sinéad rolled her eyes. Becca was always teasing her about how much she obsessed with making sure Rory existed in the kind of environment in which you could operate on an open wound. Sinéad used to have a normal attitude to germs but now believed bacteria was the enemy. As far as we could tell, Rory was the cleanest baby that had ever lived, existing in a little bacteria-free bubble. Also, he had not left Sinéad's side for a single moment since he'd been born, three years earlier. They co-slept in the double bed, while her husband, Conor, slumbered in Rory's toddler bed. Rory only played with other children if Sinéad was able to vouch they were fully inoculated and that their parents followed similar cleaning regimes.

'She's like Spider-Man,' Becca had said. 'Constantly poised to fight off evil. She needs to unclench. Let the child go and live. Get filthy. Play with worms in the garden.'

Becca had always said children were boring. She made a concession for Rory because his curly hair and blue eyes hardened even her heart, but other than him, children held no appeal. 'Too busy having a life,' she'd always say if anyone asked if she wanted children. 'Too busy having fun.'

Sinéad's only fun, these days, as far as I could tell, was meeting us for a walk or a coffee. Rory wasn't allowed to go to a playgroup or even go to nursery because Sinéad had read about one from which all the children developed E. coli. 'They are a petri dish of germs,' she had explained. 'Rory's not going anywhere until his immune system is robust enough.'

In the café, I sat down beside Becca, who had been drawing a picture using Rory's crayons.

'Be careful,' Becca said. 'Sinéad will anti-bac you if you stay still for long enough.'

'You have heard of the concept of germs, Becca?' said Sinéad, picking up Becca's purse and giving it a once-over with the wipes. 'They're everywhere. And also lethal.'

Becca took back her purse. 'Thank you for that, Sinéad,' she said, smiling and resuming her drawing. 'If you hadn't cleaned it, I might have *died*.'

I leaned down and kissed the top of Rory's little blonde head. 'How is my little godson?'

'Hello, Auntie Cat,' he said, putting the piece of Lego into his mouth, before Sinéad quickly pulled it out again and wiped it.

'*Our* godson,' said Becca. 'Remember, we *share* him.'

'I thought you didn't like children,' I said.

'Only Rory,' she replied. 'When he's old enough, I'll bring him to music festivals and teach him how to drink shots of sambuca. But until then,' she looked at Rory, 'you'll have to stay with the grown-ups and be boring. Sorry, kid.'

Rory smiled at her. 'I like your drawing,' he said.

'It's a depiction of what's going on in my brain,' she told him, earnestly. 'Just a big scribble.'

Rory nodded. 'I like it,' he said.

There was no reason for Becca to change her life, because things were going brilliantly well for her. She was happily cohabiting with her long-time boyfriend, Ryan, and lived in a gorgeous house facing the sea and was always going on weekends away.

Alison came over to take our orders.

'I'll have a soya decaf and a gluten-free muffin,' said Sinéad, 'and an organic, locally sourced apple juice.'

'Naturally,' said Alison, as Becca gave me a look. Dairy and gluten were also on Sinéad's hit list.

'Flat white, thanks,' Becca said. 'And a scone. Extra butter, extra jam, extra gluten.'

Alison smiled at me. 'And you, Cat?'

Normally, I had a scone and coffee, just like Becca, but I thought it was a perfect 'yes' opportunity. 'What else do you have?' I asked.

'Oh... um...' Alison looked up at the blackboard. 'Well, what do you feel like?'

'I don't know,' I said. 'But whatever you offer me, I'm going to say yes.'

Alison, Becca and Sinéad all looked at me as if I was mad.

'It's a new thing,' I explained. 'Say yes to everything. Get more out of life.'

'I should do that,' said Becca. 'Open my horizons.'

'Me too,' said Alison. 'I can't remember the last time I went out spontaneously without it being scheduled five months in advance.'

'Yes is truly the scariest word in the world,' remarked Sinéad, her eyes wide open. 'I mean, things *happen* when you say yes.'

'That's the point,' I said, with the air of the seasoned yes-sayer as though I was a dangerous thrill seeker, instead of just someone looking for breakfast. I turned back to Alison. 'What do you think I should have?'

'Okay,' she said, 'so something out of your comfort zone... what about a hot chocolate...?'

'Hot chocolate? You mean, no *coffee*?' Actually, I had been wrong. This was scary.

'No coffee,' she said. 'And French toast with maple syrup?'

'I'm not sure I like French toast with maple syrup,' I said, already backtracking and beginning to panic at this brave new world of breakfast.

'Have you ever had it?'

I shook my head. 'But... it's not my thing...'

Alison smiled. 'Well, then, that's what I am going to offer you. What do you say?'

'Yes!' I said, as Becca and Sinéad gave me a round of applause, as though I had done something that had taken real courage.

'So,' I said, as we waited for our food, 'how is the television awards thing going?'

Becca was organising the biggest night in Irish entertainment, the Irish Television Awards – the ITAs, which was happening in a few weeks' time. Beamed live on TV, it was something of a national event, with everyone studying the good, the bad and the ugly outfits, who won and who missed out, and what scandal and stories emerged from the night. I'd never been invited as it was really only for the big shows, with the huge audiences. *Farming Weekly* wasn't really on anyone's radars, apart from those whose idea of dressing up was washing the wellies under the outdoor tap.

'They are still insisting on having an ice sculpture,' said Becca, 'even though I have said repeatedly that they are so *over*. And it's the summer, so it's going to melt so much quicker. And then we're trying to source a golden carpet from Italy. I've put my foot down about the red. I said I thought we were brought in to make this year different?' She rolled her eyes. 'And then I had to have a meeting with the lighting guy, and then talk to staging and the sound team. And then I checked the chairs at the hotel and discovered they are truly horrible. We'll have to hire them in.'

Alison slipped in behind me and placed our food in front of us, along with Rory's juice. Sinéad quickly wiped the cup before giving it to Rory, but I was absorbed in the over-the-topness of my food. This was definitely an indulgent step up from my basic brekkie. My hot chocolate was topped with whipped cream, a flake and a sprinkling of hundreds and thousands, and my French toast looked impressive, golden and glistening, the maple syrup rolling off, like a slow-moving river. It was the kind of treat you might order if it was your birthday, not just a very ordinary Saturday.

Rory's eyes lit up, but Sinéad distracted him with a slice of dried apple and a rice cake.

'Dig in,' said Becca to me. 'Go on.'

I did, and it tasted amazing. 'Thank you, Alison.' I waved over to her. 'Delicious.'

Becca buttered the end of her croissant and popped it into her mouth, looking enviously at mine. 'I think I might do your "yes" thing too,' she said.

'What would you say yes to?' asked Sinéad.

'Ryan's always on at me to stop working so hard,' she said. 'Relax a bit. Maybe I should do that. Be a bit more Zen. A bit more alternative. Join a yoga class. Get fit, that kind of thing.'

'I'm not sure if I can,' said Sinéad. 'If I start saying yes, then our whole life could just collapse.' Sinéad looked at the time on her phone. 'We've got to get to the chemist before Rory's lunch,' she said. 'He's run out of his vitamins. And his fish oils.'

'The child is going to be a genius at this rate,' said Becca. 'All this no TV and omega-3s.'

We all looked at Rory, who was picking his nose with a piece of Lego.

'There are more germs in a toddler's nose,' said Becca, 'than in a public toilet. Just FYI. I think it's too late now,' she added, as Rory put the piece of Lego into his mouth. 'He's got the lurgy.'

Sinéad rolled her eyes. 'Maybe you should say yes to being a more supportive godparent to Rory.'

Becca laughed. 'That's exactly what I'm trying to do,' she said. 'I am just trying to show him that there is more to life than zapping germs.'

'I'm just trying to keep us alive,' said Sinéad. 'But if you think I *shouldn't* be trying to protect my son, you can lecture me when you have your own child.'

Becca nodded. 'I'm sorry, and you're right. What do I know? The only thing I've ever managed to keep alive is my spider plant and even that's looking a bit peaky. Look, I'll shut up and keep my nose out. You're doing an amazing job. Look at this child.' She put her arm around Rory and squeezed him. 'He's fabulous. And he is a genius. Apparently, Einstein couldn't speak before he was eight and always stuck things up his nose.'

3

It was late afternoon when Sinéad took Rory home for a nap, and Becca and I went for a walk. There was a golden glow in the air, the warmth of the day beginning to cool.

Sandycove is just a seashell's throw from the Irish Sea, with a small cove which is, obviously, sandy, a harbour, boats scudding across the waves. The sea was a magnificent backdrop, the glinting light, the sight of a storm on the horizon, the flotilla of yachts. In the winter, huge waves crashed over the sea wall, but now, in summer, it was a beautiful, shimmering deep-blue mirror. Seagulls swooped overhead, wings spread out, floating on a passing air current.

On we walked, curving along the edge of the beach, sticking to the path and up the slope to the Forty Foot. It's just an old bathing place where a small promontory pokes out to sea, a daily pilgrimage for hardy, seaworthy Dubliners. The only time no one swims is during a storm, and even then, you see the daily bathers gathering in the curving arm of the harbour, along with the seagulls, while the Forty Foot is battered, water surging over the rocks, the whole world shaken to its core.

To one side, there is a row of covered benches, where the swimmers strip off before either diving in or sedately stepping down to the sea. I thought of Lorraine's challenge to get me in there, but just because I lived by the sea didn't mean I wanted to get *in* it. As teenagers, only if it was a very rare heatwave and we were in danger of melting, would we get in. But even now, I remembered the cold that chilled the marrow, instantly and completely stopping your breath and your blood from flowing through your veins.

Seeing the sea was a sight I never tired of, but I hated the thought of inching into its frozen, murky depths. The Irish Sea is no Mediterranean, and yes, it is blue and sparkly in the summer, but here in Ireland, it takes guts and determination. Which was the whole point, I imagined, like eating porridge or going to bed early. It was about doing the right thing, rather than the pleasurable thing. All year round, there were the hardy sorts, in their old dressing gowns or dryrobes, ideal for changing and keeping hypothermia from finishing you off.

'Lorraine wants Mum and me to really challenge ourselves,' I told Becca. 'I mean, it's one thing having chocolate for breakfast, but it's another getting in the sea.'

Becca shuddered. 'There is no way I'm getting in there,' she said. 'Just say "no" to that.'

'But... I'm either saying "yes" to things or I'm not. If I'm selective, then it's not really a challenge.'

'You mean it's not á la carte?' said Becca. 'You can't choose what you want?'

'Well, then it's not a challenge,' I replied. 'And I promised...'

'That's where you went wrong,' remarked Becca. 'Never promise anything. Especially when it comes to being cold and wet.'

But it was too late, I'd already promised. I'd have to do it. I just had to find the right moment and go in for two seconds and then never, ever do it again.

We passed through the gate, under the arch and the old metal Forty Foot sign, and sat on a wall to people-watch. There was always an eclectic bunch down here, all shapes and sizes, ages. They chatted to each other, some were laughing, a group of sixty-something women were giggling, one wiping her eyes from laughing so much. Two men sat together, drying off in the early-evening sun. This place was different, you realised. Everyone seemed happy.

I recognised Lorraine's neighbour, Margaret, who was talking to another woman, with a long grey plait, wet from the sea. Perhaps in her early seventies, her skin wrinkled and bronzed as she shimmied under a towel, drying herself.

'I haven't used soap for years,' she was saying. 'There's really no need...'

'But aren't you worried about not being clean?' said Margaret, struggling under a towel dress, the kind with elastic at the neck.

'The sea cleans me,' the woman was saying. 'It's all I need.'

'Nora's not worried about anything like that...' another woman said and they all laughed.

Becca was talking. 'It's only a month to the Irish Television Awards,' she was saying. 'It's the biggest event we've ever taken on and I've started to wonder what's next? Bigger events? Can you ever go back to the small launches of a new product or the opening of a new bar? Or does it always have to grow? Sometimes, I wouldn't mind some time off, like Sinéad.'

'She's on maternity leave,' I said.

'Well, a sabbatical, then,' she replied. 'Just do something different.'

I was about to speak again when a voice interrupted me.

'Hello, Catríona,' It was Margaret, now dressed in navy shorts and a while short-sleeved shirt. Beside her, the other woman with the long grey plait was dressed in a blue, faded towelling dressing gown and men's sandals. 'This is Nora. Nora is the one who started off all the swimming.' She smiled at me. 'Have you come to join us?'

'The thing is,' I said, 'I'm a bit of a wimp. I really feel the cold.'

'Ah!' Nora smiled. 'But that's what everyone says and then they wonder why it took them so long to get in.'

'But I thought you were challenged by Lorraine to say "yes" to things.' Margaret turned back to Nora. 'Lorraine suggested that Catríona's mother did a parachute jump and that Catríona should swim in the sea.'

'You got off lightly, so,' laughed Nora. 'Anyway, we're always open to new members. Try it, you might like it.'

'She's an enabler,' said another woman, who had just walked up to us. She was wearing a loose, leopard-skin jersey dress and sequinned flip-flops. 'The zeal of the converted. She has us all obsessed now.' She smiled at me. 'I'm Brenda. We're here every evening, around this time.'

'Nora, wait up!' Another woman walked towards us, dressed in a long kaftan. 'Are you walking home?'

'This is Dolores,' said Nora. 'And that fella over there is Malachy…'

A tall, gangly man in his mid-thirties with red curly hair gave me a shy wave.

'We're here every evening,' added Nora. 'You can always bring a tot of brandy to warm you up afterwards.'

'Or one of those fancy robes,' said the third woman. 'Everyone's getting them now. Fierce warm they are. Fleece on the inside, instant heat.'

'Well, then,' said Nora. 'No excuse. Here, everyone is equal. You leave your life and everything else behind on dry land and you just get in.'

'Baggage,' said Brenda.

'Yes, emotional baggage, what you lug around all day every day, and then... well, you become...'

'Weightless,' said Dolores. 'It's all washed away.'

They all smiled at me, sensing I was close to saying 'yes'. There was something about them, their skin clear, their eyes bright. They did look as though they were enjoying themselves.

Becca nudged me. 'Go on,' she said. 'Say "yes".'

'*You* say yes!'

'They didn't ask me, they asked you!'

Before I knew it, I had committed. 'Yes,' I said. 'Yes, I will.'

4

If I was to do this, then I needed something to swim in. And I knew where my old swimsuit was – in a bag, in the wardrobe of my old bedroom, probably mouldy and musty, but as it was going to be a one-swim-only experience, it would do.

Mum answered the door.

'Hello, sweetheart,' she said, giving me a hug. 'How are you after last night? Wasn't it lovely? I stayed and cleared up with Lorraine and didn't get home until after 2 a.m.'

I followed Mum through the house, past my old school photographs and my graduation one, the picture I drew when I was in junior infants of the three of us, all with huge heads and bigger smiles and holding hands, which Mum had framed all those years ago and refused to take down.

'The only thing is that Lorraine is still on at me to do that parachute jump...' she said.

'That's too much. But I have agreed to swim. I was just down there with Becca and I said I'd join them tomorrow. So I need my old swimsuit.'

'You're brave,' Mum said. 'I've signed up to a Pilates class. But there might be something in Lorraine's plan. Even signing up for Pilates made me feel… oh, I don't know… somehow it made me feel as though I *already* had a more interesting life. I think it's a mindset thing. Some people are born with it, and others have it thrust upon them.'

'Lorraine is definitely the thrusting type,' I said.

'I was thinking,' Mum continued, 'even just knowing that you have to say yes to everything gives the world a frisson. As though you are both scared and excited, as though anything could happen next.'

'I'm just scared,' I said.

'So am I,' she admitted. 'What if Lorraine makes me do the parachute jump?'

'You're not doing it,' I said, firmly. 'That's just crazy. There is no way you are throwing yourself out of a plane and plummeting to certain death.'

She shook her head. 'No way. Lorraine's emailed me the forms,' she went on, 'I'm pretending I haven't seen them. Maybe she will forget about it?'

'And maybe she will forget about sea swimming.'

Dad was sitting at one end of the old pine table eating a bowl of soup. 'Don't tell me you're actually doing the "yes" thing as well,' he said, as I bent down and kissed the top of his head. 'Another of Lorraine's hare-brained schemes,' he tutted. 'Remember when she made you camp outside Arnotts on St Stephen's Day just because she needed a new sofa?'

'They were half-price,' said Mum. 'And I didn't mind. Not when you kept coming with hot-water bottles and flasks of tea.'

'I told you, you should have let me wait *for* you,' he said.

'She doesn't even like the sofa now,' remarked Mum. 'Says the floral print reminds her of her mother's old curtains. Quite triggering, she says.' She smiled at me. 'So, what do you think? Are we to keep going?'

I nodded. 'Let's see what happens over the next month. Not that I think we should do anything dangerous...'

'Definitely not.' Mum seemed relieved.

'But just pleasantly be open to new experiences,' I said, and Mum nodded in full agreement.

'Well, I'm having a new experience this evening,' she replied. 'Your father is taking full advantage and is taking me to a documentary about steam trains.' They smiled at each other.

'Oh God,' I said.

'I know,' she said. 'He says my mind is going to be blown.'

'Like the steam trains.'

Dad laughed. 'And I thought you were both hoping to open your minds to new experiences.'

'You're not exactly adventurous,' said Mum. 'You like the comfort of your shed too much.'

'I have everything I need,' remarked Dad. 'My shed, my wonderful wife, my lovely daughter. Why would I need new things?'

Mum turned to me. 'I've started on the decluttering. And I've been going through my paperbacks, but you know what books I *haven't* sent off to the charity shop? My Georgette Heyers. My old Regency romances. I used to love those when I was young...'

Dad looked up. 'I had no idea,' he said, as though there were still things to discover about each other. 'I thought you only read non-fiction.'

Mum gave a nod. 'I'm a fan of pure escapism as well though. I hadn't thought about them for years. All's well with the world when you are reading Georgette Heyer. But when I was in school, our English teacher frowned on anything that wasn't W. B. Yeats or one of those types, and once, when I mentioned I was reading a new

Georgette Heyer, he said, "Are you trying to make your brain regress, Miss Matthews?" And everyone laughed. It was the first time I understood that books weren't just books – there were acceptable books and *unacceptable* books.' She shrugged. 'It's funny the things you can be shamed for.'

Dad nodded. 'I was shamed because my blazer was too big. It had belonged to my uncle Anthony who had gone to the same school twenty years before and he was, shall we say, very broadly built. He couldn't help it – big shoulders, big chest, bigger appetite. And then there's skinnymalink me, no flesh on me at all... and couldn't kick a ball down a field.'

They looked at each other, briefly, full to the brim with love and affection, the way they always looked at each other. Except, Mum looked away, and Dad reached for her hand.

'Now, not to alarm you...' said Dad.

I was, of course, immediately alarmed.

'But we've had a health scare,' he went on, glancing at Mum.

'What kind of health scare?' I said.

'Nothing – absolutely nothing to worry about,' said Mum. 'I'm all-clear. A lump on my breast. And it's benign. I just thought I'd tell you now there's nothing to worry about.'

'So, if it *was* something to worry about you wouldn't have told me?' I said.

'Well...' said Dad.

'We would have done,' said Mum. 'Of course we would have. But it's just that this is good news.'

'You're definitely all-clear?'

Mum nodded. 'I went for scans, all sorts. Poking and prodding and nothing there. Except...' She looked at Dad again.

'Except your mother's now got it into her head that life is short,' he said.

'Which it is,' she continued, 'and it is why Lorraine started on the "yes" thing. I told her about the lump, and so she's been on at me not to waste a second more.'

'But you haven't wasted your life.' I was trying to take all this in. 'Why didn't you tell me?'

Dad looked just as scared as Mum did. And that was the problem, I thought. It was hard enough being scared for yourself, but being scared for someone else was worse.

'Because we wanted to make sure we knew all the facts,' said Mum. 'And now, it's passed, everything is fine... and yet... I don't know...' Dad was still holding Mum's hand. 'I came home from the party last night and burst into tears. It's as though I've done the being strong bit and now the shock has hit me. But I'm fine... I'm fine...' She came over and put her arms around me. 'I'm fine, your dad's fine, and all is well. I just want to make sure I don't waste this precious life. I mean, the thought of jumping out of an aeroplane is my nightmare. But here I am, retired, and facing the rest of my life doing nothing. And so... well, I have to at least think about it. I want to feel *alive*.'

'Have you ever considered quilting?' I said, but Mum ignored me. It seemed her mind was made up.

When I said goodbye, standing in the hall, swim bag in one hand, I hugged Mum goodbye, harder and longer than I ever had before. 'I love you,' I said.

'I love you, Cat.' She smiled at me. 'Everything is going to be more than fine. I promise.'

I nodded. 'Why don't you come for a swim with me?' I said. 'A little less terrifying than a parachute jump.'

'Maybe...' She smiled at me. 'But,' she went on, 'we'll keep going, the two of us. And we may have a bit of fun along the way? We have nothing to lose and everything to gain.'

5

Mum was right. We had everything to gain. Life was far too short and we should never take it for granted. We needed to make the most of every second we were alive.

I walked to the village, feeling a little shaken after Mum's revelation but cautiously optimistic and even excited about saying yes to things. I just wasn't prepared to have to say yes again, quite so soon.

The village of Sandycove is bookended by a church and the old pharmacy, now a doctor's surgery, and in between are two boutiques, a delicatessen, a butcher's, a lovely flower shop, Sally-Anne's bakery and Alison's café. Now, in July, there were profusions of blue and pink hanging baskets on every lamp post, benches which the council had placed on the side of the road where people sat with their dogs and a takeaway coffee.

At the checkout of the supermarket, where I'd gone to buy some milk, I heard a voice behind me. 'Cat! How's it going?'

I turned around to see Callum Flynn, who had once worked on *Farming Weekly* as a researcher. He was charming and friendly around the office, always happy to talk about anything but work, but spent too much time staring out of the window.

'Hello, Callum, grand... you?'

He shrugged. 'Fine... yeah... fine... not a bother... you know...' He looked completely dejected.

'Is everything okay?' I knew he was married and had a daughter and that he lived in Dún Laoghaire, just up the road.

'Well,' he said, 'not the best, to be honest. Denise, my wife, my... soon-to-be ex-wife asked me to move out.' He looked away for a moment. 'Yeah, so not really at the peak of my game...'

'I'm so sorry...' I said.

'I don't know why I'm telling you all this...' he muttered.

'It's okay.'

'I've been trying to keep it all together and be positive. I want Denise to be happy more than anything and if she's not happy and if I'm not making her happy, then she is right to ask me to leave...'

'I suppose...' He looked stressed, which was unusual for him, as I recalled he was so laid-back to the point of horizontal and would come into our office and chat about a cloud he'd seen on his way to work or how your whole personality was dominated by whether you were a side sleeper or a back sleeper. We all really loved him but we didn't have time to ponder the esoteric aspects of life.

'I mean,' he went on, 'she says I haven't found my groove in life and she's fed up of propping me up. It wasn't my fault that the only thing I am good at is acting. I tried to explain to her that the problem is that there are thousands of people who are much better at acting than me.' He looked at me. 'It's not fair, is it? The one thing I can do, I'm not much good at.'

'It's not fair,' I agreed, my heart going out to him. 'Do you want to go for a cup of tea? Alison's stays open late on a Saturday.'

Five minutes later, we were sat opposite each other at the back of the café. Callum pushed back his thick blonde hair. He hadn't shaved in a couple of days and his pink T-shirt looked as though it could do with a wash.

'Where are you living?' I asked him.

'Couch-surfing,' he said. 'And it means Loulou – my ten-year-old daughter – can't stay with me because Denise says she can't sleep on a sofa in a friend's house. I was just looking at the rooms-to-let ads on the noticeboard at the back of the shop. I'm going to ring some of them.'

'I hope you find somewhere,' I said.

'Unless...' He stopped. His eyes were big, with a Bambi quality to them.

Oh no. Please don't ask, I thought. Because I was going to have to say yes.

'Unless,' he went on, '*you* might have a room going? Just until I sort myself out...?' He gave a beseeching smile. 'Please?' His voice wavered a little.

I thought of my pact to say yes. To everything.

'Yes,' I heard myself say.

'Yes?' He looked in shock. '*Really*?' A grin spread across his face.

'Yes,' I said again, feeling panicked. I didn't want a lodger. I liked living alone. I knew the yes thing was about being out of your comfort zone, but having a strange man living in my house was beyond all that was reasonable. But a deal was a deal. And poor Callum needed help, that was obvious.

'Could we start tonight?'

'Tonight?'

'I could go and collect Loulou and we could come over?' He looked at me. 'If you're sure, as in really sure, as in completely, properly, actually sure?'

'I'm sure,' I said. I wasn't sure, however, at all. This 'yes' business was getting scarier by the minute. What next? Lion taming? Grizzly bear-baiting? A round with Kellie Harrington in the boxing ring?

A huge grin spread over his face. 'This is brilliant!' He'd taken out his phone and started scrolling for a number. 'I'll pay you, obviously,' he went on. 'But best of all it will give Loulou somewhere to go on Saturday nights. Do you have an extra room for her?'

'My study. Well, box room...'

'She said yes, everyone!' he called out to everyone in the café. 'She said yes!'

All the customers looked up and smiled.

'Congratulations,' someone called out.

'Have a lovely life together!' said another.

'We're not...' I began, as Callum said, in a louder voice: 'Thanks, everyone! It's been a struggle since Denise chucked me out, but I'm getting back on my feet now, thanks to this lovely lady.'

'Aww,' said one woman, wiping away a tear.

Callum turned back to me. 'I'll just go and get my things and I can be at yours in an hour. That all right with you?'

It had to be, I thought, blaming Lorraine, blaming Mum, blaming Callum for being so persuasive. It had been so much easier in the days of 'no'.

* * *

Callum turned up at mine, an hour later, with an old, battered holdall, a strange-looking plant and standing just behind him was a small girl, with two plaits, glittery runners and shorts and a T-shirt with a sequin unicorn on.

'This is Loulou,' Callum said. 'Say hello to Cat, Loulou.'

She lifted her hand in a tiny wave.

'Loulou is excited to stay with her dad again, aren't you, Loulou?'

Loulou half nodded, as though she wasn't sure.

'And Saturday nights is when Denise said Loulou could stay with me. If I got a place.' He smiled at Loulou. 'And Loulou, Cat is my new landlady.'

'Well, not really landlady,' I said.

'Yes,' said Callum. 'Officially my landlady.' They both stepped inside. 'This is great,' he remarked, looking around the hall. 'Nice poster on the wall, place for umbrellas. That's handy, isn't it, Loulou?' He poked his head into the living room. 'Oh,' he said, when he re-emerged. 'There's a problem.' Loulou and I made eye contact. 'Your television is tiny.'

'Tiny? I thought it was quite big. What do you think, Loulou?'

Loulou went in and had a look at my perfectly adequate television. 'It's normal,' she said.

'Thank you...' I said.

'Would you mind if I brought in *my* television?' asked Callum. 'Denise has been trying to get rid of it for years... just like me.' He looked away again. 'Says it's too dominating. Not like me. I need to be more dominating, don't I, Loulou?'

Loulou nodded. 'You need to get a job and find your purpose,' she said, making me laugh.

'That's exactly what I need to do,' said Callum.

Loulou seemed to be growing in confidence. 'My teacher Miss Lally says we all have to find our purpose. She made a big poster for the wall which said find your purpose and asked us what we think it means.'

'And what does it mean?' I said.

'It means don't be afraid to be you,' replied Loulou, 'and be you in everything you do.' Loulou and Miss Lally were probably the wisest people in the world. Next stop, their own TED Talk.

'And this is Steve,' said Callum, holding out the plant. 'I have had him for twenty-three years. He's a yucca. Denise was glad to get rid of him as well.'

'I think Steve needs water,' said Loulou.

'Okay,' said Callum. 'So why don't you go and water Steve and I'll go and get the TV.' He smiled at me. 'You will love it. It's big.

Amazing sound. Incredible resolution. It turns every living room into a cinema.'

I wasn't sure I wanted my living room turned into a cinema, but I didn't feel able to object, not in this brave new world of 'yes'.

Callum raced out to his car and returned, staggering a little under the weight of a television the size of a door.

'Be back in a moment,' he said, stumbling into the lounge, 'will just wire it all in.'

Loulou ran some water over Steve's roots and then placed him on the kitchen windowsill.

'Would you like a drink, Loulou?' I said.

She nodded. 'Yes, please. Do you have any apple juice?'

'No, I have...' I looked in my fridge. 'Water?' I said, as we heard Callum, shifting my old television to one side and hefting his into place.

She shook her head. 'I'm okay.'

'Tea?'

She shook her head again. 'It's fine.'

'Why don't we go and make up your room?' I said. 'I've got a camp bed and some nice bed linen.'

She nodded and followed me upstairs.

I had lived alone for eighteen months – ever since I had left PJ behind in Spain – and had loved it. Now, I had a lodger *and* a lodger's child. I reminded myself that life was short and precious and Callum needed help and I was in a position to lend a hand.

'I like your house,' Loulou said as we went up the stairs. 'It's really nice. Tidy. Our house is messy. Mum says that she can't focus if the house is too tidy, but she used to complain about Dad because he was messier than anyone, even me. He would leave his shoes right in front of the door and Mum would always fall over them, and he would leave cups in the sink. He had to leave, didn't he?'

I turned around to face her on the landing. 'Well, maybe he will learn to be less messy? And find his purpose. What do you think?'

She shrugged and looked away. 'I don't know.' Her voice was quiet. 'Mum said that she loves him but she can't live with him.'

'And how do you feel?'

'I can live with him,' she said. 'I like living with him. And I don't mind his mess. Or the TV. Miss Lally says that Mum and Dad love me and that won't ever change.'

I felt like giving her a hug. 'That will never change, Loulou,' I said.

From downstairs, we could hear Callum shifting the TV into place and fiddling with the wires. It sounded like he was settling in for a very long stay.

'Come on,' I said. 'I need you to choose a duvet cover from the hot press. And then I can make some dinner? Okay with you?'

It was strange suddenly my life and my house being so different, but it was a nice feeling. Having a lodger wasn't something I had planned, but life was already more interesting. Who knew what else lay ahead?

6

On Sunday morning, Loulou was in the living room reading a book, one of my rugs over her. We'd eaten pizza the night before and watched television and then Callum had put Loulou to bed, and I had gone up and read in bed.

Now, in the morning, I asked her, 'Did you sleep okay?'

She nodded. 'I always wake up early. Mum says I was born like that. Dad can sleep all day, Mum says. So, I just read until he gets up. My favourite writer is Jacqueline Wilson. I read all her books.'

I sat on the sofa beside her, wondering what happened next. I didn't have much experience of children, just Rory, and now I had a ten-year-old lodger.

'Would you like some breakfast?' I tried to think what children liked and thought of my meal the day before. 'French toast with maple syrup? Hot chocolate?'

'Really?' Loulou was suddenly animated.

'And cream on top of the hot chocolate? With a flake?'

She jumped up, excited. It was lovely to have this kind of effect on another human being. Loulou's happiness was infectious. This was very different to my usual Sunday mornings which were

normally spent reading the paper, listening to the radio and eating puritan wholegrain toast and marmalade.

'I'll find a recipe,' I said. 'And go to the shop. Funnily enough, I don't keep whipped cream and flakes in the house.' I would from now on, I thought, for at least as long as Loulou was staying.

Callum didn't wake up until after 11 a.m., and by that point, Loulou and I had made our breakfast, cleared away and she was back reading her book in the living room.

'God, I slept well,' Callum said, yawning, his blonde hair all over the place. 'Your spare bed is amazing. Better than Hugh's sofa bed, I can tell you.'

'I've cleared out a cupboard that you can put your own food in,' I said, quickly. 'And a shelf in the fridge.'

He nodded. 'I'll get something to eat on my way home. I mean, to Denise's. To Loulou's...'

It can't have been easy to have to start again and although I could already see why Denise might just want to be rid of him, he was a good person. Maybe Denise just couldn't stand the massive TV any longer.

Once he and Loulou had gone, I tidied the house, caught up with laundry and finished the newspaper. I took out my old swimsuit and towel and hung the bag ready for my swim later.

My phone rang. An unknown number. Strange, on a Sunday afternoon.

'Hello?'

'Catríona Jones? It's Tom Doherty here... we haven't met...'

Tom Doherty. I knew exactly who he was. Everyone did. What was he doing calling me? He'd arrived at the television station two years earlier, straight from the commercial sector, in a blaze of publicity, everyone wondering if this youngish man from Galway was talented enough and confident enough for such a big job as Head of Entertainment. And it seemed as though he was. In a short

time, he'd commissioned brand-new shows and steered many of the ones he'd inherited to even greater success. At last year's Irish Television Awards, his programmes had swept the board.

Even my team on *Farming Weekly* had taken notice all the way from our grotty building at the far end of the campus where we were relegated, along with our rattling windows, inconsistent heating, foul-smelling microwave and limescale-encrusted kettle. Meanwhile, 'Entertainment' was housed in the gleaming new building which had plush green carpeted offices, a large open-plan layout with booths for meetings and shiny workstations and clean, modern kitchenettes.

'So, Catríona...' Tom continued.

'Cat,' I said. 'Everyone calls me Cat.' I wondered why he was calling. Maybe he had the wrong number?

'Okay, thanks, Cat.' He had a soft, warm accent, a far cry from some of the braying rugby-types who normally inhabited the corner offices. 'Look, I'm sorry for calling so late. It's just that a situation has arisen.' He paused. 'Barbara Brennan has broken her leg. Not sure how or exactly why she was up a ladder on a Sunday morning, but that mystery will have to remain unsolved. She's currently in A & E, unable to move. She's going to be out for the next month, at least.'

'Oh dear,' I said. 'I hope she's okay.' Barbara was the co-host on *The Daily Show*, one of those people who seemed to have been on television *forever*.

'She'll be *fine*,' he said, firmly. 'But we're in need of someone to stand in for her tomorrow.'

'Tom,' I said, 'I think you might have the wrong person. I'm Catríona *Jones*. I am a reporter on *Farming Weekly*... it's the farming—'

'Yes, I know who you are,' he said. 'And I definitely have the right person. That is, if you are the Catríona Jones who presented

that brilliant report when the cow charged into you. I'm still laughing about it...' he tittered.

'My producer Mike also thought it was hilarious as well.' I still wasn't sure why that would have made Tom Doherty interested in me.

'It was...' – I could hear him trying to find the right word – '... charming. And sweet... and brilliant, it really was. I watch *Farming Weekly* every Sunday morning. Today, I saw your piece on goats and cheesemaking... you're a great interviewer. I really liked it,' Tom went on. '*Loved* it, actually.'

'Thank you,' I said, surprised. Even I never watched the show, which was broadcast at 8 a.m. on a Sunday morning. The first few weeks, I had watched myself back and had been so mortified that I soon learned not to make the same mistake again. But I loved my job, having begun as a researcher on the show and risen to become one of the reporters for the last year. However, I didn't know what any of this had to do with Tom Doherty. He was big time. *Farming Weekly* was very small indeed, almost anonymous really, mistakes could be made – and learned from – and the only people who followed me on social media were my friends and a few odd farmers who never did anything more than 'like' my posts of the sunset over the sea at Sandycove.

'Well,' he went on, 'I wondered if you might be available to present *The Daily Show* tomorrow while we see how Barbara and her leg are.'

I was silent for a moment trying to take it all in. *The Daily Show* had something of a cult status in the hearts and minds of Irish people, everyone from students to residents in care homes tuned in every afternoon to watch the slightly odd presenting couple of David Fitzgerald, ageing former crooner with band The Celtic Heartbreakers, and the blue-rinsed Barbara Brennan, who seemed perpetually teetering on the edge of inebriation. Covering every possible topic imaginable, the show was topped with a heavy dusting of frivolity. You could be sure nothing unsettling would be mentioned or life's dark recesses hinted at. Instead, it was a place where everyone smiled in joyful daytime-TV technicolour – from the yellow sofa to the pink cushions, to David's pastel linen suits. All things bright and wonderful... and utterly inconsequential. Unless, of course, you were asked to present the show at the very last minute.

Being a television presenter hadn't been part of my plan. What I did dream of was making documentaries, programmes about real people. I wasn't cut out to present daytime television. That was an art in itself, making it look easy and effortless, like gliding swans. I wasn't like Susie Keane who presented *Quiz Me I'm Irish* on Saturday nights with her glitzy dresses, megawatt smile and sexy wiggle.

'I know it's short notice... and it's Sunday afternoon but... look, just say no if you can't... but maybe I could come and meet you? We'll talk everything through, but I just want to say how grateful I am that you might even consider this proposal at such a late stage.'

Tom Doherty, I thought, was obviously incredibly good at getting people to do what he wanted, but *The Daily Show* was too big and too scary to even contemplate. And although I knew I'd promised Mum that I would say yes, there had to be a way to say no. Live television at such short notice should surely be inadmissible?

'We could meet in The Island,' I found myself saying. 'My local pub, in Sandycove.'

smiled again. 'I'm in exile. I'm here under duress. But I go back as much as possible, breathe in enough Galway air to keep me going in the Big Smoke. As I was driving along the coast,' he went on, 'I saw some swimmers wearing those expensive dryrobe things. In Galway, you'd be laughed out of it. We throw ourselves into the sea wearing only our underpants.'

I laughed. 'You'd be arrested for that kind of behaviour here,' I said. 'If you're not wearing a couple of hundred euro on your back getting into the sea, then you aren't allowed to swim.'

Now, he laughed, his eyes focused on me. Was this a job interview? I liked him, though. He wasn't what I had imagined him to be. He was just so normal and *nice*.

'Drink?' Tom said. 'Crisps? Nuts? Scampi fries? All of the above?'

'I'll have what you're having,' I said.

'Just a Sunday afternoon pint,' he said, signalling to Mick, who worked behind the bar at The Island.

'So, where do *you* live?' I asked.

'I'm in town,' he said. 'Small flat. Modern. Clean. Devoid of any personality whatsoever. My mother came up and took one look around and made me go and buy some cushions. *Then* she sent up a blanket type thing that she says is for the sofa. But I can't work out if it's just for display or if I'm meant to drape myself in it. I was watching a hurling match and I was freezing. Aha, I thought. The blanket. Finally it gets to fulfil its destiny. So, I shook it out over me and lay under it, but then felt so ridiculous, like a Victorian lady suffering from typhoid – isn't that what they all had? – I threw it off and put a jumper on instead.'

'The poor blanket,' I said. 'Anyway, I think it was syphilis.'

He nodded. 'Probably. Anyway, the blanket is still lying there, crumpled and useless.'

7

Tom Doherty was sitting in the small, leafy courtyard of The Island, in the shade of a large palm, his back to a white-painted brick wall. He was wearing a loose white linen shirt, the sleeves folded up, and a pair of navy cargo shorts. On the table was a pint of Guinness. He glanced up, smiling. I'd only ever seen him from afar – in the canteen – and close up, he was remarkably good-looking: tall, broad, dark hair corporate-regulation short, eyes pale green, the colour of the sea.

He stood up and held out a tanned and freckled arm. 'It's so good of you to come,' he was saying. 'And it's a Sunday evening. I feel terrible to have disturbed you.'

I sat down across from him, placing my swim bag on the bench beside me. I was determined to go for my quick dip, get it over with, box ticked, and home again. Lorraine off my back – until, at least, her next hare-brained scheme. I vowed not to get involved.

'I don't know Sandycove,' he said, 'being a blow-in from Galway. But it's beautiful. And a bit posher than I'm used to.' He smiled.

'Do you miss Galway?' I asked.

'You mean the land of the horizontal rain? Yes, every day.' He

'I think we can all identify with the blanket,' I said, making him laugh.

'Some of us more than others,' he replied, just as Mick stood beside our table.

'Now, what will you have?' said Tom. 'You don't have to just have a pint, you know. Isn't it officially happy hour?'

Mick had been behind the bar in The Island for years. He'd talk to anyone, about anything. 'It's always happy hour in The Island,' he said. 'Even when we're closed. It's a state of mind.'

Tom nodded. 'Indeed. Happy hour should not be determined by publicans trying to sell vats of cheap cocktails...' He looked up again at Mick. 'Which I am sure you don't.'

Mick shook his head. 'Our cocktails are never served in vats,' he said. 'Just the appropriate glass. And they are certainly not cheap. Ten euros for a martini.'

'But worth it?' said Tom.

Mick nodded. 'Every penny. For those special occasions.' Mick gestured towards Tom's pint of Guinness. 'We'll have you back here when you are more inclined...'

'Definitely.' Tom smiled at me. 'Sure you can't be tempted by one of this establishment's finest cocktails?'

I smiled. 'It's 4 p.m.,' I said. 'And a Sunday. Just a Guinness, thanks, Mick.'

When Mick had gone, Tom turned back to me. 'You've lived here all your life, then?'

I nodded. 'I grew up here and live just outside of the village.'

'Who do you live with?'

I'd met this kind of Galway person before, the kind who didn't see the value in small talk, got straight to the point.

'No one,' I said, 'except, as of last evening, a lodger. And his daughter, who will be with him every Saturday night.' And probably with me every Sunday morning while Callum slept in.

Tom nodded, still smiling. Perhaps this was a kind of job interview and he was asking questions to see how I behaved. 'So tell me about *Farming Weekly*,' he said, 'what do you like about working on the show?'

And so I spoke about the people I met while reporting, the fact that we were broadcasting to a niche audience, that we were bringing in serious subjects along with entertaining pieces, such as my piece with the cow and the mud.

He laughed again. 'You can't take live television too seriously. It's only TV. Not brain surgery.' He gave me a look. 'But then again, when it comes to the ITAs, I take it very seriously indeed. I'm hoping to soon be able to clutter up the awards cabinet a bit more. I used to be competitive on the hurling pitch. Now, I just like seeing my shows win awards.'

Mick placed my pint in front of us and I thanked him.

'Let's get down to business,' said Tom. 'Now, I've just been on the phone with Barbara. It's been confirmed as a fracture. Bed rest, one of those big boot things, hourly gin and tonics, that kind of thing. So, we need someone tomorrow. I have a couple of other people we can ask at short notice, but I wanted to try someone new.'

'I don't think I could present...' I began. 'I mean, I don't have the kind of... experience...'

He was looking at me, eyebrows raised.

'I mean, if you are asking me to fill in for a day...' I said. 'I just don't think I am what you are looking for.'

'I'm not,' he said.

'Not what?'

'Not asking you to fill in for a day.'

'Oh...'

'I'm asking you to fill in for four weeks, to the end of the run. We come off-air for two weeks and then it's the autumn schedule. I have wanted to shake *The Daily Show* up for some time, bring in new talent, broaden the range of topics on the show, increase our viewership, change the demographic. I want younger women watching the show, not just our wonderful older viewers. And with Barbara out of action, this might be an opportunity to try something – some*body* – new. Would you like to do it? Would you be available until thirty-first of August?'

Say no, every fibre in my body was screaming at me to say no. This was daily, *live* television. For four *whole* weeks.

'It's a small team,' Tom was saying. 'There's the crew, obviously, the make-up and wardrobe gang, and then editorial. Our producer, Angela Browne, has recently come back to Ireland after being at the BBC for years, and there's Ava Smyth, our researcher, and, of course, David Fitzgerald. Needs no introduction. We will pay you double what you are currently getting on *Farming Weekly*. And if you start tomorrow, take it easy, nothing too difficult to get your head around, and then you'll be off and flying.' He smiled at me again. 'So, what do you think?'

Live television? Terrifying. Tomorrow? It was too soon, too rushed. There was no way. Tom was looking at me, smiling, waiting for my answer.

'I'm not sure...' I said.

'Is it David?' he said. 'Because if it is, don't worry about him. He's got a massive ego, obviously, but so has everyone else who is on-screen. He'll be nice to you, I promise.'

I'd spotted David a few times in the main canteen at the studios. One time, there had been a group of senior citizens for the day as extras on the soap that was filmed on campus. David signed autographs, posed for selfies, hugged everyone, made everyone laugh – one woman nearly buckled over – and was treated like a rock star.

'I don't want to make a fool of myself,' I said. 'And I think I am very likely to make a fool of myself.' I thought of me skidding along in cow dung. I wasn't sure I wanted to make an eejit of myself every day for the next four weeks.

But Tom laughed. 'Ah, if that's all it is,' he said. 'But don't you think it's when you stop worrying about making a fool of yourself in life, you can really live? When I used to play a little bit of hurling, in one match I hit the puck into the other team's goal, I face-planted the ground. I ripped my shorts. Badly. I stood up, mortified. And thought to myself, I will have to leave town. This can never happen again. I will never see my parents again.' He was laughing now. 'I was seventeen for context,' he said. 'Anyway, when I slunk into the changing rooms afterwards, the lads were laughing so hard, we thought we would have to have them resuscitated. One of the lads, who'd lost his grandmother the previous week, couldn't breathe with laughing.' Tom began laughing himself and I found myself laughing. 'They didn't think I was an eejit. They were just happy. And I went home that day feeling on cloud nine. Okay, so we'd lost the match, but it was all grand, I'd put myself out there, so it hadn't worked, but we'd had fun. And that's all I want from you, is to have fun.'

Seize the day, Lorraine had said. Live life to the full. But I couldn't, I told myself. I didn't want to. It was terrifying. And yet... there was something inside me, amongst the terror and the fear, a small kernel of excitement.

'Yes,' I heard myself say.

Tom smiled. 'Great! What about being in the offices at 9.30 a.m.? Come to my office and I'll bring you down to meet Angela and the team.'

8

The weather was still warm, the sky bright, as we walked on to the street.

'Tom!'

I looked up to see a woman, in a towelling dressing gown, her black hair pushed up in a type of bird's nest. It was Brenda, one of the women I'd met with Margaret and Nora the day before.

'What are you doing in Sandycove?' she asked.

'Just having a meeting with Barbara's stand-in.' He smiled at me. 'Cat Jones, this is Brenda O'Brien, *The Daily Show*'s make-up maestro.'

'We met yesterday,' said Brenda, smiling at me. 'Hello again. You're coming swimming with us, aren't you? And *The Daily Show*... you're very brave.' She slipped her arm through mine. 'Don't worry, I'll take care of you.' She turned back to Tom. 'So it's true then that Barbara broke her leg?'

He nodded. 'It will heal quite quickly, they think. But absolutely no weight on it and so Cat is stepping into the breach. I didn't know you were a sea swimmer, Brenda?'

She nodded. 'Every day. Sorts me out. No need for pills, just a sunset swim. I return home like a Buddhist monk without the need for the endless praying and chanting.'

I wasn't convinced nirvana would be found in the chilly depths of the Irish Sea.

'Didn't you say you were going to join us?' she said to me, peering, as though she'd only just recognised me. 'Well, come on, there's no time like the present. The power of now, wouldn't you say?' She looked up at Tom. 'Will you join us, or are you too important?'

'I can't,' he said. 'I have a cat that needs feeding. Another time, I promise.'

'Well, come on then,' said Brenda. 'Have you got your togs?'

I held up my swim bag. 'I have them here,' I said, turning and shaking Tom's hand. 'See you tomorrow.'

He seemed surprised and amused by the fact that I was suddenly going swimming.

'It's a kind of dare,' I explained. 'Seize the day. Say yes to life. That kind of thing.'

'Well, don't drown,' he said. 'Brenda, keep her alive. We need Cat in one piece. I don't need another presenter signed off.'

Brenda and I walked from the village, across the road which always had sand along the edges, blown in from high winds, past the Sea Shack restaurant and towards the beach.

'How cold is the sea?' I asked.

'Very,' she replied. 'If you want warm water, take a bath. If you don't want to risk jellyfish or seals, go to your local pool. If you don't want risk and danger, never leave your house. The whole point is to immerse yourself in another world, get out of your depth, where you can't touch the bottom. Get so cold, your body has to find another way of keeping you warm, it fires up the body's very own central heating, your own thermodynamic system. Years ago, when we were wearing animal skins, we were permanently cold, but our bodies worked efficiently...'

'But didn't they all die by the time they were thirty-five?'

She laughed. 'Yes, so it's a good thing that we discovered fire, but we do need to crank up the old internal thermodynamic heater from time to time. It's a primal thing.'

We had walked up the hill and ahead of us the Irish Sea in all its choppy grey glory sparkled. We ducked under the old wrought-iron Forty Foot sign.

'There they are. Nora is the one with the plaits,' she said, quietly, as we walked towards the group. 'And you already know Margaret. Very religious. But actually very nice. Margaret recruited Malachy from her church group; Nora and Margaret are neighbours; Dolores was swimming here and then just joined in with the chat one day and became one of us; and I met Nora through her daughter, Tabitha. Anyway, time for a dip. Ready?'

We stood in front of the group who had turned towards us. Nora reminded me of an Indian mystic, small, wrinkled and wearing a smile of someone who had discovered the meaning of life. 'So, you've finally made it,' she said.

Brenda introduced us. 'Margaret,' said Brenda, 'you know Cat, don't you?'

Margaret nodded. 'We met at her mother's retirement party. My neighbour Lorraine never seems to tire of a party. Any excuse, it seems.' She smiled. 'But isn't that what community is, coming together and celebrating?'

Malachy stuck out his hand. 'Malachy,' he said. 'Good to meet you.' He was tall, super-skinny and with red hair that stuck up in all directions. His whole body was covered in freckles and his smile was gap-toothed and instantly sunny. I liked him immediately.

Nora moved her towel and bag up a little bit to make room for me on the old cement benches, which everyone changed at and where they left their belongings as they went for their swim.

'Do you have any advice for a first-timer?' I said.

'Well...' Nora tried to think. 'I would say that your body will go into paralysis, that you won't be able to move any of your limbs... and you may feel as though you are drowning...'

'What?' I said. '*Really*?'

'If that happens,' continued Nora, 'just shout for us and we'll throw you the life ring... but often the paralysis extends to your vocal cords and you can't do anything, just sink...' She had started to smile.

'Nora,' said Margaret. 'Stop scaring her.'

'Ah, she'll be grand,' smiled Nora. 'Get in, swim about, get out again. No bother to you.'

'I think of it as entering another world,' said Brenda. 'Like I've had enough of this one and just want to step out of it for a while. I'll deal with all the troubles later.'

'Like Narnia,' said Malachy.

'It's definitely as cold,' agreed Brenda.

There was a voice behind us.

'Don't go in without me!' It was Dolores, rushing beside us, throwing her bag on the bench, stepping out of her shoes in one movement and then pulling off her dress to reveal her blue and white flowery swimsuit. 'I thought I wasn't going to make it,' she said. 'Thank God I did. It hasn't been a good day.' She turned to me. 'This is your first time?' Dolores's hair was piled on her head as though she'd pinned it up a week ago and slept on it every night. She had a tattoo of a cat on the top of her arm. 'Oh! I wish it was my first time,' she said, not waiting for my answer. 'To have that feeling, to be a newborn again!'

I had managed to get my swimsuit on without flashing anything and stood for a moment in the light breeze of the evening. I hadn't worn it for years, and the elastic was stretching a little on the legs and it was not the most stylish of items. Anyway, this was going to be a quick swim – my first and last – and as I was starting a new job in the morning, it was just a way to take my mind off it. I had to call Mike at *Farming Weekly* and let him know... My mind raced at all the things I needed to sort out.

'Ready?' said Brenda.

I shook my head. 'I don't think so...'

'Come on, it's now or never.'

She took my hand and we stepped over the rocks, through the shallow pools. Ahead of us, Malachy stood poised at the edge of the far rock, hands in prayer position, and then flipped himself, head first, neatly into the water.

Nora held on to the railings and lowered herself in, while Nora stepped forward and smoothly entered the water. Margaret stood, with one hand on the railings... and seemed to be singing, '*Pardon for sin... and a peace that endureth... thine own dear presence to cheer and to guide. Strength for today and hope for tomorrow, blessings all mine, with ten thousand beside...*' She pulled her goggles on over her eyes, stepped quickly into the water and soon had pushed off into a breaststroke. I could still hear her as her body carved through the black still water. '*Strength for today and hope for tomorrow...*'

'I'll go first, okay?' said Brenda, letting go of my hand, and stepped down into the sea.

I followed her, taking the first step down, and then the second and suddenly my feet were licked by the sea's icy tongue and cold pulsed through my body. I stifled a shriek. Brenda was already front-crawling through the water. I would go in, but that was it. Never again. I could explain to Brenda that I had developed a terrible skin condition from the cold and that, much as I wanted to continue, I really just couldn't.

It was up to my knees now and then thighs and then hips, the cold shooting up my body. It was so much worse than I could have ever imagined. The Forty Footers were paddling in a semicircle in the sea, looking at me.

'You need to just go for it,' Dolores said.

'Just throw yourself forward,' encouraged Malachy.

'Get your hair wet,' added Brenda. 'That's the best way.'

'Just fecking get yourself in,' said Nora.

Five pairs of eyes all fixed on me. I had no choice but to go for it.

I pushed myself forward and plunged in, eyes squeezed shut. The water rushed over, enveloping me within its clutches. The cold spread in rivulets across my scalp, down my spine and in every crevice, nook and cranny. The sea had taken me and subsumed me, my ears full of bubbles, my brain full of nothing, my whole body tingling. And then, suddenly, I resurfaced, to a round of applause from the Forty Footers. The sun sparkled over the sea and suddenly I wasn't cold, in fact I was warm, and what was more, instead of having being subsumed by the sea, I was part of it, as though it had moved to make room for me, as though it wanted me here. Or maybe I had swallowed a whole load of hallucinogenics along with sea water, but I did feel different and, as Dolores had said, newborn. In fact, I felt more alive that I could ever remember, as though this was the very thing, the only thing, we should be doing with our bodies.

For a moment, I thought I'd forgotten how to swim and I sculled around, paddling my hands, but then I slipped forwards and felt an arm sweep above me, and then the other, and I was swimming. I was warm and cold at the same time, and it felt wonderful, almost euphoric, excited but totally and utterly calm. I was certain that I wanted to seek it out again.

Afterwards, as we changed at the benches, wriggling back into dry clothes, becoming once more landlocked and grounded, all the Forty Footers showed a really sweet pride in my achievement.

'Well, I was most impressed,' said Dolores. 'You looked like a mermaid out there, as though you'd spent all your life in the sea.'

'Very impressive,' added Malachy. 'My mam used to say that there was no point in being on the sidelines of life and you went straight in.'

'You were fab,' said Brenda, giving me a nod. 'Like a duck to water.'

'I think we'll keep you,' said Nora, winking at me. 'Something tells me you enjoyed yourself out there. You look as though you've been dipped in magic potion. If you want to come and join us at sunset every evening, then you are most welcome.'

'I'd love to,' I said. 'I really would.'

* * *

At home, I stood under my shower until the hot water ran out, warming me from the outside in. It was only then that the nerves about the following day began to kick in. What had I agreed to? Why had I said yes? I needed more time. But then I remembered what Brenda had said about taking the plunge. Maybe this was better, to just get going. Any longer and I would probably become paralysed by stage fright.

I called Mum to tell her the news, and texted Becca and Sinéad. And then I phoned Mike, my *Farming Weekly* producer, to ask if he was happy with me standing in for Barbara.

'It's grand,' he said. 'Tom Doherty already called me. Big time, eh? Just still say hello when we meet in the corridors.'

'It's only a few weeks,' I said. 'And then I'll be back. Okay?'

'As long as you promise to make me laugh on *The Daily Show* as much as you made me laugh on *Farming Weekly*?'

'Promise.' I hoped this time that I would make people laugh with me, rather than at me, but I also felt weirdly excited by the prospect. Everything was like sea swimming. You never wanted to get in, but when you did, it wasn't ever as bad as you had feared. Or at least I told myself that. Otherwise I wouldn't be able to get out of bed the following morning, too scared to leave the house.

THE JONES FAMILY!

Mum: Morning! Good luck today! So excited for you.

Dad: Break a leg.

Me: Thanks. What are you two up to?

Mum: Going to start on the decluttering.

Dad: A full day planned. An early-morning yoga session, followed by a breakfast meeting with George Clooney, a songwriting session with Paul McCartney, quick trip to Paris for lunch with Catherine Deneuve, the afternoon spent chatting with the Dalai Lama about the meaning of life, and then home for tea and your mother's delicious lemon drizzle cake.

Dad: Sorry. Forgot. In the shed all day. But I'll have the TV on to watch you. GOOD LUCK.

Me: See you later. Love you xxx

9

The thermodynamic good-mood effect of the sea evaporated the following morning when I began my stint on *The Daily Show*. I had woken up feeling nervous and had driven to television centre, wishing that I had said 'no' to Tom Doherty.

Callum was in bed when I left, which was a relief because he had a tendency to see me as a therapist and the previous evening had made me a cup of tea and had begun to talk about Denise and how he didn't know if he'd ever manage to get her back. I listened and made soothing sounds and let him talk. He seemed to need someone to listen to him, and I felt sorry for him, being at a loss about life and missing Denise and Loulou. In the end, I had to go to bed. It was past 11 p.m., and I managed to escape, leaving him sitting on the sofa, under my rug, with a big cup of tea and three biscuits. 'Thank you for listening,' he said, giving me a sad smile as I left. 'It's very kind of you.'

I arrived at TV reception and waited for Tom, sitting on one of the black leather sofas in front of a low smoked-glass table, my feet on a deep-pile rug. The cabinets on either side of the waiting area, just before the curved staircase swept upstairs to the offices, were filled with awards.

People came in and out of the revolving door, waving to the receptionist, running up and down the stairs, talking in loud voices. 'I know, Robert, but that's not how narrative works...' I heard one man say, who was wearing neon socks and massive black-framed glasses. 'So, I said I am never working with him again... *never*. He asked me to make him a coffee! I know!'

A woman with blonde hair cascading down her back, wearing high strappy sandals and a long, tight blue dress, walked into reception. 'Hi, Cathy,' she said, dazzling with her teeth, and waving just the tips of her fingers.

'Morning, Susie.'

It was Susie Keane, one of the country's biggest stars who was always on the cover of magazines. I'd read this month's *Woman's Way* in the hairdresser's last week, where Susie had posed barefoot, in jeans and a vest top, holding a Labrador puppy, and spoken wistfully about how she loved being single because it made her feel more 'powerful'. 'But I wouldn't mind it if Mr Right came along,' she had said. 'Someone who will treat me like his princess. Is that too much to ask?' Looking at Susie, it was hard to believe that she was single. She had to be one of the most gorgeous women in Ireland – small, petite, a fabulous smile. Women like her were never on their own for very long.

Tom came down the stairs, smiling when he saw Susie. 'Good morning,' he said. 'How's it going?'

'Better,' she said, 'now I've seen you.' She laughed but I couldn't see her facial expression.

Tom seemed to try to get around her, but she was blocking his way. 'Sorry,' he said, 'just need to...'

She went the same way and then, as he bobbed back, so did she. 'How was your weekend?' she said. 'Get up to anything?'

He shook his head. 'Nothing wildly exciting. You?'

'Oh, you know me. I'm *always* wildly exciting.' She laughed again.

Tom smiled back at her. 'Look, I'll call over to your desk later and see how you're getting on.'

'I won't be around,' she said. 'I'm only here for an interview with *Cailín Deas* magazine. We're going to meet in the canteen.'

'Great...'

He went to move past her again, and she stepped forward, her blonde hair falling over one eye, and she laughed. 'Sorry, Tom...'

'I'll see you when you're back in the office... I just have to...' And he placed one foot to one side, but she slipped her arm through his.

'I need your advice,' she said. 'What shall I wear for the photo shoot? Should I dress sexy Saturday night, or soft Sunday morning...'

'I don't know,' he said. 'I really don't...'

'Oh, you're useless to me,' she said, laughing again, but he was trying to extricate his arm from her grip.

'I'm late for a meeting,' he said, giving me a wave.

Susie turned to look at me, her face curdling, her smile frozen. And then, as he turned back, she smiled beautifully again. 'Come and find me later,' she said. 'We'll have a coffee. Call me?'

He nodded vaguely. 'Bye, Susie!' he said and then made straight for me, holding out his hand. 'I was half-afraid you wouldn't turn up.'

Susie had continued up the stairs and was gone.

'I thought about it,' I said to Tom. 'But I couldn't think of a convincing enough excuse.'

'If you'd said you died of hypothermia in the sea, I would have believed you.'

'Should have thought of that one. Sorry I can't make it. I'm dead from the cold.'

He laughed. 'Come on upstairs,' he said, 'let me introduce you to the team.'

The Daily Show occupied a small pod of desks in the middle of a vast open-plan office.

Tom brought me over to a small woman with cropped hair, dressed in jeans and a T-shirt. 'Cat,' he said, 'this is Angela Browne, the producer...'

'You are very welcome to the show,' she said, shaking my hand enthusiastically. 'New blood. My favourite kind.' She smiled at me. 'It means we can try out a few new things.'

Ava Smyth, the researcher, was dressed head to toe in black, with backcombed hair, red lipstick, and her eyes were lined with thick, smudged black liner. 'Welcome to the Twilight Zone,' she said.

I laughed. 'Is it that bad?' I asked.

She nodded. 'Worse. It's the show where words are spoken but nothing is said, where people do things but nothing is done. It's a Bermuda Triangle of inanity. People get lost in here and they can't find their way out.'

Angela laughed. 'Ava really loves it here, can you tell?'

'How long have you been on the show?' I asked Ava.

'Two years too long. Hopefully, I'll be gone before they kill my spirit. I'm being slowly driven mad here. One day, you will find my withered body slumped over my keyboard, finished off by writing my millionth brief on how to make soda bread.'

'I'll leave you in these two's capable hands,' said Tom, smiling. 'Good luck, and remember it's only television. We're not saving lives. See you in the morning meeting.'

When he'd gone and Angela had shown me to my desk, she said, 'We have a daily meeting every morning at ten. It's a chance to go through the day's show and what to expect. Why don't you make yourself a coffee in the kitchen and then hopefully David will be here?'

I returned with a mug of instant coffee to find David – who had been on my television screen for decades – sitting at his desk. He looked smaller than he did on television and quieter, as though he'd turned the volume down on his personality. He was shorter than me, dressed in soft leather loafers and a loose, pale pink linen suit, the sleeves pushed up to his elbows, a loose white T-shirt underneath. It was like a look from another world, another era, but it suited him. His skin was mahogany-tanned, his teeth whitewashed.

He shook my hand. 'Thank you for filling the breech left by our dear Barbara,' he said. 'Big shoes to fill. Size eights, if I am not mistaken. But just read the autocue, say your lines, smile at the camera, and that's all there is to it. Easy-peasy.'

I didn't say much in the meeting, just tried to listen and pay attention to what was going on, my pile of briefs and notes in my hand. The jittery feeling only abated a little in the make-up room when I met Brenda, from the Forty Foot. She was super-stylish, now on dry land, raven hair with a streak of white, dressed in black trousers, a loose leopard-skin shirt and flat black sandals.

'So, how are you getting on?' She patted the large chair placed in front of a mirror. 'Come on,' she said, 'take a seat in the psychiatrist's chair.'

The room was brightly lit, but there was incense burning in one corner and Mozart playing on an old CD machine. There was a large poster on the wall of a woman diving deep into the sea and the words, 'And into the ocean I go to lose my mind and find my soul.'

'So, how are you holding up?' said Brenda, once I'd sat down. 'Feeling okay?'

'Not really,' I admitted. 'I'm terrified.' My heart was racing and sweat prickled my whole body.

Brenda nodded as though it was entirely normal. 'They are all terrified,' she remarked, 'all the presenters.' She unzipped her make-up bag and laid out palettes, brushes, pots, and then, scrutinising my face, said, 'Being terrified is why they do it. Thrill seekers, adrenaline junkies, white-knuckle riders... people who want to risk it all...'

'I'm not like that,' I said. 'I feel like I am going to throw up.'

She nodded. 'Normal response, I would say.' She began dabbing at my face with foundation. 'If you are feeling overwhelmed, then do what I do, go to your happy place. Mine is' – she nodded towards the poster – 'the sea. So, how did you enjoy it yesterday? Did you feel worse after you came out or better?'

'Better,' I said. 'I was cold but also warm, it was so weird.'

She smiled. 'Cortisol. If you keep going, then you start creating a positive dopamine pathway as well. If you know you can go into the sea for the first time and come out feeling better about yourself, you can do the same on live television.'

'Feel the fear and do it anyway?'

'Don't fear the fear, I would say. Just accept fear as something transient. It comes, it goes. Nothing is forever.'

'How long have you been swimming?'

'Eight years,' she said. 'It started because I was in constant pain with my fibro and it really helped. And then a relationship ended... badly... you know, the usual. And menopause, of course. That's a barrel of laughs, I can tell you. I wonder how many times in our lives we are broken and then heal again. I must be on my seventh or eighth go by now.'

'And swimming helped you?'

She nodded. 'It's my therapy. The waves, the cold, the floating away from land... I have my Mozart, my dog, Arthur, and the sea. I couldn't live without any of them. Or the Forty Footers. Nora... she's been sea swimming for decades. She's one of those no-nonsense people who will never stop. She's always doing something, whether it's volunteering at the food bank or campaigning against something or other. Margaret's a churchgoer, but we won't hold that against her. She started coming a couple of years ago when her mother was very unwell and she needed somewhere away from hospitals and all that. Her mother died a year ago now, and she says she wouldn't have coped without our daily ritual. And there's Dolores, battling her own demons. But then again, who isn't? She goes to an AA meeting every day, she won't mind me telling you as she's very open about it. And then there's Malachy, such a nice young man, lives with his mam, works in the council and I think we're just a little breather from life. He's shy and a bit awkward, but he's part of the tribe now and I swear he's a million times more confident than he was. When there's a storm, Nora insists we still meet and have a flask of tea and watch the spray... You feel the call of the waves. Without it, I don't know what I would have done.' She smiled at me and looked at my face and then started brushing on mascara. 'I savour every moment. Once you realise that there is a reason for everything, life suddenly becomes endlessly fascinating. It washes away all the negative vibes. I would not have managed to find the strength to leave my last relationship without it.' Brenda gave me a shrug. 'The power of the ocean. Don't underestimate it. It changes lives.'

I nodded, taking it all in, realising how much I already liked this group of women – and man. I would never have met them if I hadn't gone swimming, and now I wanted to be their friend, I wanted to find out what next life had in store for all of us. Every day was a new page in life's adventures, if you were out there, doing things, saying yes, then you couldn't help but have a more interesting life.

When she finished her make-up ministrations and I stood up, Brenda surveyed me. 'You'll do,' she said with a nod. 'Not everyone can scrub up as well as you. Good bones. Amazing face. Excellent hair. Gorgeous smile.' She winked and waved me off at the door. 'Good luck!' she called as I walked down the corridor, legs still shaking, towards wardrobe. 'Remember the sea!'

10

As we perched on the sofa, under the glare of the studio lights, our clipboard of notes in front of us, David turned to me. 'I never say, have a great show… I always say, see you on the other side…'

I opened my mouth to speak, but nothing came out. I tried again, but my mouth was so dry, I couldn't even begin to make sounds. Martin, the floor manager, was standing to one side, talking to Dmitri, one of the camera operators.

'Right,' David said quickly, realising I needed the verbal equivalent of a defibrillator. 'Deep breath and remember that everyone at home wants you to do well. All they want is light relief from the relentless drudgery of domestic life. They want nice, frothy chat, they don't want you falling on your arse, being nervous. They *want* to like you. Okay?'

I nodded, eyes wide, like a startled fawn.

'Now,' he went on, urgently, 'when the red light goes on, stare down the barrel of the camera. Imagine you are talking to someone you like, someone you love. I always think of my old mam, gone twenty-five years now, but in my world, she's at home watching.

And relax the shoulders, unclench the jaw and say "sausages" ten times. Say it now.'

'Sausages?'

'Yes, ten times, quickly,' he ordered.

I obeyed and then he said, 'Now say, Sammy says sausages sound spicy.'

I obeyed again.

'Better,' he said. 'Suck in your cheeks and then out, repeat as often as you can. Gets the mouth moving and you are less likely to trip over your words.'

'Thank you.'

'And remember to smile. No slapped arses, no sourpusses. We're on television. Not the Cavan bus bringing us home from the chicken factory.'

I nodded again, my mind jolting from sausages now to chickens and trying to smile.

Angela spoke in our earpieces. 'Ten seconds to live. Standing by... eight... seven... six...'

It was at this point that I lost track of time, space, my own name and what on God's earth I was meant to be doing. I was going to have some kind of breakdown on live television. My mind went utterly blank. This had all been a terrible mistake. I wasn't *meant* to be on television. I had loved being a reporter, heading out to meet interesting people and being part of a small, tight-knit team. This was the big league, Manchester United vs Roscommon Rovers, and I wasn't ready. Instead I was in the middle of a live-action fever dream, a waking nightmare.

Angela's voice interrupted my thoughts. 'And we're live.'

The camera took on a suddenly menacing presence as its red light clicked on and moved closer. I tried to remember what David had told me about staring straight into the camera, as though a tiny viewer was tucked right inside.

'Good afternoon!' David boomed, sprouting into life, as though injected with a mood-bursting elixir. 'You're very welcome to *The Daily Show*!'

David was magnificent, his charisma in full sail. As he talked, I found myself mesmerised by his face, lost in the smooth skin and his tight, bright smile which made him look like he was the happiest man in the world and there was no one you would rather spend time with.

'And you may be surprised not to see Barbara,' said David, still talking into the camera, 'as you all know her to be my wonderful friend and co-presenter. Sad news...' He pulled an appropriate face. 'Barbara fell off a ladder and has banjaxed her leg.'

In my earpiece, I heard Angela shout, 'Camera two!'

David swivelled his head and looked straight down the middle camera. 'Get well soon, Barbara! And stay off any ladders!' He laughed, then swiftly straightened his face. 'No, but seriously, *do* stay off ladders, kids, ladies... even gents. Dangerous, *dangerous* things.' He switched to another camera. 'But good news, standing in for Barbara today is a brand-new presenter, a reporter on the Sunday morning show *Farming Weekly*...' He turned to me. Welcome to the show, Catríona Jones...'

'Thank you, David,' I managed. 'Delighted to be here, and yes, Barbara, get well soon.'

'Everyone calls you Cat, is that right?'

'That's right,' I said.

'Well, luckily, I like cats,' he said. 'Human and feline kind. Now, back to the show...' He gave a dazzling smile to the camera. 'Today we talk to a woman who makes candles in the shape of animals... I wonder does she do cats, Catríona?' Another laugh. 'And we'll be talking to our fitness expert about the importance of foot yoga...'

'Now, to you, Cat,' said Angela in my ear.

I looked straight down the camera, just as David had done, ready to read the autocue.

'And if you thought you didn't need to up your fashion game just because you're grieving,' I heard my voice say, 'Sabrina Kelly, our fashion guru, will be here with funeral attire. How to look dignified *and* stylish... And our fabulous resident chef, Betty, will be on hand to bake her famous soda bread.'

'Delicious,' said David. 'Nothing better. Now, let's begin the show with a real-life story.'

Sitting across from us was a ruddy-faced woman, smiling shyly at me and David.

'Thank you, David,' I read, feeling as though I was having an out-of-body experience. I had to react in a totally different way to how I was feeling inside, like a swan swimming, all calm, all serene, but my insides were churning. 'Well, as you all know, we like to feature stories of remarkable animals on this show, creatures doing incredible things, but have you ever heard of a sheep saving someone's life?' I somehow remembered how to smile. 'Fidelma O'Reilly was on an ordinary walk near her home on the Dingle peninsula when she slipped off a cliff... but she was saved by a sheep.' I turned to Fidelma. 'Truly remarkable,' I said. 'Now, tell us what happened that fateful day.'

'Well,' Fidelma began, 'I was on a walk... and it was a lovely day, you know the kind of day... and there were sheep. And I took no heed, being on a cliff and all I was thinking about was buying a new air fryer. You see, my sister has one and says they are only marvellous and I was thinking where should I buy it, should I get the same as hers or a better one? You know what it's like...'

'You were on the cliff,' I prompted her.

'I was wearing a jumper,' said Fidelma. 'Ironic, you might say.'

'Ironic, how?' I asked.

'It was wool,' she said, 'and it was the jumper which the sheep used to pull me out. I sometimes think that maybe it thought I was one of them.'

She went on to tell her story about how she was out walking along a cliff path and slipped, falling three feet to a rocky outcrop and fracturing her shoulder. Somehow, a sheep came and she was able to hang on and it pulled her to safety.

'Marvellous, marvellous,' said David. 'A wonderful story, wonderfully told. Well done, Fidelma. Now...' He looked right down the camera again. 'Have you had a fashion crisis at a funeral? No? You might think that all you ever need to do is wear black, but after the break we'll be showing you how to look graceful at the grave and how to bring a bit of flair to the funeral.' David's smile froze on his face. 'Back after these,' he said, as we went to an ad break.

'Was I all right?' said Fidelma. 'It's just that I lost my train of thought a couple of times.'

'You were fabulous,' said David, taking one of her hands in both of his. 'Thank you for coming, we really appreciate it.'

'Get ready for funeral fashion,' said Angela in our ears. 'To Sabrina now.'

The rest of the show was a blur, but I think I managed to read the autocue without looking totally bewildered, taste the soda bread without choking and attempt some foot yoga without falling over.

Finally, as the credits rolled, David, Martin, Dmitri and the other crew members rushed the set, heading straight for Betty's soda bread, buttering it and scoffing it with a fervour last seen at a chimps' tea party, while I stood apart slightly, in a daze, wondering what had just happened.

Angela joined me. 'You did it! You were amazing,' she said, hugging me.

'Really?'

She nodded. 'You were so calm and together.'

'Calm?' I said. 'Are you sure you're talking to the right person? I don't think so.' I held up both palms for inspection. 'Look, clammy. The hands of a person on the verge of a nervous breakdown.'

'You brought something else to the show today... just having you here made everything different – younger, less cosy...'

'Angela,' I said, 'I interviewed someone about the joy of brass rubbings...'

'Yes! And you made it sound interesting. *I'm* even thinking of heading off to my local church and rubbing away. And I hate *all* churches. Just the whiff of incense is enough to trigger a panic attack. But anyway,' she went on, 'you being here is an amazing opportunity for us to bring in a more contemporary element. With crisis comes opportunity and all that and it's a chance for us to try out a few different things. I was hoping that we could bring in a couple of edgier items, talk about more *serious* things, *as well as* the joys of brass rubbing.'

Back in my dressing room, I took off my make-up and I looked at my phone – forty WhatsApp messages, and fifteen missed calls.

Mum: You were wonderful!

Becca: Loved every second. Can't wait to hear the low-down.

Sinéad: Rory and I loved you! See you soon! Tell us everything!

The team had a debriefing meeting and a chat about the following day's show.

'You remembered to breathe,' said David, 'which was a good thing. And when you spoke, words came out. And, this is unusual, the words were intelligent and coherent. Doesn't often happen to neophytes, I can tell you. And more than that, you were delightful. Keep it up.'

I smiled at him. 'I'll try.'

Finally, I was free to go and I sat in my car and exhaled. And then, I started the engine knowing that soon I would be in the Forty Foot. I now had a very good cure for all the on-air stress, the clammy hands, and the beating heart.

THE GIRLS!

Becca: LOVED IT!

Sinéad: Best thing I have seen for ever.

Becca: Loved your make-up. You looked IN-CRED-IBLE.

Sinéad: Beautiful. We'll be watching tomorrow!

11

When I parked at the Forty Foot, the air still warm, the sea was calm and quiet, eddying and swirling around the rocks, the sun just beginning to set. Sinéad texted me:

Need to get out of house. Conor has meeting and we need to be quiet. Fancy a walk?

I texted back:

At Forty Foot. Another sea swim! Be finished around 8 p.m.

Feeling slightly drained and tired, I walked up to the rocks and saw Brenda waving to me from the changing benches. Beside her, Nora was in her swimsuit, fiddling with her plaits, and Malachy was pulling off his T-shirt.

'I knew we'd reel ye in again,' said Nora, smiling when she saw me. 'Like a fish.'

'It was all your talk of negative vibes,' I said to Brenda.

She grinned. 'That always works,' she said. 'Did I sound like I knew what I was talking about? I don't. At all. All I know is a swim in the sea keeps me on the mental straight and narrow. Wouldn't you say, Nora?'

Nora was smiling. 'I do indeed, Brenda. You have to find your own particular cocktail for good health. Takes a bit of time to find the exact ingredients. My cocktail consists of sea swimming, cycling and the odd tot of whiskey.' She turned to her side. 'Malachy? What's yours?'

'Um...' He was wearing just his blue and yellow trunks now; his long, thin body was pale as a morning moon. 'Mine is sea swimming, Mam, obviously, and... I'd like a dog one day to bring up the Dublin mountains. But until then, it's just the sea and Mam. And fruit cake. God, I love a bit of fruit cake.'

'Sorry I'm late!' Margaret was rushing towards us. 'I needed to help coax a recalcitrant cat from a very large beech tree.'

I changed alongside Brenda. 'By the way,' she said, 'you were great today. We were all so impressed. I always watch the show with the wardrobe girls, we have a cuppa while it's on. And we were all in agreement that you were fab.'

'Thanks, Brenda,' I said, thinking how kind she was, her words helping to balance out my imposter syndrome.

'And by the way, I can take off your make-up after the show. Don't be doing it yourself. Come in to me. I used to always take off Barbara's, and she used to say it was the start of her wind-down.'

We stood at the edge of the steps. Ahead of us, Margaret was again singing her hymn before beginning her stately breaststroke, like a regal duck, dignified and waterborne. Nora over-armed straight out to sea and then began to float and drift where the water changed from shoreline to deep water. Malachy was diving off the rocks and swimming around and then pulling himself up again. Brenda left my side and began paddling around, eyes closed, as though meditating.

I stepped into the sea, the cold soaking into me, bringing me to near-freezing point, almost painfully so, but this time I was more confident. The discomfort was only temporary, I now knew, and I pushed off, my body slicing through the sea until I was submerged, my head under, eyes scrunched shut. Away, and beyond, were voices, people, but here I was in a whole other world, just the sound of darkness, if that made sense, a space where you didn't think but where time seemed almost suspended. And then, the moment was over, and I swooshed up, my head breaking the surface, and I was back in the real world.

I was smiling, I realised, as I began to paddle about. Brenda had been right. Being in the water was the perfect antidote to live television. If I was going to stick it out for four weeks, then I needed something to take me away from real life and if it wasn't going to be hallucinogenics, then sea swimming was going to be my drug of choice and it felt good.

* * *

When I was changing into my clothes and drying myself, I thought back on the day, from the moment in reception, to meeting the team, to hair and make-up and then the rush of the show. One hour felt like ten minutes, there was little time to think, and I'd followed David's lead, as he'd powered through, from reading the autocue to asides and quips, being effortlessly and totally in charge. Thanks to David, I was feeling more comfortable. He was someone I could learn from, his cool, his confidence in front of the camera, his ease with the guests.

'Hello!'

It was Sinéad, pushing Rory in his buggy.

'Hello,' I said, giving her a hug and then reaching down and kissing Rory. 'How's my favourite godson?' I said to him.

'I fine, tank you, Cat,' he said.

After introducing Sinéad and Rory to everyone, we waved goodbye and walked towards the beach. Sinéad's husband, Conor, had taken up the option of working from home for the last year, but his move was slowly driving Sinéad mad.

'Conor has work calls,' she explained, 'so, we came out for fresh air. It's the LA office again, and Rory and I have to be completely silent while Conor shows off to everyone on his Teams meetings. I've seen a completely different side of his personality. He actually used the word "man" as in "how you doing, *man*?"' She shuddered. 'I don't even know him any more. Exactly who am I married to?' She tucked Rory's blanket over him. 'Anyway, what about you? How was *The Daily Show*? You were amazing, by the way.'

I knew friends *had* to say that kind of thing, but it was nice all the same. 'There was a moment when I was on the verge of having an on-air meltdown,' I confessed. 'I was worried I was going to cry live on TV.'

Sinéad laughed.

'No, I mean it,' I said. 'I could be the first person on Irish television who breaks down and crawls off set in the fruitless but desperate search for vodka.'

Sinéad laughed again. 'Sometimes,' she said, 'I wish we were all students again, living together, eating toast and watching daytime TV... and now it's me eating toast on my own and you *presenting* daytime TV.' She checked her phone. 'Conor's texted. I'd better go back,' she said. 'He says he's finished and do I want to watch another episode of our Netflix series? Honestly, it's all about him, it really is.' She hugged me goodbye. 'So, are you a sea swimmer now?'

I nodded. 'I might be,' I said.

'Well, at least I know where to find you if we need to make ourselves scarce again.'

* * *

When I arrived home, damp from the sea, feeling the same invigoration and joy that I had the previous evening, Callum was watching television, eating baked beans on toast, using one of my cushions to rest his plate on.

'Bravo,' he said, smiling at me. 'I thought you were a very welcome addition to the show. I watch it every day. Well, I have done since the acting... and everything else... dried up. That David looks as mad as a hatter though.'

I perched on the armchair beside him. The sofa was saggy and crumpled, the other cushions which weren't being used as a resting place for a plate were piled in one corner as though they'd been used as a pillow and my rug was rumpled as though it had been wrapped around Callum all day. It had been a warm, beautiful day and he had spent it inside, in front of the television. My heart went out to him and I reminded myself that I didn't mind being his sounding board.

'So how was your day?' I asked.

He shrugged. 'Same as always. Woke up. Dozed a bit. Tried to work out a plan. That's what Denise says I need. A plan. I just don't know how everyone I know has plans. Do you just *make* plans? Do plans find you? Do they just come into your head?'

'A bit of everything, probably,' I said. 'You decide what needs to be done and you work out the steps to get there.'

'I know I need to eat, I know I need to go and see Loulou. And get dressed and brush my teeth. The basics. But anything more is beyond me. I've always felt a bit overwhelmed by plans,' he said. 'I mean... just making this...' He held up a forkful of beans. 'It took a while. Toast, heating the beans. Finding the plate. Once upon a time, Denise thought I was a fecking marvel. That was when I was a man about town, acting in the Gaiety Panto every year, a few touring shows, the run of Druid plays. Life was in the palm of my hand... Was that me? And asking Denise out that time, and then being together enough for her to fall in love with me. And then... somewhere along the line, I started to lose my grip on things. I was put on antidepressants and they did the trick for a while...' He sighed. 'It's as though I'm like a train that has gone on the wrong track...' His eyes were full of tears. 'I need to be a better father, a better... well, a better person, really. I just don't know how.'

'You'll find yourself again,' I said, gently. 'I know you will.'

'I hope so,' he replied. 'Because I used to really like the old Callum. Not sure if I like the new version all that much.' He wiped his eyes. 'Sorry.'

'It's okay.'

'Just need to get the old noggin straight. And I have to try to think of a career for me to do. Only... every night I go to bed thinking: tomorrow I will wake up and know what I am going to do for the rest of my life. And then I wake up and it's just... I don't know... overwhelming. Where do people even start?' He smiled at me. 'By the way, I've left the first week's rent in an envelope on the kitchen windowsill, under Steve. Do you want some beans? There's more in the can...'

'No, it's fine,' I said. 'You save them for yourself.'

THE JONES FAMILY!

Mum: Today's 'yesses' include joining a salsa class, going for an extra-long walk with Lorraine, and your dad is opening that bottle of red wine that we've had in the cupboard for years!

Me: Great. Mine include wearing silver shoes on TV, having pickle in my lunchtime sandwich and eating the chocolates in the office.

12

My first week on *The Daily Show* was spent in something of a haze. Every morning, I had to drive past my old office on my way in, gazing somewhat wistfully through my windscreen at the dilapidated building, where my old colleagues were busy working on the next edition of *Farming Weekly*. Being on *The Daily Show* meant I missed that ease and comfort of familiarity, but I'd said *yes*, so there was nothing to do but to plunge on.

My new office was bigger and grander than my previous one, the carpet tiles were a bright, grassy green and none had stains of decades-old spilled coffee or someone's lunch from the 1980s. The lighting was brighter, the air was cooled and the large glass windows looked out on to a generous green space, with trees and bronze sculptures, where people would take their lunches or hold meetings.

Beside our pod of desks, in the open-plan office, was the *Quiz Me I'm Irish* team, all working away for that Saturday's show. On the other side was the sports department, where several large televisions blasted out various international matches or events. They ate crisps noisily from breakfast time, shouted out scores to each other and spent the rest of the time either mercilessly teasing each other or flicking paper clips at one another.

One morning, as they scooted around on their wheelie chairs, Ava, our researcher, looked at me. 'Don't they say the modern office is where your soul goes to die?'

My week soon became a routine, arriving by 9.30 and heading to the morning meeting, held in a small conference room, at 10. The meeting was Angela's opportunity to talk all of us through that day's show, guests, running order, potential problems and pitfalls, and editorial direction.

The rest of my day was spent reading the briefs prepared by Ava, making notes and then heading down to Brenda in make-up and the girls in wardrobe. I had been bought some dresses which were a little more me but still far too glamorous. When I looked in the mirror, all made-up, dressed-up, glammed-up, all I could see was a glossier version of myself. In real life, which is what I had begun to think of my world outside of this place, I only ever wore jeans and tops and minimal make-up. Here, in this unreal world, I could barely recognise myself. It was acting, I had realised, thinking of David and the way he sprang into life once the cameras were rolling, radiating the kind of charm and warmth that would seem fake in real life but entirely appropriate in this over-the-top world.

I was beginning to develop my own little persona on-air, a more confident version of myself, someone smilier, happier, even giddier. I laughed at David's jokes, made a few of my own, stood taller and stronger. David, I had noticed, would consume a can of Red Bull before going on-air, which gave him that slightly wired, electrified personality. I began having a shot of espresso in the minutes before air, feeling my body ping into action.

Every day, under the hot lights, in this fake sitting-room set,

Angela would announce in our ears, 'Ten seconds to live.' And I would sit up straighter and stare down that camera, heart thumping in my chest, the caffeine doing its thing, adrenaline doing the rest.

The make-up room had become something of a safe place for me. After the show, with the lights turned to low, Brenda would remove my make-up by rubbing my face with rose-scented oil and warm muslin cloths, her Mozart playing on her tinny CD player.

I would crawl into the make-up chair, feeling exhausted. Already, it felt like I had been on the show for months.

Brenda would press a cloth to my face. 'You relax now,' she would say, in her therapist's voice, '... close your eyes.'

I would sink back in the chair, the room warm and dark, feeling all that energy leaving my body, make-up being removed and transforming me back into the person I recognised. In a little while, I told myself, we'd be both in the sea, bobbing about, like seagulls. It was that thought that kept me sane during the day. I realised I was craving my swim, needing that dopamine rush of the cold and the warm, the washing away of the day.

After one show, Brenda said: 'Great show. Loved the item on making the perfect cup of tea. I think it has to be leaves too. Teabags aren't the same. It's fascinating what you can learn about making tea, don't use boiling water for coffee, always for tea.' She rubbed away my mascara in a delicate swoop around my eyes. 'I was watching a really good programme the other night,' she went on, 'all about us rushing about, racing through traffic, running for planes... the excitement of the doorbell when the online shopping arrives. Our ancestors didn't have that kind of adrenaline constantly pumping through our bodies. Apparently, we've forgotten how to wind down and let it all dissipate naturally...' She smoothed cream over my eyelids. 'I was thinking of all of my lovely presenters... having to deal with modern life and having to make live television. I don't know how you do it. Rather you than me. Presenters crave the adrenaline and the fame. Well, most of them do. Meanwhile, I am very happy to just settle in with my cat Arthur and only do the things I actually want to.' She gave my face the once-over. 'There you go, all done. Back to your beautiful, natural self.'

Later, I had floated on my back in the sea, letting the water ripple over me, half-submerged like a piece of driftwood. If I hadn't had that, it would have been really hard. No wonder people turn to alcohol or chocolate. How else do you cope with that mass of energy and adrenaline in your body? Swimming just soothed it all out of you. Some evenings, as I held the handrail, stepping into the sea, my hand was visibly shaking with all of the cortisol and adrenaline. And then, as I pushed off – still freezing, still wanting to scream with the horror at the cold – somehow I would begin to be soothed, I would relax, as everything was washed away.

* * *

By the end of my first week on the show, I was more settled and confident in my new role. The butterflies were less evident, the hands less clammy and I felt more comfortable with my daily routine.

In the morning meeting, we sat around the long table, listening as Angela briefed us on the content for that day's show.

'Well,' she was saying, 'happy Friday. Just to say well done to Cat, who has survived week one on *The Daily Show*...' She looked over at me. 'Anything you have to say, Cat? Happy with the way things have gone?'

'I think so,' I said. 'I mean... I'm learning a lot, but most of all I am learning how much I have to learn. If that makes sense.'

David nodded. 'I stopped learning a long time ago,' he said.

'Learning is very tedious. I find you need to white-knuckle life, it's not an education, it's an experience... when you're bored of broadcasting, then it's time to retire. *Not* that I am close to retirement age.' He gave a laugh. 'Oh no, not by a long shot.'

Tom cleared his throat. 'I think Cat has done remarkably well,' he said. 'It's not easy being parachuted on to a big show like this. The breadth of topics you've gone through, the fact that you're still smiling is brilliant. I'm really pleased with how well you've done.'

'Thanks, Tom,' I said.

'I concur,' said Angela. 'Thank you, Cat. You've been great. Right, let's push on with today's show. So, we have Betty coming in to cook today. Fun ways with porridge... you know, nuts and seeds, stewed fruit...'

'Fun?' David queried. 'Porridge is the least fun food I can think of...'

'Some people like it,' said Angela. 'In fact, I would say most people do.'

'I don't,' remarked Ava.

'Nor do I,' echoed David. 'And it's summer. Not exactly porridge weather. And oats are what I would describe as a desultory breakfast, more suited to horses and healthniks and those awful people who always go on about their digestions, the gut nuts...'

Angela and Ava looked at each other as though David might have a point. 'We could ask her to do something else,' said Angela.

Ava looked at her notes. 'Betty also suggested seven ways with boiled eggs...'

David closed his eyes. 'Now that is just disturbing. I can't... I just can't...' His words faded on his lips.

'But Betty is a national treasure,' said Angela, 'if she wants to make porridge in August, then she is more than welcome to do so. Betty is soothing and calming in a crazy world. She's like an idealised version of everyone's nan.'

'We do need to be soothed,' agreed David. 'Only I prefer to be soothed with a nice glass of Châteauneuf de Pompom or whatever is going...'

'But,' went on Angela, 'maybe we could mix it up a bit. Along with Betty, maybe introduce another chef who can be the polar opposite. I have someone in mind...' She smiled at us. 'Leave it with me.'

As we were all shuffling out of the meeting, Tom turned to me. 'Do you have time for a quick word? In my office?'

I walked with him along the corridor.

'I just wanted to see how you were getting on,' he said, smiling at Claire, his PA, sitting just outside his office, opening the door and motioning for me to step inside. 'Take a seat.'

The room was a large corner office, with a desk in the middle and a small, round conference table to one side. On the wall was a framed vintage poster of the Galway Gaelic Football team holding up the Sam Maguire Cup and on the desk there was a photograph of a younger-looking Tom with an older couple, his parents probably. He was tanned and both of his arms were thrown around them, looking as though they had been caught in the middle of a joke.

'I'm so sorry not to have been able to meet with you this week, I've just had too many meetings and we're trying to plan the autumn schedule. Contracts to be renewed, that kind of thing.' He was always so smooth and confident. 'But I just wanted to thank you for everything you have done this week...'

I braced myself for constructive criticism. Executives at Tom's level were well known for meting out feedback, however bald and honest. There were some who were famous for their tendency not to stop until they had reduced grown men to weeping messes. But Tom smiled at me.

'And I think it's going well,' he said. 'Really well, in fact. Yesterday, particularly, I thought you'd really found your groove. Talking to that woman who was crocheting Liberty Hall made me laugh... when she said that she crocheted her own underwear and you looked straight at the camera. Excellent.' He grinned. 'Loved it. You have the right mix of respect but a knowing wink to our other audience – the ironic crowd.'

'There are *two* audiences?' I hadn't known I was being ironic, nor did I remember looking straight at the camera. But I realised there were ways you could use the camera as another way of communicating, so you weren't just performing, you were also playing. David, I realised, did it all the time. It gave another dimension to presenting.

He nodded. 'There are many different audiences, all working on different levels. David plays to many of them, I think you are playing to the ones even he doesn't quite reach.'

'I've been really nervous,' I admitted.

'Well, you are managing it all very well,' he said. 'I always say to presenters, give it all you've got, but remember, we're not curing cancer. Now, I just wanted you to sign your contract... if that's okay... you don't have an agent, do you? So, you have to do it yourself...'

There was a voice outside. 'Don't worry, Claire. He's expecting me.' It sounded like Susie Keane. She knocked and opened the door. She looked the same radiant self I had seen on Monday morning – blonde, wavy hair, that beautiful heart-shaped face, the small red lips. 'Tom, I just thought...' she began but stopped when she saw me. 'Oh, I didn't realise...'

'Susie,' said Tom, 'have you met Cat Jones, who's filling in for Barbara on *The Daily Show*?'

Susie shook her head. 'No,' she said, stepping into the room, bestowing that beautiful smile of hers. 'So lovely to meet you.'

But before I could speak, she had moved on, back to Tom, the smile snatched away.

'Tom,' she said, looking right at him. 'I thought we could go for that drink you owe me later? It is Friday, after all, and I can't be expected to stay in on my own. And you did promise, didn't you? Remember?'

'I'm not sure,' Tom said.

Susie turned to me. 'This man said that he would buy me a drink if the audience figures for my show beat last year's. And they did. But still no drink!' She turned away, pouting.

'I said I would buy the *whole* team a drink,' remarked Tom. 'I owe *all* of them. It's just that I said I'd meet some of the lads from my five-a-side team for a quick kick-around and then a few pints. We can organise the team drinks for next week?'

'Or you can tell your five-a-side friends that they can meet next week?' she said, smiling at him. 'What do you prioritise? The *Quiz Me* team who are bringing in record viewers and the most popular show in the country...' She glanced at me. 'No offence.' She faced Tom again. 'Or a kick-about with the lads?'

'I'll let you know,' he said. 'I promise.'

She was about to say something more and then stopped. 'Okay, talk later.'

When the door had closed behind her, Tom seemed unruffled as though entirely unmoved by the sexiest woman in the country making a move on him. But perhaps, as Tom was surrounded by talented, beautiful people all day, he was immune. But I could see why Susie liked him. There was something about that calm manner, as though he could handle anything, as though you would trust him with your life.

'You're doing brilliantly,' he said, pushing the contract towards me. 'Keep going. Only three weeks left.'

'Thanks...' I signed my name where he pointed.

'And how is the swimming going?'

'Still cold,' I said. 'But surprisingly amazing.' I told him how I had been swimming every night this week. 'I almost can't remember life before it. I love it.'

He smiled, nodding, as though he understood. Swimming was part of my life now and I found myself checking weather forecasts and tide times and even listening to the sea area forecast as though it had any relevance to me at all.

LORRAINE!

Lorraine: How are you getting on?

Me: With what? The show?

Lorraine: Saying yes! Your mum says you've been very busy. Just want you to admit I was right.

Me: I've been sea swimming every day, I have a lodger and a new job.

Lorraine: Told you so.

Me: Looking forward to going back to my nice, quiet old life. Three weeks to go.

Lorraine: There's no going back. I promise.

13

After my swim that Friday evening, the sky was still bright and warm and I walked back along the beach, towards where my car was parked. On the grassy bank doing yoga was a group of women. I'd seen them there before and I'd never taken any notice of them as there were often people making the most of the long evenings. On other nights, there was a tai chi class, sometimes there was an aerobics class, and another evening, a small group of artists had set up their easels and stools and had painted the light glittering on the sea.

'Feel the earth beneath your feet,' the yoga teacher was saying. 'Feel the energy from the earth infuse your body with its innate goodness. You are strong warrior women, you are descendants of Celtic goddess Queen Méabh, her spirit is in all of us... feel her rise within you...'

I noticed one woman at the back of the class was lying down, as though she was either asleep or on strike. She looked familiar – long, smooth dark hair spread out behind her, a red hooded top. Becca!

I crept closer, peering from behind the wall.

'Becca!' I hissed. 'Becca!"

She turned her head, eyes lighting up when she saw me and then, without a word, began rolling like a sausage towards me. Just as she got to the wall, she hopped over it and grabbed my sleeve. 'Run!' she hissed. 'Before they break my spirit, never mind the one belonging to Queen bloody Méabh!'

The two of us ran along the seafront and spied on the group from a distance.

'What the hell was that?' I said.

'Spiritual yoga,' she replied. 'I thought I was going to lose my mind.'

'But you hate yoga,' I said.

'I do,' she said, nodding fervently. 'I really hate yoga. I still hate yoga. It's so not me. That was the first and last time. But I was thinking of you and all your yes business and I thought I should get out of my comfort zone, and Sarah-Jane in the office is really into her crystals and burning sage and all that. She nearly firebombed the office last week when she lit some incense and it fell onto a file of papers. But while the rest of us were freaking out and screaming, she was totally cool. It doesn't matter, she kept saying. We're all fine. Nobody died. "You're too Type A," she said to me. "Type As can't cope with chaos. They like everything planned and organised and life all folded into little triangles. You can't Marie Kondo *everything*. Relax and let chaos into your life." And so, I thought I could prove that I could cope with chaos and when she suggested spiritual yoga, I said yes.'

I laughed. 'You've gone mad.'

'I have.' She nodded. 'I really have. Could it be the menopause?'

'You're thirty-two!'

'It could be, though.' She shrugged. 'My body feels strange. Anyway, fancy a drink? Undo all that yoga shite?'

'Love one.'

'Sarah-Jane isn't going to be working for us for much longer,' went on Becca, as we walked to The Island, 'so at least she won't make me go to another spiritual yoga class. She told me earlier that she doesn't feel as though her "destiny" is in events because by its very nature events is about planning for the future and she is only interested in the "is-ness of now".'

'The is-ness of now?' I repeated.

Becca nodded.

'So she can only work in an industry which is about the present tense. Like live television, once it's gone, it's gone.'

'She should come and work with you,' Becca suggested.

'I don't think crystals and incense would go down well,' I said. 'So, are you embracing the unpredictable, letting it all hang out? Stop being such a control freak?'

'Me?' She clutched at her breast. 'Control freak? Have you met Sinéad? She won't let her child have a fecking ice cream. The poor boy thinks the world smells of disinfectant. She is so uptight, I am amazed she can sit down.'

I laughed. 'Becca!'

'It's true! I've never been that bad, I just take my work seriously. Except, I think I'm starting to lose interest. I don't know what's happening to me. The other night I actually watched a *film* with Ryan, rather than catching up on some work. He kept checking on me to make sure I was still breathing.'

At The Island, we went straight into the garden and sat at the same table where I had met Tom. It seemed an age now.

'What will you have?' I said to Becca.

'Gin and tonic,' she said. 'And a packet of Tayto.'

'Two gin and tonics,' I called over to Mick. 'And a packet of Tayto, please.' I turned back to Becca. 'So, if you don't like yoga, what else are you going to say yes to?'

Becca pulled a face. 'Whatever presents itself to me,' she said. 'I am going to stop being so adamantly prescriptive. Let a little flow in. Ease up a bit. But don't tell annoying Sarah-Jane, okay?' She held up a strand of her perfectly straight, perfectly smooth dark brown hair. 'Remember what this used to look like?'

'Curly?'

'Understatement.' She thanked Mick as he put down our drinks. 'More like I had my hand in a socket while standing in a bucket of water. How long have I been straightening it for?'

'Ten years?'

'Fifteen. But... I don't know, call me crazy, but I was thinking of leaving it natural...' She gave me a questioning look. 'What do you think?'

'I think it would be lovely...'

'I feel scared though,' she said. 'As though I would be naked or something. Straight hair is part of my armour, but I still want to do it. And another thing that's worrying me is that I'm turning into my mother. I look in the mirror and see her face staring back at me. Except she has frizzy hair. And the way I now can't drink caffeine after 2 p.m. or the fact that I have started to find David Attenborough attractive...'

I laughed. 'You mean, you haven't until now?'

'Not really,' she said, seriously, 'but my mother has been lusting after him since *Blue Planet*. No wonder Dad was a disappointment.'

I laughed again. 'But turning into your mother is inevitable,' I said. 'And your mother is lovely.'

'*Sometimes*,' replied Becca, taking a Tayto packet, ripping it totally open and placing it between us, so we could share them. 'Ah, she is, she's a dote. But I don't want to turn *into* her. I can't let myself totally transform into her.'

'Resistance is futile,' I said.

She laughed. 'Probably. But you know I've wanted to run my own company since I was in school. You know I've never wanted to have children or get married or do any of those boring things that everyone else does. And I would have thought by now it would get easier, that I would know what I want and where I'm going, but sometimes I wonder if this is all there is for me. And that the scariest thing I can think of doing is going to yoga or not straightening my hair.' She held up her gin and tonic. 'Here's to us, being out of our comfort zones and feeling scared.'

'Here's to us,' I said. 'And to frizzy hair and all who are adorned by it.'

She laughed. 'So, you're still saying yes to everything?'

'I have to,' I said. 'I can't let Mum be on her own.'

'Well, I'm in it too, now. I can't let you be on your own, either.' She smiled. 'Isn't that's what friends are for?'

14

I hadn't seen much of Callum during the week, but I had seen signs that he had been eating, which I was relieved about, and that he did occasionally leave the house. He wasn't messy in the way that Loulou had suggested he might be and instead was obviously making a huge effort to put his shoes away and the kitchen was always as I had left it. Just a half-tin of baked beans in the fridge or McDonald's wrappers in the bin were the only signs that he was alive and functioning.

On Friday night, he came into the kitchen as I was making some pasta for myself.

He looked better than he had a week ago, I realised. Maybe sleeping on people's sofas had been really stressful and at least having a bed and a place to return to had made life easier for him. 'Just checking that you're okay for Loulou to come here again tomorrow?'

'Of course,' I said. 'I've got the breakfast things in for her and apple juice. And I put a lamp beside her bed so she can read.' Loulou, I had realised, was part of the lodger package. Not that I minded being an accidental landlady, but it was, admittedly, far more than I had bargained for. 'What are you going to do with her tomorrow?'

'I thought we could have a takeaway,' he said, 'and watch *Quiz Me I'm Irish*... do you like it? It's our favourite show, with the lovely Susie Keane...' His eyes went misty for a moment.

'She sits near me in work at the moment,' I said, wanting to cheer him up.

'Does she?' He looked uncharacteristically animated, but then visibly sank again. 'She's not a patch on my Denise. Well... not *my* Denise... any longer.' He nodded bravely. 'I think she is dating again. Or at least thinking about it. A friend saw her profile on an app. I've just got to let her go, haven't I?'

I went and sat down by him. 'What do you think?' What did I know about relationships and marriage?

'I have to move on with my life,' he said. 'I've got to get a proper job. I've got to be a better dad to Loulou. Be more useful.'

'To whom?' I felt a bit like a therapist.

'The world,' he said. 'I've been doing a lot of thinking lately and life isn't just about living your own life, it's about living your life in conjunction with others.' He looked quite pleased with this psychological breakthrough. 'It's about bringing your best self to the table... it's about being useful to the people around you, to society, not just existing. I was watching it on this programme. You need to find your life's purpose, and that could be anything, really, just something that you are passionate about. You need to have a dream and you owe it to yourself to follow it through. In fact, you owe it to the world to follow it through and then you create flow and if everyone creates flow, the world would be a much better place.' He nodded at me. 'I listened to a podcast and took notes.'

Callum seemed to be moving forward, which was a positive step. 'And what's your life's purpose?' I asked.

He shrugged. 'Feck if I know. I just know I need one.'

'That's a start.'

My phone rang. Sinéad. I excused myself to answer it.

'I am calling about an event tomorrow morning, one of my mum's friends is organising it... would you like to...'

'Oh God,' I said. 'What is it? Because you know I have to say yes.'

She laughed. 'It's a clothes swap party. You bring some clothes you don't want and swap them for clothes you do want. Tomorrow morning, 10 a.m. Becca's coming. Just bring some nice clothes that no longer spark joy.'

'Yes,' I said.

* * *

The following morning, Becca, Sinéad, Rory and I gathered outside a large, double-fronted house in Sandycove, the kind with bay windows, gravel driveway and a family car the size of a minibus.

Sinéad had carrier bags of clothes hanging off the handlebars of the pushchair, Becca had her overnight bag and I had two bags of clothes and shoes. It hadn't taken me long to declutter my wardrobe, in fact, it had felt oddly liberating. I was never going to wear that pink dress which made me look half-tablecloth, half-woman, or the jacket that I bought thinking I needed to be more grown-up. I wanted only to dress in things that made me feel more like me, rather than an ideal me.

'Whose house is this?' said Becca, removing her sunglasses to have a better look.

'Her name's Sandy,' said Sinéad. 'Married to Robert. A bit annoying, but her twins go to Mindful Kids with Rory.'

'Did you bring anything nice?' I asked.

Becca nodded. 'I've brought some of my suit jackets. See, I too am trying to be more mindful. Saying yes to relaxing my look. I've been in the power suit for too long. And the heels. I am never going to wear them again. I'm saying no to uncomfortable shoes.'

'I thought we were only saying yes?'

'Okay then, so I say yes to flat shoes,' went on Becca. 'I don't know what's happened to me lately. But my feet hurt all the time. It's like they're expanding or my bones are changing. I don't know. But I can remember when I used to wear heels all day long.'

'I haven't worn anything high in years,' said Sinéad. 'Can't be bothered.'

'They've put me in runners on the show,' I said. 'The girls in wardrobe says high heels are only being worn on the glamour shows, the Saturday night entertainment programmes. Like *Quiz Me I'm Irish*.'

'I love that show so much,' said Sinéad. 'Conor and I watch it every week. He normally falls asleep during it, but it's practically our date night – him asleep in front of the television and me actually answering the quiz questions out loud. I think Susie Keane is actually friends with Sandy. She mentioned it the other day, they go to the same gym, apparently.'

'If you fall asleep in front of Saturday night television,' said Becca, 'then you have officially passed from youthful adulthood to middle age. You have crossed the Rubicon, Sinéad. You and Conor are middle-aged, at thirty-two.'

Sinéad nodded. 'It's true. The man is thirty-two going on seventy-two. He has started wearing vests because he says he is cold working from home, so he went out and bought himself a pack of three. Says they have changed his life and started going on about his kidneys and how they should be kept warm at all times or you get some kind of... I don't know, cold kidney disease. And he's telling me this while I am trying to make Rory his breakfast before he has to go back to having one of his incredibly loud Teams meetings, mug of tea in his hand, and then he leaves it where he puts it down. I found one behind my peace lily earlier. Crusted over with green mould. My *favourite* mug.' She shuddered. 'I almost died. "Did you know, Conor," I told him, "that you have now brought spores into the house which could kill Rory?" His immune system is too underdeveloped.'

Becca gave me a look. 'At least,' she said, 'Conor's kidneys are warm. Wouldn't want to breathe in killer spores with cold kidneys. Now, shall we go in and swap some clothes?'

Inside, the interior decor of the house was a very limited palette – pink. From the floral wallpaper, the stair carpet, the hand-painted French armoire in the vast hallway, to the gaudy chandelier. The kitchen was just as pink – a sparkly pink terrazzo floor glittered beneath us, the walls painted a pale pink, the kitchen units a deep magenta. It also looked like a posh jumble sale, with a frenzied, almost hysterical atmosphere. Women were going around with piles of clothes over their arms, a look of feverish ecstasy in their eyes, as they tore off their clothes and wriggled into dresses in full sight of everyone else, and then accosted anyone squeezing past, demanding their opinion – 'Should I take this? Does it suit me?'

'This is what it must have been like in the last days of the Roman Empire,' said Becca, as we hung up the clothes we were donating on one of the rails.

'I'm feeling a little insecure about the clothes I've brought,' I said. 'I feel as though you get judged on your cast-offs.'

Sinéad was standing to one side, anti-baccing Rory and pulling a mask over his face. 'There's too many people in here,' she said. 'I didn't think it was going to be like the January sales in Brown Thomas. He's going to get ill.'

'I'll mind him,' I said. 'Don't worry. You go and have a look around. I don't need any new clothes.'

'Are you sure?' Sinéad looked excited as I nodded.

After cleaning my own hands, under the watchful eye of Sinéad, while she browsed along with Becca, I played I spy with Rory.

'Hello...'

I looked up to see Susie Keane standing in front of me.

'You're the new... the stand-in... the...' She shook her head. 'Whatever you are!' She laughed so charmingly, I could have sworn she wasn't being rude.

'Yes, yes,' I said, 'that's me, the new whatever!'

'So, how are you finding it?'

'The clothes swap? I don't need anything...'

'No...' She gave me a sharp look. 'I mean, television. Entertainment. The team. People like... Tom.'

'Fine,' I said, carefully. 'Everything's fine.' Something told me that she wasn't really interested in my emotional well-being and definitely wasn't here to make friends.

'Good,' she said. 'That's good.' She gave me a look. 'Now, do remember that there's a hierarchy. Some of us have been working towards certain goals for a long time and others should wait their turn.'

I wasn't sure if she was talking about work or about Tom, but something told me it was the latter. 'I am not working to any specific goals and if I was, I would be happy to wait my turn.'

She smiled and was back to the beautiful Susie Keane again. 'I'm so glad you understand.' She glanced down, a disgusted look on her face. 'That child is covered in blood.'

'Blood!' Rory had blood pouring down the side of his face, but he looked completely fine, no tears, no pain. 'Rory?'

'Ketchup!' he said, delighted. 'My favourite.'

Who knew what bacteria lurked on an old bottle of ketchup?

'Rory!' I shrieked, swan-diving towards him and hoping that Sinéad was too enraptured by new clothes to see that her son was teetering on the cusp of an E. coli death. I quickly tried to clean him with a cloth I found under the sink, before Sinéad and Becca finally emerged, bags bulging with their swaps. I looked at Rory and realised that the left side of his hair was encrusted with ketchup.

'Rory,' said Sinéad, kneeling down in front of him. 'What's in your hair?' She looked at me, terrified. 'Is it blood?'

'It's...' I had to come clean. 'It's ketchup. He found a bottle.'

For a moment, a thousand emotions flickered through Sinéad's face, as though she was battling with trying not to explode. Maybe it was that glow of new clothes, only enhanced by the fact that they were free, that softened Sinéad. She laughed.

'Rory!' she scolded. 'Silly boy. You're meant to *eat* ketchup, not cover yourself in it.'

'I *was* twying to eat it, Mummy,' he said, seriously. 'But was too slipperwy.'

And she laughed again, all thoughts of E. coli and bacteria pushed away.

Becca looked at me and gave me a secret thumbs up.

'So,' I said, 'what did you get?'

'A nearly brand-new Sweaty Betty hooded top,' Sinéad said. 'And a T-shirt and a pair of leggings.' She raked through her opened bag to show us. 'And they are all from Elizabeth O'Neill. Bought them for her new life as a fitness fanatic, which never materialised. And...' Sinéad looked thrilled, 'Elizabeth is *ob*-sessed with washing with laundry sanitiser. And obviously, I will wash them as well...'

Becca smiled at me, as though to say that Sinéad hadn't *totally* changed.

'What did you find?' I asked Becca.

She shrugged. 'The weirdest thing,' she said. 'And I don't know why. I was just drawn to them. Again, hardly worn and...' She reached into her bag and drew out a pair of Birkenstocks. 'They're lined,' she said, breathlessly, 'with sheepskin.'

'Wow,' said Sinéad, taking one. 'Amazing. And nearly new.'

'They were an unwanted Christmas present,' said Becca. 'This woman said her husband bought them for her because she complained that her shoes hurt. Anyway, she unwrapped them on Christmas morning and was horrified that he saw her as a Birkenstocks kind of person. But the thing is, and I never knew this, I *am*. It's like my inner earth mother has been activated. She was dormant all my life and now she is awake.'

'Did you give away your shoes?'

Becca nodded. 'To the same woman. She grabbed my Dior heels, screaming with delight. Look, there she is...' Across the room, a woman was strutting around in a pair of nearly new vertiginous heels. 'I just can't wait to put these on,' said Becca. 'I just have a feeling that once they are on, I won't take them off.'

'And this is the woman who once spent three hundred and fifty euros on a pair of high heels which she couldn't walk in.'

'Car to bar,' said Becca, tying up her curls into a ponytail. 'But that was then. This is now. I only wear Birkenstocks.' She looked absurdly pleased, as though she'd just discovered that George Clooney was moving into the house next door. 'And I found this for you, Cat.' She held up a bag.

Inside was a nearly new bright blue swimsuit and a navy towelling poncho.

'Madeleine was giving these away,' said Becca. 'She's just bought herself a camouflage dryrobe. Says she wouldn't be caught dead in her navy towel any more.'

'But I will,' I said, thrilled. Now, I wouldn't have to be seen in my nearly transparent suit and I would have a much nicer towel to change behind.

THE FORTY FOOTERS!

Margaret: High tide at 7.32. Shall we meet at 6 p.m.?

Nora: Thank you, Margaret. See you then.

Brenda: Fab. TY.

Dolores: Beautiful day today. The sea is sparkling.

Nora: You're up early?

Dolores: You know me, early bird gets the worm.

Malachy: I'll be down after work. Have a good day, everyone.

15

Late on Saturday afternoon, I walked to the Forty Foot where the gang were all meeting. I'd already been added to their WhatsApp group – a move which made me feel as though I had been accepted into a special swimming club. The WhatsApp was busy with times to meet and other useful information. It seemed to be led by Margaret, who would post the times of high tide and forecast every morning, as though she was the weather monitor. She would also post what she thought of as relevant community information such as:

James' Deli has a very good supply of courgettes.

Or:

Delicious sour-dough bread in Sally-Anne's, new recipe.

Or:

Remember The Great Sandycove Bake-Off in two weeks. I have application forms.

Today, being a Saturday, the beach was jam-packed with day trippers and picnickers, families with children playing on the sand, everyone hot and tired, and falling into the sea to cool off. The Forty Footers were there already when I arrived, changing in our usual space at the far end of the benches.

Nora was in her swimsuit and sat with her back to the wall, her legs sticking out, her face in the sun, eyes closed.

'Have you got your SPF on?' said Margaret.

'I'm just getting my vitamin D,' said Nora, eyes still scrunched closed. 'We can't live without sunlight.'

'But don't overdo it,' cautioned Margaret.

'Balance in everything, Margaret,' replied Nora, opening her eyes and turning to her. 'I have found,' she said, smiling, 'that we spend all our lives either doing too much of one thing or not enough of another, and finding the right proportions of everything – the good, the bad, the ugly – is where happiness lies.' She poked Margaret with her toe. 'This one here is too scared to have any of the good in her life. She only eats sprouts and never cream cakes. She only watches the news and never a Robert Redford film.'

'I *have* watched a Robert Redford film,' said Margaret, who was stepping out of her shorts, her swimsuit already on. 'Once. He was a journalist. I think.'

'If you can't remember Robert Redford then you didn't really watch it,' said Nora.

'Finding balance is not easy,' added Dolores, 'not when you're an all-or-nothing woman. I'm either on or off.' Malachy was beside her, rolling up his towel and neatly folding his clothes. 'This one is always *off*. Should be having fun at his age, going to discos. Do they still even have discos these days?'

Malachy laughed. 'Don't ask me, Dolores. How would I know, if I'm always off?'

'Do you mean that Malachy never goes out?' said Brenda, who had changed into her leopard-skin swimsuit.

'I do,' Malachy insisted. 'I go to work, and I swim here. But on the whole, I'm very happy staying at home with Mam.' He turned to me. 'She's got a touch of dementia. Well, more than a touch.' He looked away. 'I go home after work, check on her, make sure she's all right, and then come here, quick swim, and back home to make dinner. Eggs usually, but tonight we've got fish and chips. She loves it.'

'You're a good boy, Mal,' said Brenda.

'She's my mam,' he replied, shrugging. 'She looked after me for all those years. And anyway, I don't want to go to discos.' Everyone was looking at him, nodding sympathetically and he blinked a little, looking out to sea.

'I'm doing this saying yes to everything,' I said, changing the subject to take the heat off Malachy. 'I wouldn't be swimming with you if I hadn't started forcing myself to say yes to scary things.'

'Nothing scary about swimming,' said Nora.

'My mum's friend Lorraine, Margaret's neighbour, told me I needed to get out more...' I added.

'Like our Malachy,' said Brenda.

'And I said yes to having a lodger,' I went on. 'And I started a new job...'

'Which she's very good at,' remarked Brenda.

'And...'

'Met any nice men?' said Dolores. 'Said yes to anyone nice?'

I shook my head. 'I'm not interested...'

'What about this lodger?' asked Margaret. 'Is he an *eligible* bachelor?'

I shook my head. 'Definitely not.

Dolores leaned closer. 'My problem is *always* saying yes. I've had to learn how to say no. Couldn't ever say no to a drink, to staying up late, to having a party. I'd have a party on my own, no problem. Who needs actual friends when you've got a nice bottle of red wine? Or two, or three... That was another problem – not being able to stop at one.'

'You're doing brilliantly,' said Nora. 'We're really proud of you.'

'You know what we should say yes to?' I suggested. 'A hot tea... I could bring a flask.'

Margaret brightened. 'I have the perfect one,' she said. 'It makes enough tea for ten people. I bought it for a church trip to Russborough House years ago and it hasn't had an outing since. I'll be on tea duty.'

'And I'll be on biscuit duty,' I said.

'Good idea,' said Nora. 'There's always room for tea. Right, who's ready? Shall we go in?'

And so we did, Malachy leaping in from the far rocks, Margaret launching herself after singing her hymn... and I stepped in, welcoming the cold.

* * *

After our swim, Margaret left to do the flowers in the church, Brenda was going to her choir rehearsal, Malachy had to go home to his mam and Dolores had her 'meeting'.

'Good luck, Dolores,' said Nora, as we walked down the slope, her wheeling her bike. 'Where are you off to?' she said to me. The sun was still high in the sky, the whole stretch along the coast full of locals out enjoying the light and bright evening. 'Would you like to come beach cleaning with me? Takes about half an hour. We pick up after the day trippers. Just a quick tidy-up.'

What I really wanted to do was go home and relax. I knew

Callum was bringing Loulou back to the house for her night and for some reason I felt a responsibility to make it nice for her. But I had made a promise to Lorraine.

'Yes,' I said, 'I'd love to.'

I had to try to keep up with Nora's fast pace, her long grey plaits wet from the sea, soaking into her T-shirt.

'How long have you been beach cleaning?' I asked.

'Since forever,' she said. 'We used to just pick up things like old bottles and fishing nets. Now, it's quite shocking what people leave behind.' She shook her head. 'I decided a long time ago not to try to get into the minds of people who leave their rubbish behind. But if we don't do it, then who will? And I've been playing on this beach since I was a small child, so I'm happy to do my bit... Now, here we are...'

There were still some sunseekers sitting on their towels, but most of the families who I had seen earlier when I walked up from the car had gone. The sand, now that I looked, was dotted with rubbish.

'We're on rota,' explained Nora. 'Two of us every evening. I do every couple of months. Sean calls us the Flotsam Army.' She looked up as a tall man, around my age, dark hair, wearing a faded Greenpeace T-shirt, walked towards us.

'Evening, Nora,' he said. 'Good to see you.' He smiled at both of us.

'This is Sean,' she said to me. 'Sean, the general of the Flotsam Army.'

He laughed. 'Oh, I think it's a very egalitarian army,' he said, 'if armies can be egalitarian. My job is just organising the rota,' he said, smiling at us both. 'It's hardly general level.'

'I've brought Catríona with me,' Nora said. 'She said she would give us a hand.'

'Cat...' I held out my hand.

'Sean,' he said, smiling. 'Right, shall we get going? Nora knows the drill. Need a bag?'

From her pocket, Nora plucked a neatly folded square, which she unwrapped to produce a large plastic bag. 'Do you have a bag for Cat? And a picker?'

Sean handed me a large cotton shopper and a litter picker. 'Just put in anything that shouldn't be on the beach and I will sort it out when we've finished. We have the throwaways – the stuff that just goes in the bin; the donations – stuff that perhaps can be sent to the charity shop, the clothes, the toys, that kind of thing; and the recyclables, the plastic, that kind of thing. Right, I normally set a timer for thirty minutes and we do as much as we can.'

I took my bag and Sean pointed me in the direction of the far end of the small beach.

'You go as far as the life ring,' he said, 'and to the large boulder.'

It was depressing to think quite how much rubbish you could find tucked in between rocks, bottles half-submerged in sand, a whole bag of a half-eaten picnic, but we carried on until I found myself just beyond the life ring.

'Everyone finished?' said Sean, who had two bags filled with rubbish. 'I'll just go through it now and then I need to get home.' He smiled. 'Having a two-year-old and a six-month-old means that I can't leave Sarah for too long.'

'When are you heading away?' asked Nora. 'In that old van of yours?'

'We bought a camper van,' Sean explained. 'It's currently sitting outside the house needing a new fan belt and whatever else. But we're heading down to Bantry on Monday.'

For a ridiculous moment, I felt a little disappointed that Sean not only had a partner, and children, but a camper van – and they were heading to West Cork, my favourite place in the world. I wanted someone in my life, I realised, someone to share things with, someone to go home to. It took me by surprise how visceral the feeling was. I wanted what Sean and Sarah had – this family I knew nothing about and yet had something I wanted.

'Would you like me to put you on the Flotsam Army rota?' said Sean. 'It's once a month or thereabouts, quick thirty-minute tidy-up, sort through.'

Of course I had to say 'yes' to being on the rota. 'I'd love to,' I said.

After we had finished, I walked away feeling good about myself – the opposite to feeling *fed* up, this was full up. It might not last, it could drain away so easily, but to know that there were places you could go and things you could do that filled you up even a little was heartening. This was what it was like to make a difference. A small – tiny – difference, but it felt good all the same.

16

When I arrived home, Loulou was lying on the sofa, watching the television, a bag of Maltesers on her lap. Callum was in the armchair next to her.

'Hey!' I smiled at her, but she put her finger to her lips, after pressing pause on the TV remote.

'Shhhh. Daddy's asleep. He doesn't like being woken up.'

'Okay,' I said in a whisper, sitting on the arm of the sofa. 'What did you guys do that was so tiring?'

'We went to the cinema,' she whispered. 'And then we went to see Granny and Grandad, which Daddy hates because they always criticise him.'

'Really?'

She nodded. 'They think he should get a proper job. Grandad says he could go and work for him if he would just get off his arse...'

'He said that?'

She nodded. 'Grandad has his own business and he said that Daddy didn't inherit any of his brains.'

'No!'

'It was really mean of them, wasn't it? Mummy says they aren't the nicest parents to Daddy, even though they are nice grandparents to me. It's not fair, though. I would prefer them to be not nice to me and nice to Daddy.'

No wonder Callum was so tired, I thought. It was hard to keep going when you had no support from family.

I sat next to her. 'So what are you watching?'

'*Tracy Beaker*,' she said. 'She's a foster child and doesn't have a mother or a father. Well, she has a mother, but she's useless, and her father doesn't exist. So Tracy has to survive on her own.'

'Maybe I could watch it with you?'

'Would you?'

'It sounds really interesting.'

Loulou wriggled closer to me, and balanced the Maltesers between us. 'Would you like one?'

'Are you sure?'

She nodded. 'Very.'

'I'll just take one.'

'I could count them out and we will have exactly half each?' And she did. Except there were nineteen and she took the extra one.

For the next hour, we watched two episodes of *Tracy Beaker*, Loulou answering all my questions, while Callum slept on, a slight snore rumbling from him, making Loulou pull a face and giggle at me. I wondered what she was feeling, spending Saturday night with a stranger, rather than her Dad. I contemplated giving him a sharp nudge, but decided he was a virtual stranger, not someone I could wake up and remind him he had a child to look after.

Eventually, his eyes flickered open, like a man waking from a coma. He turned his head to look at us. 'Sorry about that,' he said, looking a bit sheepish. 'How long was I gone, Loulou?'

'Not long,' she said, as though she wanted to protect him.

'We should think about dinner,' he said. 'Cat, would you like to join us? Takeaway? Pizza?'

'There's an amazing place in the village which does wood-fired pizza... *and* they do salted caramel ice cream.'

Loulou jumped up. 'I'll lay the table,' she said.

'And I'll order...' said Callum. He smiled at me. 'Thanks, Cat.'

It was strange, but I realised I was getting something out of having them around, even watching television with Loulou had been fascinating. Having a child around opened up another universe, and that was the thing about saying yes, doors opened into other worlds, and life became kaleidoscopic in colour and variety. I hadn't thought of myself as bored, as such, before. But I was definitely more interested now... in *everything*.

In the kitchen, Loulou opened the drawer, took out napkins and a tablecloth and then arranged everything beautifully. 'Can we eat like princesses?' she said, excitedly. She even lit a candle and, just as we stood back to admire her work, the doorbell rang.

'Pizza's here,' I said.

'I can't believe it!' Loulou said, thrilled at the timing. 'It's like magic! Thank you, Cat.'

Callum walked in. 'How about we eat in front of the television. *Quiz Me I'm Irish* is about to start... if anyone would like to join me?'

Loulou glanced at me. 'I might stay here with Cat,' she said. 'If that's okay, Daddy?'

A look of hurt flickered over his face for a moment. 'Of course it's okay, sweetheart.'

Loulou looked down for a moment as though she, too, was tortured by something. Your parents' relationship was sometimes overwhelming, I thought, and your own relationship with your parents could be sometimes confusing. Poor Loulou, and poor Callum.

'If that's what you prefer?' he said, trying to smile.

She nodded again. 'Yes.'

'Well, I can join you two here, then,' said Callum.

'You watch the TV,' said Loulou, 'and we can just eat here. We were going to eat like princesses.' She looked at me. 'We were... but... I don't mind...'

'It's fine,' said Callum. 'You just come and join me when you two are done being princesses.'

He turned to go and Loulou caught up with him and hugged him from behind. 'We won't be long, promise,' she said.

He ruffled her hair. 'You take your time.'

'I've got some apple juice,' I said, when she came back into the kitchen, 'and we'll use my special glasses?'

Facing each other at the table, we used our napkins to dab at our mouths princess-style and we chatted about school and *Tracy Beaker*, and which was the best Ben & Jerry's flavour, and in the background, from the TV, I could hear the voice of Susie Keane and I remembered her being not so charming at the clothes swap when she seemed to be warning me off Tom.

17

At the Monday morning meeting, Angela was speaking. 'So, after Percy the dancing pug,' she said, 'we'll have Maura and ways to keep cool while having a hot flush, and then to Lisa for her segment on ways to tie a scarf.'

'I favour the folding it in two, and then tucking the ends through,' said David. 'Learned it from the girls in wardrobe. They have all the new moves.'

Angela's phone rang. 'Sorry,' she said, 'I just have to... Ah, Betty! How are you?'

'Betty Boyle,' said David to the rest of us, 'the world's most basic cook.' He sat back in his chair, his loafers up on the desk. 'Do you know, once upon a time, we used to smoke at our desks? All of us puffing away, the whiskey would be brought out at lunchtime on a Friday... ah, happy days.'

Beside us, Angela was still on her phone call. 'Oh, that's terrible,' she was saying. 'Oh no. Poor thing. And was his death...? I mean, did he die...? Was he...? Oh... it was painless. Well, that's good to know. And he died in your arms? Ahhh... you're right, that's real love. He was your best friend, of course he was. No, you'll never find love like that again. No, of course you take as long as you need. No, you can't hurry grief. Yes, he *was* adorable. Yes, his face was like an angel's. No, nobody minded when he defecated... you can't help it when you get old... I know, you're so right, it *will* happen to all of us. I know... I know... Lots of love. Slán.' She ended the call and looked at us. 'That was Betty... Mr Potts has died... she won't be able to be on the show for the next few weeks.'

'Ah, that's terrible,' said Ava. 'But wasn't he really old?'

'He was seventeen,' said Angela. 'Ancient, in other words. It was time for him to go. When you get to a certain age, it's only right that you let them go...'

'Not necessarily,' insisted David, glancing at Tom. 'Some can continue on forever... it's the rest of the world that gets old...'

'Who is Mr Potts?' I asked.

'Betty's teacup Yorkie,' said Angela. 'You didn't see him last week because he was in the vet's. But he passed away in her arms last night.'

'He was an ankle biter,' said David. 'And you know I like to go sans socks? Well, there was no protection against his surprisingly sharp teeth. He was half-dog, half-shark.'

'Poor Betty is very upset,' said Angela, 'and needs to take grieving leave.' She looked over at Tom. 'She's going to call you shortly to sort everything out. She's wondering if the station would pay his cremation costs?'

'Cremation costs?' said Tom. 'Why on earth is that our responsibility?'

'Because she says he was a TV dog. When he was younger, he'd been cooking with her, tasting the food, sitting on the work surface.'

'Before my time,' replied Tom. He looked at me and smiled. 'But don't we have a taxidermist on today's show? Maybe that would solve Betty's problem?'

'Tom!' Angela swiped him with her hand. 'Poor Betty. Don't even suggest such a thing about Mr Potts.'

Tom laughed. 'Don't worry, I will talk to her, sort things out, arrange grieving leave.'

'So, who will be in place of Betty?' I said.

Angela looked suddenly excited. 'Well,' she said, her eyes shining, 'there could be a silver lining, because this morning I received a phone call from the agent of... well, he's only the best chef in the country. I've never been to his restaurant, but I bought his book... My God, that chicken dish with olives... to die for...'

'Olives? The devil's eyeballs,' said David. 'No one *I* know eats olives.' He looked at Angela suspiciously. 'Who is this charlatan? Suddenly I miss Betty and her porridge and endless eggs.'

I felt ill suddenly. And it wasn't the mention of a surfeit of eggs. I had a strong inkling where this conversation was going.

'It's only PJ Doyle!' said Angela, delighted.

My inkling had been right. With difficulty, I struggled to keep my rictus smile from fading.

'I am thrilled,' Angela went on. 'The *enfant terrible* of Irish cuisine... he'll shake things up a bit! No soda bread or apple tart or... I don't know, *ordinary* things. He'll do... snails or seaweed or things like that.'

Under his tan, David suddenly appeared a shade of green. '*Snails?* Is this 1845? Are we in a famine that no one told me about? I thought we'd *evolved*, *unlike* the prehistoric snail. We now eat *actual* food that tastes nice.'

'I know, I know...' said Angela soothingly. 'Don't worry, I am sure he won't do anything with snails, I just wanted to show how different he is to Betty. There's this recipe in his book for fish that you just marinade in lime juice and that's it... no cooking.'

David looked faint. 'Raw fish? Holy mother of God. Our core audience is the good people of Middle Ireland who do not eat snails or raw fish and certainly not olives. They'll be switching channel to watch Mr Truly Talentless Valentine O'Malley and his conveyor belt of has-beens.'

'I just want to try out a few new ideas,' said Angela. 'And PJ Doyle is one of them. He will bring a certain kind of exciting chaos to proceedings, an element of unpredictability... He's going to be with us for the rest of the summer. And it's going to be fun. I'm going to see if he can come in today. It's a bit short notice, but according to his agent, he's a very recent convert to the show. His agent said it was most unusual as he normally says no to everything. Can you believe it? PJ Doyle watches our show!'

'Jeepers,' said David, 'he sounds even more of an eejit. And why the sudden interest in our show? It doesn't make sense.'

I sat, only half listening, thinking of how much PJ was going to spoil everything.

18

PJ Doyle and I had first met three years earlier at a Food Ireland lunch to promote home-grown and home-made produce. Mike, my old producer, had commissioned a report and, microphone in hand, I had found myself standing in front of PJ Doyle, one of the best new and upcoming chefs on the Irish cooking scene.

It was a couple of days later, when the interview had aired and my phone had rung.

'Cat,' the voice had said, 'it's PJ Doyle.' I didn't stop to wonder how he had tracked me down because he made it sound totally normal. His confidence was so unusual. 'Look,' he went on, 'I wondered if you and some friends would like to come to the restaurant – chef's table, the works – just to say thank you for being so charming the other day. Not all journalists are as thorough and fair with their questions.'

I began to say no. 'It's very kind of you bu—'

'It's only dinner,' he said. 'And you'd be doing me a favour. I need the chef's table to be full because I like to keep an eye on my trainees... and surely you have a couple of friends who would like a night out?'

Becca was always up for food and Sinéad was nine months pregnant and had only that day told me she needed one last night in Dublin's city centre before she had the baby. 'Well...'

'What about this evening?' he went on. 'No strings attached. It's just a meal to say thank you for not asking me why I don't serve burger and chips at the restaurant or any of the brainless inanities I keep having to flap away.'

'I could ask some friends,' I said.

'Great.' He sounded pleased. 'Seven thirty?'

* * *

It ended up being an amazing night. Sinéad wasn't drinking, obviously, but the three of us enjoyed every single morsel of the nine-course menu which we were served.

'You know,' said Becca, as she polished off the sea salt and Wicklow honey caramel fondant, 'I think PJ Doyle might be a genius. And, Cat, he *likes* you.'

Carried away by the wine and the lovely food, I was also absurdly flattered by the attention. And so, when PJ rang the next day to ask me to his for dinner, just the two of us, I said yes.

Things progressed very quickly. Within a week, he told me he loved me and soon he was coming back to mine straight from the restaurant. I even changed my hours to fit in with his and, for a couple of months, I thought I had found The One.

Except for the criticism. At first, I thought it was just normal feedback or observations but then he would sulk about something he had 'noticed' in me, that I wasn't quite the person he had thought I was, and however much I tried to convince him I was, it would still take him days to forgive me. Now, looking back, it all seemed so crazy to think that I had desperately tried to prove myself to him. Once, he even became annoyed when I had used one of his Japanese knives to slice my breakfast banana, but when I'd tried to tell him that the knife didn't matter and his sulking wasn't going to get us anywhere, he acted like the incident hadn't happened, and I began to question if I had imagined it.

And then, finally, in a small restaurant in Bilbao, where we had to breathe in a special mist and, for one course, eat blindfolded, I'd snapped. Exhausted from months of trying to please him and to stop him from the silent treatment or anger, I'd had enough. We'd gone for a weekend because he wanted to try as many of the two- and three-star Michelin restaurants as possible in forty-eight hours. It was at the final one when I reached the end of my patience and ability to listen to a man who wasn't interested in conversation, only in the sound of his own voice. Every time I had offered an opinion or critique, he had silenced me with a look or even a finger in the air.

'But it's potatoes with oranges,' I'd said. 'It's horrible.'

'If you don't cook professionally,' he'd replied, 'then you don't get to criticise.'

I'd seethed. 'I don't want to be here any more. And I don't want to be with you any more. You're just too hard to please.'

I'd folded my napkin up and climbed, with as much dignity as I could, out of the chair – it was ridiculously oversized and I had felt like a toddler the whole time.

'Where are you going?' shouted PJ, his face already red. In a moment, he would explode, I thought. He tried to get off the chair, but I had a head start. 'I'll see you back at the hotel! Wait there for me.'

Except I didn't wait. At the hotel, I packed my bag and left, which took all of fifteen minutes. Heart beating, but determined, I took a taxi to the airport – suppressing any instinct to tell the driver to drive for his life – where I managed to get on the next flight home.

Back in Sandycove, I blocked PJ on everything and refused to talk to him. Cowardly, yes, but totally necessary. He wouldn't have let me go if I'd let him talk to me. He would have had me convinced that he was right and I had done a terrible thing by leaving him like that.

Becca and Sinéad both confessed that they had never liked him.

'You said he was a genius!' I'd said.

'I had drunk a *great* deal of wine that evening,' explained Becca. 'I momentarily had lost control of my senses.'

'And I was too pregnant to even think straight,' said Sinéad. 'My waters broke that night, remember? I think it was that food which induced it.'

'I can't deny he is a great chef,' Becca had acknowledged. 'But he was just too intense. You just didn't seem happy together.'

'You just need to find someone nice and uncomplicated,' Sinéad had added. 'Someone who doesn't love food to an abnormal extent.'

'God, yes,' agreed Becca, passionately. 'None of this food-is-art shite. The kind of person who likes cheese on toast or Supermac's chips. Someone *normal*.'

'Someone,' said Sinéad, 'who doesn't sulk.'

We'd been together for a year – a year too long, to be honest, and as soon as I was back in Dublin, I felt the relief of not having to deal with him, listen to his rants or do as I was told. Our paths had not crossed since I'd walked out of that restaurant, but I dreaded meeting him again. PJ was not the kind of person who liked being made a fool of.

19

I managed to avoid PJ before the show. Guests were kept in the green room ahead of broadcast, but the chefs, because they had to be in the preparation area, were given free rein. In my dressing room, I did my speech exercises, worried about what PJ would say to me or how he would treat me. I didn't go on set until moments before the camera was rolling, and then slipped on to the sofa beside David, picking up my clipboard of notes.

'Sorry,' I said, smiling. 'Bit delayed. Problem with a button.'

Angela's voice in my ear. 'Everything all right?'

I gave the camera a thumbs up. Talking to someone whom you could only hear was still something I was getting used to, as though you were having conversations with your inner self, out loud.

'Right, guys,' said Angela. 'Get ready. Ten... nine...'

'I've just met PJ,' said David. 'And I take it all back. He's not an eejit but such a charming man.' He smiled. 'Absolutely lovely. Said he wouldn't dream of doing anything with snails.'

'...And we're live,' said Angela. The red light on camera one flicked on as David, as he always did, sprang into life.

'Good afternoon!' said David. 'And you're very welcome to *The Daily Show*. I'm David Fitzgerald...'

There was a split second – any silence on-air is always too long – before I managed to find my voice. 'And I'm Cat Jones.'

'We've got a wonderful show today, don't we, Cat?'

'We do,' I said, reading the autocue. 'We have the star of the new dating show *Where's My Ride?*... Noel Percival from the police drama everyone is watching, *Sod's Law*... a taxidermist on the new way of keeping your pet with you forever... and a discussion on how to communicate with teenagers...'

'And someone who is excellent at communication through the language of food,' went on David, managing to get through the terrible script still with a smile on his face, 'we have one of Ireland's very best chefs, the incomparable, the daring and brilliant PJ Doyle...'

* * *

During the show, out of the corner of my eye, while we were interviewing the taxidermist who was able to recreate your deceased cat, dog or, even in one case, budgerigar, I could see PJ entering the kitchen area.

'Final question,' Angela said in my ear.

'So, Teri,' I said to the taxidermist, 'is there an animal that is just too difficult to stuff?'

'Elephant,' she said, immediately. 'My spare room's not big enough. It's only a two-up, two-down in Cabra.'

From the kitchen area, I could see PJ looking over at us, craning his neck as though desperate to get in on the action.

David was laughing. 'The elephant in the room!' he said. 'Get it?'

Teri smiled politely, but it was clear from the expression in her eyes that she didn't.

'Take a break,' said Angela.

'And we'll be back with super-chef PJ Doyle after these...' I said, straight down the camera. PJ was going to be fine, I told myself. We would just be perfectly pleasant and professional to each other, no one would ever know our history, and surely he wouldn't still carry any resentment towards me because of the way I'd ended things.

David and I had to walk briskly across the studio floor to the kitchen area, but David was waylaid by Brenda. 'You're a bit shiny,' she said, flicking the powder brush at his face. 'Needs dampening down. You're like a conker.'

I had no choice but to walk towards PJ on my own. He stood, watching me approach.

'Oh, Cat,' he said, 'how lovely to see you.' He held out his hand. 'Do we kiss? Shake hands? Rub noses? What do old lovers do?' He was wearing a too-tight T-shirt cut to show off his arms, which were muscled from years of meat-cleavering as well as hours in the gym with his PT.

I had to keep smiling. My microphone was off, but in a studio there were cameras everywhere.

'They greet each other politely,' I said.

'The last time I saw you your backside was leaving that restaurant in Spain,' he said. 'There was I, looking forward to the next course, and off you go. And you don't return. Nor do you answer any of my messages. Frantic they were. I was worried about you.'

At the time, I had told him I was leaving and that it was over. I couldn't stand another of his rants about someone else, or about veganism, or the customer who ordered ketchup for his meal, or when I told him once that the soup I had made had a stock cube in it, rather than the congealed jelly that he had put in my fridge, and he had gone on and on about flavour and taking care over food and additives and whatever. I had had enough, I remembered, hearing his voice going round and round in my head. But now, I felt foolish. There had to have been a better way to end things, rather than run away.

'Sorry,' I said. 'I shouldn't have just gone like that.'

'Finally.' He stared at me. 'Took you a while.'

'Everything okay?' said Angela in my ear.

'Grand, grand…' I turned around in the direction of the producer's box before turning back to PJ, trying to look neutral again.

'What should you have done?' he said. 'How should you have done it?'

'I should have…' I stopped.

'You should have what?'

It was all coming back to me now. PJ always remained laser-focused until he had got you to say what he wanted you to say. It could be promising never to use a stock cube or a particular knife again, it could be swearing never to opt for a vegan diet, it could be agreeing that ordering ketchup in a proper restaurant was a personal insult to the chef and showed that you had no regard for decent food and therefore yourself. With PJ, the only way to manage him was to give him what he wanted.

'I should have stayed and we could have talked it through.'

He nodded, half-satisfied, but not enough. 'Why did you leave at all?' he said, his voice now sweet and wheedling. 'I mean, there we were, on a gastronomic adventure, eating in the finest restaurants of northern Spain…'

'I just couldn't listen to your anti-vegan rant any longer,' I said.

'Thirty seconds,' said Angela.

'I can't stand vegans!' he spluttered. 'They're so fecking…' He struggled to find the right word. 'They're so incredibly annoying!' I braced myself for him to say something mean, something that would cut me down to size. But his face softened as he looked over my shoulder. 'Ah, here's the man himself.'

'Ten seconds,' said Angela, in my ear, as I turned up my microphone.

'Looking forward to this,' said David, striding towards us. 'Feeling a bit peckish.'

'Coming to you now,' said Angela. 'Stand by... And we're live.'

I faced the camera. 'Welcome back,' I said. 'And we're all in for a treat now... We're delighted to be joined by the country's most exciting chef, the great PJ Doyle...' I turned to PJ. 'What are you making for us today, PJ?'

PJ was a complete natural. He transformed himself into a charming, sweet, gently spoken man, who made eye contact with David and me, smiled down the camera, peppered in a few self-deprecating jokes, some invaluable culinary tips, a nod or two to his favourite suppliers, a shout-out to his 'amazing gang' back at the restaurant, and in the end produced a plate of food which looked – as it always did with PJ – visually stunning. He looked right down the camera, a twinkle in his brilliant green eyes, which was both sexy and playful. God, he was a good actor, I thought. No wonder so many people were taken in.

'Now,' said PJ, 'who is going to taste it?' He held up a forkful of food and looked straight at me. 'Cat, will you have some?'

I wanted to say no, but I hadn't used the word in quite a while and I wasn't about to start now, knowing Mum was probably at home watching me. 'Yes,' I said, just as the fork came straight for me and there was nothing I could do except open my mouth and begin to chew. 'Mmm, delicious.'

PJ leaned over again to me and dabbed at my mouth with a tea towel. 'Few crumbs,' he said. 'There...' And then he tucked a strand of hair behind my ear. 'Good?'

'Yes...' I said again.

'Ten seconds to roll credits,' said Angela.

'And that's it from Cat and me,' David was saying. 'But, most of all, that's it from our star chef, the utterly brilliant PJ Doyle...'

'Back tomorrow,' I said, remembering to smile.

And the credits started rolling and David slapped PJ on the back. 'Now, much as I adore our Betty and her soda bread, this was a real change in the right direction. Just what our viewers are crying out for – edgy, interesting food. Who would have thought about toasting hazelnuts or smoking herbs? In my day, smoking herbs meant something entirely different.' David laughed as the crew had joined us, trying to get to the food before it was gone.

I turned and began walking away.

Angela was in front of me, looking excited. 'Great show! Oh my God, *all* of it. But especially PJ... or *Peej* as he says we should call him. He was so good, don't you think?' she went on. 'I mean, we all love Betty, but Peej is so *untamed*... I mean, we all know how to make her apple tart and chowder by now... it's definitely time for something new. And did I sense a little bit of a frisson... a bit of *chemistry* between you?'

'I don't think so, Angela,' I said.

'You seemed to be talking quite intently before the show,' she continued, 'what were you talking about.'

'Oh, he's just very passionate about food,' I replied. 'He was telling about what he was going to do.'

'It's just that I heard him say something about old lovers?' She looked at me. 'And the way he touched you. Look, Cat, if there is going to be a problem with you two working together, we could all sit down and talk it through? What do you say?'

'It will be fine,' I said, not wanting to make a fuss or any demands. 'Honestly...'

'Really?' She peered at me.

'Really. And I've got to go...'

'You go, you go!' She waved me away. 'But tell me if you are ever uncomfortable or if there is anything I can do? Okay?'

I nodded. 'Thanks, Angela. I appreciate it.'

It was only for a couple more weeks. How difficult could it be?

20

In the make-up chair, I thought I might actually cry. Brenda was changing the CD on her ancient player, while I began wiping off all the foundation from my face, hoping she wouldn't see how rattled I was.

'I'll do that,' said Brenda, turning towards me. 'We put it on, we can take it off again.' She smiled at me and then she peered closer. 'What's wrong?'

'I'm fine,' I said.

'It's that chef fella, isn't it? I was watching the show and I thought there was something between you. What is it?'

'We went out with each other,' I said. 'And he was…'

'Controlling? Toxic?'

I nodded. 'I wasn't perfect either.'

'No one is,' she said. 'But controlling behaviour is unacceptable. I've had one of those myself, as I've told you. Still have to see him every day because he's my postman. We've been separated for a few years now, but he acts like he is desperate to get me back, as though I broke his heart. I didn't, by the way. The man is incapable of love, he just doesn't like *not* being in control.'

'I think it's the same with PJ.' I sighed.

'People like my postman and your PJ, they just want to disturb you, shake you up. They *want* you to be crying, upset, that's when they feel most powerful. Be at peace with your peace. Don't rise to anything, don't respond, eyes front and carry on.'

'Thanks, Brenda.'

She smiled kindly at me. 'And sea swimming. Feel the power of the sea. And don't give him a second's thought. Promise me?'

I nodded.

'I'll see you at the Forty Foot, later, yes?'

'I wouldn't miss it for the world.'

* * *

Just as I was leaving the office, I heard Tom's voice behind me.

'Cat! Hold up!'

I waited for him and he walked towards me.

'Great show,' he said, smiling. 'I didn't catch all of it because I was on a Zoom meeting, but it was on in the office. Are you walking to the car park?'

I nodded, wondering about him and Susie. It was none of my business, obviously, but what she had said to me at the clothes swap had confused me. They weren't an item, as far as I could tell, but she felt confident enough that she could warn other women off.

Tom and I descended the curving stairs to the main reception area, as he continued talking about the show. 'I thought PJ worked well, did you?' I felt him look at me.

'Yes... yes, he worked well.'

'You didn't mind... when he...?' he began. 'I mean... he seemed a little flirtatious with you.'

'Was he?' I gave a confused smile as though I had no idea what he was talking about.

'You're okay with it?'

He was still looking at me.

'Yes, of course,' I said. 'I didn't notice anything. And it's all fine.'

He nodded, and then turned to wave at Cathy on the front desk.

'Goodnight, Tom!' she called, giving him a special wave.

'Night, Cathy,' he said. 'Hope we win at Croke Park. Up Galway!' He turned back to me. 'Us Galwegians have got to stick together,' he said, as we stepped outside and walked towards the car park. 'We're on enemy territory.' He smiled at me.

I smiled back. 'You must feel permanently surrounded...'

'Oh, I do,' he said. 'Dubliners, everywhere I turn. Mam worries about me,' he went on. 'Thinks I am going to start supporting the Dubs in the All-Ireland and start speaking in a Dublin accent. Last time I was home, she gave me a present of some Aran Island socks. Just so your feet are in the west at all times, she said. Thing is, and I daren't admit this to her, but they are way too scratchy and slippery. I put them on, dutiful son that I am, and almost broke my neck trying to make myself a cup of tea. Took them straight off.'

I laughed. 'Traitor,' I said. 'And what about your dad?' I wondered about the photo on his desk.

'We lost Dad two years ago,' he said. 'Mam's fine. Busy and all that, but I try to go home as often as I can, just to cut the grass, eat some decent food and watch a match in the pub. It is exactly the antidote to all this...'

I thought of my own antidote – swimming at the Forty Foot, diving into the sea and disappearing under the waves.

We stood beside an old yellow Renault and Tom took his keys out of his pocket and turned to the car. 'Let's just hope my old jalopy starts,' he said. 'This morning I lurched most of the way here, like some overexcited dog on its way to the park.'

'This is *yours*?'

'You sound surprised,' he said.

'You do surprise me,' I said. 'But in a good way... I don't know... it's cute.' I smiled at him.

'I'm not into big cars,' he explained. 'And I like this one. It's worth the lack of heating, the worry if it's going to start every morning, the fact it seems to have a mind of its own. And it makes me feel ten per cent more French...'

'French?' I laughed again.

'I really like France,' he said. 'I go there every year on holiday and I even bought a striped top last summer... even my cat laughed at me.'

'You're a *cat* person?' Why was I sounding so surprised at everything he said?

'Yup. My passion for my cat is as great as my passion for France. In fact, I have a French cat. His name is Pierre. I say bonjour to him every morning.' He was smiling at me.

I smiled back. I had assumed he was just another one of those super-confident, sleek-car-driving executives, but he didn't take himself as seriously as most other men at that level.

'What are you doing on this fine Monday evening?'

'Swimming,' I said.

'Of course you are...' He smiled again at me.

'What are you doing?' I asked.

'Five-a-side. Couple of pints. Home to Pierre.'

'French food?'

'Definitely.' He grinned. 'Fromage in some form.' He opened his car door. 'I'll see you tomorrow.'

'Safe drive home.'

'You mean, lurch home?'

'Safe lurch home, then.'

I started my engine, just as my phone rang. I pressed the Bluetooth. 'Hello?'

'You left so soon.' It was PJ. On a new phone number so he wasn't blocked. He'd clearly kept hold of my number.

'Yeah... I had to go...' Be at peace with your peace. In the make-up chair, it had made sense, but now I was trying to remember what to do. I thought it just meant don't rise to the bait, be calm and don't become emotionally involved.

'Cat,' he said, 'I just want to say I forgive you...'

'You forgive me?'

'Yes, I do,' he said. 'We all make mistakes and you're fallible... Anyway, we can move on. So, what did you think?' PJ pressed.

'Of what?' I was thrown.

'What did you think of me on the show? Do you think it worked? How was I?'

'Fine... you were great.' It was really hard to know how to manage him. He was the kind of man you didn't want knowing anything about you because he would retain the smallest piece of information, tuck it away, ready to be used to his advantage, to gain power over people. I had often thought it must be exhausting to be PJ, to work so hard in charming the right people and overpowering the others.

'I hope you don't mind me being on the show...'

'Of course not...'

'Because they've asked me back. Loved what I did. That woman, whatever her name is...'

'Angela.'

'Whatever. She said I brought edginess to the show.' He laughed. 'God, these television people are so up themselves, aren't they? I mean it's a crappy daytime TV show. No one is watching apart from people with no lives.'

'Actually, the audience figures are huge,' I said, defensively. 'So that's a lot of people with *no lives*, as you put it. And Angela is amazing...' That was what he did. He needled until you reacted. I had so quickly forgotten Brenda's words about being in your peace. He rattled me so easily. 'I've got to go,' I said. 'I'm driving.'

'See you, Cat,' he called out. 'See you when I'm next on. Can't wait.'

THE JONES FAMILY!

Mum: The show was great! Well done. By the way, call in for tea sometime. Am entering The Great Sandycove Bake-Off. Don't know what to make.

Me: Your lemon drizzle of course! Will call in later.

THE GIRLS!

Sinéad: Are you going to TV awards? Becca wants us to go?

Me: I don't think so. *The Daily Show* team are going, but I'm just there for so short a time.

Becca: The two of you are coming. No debate. I need two people there who aren't insane.

Sinéad: Conor's Mum says she will mind Rory, but I don't know if I trust her. She once gave him a slice of toast which had been on the floor.

Becca: He'll be fine. She brought up Conor, didn't she?

Sinéad: That's what I'm worried about.

Becca: Ha ha.

Sinéad: Why was PJ on the show? Whose idea was that?

Becca: He's still got that mad look in his eyes, like a rabid dog.

Sinéad: He looks like a very angry potato.

Becca: Or a mass murderer. He's a walking 'Wanted' poster.

Sinéad: Cat?

Me: It was the producer's decision. Nothing to do with me.

Becca: Obviously.

Me: I'm just trying to be professional. And nice. It's only a couple of weeks. How bad can it be?

Sinéad: You'll survive! I know you will!

Becca: You should make sure you are up to date with your tetanus shot, however, just to be on the safe side.

Sinéad: And insect repellent. Spray right in his eyes.

Me: It'll be fine! Promise! xxx

21

In the sea, I paddled around, flipping onto my back, letting the cold soak into my body, every tension and muscle ache easing out. Here in the sea, we were all the same. You didn't know anything about anyone, we were all equal, everything that set us apart, that set us above or below someone else was gone. It wasn't as though I was suddenly transformed into a better version of myself every time I got out of the water, but it was almost that I left something behind, all the things that kept me down were washed away. It was as though I was reset each time I swam, unencumbered by all the earthly judgements that we make and are made about us. I still stayed close to shore, floating about, breaststroking around, my face and hair saturated, and every day I felt a little less anxious about being on live television. I woke up each morning with the knot in my stomach a little looser, my breathing a little deeper. I found myself thinking about my evening swim during the day, knowing that whatever happened, later on, I'd be in the sea where nothing mattered except keeping afloat.

'I like your poncho,' Brenda said, as we dried off and I'd wriggled out of my swimsuit. 'I swear by mine,' she said, pulling at her hooded leopard-skin towelling poncho which made my navy one look very plain. 'Means I don't expose anyone to the wonders of my body.'

Dolores, who was standing beside her, grinned. 'You see all sorts here. I once saw a man who was sitting down, totally naked, drying his toes, meticulously topple forwards and land on another man, who was trying to change under a towel. They both screamed.'

'Well, I don't care,' said Nora, who always dressed quicker than anyone because she stripped off efficiently and dressed herself equally efficiently. 'If people want to look at my naked form, then let them.'

Margaret was wearing a towel which was elasticated around her neck, like a dress without arms and, trapped within, she fought a daily valiant battle to change. 'This was my mother's,' she explained to me. 'She used to come down here every day, didn't she, Nora?'

Nora nodded. 'We still miss her.'

'And I looked at it, and I thought, what do I do with it? It was possibly one of her most used items of clothing. It was either drying over the rack at home, or in her bag ready to be taken down here. And so it was this thing that brought me here. And it is here where I found her again.' She gave us a small smile. 'She's very present, just at this spot. I sing her favourite hymn every time I swim. "Great Is Thy Faithfulness". I like to think of the words which fortified her and which fortify me.'

'It was her happy place,' said Brenda.

Margaret nodded. 'I suppose it was. You could even say it was her spiritual place. She'd stopped going to church before I was born, even though her father was a Church of Ireland rector... she hated all that gathering and organising and having to be good. She was a single mother and she would sing hymns to me and then every day would come here and swim.'

'She and I were old pals,' said Nora. 'Neighbours for years and years...' She smiled at Margaret. 'Knew this one since she was a tot.'

'It's my happy place as well,' said Malachy, who was dressed, his towel rolled under his arm. 'You need somewhere to go, don't you?'

Nora nodded. 'You really do.'

'Some people find it in the pub,' said Brenda. 'Some people's happy place is Lansdowne Road, watching a rugby match. Others, if they are lucky, it's their home.'

Dolores spoke. 'Mine *was* the pub,' she said. 'This isn't my happy place. I can't say I'm *happy*. It's just that I know if I don't come, then I may go back to my old happy place.'

The others nodded, as though they understood what she was saying.

'My happy place is my bed,' said Brenda. 'Me and Arthur, a cup of warm milk, *Marriage of Figaro*... and I start to relax.'

'Why do you swim then?' I asked.

'It's my meditation and my therapy,' she said. 'I can talk to myself out there better than I can here, on dry land. And once I've done my talking, I can go home and feel better.'

'Where's your happy place, Cat?' asked Malachy.

I tried to think. 'Maybe my dad's shed? He fixes things and he's got this shed which is full of clutter and a little gas stove and the radio is always on, and he's just there... it's so peaceful.'

Nora nodded. 'Sounds like a happy place to me,' she said.

After we'd dried off and were back in our damp and crumpled clothes, Margaret produced a large flask of tea and several chipped cups with a little rose pattern on. 'As promised,' she said. 'Now, don't worry about breaking the cups. They were my mother's wedding china and for years I've lived in fear of one smashing, but now I've come to the conclusion that they should be used rather than sitting in a glass cabinet gathering dust. And I know *she*'d want us to use them. So, this evening I would like us to raise a toast to my mother.'

The flask was passed around and we each filled up our cups. 'It's her anniversary this evening and I would be honoured if you would raise a cup to a life well lived.'

I produced a packet of chocolate shortbread, and handed it to Brenda beside me. 'Pass them on,' I said.

'Here's to a life *very* well lived,' said Nora, smiling at Margaret and holding up her cup. 'Here's to your mother... a wonderful woman.'

'Strength for today and hope for tomorrow, blessings all mine, with ten thousand beside...' Margaret held up her cup again. 'Hope for tomorrow...'

'Hope for tomorrow,' we all echoed.

'It's been five years,' Margaret said. 'I just treasure having a mother who loved me...'

'Halleluia,' said Dolores.

'...Who was always there for me...' went on Margaret.

'We can't all say that,' said Dolores.

'And who was my best friend,' Margaret concluded.

'You were lucky,' interjected Dolores.

'I most certainly was,' agreed Margaret.

'I'm lucky with my mam,' said Malachy. 'She's still here, which I am taking as a win. I don't know what I'd do without her. Sometimes I think if I'd not been blessed with such a good mother, I might have been more inspired to perhaps...' he began to blush '... find a girlfriend. It's just I don't like leaving Mam alone. She always said she liked talking to me, and I like talking to her... and...' He shrugged. 'Some people might think that that was sad, I suppose.'

'It's not sad, it just means you've got a good mother,' Brenda said.

'You could spend forever pondering the what ifs,' said Nora. 'We must celebrate the just ares.'

'What if I hadn't married Michael-John?' said Brenda. 'It would have saved me twenty years of headache,' she said. 'In the end, he ran off with one of my friends. And I was delighted. Changed the locks and got on with my life. Didn't learn my lesson, still ended up entangled with Postman Pete.' She drained her plastic cup. 'Any more of this going, Margs? Thinking about men always makes me gloomy.'

'Let's not be gloomy,' said Margaret, topping up our cups with a couple more drops of tea each. 'Not today, not when we are celebrating Mam's life.'

'My mam wasn't a very nice woman,' said Dolores. 'Neither was my da… When I am in the sea, I sometimes think of them and wonder what they'd make of this girl who is now middle-aged, baggier and saggier, older and not much wiser.' She drained her cup. 'Would they be sorry for not being kinder?'

'You can't wait for people to be sorry,' said Malachy. 'My mam always says that. You forgive and let go…'

'Easier said than done,' remarked Brenda, as Nora nodded along.

'What about you, Cat?' said Dolores. 'Do you get on with your parents? Are they still with us?'

I nodded. 'Both are, thankfully. Mum's fine – she had a bit of a health scare but all's well… I hope.' I smiled at them, thinking of Mum. Please stay well, I thought. And safe. And stay away from parachutes. Better still, stay away from Lorraine.

They all nodded. 'Good to hear,' said Dolores.

'You know,' said Nora, 'one thing I regret is not taking more risks. Not being braver.'

'I would say your dalliance with a certain Finty O'Brien was pretty risky,' said Dolores. 'Didn't I recall you taking off to see him?'

'Ah,' smiled Nora. 'Sometimes you've got to see where the road takes you. That particular road took me to the edge of a cliff. Literally. The man was living on the edge of one. But... it was a road worth taking. And a risk worth taking.'

'Right?' said Margaret. 'Everyone finished?' She began collecting up the cups, and putting them into her plastic woven bag. 'We'll do it all again tomorrow.'

* * *

After my swim, I called in to see Mum. Dad was out in the shed.

'I loved the item on making clothes for your pets from old jumpers,' she said. 'That pug in the tracksuit was a little dote.'

'He tried to bite David during the ad break,' I said. 'David managed to fend him off with his clipboard. And then, as soon as we were live again, the dog was like butter wouldn't melt in its mouth.'

Mum laughed. 'I thought David looked a little wary of him. And what about that awful PJ? Why on earth is *he* on the show? Who does he think he is, putting your hair behind your ear.'

'It's fine,' I said. 'Honestly. It's just an unfortunate coincidence and what can he do on live TV?'

'I suppose...' Mum looked doubtful. 'Anyway,' she said, as she filled the kettle. 'I've a confession to make.'

'A confession?'

She looked pale and strained. 'I have to admit,' she said, 'it's been something of a burden all these years. Guilt, you see. But once you start a lie, there's no going back.'

What could she be referring to? A secret love child? An affair?

'Go on,' I said, cautiously.

'It's all Lorraine's fault,' she went on.

'Isn't everything?'

'Well, you know she's made me enter The Great Sandycove Bake-Off...'

'You said in the text...'

'And of course, I said yes.'

'Naturally.'

'Well... that's the thing... I don't know what to make.'

'Your famous lemon drizzle, obviously,' I said. '*Everyone* loves *your* lemon drizzle.' It was the only cake Mum ever made and was utterly spectacular.

'Well, that's the thing. It isn't strictly speaking *my* lemon drizzle. I've been buying it from Sally-Anne's in the village for years.' She looked stricken. 'It's a terrible lie I've been caught up in. I've lost sleep over it and I decided to come clean.'

'How on earth...? *Why* on earth...?'

But it was starting to make a bit of sense. Mum had never been much of a baker, always too busy and too tired to rustle up any kind of cake and I had long resigned myself to the sad truth that mine was never going to be one of those mythical mothers who won first prize at local fetes for their tea bracks, filling the house with the aroma of freshly baked goods.

'I was at a weak point in my life. Do you remember? It was Mary's fiftieth and you know what your aunt is like. Mrs Perfect. That brown bread? Amazing. Her cheesecake? Award-winning. Her Christmas cake? Perfection. And anyway, you know that teasing she does – *you can't cook anything, oh, what have you made for us today? Cardboard again?* And... well, I don't know, but I went to Sally-Anne's, bought a cake and then when Auntie Mary turned up, I found myself taking off the paper wrapping and... putting the cake on a plate and... well, let's just say, I was economical with the truth. She asked if the cake was mine, and I said yes it was. She never asked if I *made* it. And do you remember, you turned up?'

I nodded. 'You told me to drop in and say hi.' I remembered that day, fifteen years earlier, Mum looking slightly pink with what I had thought was pleasure at long-overdue appreciation from her scary older sister.

'I still can't tell Mary. I'd never hear the end of it. But I just can't lie any longer. I will just have to make a cake. On my own. No cheating, no lying, no guilt.' She looked scared but determined. 'I can do this,' she said. 'Even I can make something half-decent. Surely?'

I nodded. 'Of course you can. If I can become a sea swimmer, then you can make a cake all on your own.'

THE GIRLS!

Becca: Fancy a walk after your swim? Having a stressful day and need to get out and enjoy the evening.

Me: Definitely. 7 p.m.?

Sinéad: Rory and I will join you. Conor has another Teams meeting. 🙄

Becca: Too busy with the ITAs. Thinking of giving it up and becoming hermit or something.

Sinéad: You mean, give up all mod cons, your luxury house, a glass of expensive wine?

Becca: I mean, a luxury hermit. Just someone with no stress. Someone who just gazes into space and has time to think.

Sinéad: Let me know when you want to swap lives? Or come and babysit Rory!

Becca: You won't let us, remember?!!! How many times have we offered and you say you are not ready to leave him. You just don't trust us.

Sinéad: I do trust you. I just don't trust you yet. But I will.

Becca: The offer is there. Whenever you decide to take us up on offer. See you both tonight. xxx

22

The days began to fly by, as I stumbled through the week, feeling as though I was gaining confidence a little more each day. In the mornings, I picked up my towel and swimsuit from the hot press where they'd been drying overnight and put them in my bag, and then, when I could feel the nerves building, I imagined myself at the Forty Foot, all stress and tension dissolving in the sea.

At *The Daily Show*, I was beginning to really feel part of the team. And it wasn't just the editorial but the crew on set, the camera and lighting people, the girls in wardrobe, Brenda. And I loved meeting all our interviewees, they would turn up nervous but excited and I loved watching them open up on camera. I started having fun on-air, learning how to foxtrot with a dancer from *Twinkletoes-tastic*, a new Sunday evening dance show, or holding puppies for a segment on an animal rescue charity.

And then, on my way home, I stopped for a swim. If it wasn't for the swimming, life would have been distinctly overwhelming. Being in the sea was a moment of peace in the day, a time to regroup, and I was beginning to see what Brenda meant – that it was almost like meditation. I'd gone every evening, meeting up with the gang, listening to their chat while we changed, and knowing that a place existed where status didn't matter and that nature was bigger than everything.

I was becoming a little more fearless as well, swimming out further and further. There was a yellow buoy about thirty metres from the shore and each day I tried to get a little closer to it, before thoughts of the seabed dropping further below me made me turn around.

This, I thought, as I propelled myself back to land, was exactly the opposite of working on television, where everyone behaved as though it was life or death or that we were changing lives. Once you were in that bubble, it was hard to see beyond it.

After each swim, Margaret now always produced a huge flask and we'd sit for ten or so minutes chatting about the temperature of the water or what we thought the clouds on the horizon meant and if therefore rain was on the way. Or the conversation would take a different turn to more personal matters, such as how Margaret was getting on in her church group and how she had been asked to perform as Florence Nightingale in the autumn show. Nora talked about her daughter who was a schoolteacher and how she was just back from her honeymoon with her new husband. Brenda talked about a trip she was planning, a 'Mozart odyssey' to Salzburg. Dolores talked of the years she'd lived in London and worked in a posh drinking club and the night she met Elton John, who was struggling with his own addiction, and they both discussed all the ways they had tried to give up. Malachy talked about work and that he'd been asked to apply for his team leader's job but he wasn't sure if he could. Everyone turned to him.

'Do it, Mal,' said Brenda.

'Know your worth,' insisted Nora.

'You'll never know if you don't try,' said Dolores.

Malachy shrugged. 'Maybe...' he said.

I didn't say much, just soaked up all their chat, drinking my tea as the sun began its slow descent.

The conversation continued on the WhatsApp group, questions about tides and weather mainly, but the odd TV recommendation or news of a dolphin sighting in the bay or how the progress of Margaret's jam-making was going. She would update us:

Labels on and having a rest in the larder.

And then there were always questions about Malachy's Mam. Nora would text:

How's your mam doing, Mal?

And he would reply:

Grand. Hasn't gone wandering for a while now.

Malachy's Mam became something of a constant point of concern. Going home, I would scan the roads around the harbour just in case I saw a woman in a nightdress, and everyone arranged shifts to keep Malachy's mam company on the days Malachy was at work.

* * *

I was in the make-up chair talking to Brenda when PJ's bald head poked around the door.

'Is Cat here?' he said, and then smiled when he saw me, as though we were old friends. 'I hope you don't mind me interrupting...' He turned his eyes on to Brenda, who, unlike most people, didn't flutter and become flustered under his emerald laser focus. Instead, she looked utterly disinterested.

'You are, actually,' she said. 'We're in the middle of a creative process which can't be disturbed.'

'I didn't know make-up was a creative process,' said PJ. 'I would have thought it was more adornment. Like painting a wall, rather than painting a masterpiece.'

'Well,' said Brenda, witheringly, 'you'd be wrong.'

'What is it, PJ?'

He gave Brenda a curt nod and then turned to me. 'You can't just pop outside for a quick chat?'

'I have forty-five minutes before we go on-air,' I said, while Brenda blended my eyeshadow. I managed to look at him from the side of my eyes. 'What is it?'

He sighed. 'I just wanted to say…' He studiously avoided Brenda, who had begun whistling quietly to herself. 'Well, it's just that I thought we didn't get off to the warmest of starts last time,' he went on. 'You know, bygones be bygones and all that. Live and let live. I'm a very forgiving person, you know me. I don't bear grudges…' He stepped into the room. 'May I?' he said, heavily and sarcastically. Without waiting for an answer he sat down in the other make-up chair. 'I just want to tell you that I think you're doing a really good job,' he went on. 'And I hope we can be friends.'

Brenda muttered something under her breath.

'Look, since we went our separate ways, I've done a lot of soul-searching and I just wanted to say that I've changed. A lot. Grown up a bit, and you were right, I was more acquainted with the inner workings of an artichoke than my own mind. Or at least something to that effect. I hope I can show you that I'm a good guy, that I've made mistakes, and even though I was humiliated and embarrassed, you were right.'

'Really?' This didn't sound like PJ. Maybe he had changed? Was that even possible?

'Anyway,' he went on, 'I've just had a meeting with Angela and she says they are delighted with me, I'm a natural. So, I just wanted to say I'll be around as much as they need me. I thought I'd just clear the air. Even though it shouldn't be my job. The onus shouldn't be on me. And I know you said sorry and that you are sorry, but it still hurts me. Here you are, going about your business, as though you didn't humiliate me. It's not right...'

'What do you mean?' I moved in my chair, Brenda's eyeliner nearly drawing a line across my face.

'You should be saying sorry,' he said, 'not me.' He waited a moment. 'I came bearing an olive branch. And you are happy for me to humiliate myself...' His eyes flickered towards Brenda and back again.

'I did say...' I began, but Brenda gave my arm a squeeze.

'Don't say a word,' she hissed, moving to stand in front of me, facing PJ. 'She's not going to say sorry because she's not sorry and because she's got nothing to say sorry for. And I think it's best if you don't engage Cat in conversation again. What happened between you belongs in the past. She has nothing to atone for. You, sir, are a bully. And an embarrassing bully at that. And by the way, your trousers are too long. You need them taking up. From now on, behave as politely as you possibly can to Catríona, and stop immediately with this ridiculous talk of apologies and humiliation. Just do your job, cook whatever it is you are going to cook and be gone with you! Leave my make-up room immediately.'

He glared at Brenda, but she refused to budge, standing, arms folded, staring back at him until he stood up and left the room. Brenda turned to me. 'Who does he think he is? Arrogant langer, if I've ever seen one.'

I laughed. The first time I'd ever laughed at an encounter with PJ. It was so much easier when you had friends on your side.

* * *

David was in particularly good form during the show, dissolving into giggles during an interview with the grande dame of Irish theatre Edna Montague, as she regaled us with stories about life on stage. 'I was playing the goddess Venus in a truly terrible play,' she said in her posh voice, 'and I turned to the director and said, Mr Keating, if you think I am removing my clothes on stage, you are very much mistaken. I may be an actress, but I am also a lady.'

'So you remained fully clothed?' asked David.

'Well, Mr Keating said, on and off stage you are a goddess... please will you reconsider? I said, only if you reconsider my pay package – pay me twice and I will appear briefly in my altogether. He agreed. And it was quite the sensation. Even though it was very tastefully done. The whole of Dublin came to see it. Except for my mother. She said I was a trollop. I told her she had Venus envy.'

David nearly lost it, tears pouring from his eyes, clutching at Edna's knees as she twinkled back at him. I'd heard her tell that story at least twice before. 'Oh my word...' He wiped his tears away with his hands. 'Edna, you're a tonic... Venus envy...'

Edna took his tie and began to pat at his face. 'I think we need a sponge,' she said, making him laugh even harder. Daytime television was utterly, completely and totally mad and you had to match the crazy energy or fail.

'Luckily,' David said, 'I have a cast-iron bladder...'

'Well, I don't,' Edna said. 'Which is why I now prefer not to emote.'

Angela's voice was in my ear. 'This is great,' she said. 'Love it!'

I smiled even harder, my cheeks aching. Across the set, I could see PJ setting up for the cookery item.

'And that's it from the incomparable Edna Montague,' said David. 'After the break, we'll be cooking up a storm with the brilliant PJ Doyle.'

Angela spoke in our ears. 'Kitchen now, please. Two minutes to end of ad break.'

David began to move across the studio as Edna's PR woman rushed towards her. 'Edna, that was wonderful. What a marvellous interview!' She gave me a special fingers-only wave that normally only pop stars give. 'Thanks so much, Cat, you and David are a dream team... love you!'

Angela in my ear: 'One minute...'

David was already standing with PJ. 'I hope there's not a quiche in sight, Peej?' he was saying. 'I'm not a fan of the quiche. A soggy, sorry mess in pastry. When one is eating quiche, one has given up on food and life.'

'Nothing worse,' said PJ, 'than a soggy quiche.' He glanced up at me.

'And ten,' said Angela, as Martin began counting us down with his hands. I focused on the autocue.

'Welcome back,' I said.

'Yes, welcome back...' David said.

'So, to cooking now,' I read on. 'And we have the fabulous PJ Doyle back with us again, to cook up a storm.'

'Lucky us,' said David.

'Oh, you haven't got lucky yet,' laughed PJ. 'But who knows?' He winked straight down the camera.

'Now,' I tried again, 'what are you cooking for us?'

'Steak tagliata,' said PJ. 'Rocket salad, parmesan and a rosemary and lemon dressing.' He held up a frying pan. 'You have to get this nice and hot. Just like Cat here. I think she might be going a bit red, do you think, David?'

David glanced at me. 'I can't see anything,' he said, confused for a moment.

'It's just the studio,' I said, trying to laugh as though this was all just banter. 'So, PJ, what are you doing? How important is it to get the pan hot?'

'Essential,' said PJ. 'You need to sear the steak, caramelise the outside, keep the inside rare...'

'I like a medium steak,' said David. 'Never rare... too much for me.'

'David, I throw people out of my restaurant for ordering medium,' said PJ. 'They have what I give them.' The steak sizzled in the pan.

'You don't ask how they want their steak cooked?' asked David. 'Doesn't that smack of dictatorship? You are the foodie Fidel Castro.' He looked straight down the camera, and gave a wink. 'The Stalin of the stove, the mixing Mussolini... the Pol Pot Noodle...'

PJ didn't laugh. 'I just feel I have worked hard and trained hard enough to be trusted to know what's right,' he said. 'If people want well done shoe leather, then go to other places.'

David decided that this was a vein of comedy which wasn't going anywhere. 'And the salad?' He changed tack. 'What is the dressing?'

PJ unsmilingly talked us through his dressing, effortlessly whisking and emulsifying, and then removed the steak, sliced it and presented it on a wooden board.

'Holy mother of God,' said David, breathing in deeply. 'Wish our viewers, or at least the carnivorous ones, were able to smell what we are smelling... Shall we taste?'

He took a forkful and just as I was about to do the same, PJ said, 'Open up, Cat,' and pushed some steak into my mouth. There was nothing I could do except try to chew it. 'What do you think? Too rare? For the babies out there?'

'It's very good,' I had to say.

PJ nodded as though, yes, of course it was. But it was too rare for me.

'Cat loves my steak,' he said, removing some fluff from my shoulder, 'don't you, Cat?'

I was still trying to chew the barely cooked meat so I couldn't answer, but whenever I had eaten it in the past, it had been exactly like this – rare, bloody, hard to eat. I would never have said what I really wanted just in case he blew a fuse.

'Melt in the mouth,' agreed David. 'It's not easy to cook steak. I usually incinerate it. You need to have nerves of steel to serve it like this. But then, that's why you were called Ireland's most exciting new chef in the Irish Food Awards.'

'It was Ireland's Best Chef, actually,' said PJ. 'But I think Cat was more of a fan of Betty. Who do you prefer? Me or Betty?'

I'd finally finished chewing. 'I like both of you,' I said, trying to smile and keep it light.

'Don't ask Cat to choose,' said David. 'You're *both* tremendous... Betty is Ireland's best classic chef... and you are Ireland's best younger chef...'

'Betty a *chef*?' PJ sniggered.

'Ten seconds,' said Angela in our ears. 'Wrap up.'

'And now that's it from today's show... we'll finish up this amazing food and we'll see you all tomorrow... be good, everyone!'

As soon as we were off-air, Martin and Dmitri and the rest of the crew began to attack the steak.

Angela came and stood beside me. 'Are you okay?' she said, quietly. 'He's not what I thought he was going to be. He's good, but there's something about him that I can't put my finger on... The socials were very lively. Twitter, Instagram. PJ is slightly... I don't know... dangerous... I couldn't quite work out what was going on.' She stopped talking as PJ came up to us.

'How was I, Angela?' He was behaving almost coyly, as though he just wanted to pleased her.

'You were great,' she said, smiling. 'Thank you so much...'

'You're very welcome,' he said, 'my pleasure.'

'But,' went on Angela, 'please don't feed our presenters on-air. They need to be in control of things. They don't want a mouthful when they might need to speak.' She smiled at him. 'Okay with you?'

For a split second, PJ didn't say anything. Then: 'Of course, Angela. You're the boss. I was just trying to be friendly, relaxed, but if you want me to be more formal... that's absolutely fine. I'm just starting out in television and there's a lot to learn.'

Angela nodded, unsure what to say. He was so clever at switching modes from arrogant to humble, from sweet to fiery. That was the thing with PJ, you never knew what you were going to get.

'I'm loving being on the show,' PJ was saying. 'I love the gang. It's so different being in the media compared to working in kitchens. Ava told me she'd rather drink her own urine than eat anything with eyes.' He chuckled. 'So funny.'

'She was being serious though,' I said. 'She's a vegan.'

The word 'vegan' used to have an incendiary effect on PJ. It would make him apoplectic with rage. He paused, as though girding himself. 'Well,' he said, 'maybe I will ask her more about it. Inclusivity and all that.' He smiled at us.

'Great,' said Angela, 'wonderful... So, look, I'll leave you to it. See you, Peej.'

'See you, Ange.' She went over to talk to Martin as PJ turned to me.

'I'd better go,' I said.

Again that flash as though he was angry.

'That woman... earlier. She really hurt my feelings.'

'What woman?' I said. *What feelings*, I wanted to say.

'The make-up woman. She said I was short...'

'She didn't.'

'She said about my trousers being too long.'

'I can't remember,' I said, moving away from him. 'I have to go... I'm going swimming.' And I left him standing on his own.

* * *

Becca and Sinéad and Rory, in his pushchair, joined me after my swim. The sun was setting, casting the world in a golden filter.

'Love the hair,' I said to Becca. 'It suits you.' The last time I'd seen her with natural hair was in school.

'You think?' said Becca. 'I just thought I'd try it out and I'm just so bored of straightening it and wearing make-up and just trying so hard. I just want to be... I don't know... maybe it's the Birkenstocks, but I just want to be comfortable.'

'It's when we get too far away from what we naturally are,' said Sinéad, 'that's when trouble starts.'

'Where did you hear such nonsense?' said Becca, as we began walking along the seafront.

'The holistic psychologist on *The Daily Show*,' said Sinéad, giving me a wink. 'She was fascinating. For a moment, I thought I was going to grow out my blonde, but me and my highlights are going to the grave together. I love them more than I love most people.'

'Come on,' said Becca, 'let's up the pace, walk a bit faster.'

'Why?'

'I need fresh air,' Becca said. 'I can't sleep lately, at all, and I think it's because I don't get enough fresh air. I'm thinking we don't amble, we walk briskly. And we'll fill our lungs, move our bodies and we'll sleep like babies.'

'Rory doesn't sleep at all,' said Sinéad. 'It's like he's decided that sleeping isn't going to be part of his skill set.'

'Rory and I have a lot in common,' said Becca.

'I am so glad you called, Becca,' Sinéad said. 'I am so glad to get out of the house. Conor decided to put together his new standing-up desk. He started unpacking it, dragging all the bits out, laying out all the screws and things and counting them, and then losing count, and the packaging was all over the place, and it looked twice the size I thought it was going to be.' She inhaled deeply, pressing fingers to her temples. 'It's very stressful living with a man who thinks working from home means taking over the home. Telephone calls made at high volume. Constant Teams meetings. Shouting at me and Rory if we make a sound more than a whisper. Honestly. I've had to watch *The Daily Show* hidden in the kitchen, on my phone, with my AirPods in. And why does he have to buy a ginormous stand-up desk, which is on some kind of pneumatic pulley thing so you can raise it up and down so it can extend even bigger?' She shook her head, as though incredulous. 'Why can't he just work at a *normal* desk?'

'It's a mystery,' agreed Becca. 'Where is Miss Marple when you need her?'

We arrived at Teddy's ice cream shop.

Becca stopped. 'I think we should all have an ice cream. Cat deserves one because she is being forced to work with her toxic ex-boyfriend. Honestly, that man. I had to watch it from behind my fingers.' She turned to Sinéad. 'Three 99s, then? Sinéad, what would Rory like?'

Rory was suddenly wide awake and looked up, eagerly, at Sinéad.

'We don't eat ice cream,' Sinéad said. 'Remember? Dairy? Trans fats? Sugar?'

'My three favourite ingredients,' replied Becca. 'Anyway, I thought we were saying yes to things, like Cat.'

'But there has to be sensible limits,' said Sinéad. 'I mean, you wouldn't drink a whole bottle of sambuca or eat a *whole* pizza.'

'You used to do exactly those things,' remarked Becca. 'Remember Malaga?'

'Yes... but...' Sinéad looked conflicted for a moment. 'We can't.' Rory looked as if he was going to cry. 'I have a banana in my bag,' she went on, quickly, before her resolve faded, rooting through the shelf under the pushchair. 'Bananas are Rory's favourite things, aren't they, Rory? And apple slices. But you two go ahead, you have one.'

Becca rolled her eyes. '*We* can't eat an ice cream in front of a child,' she said. 'I think we'd be sent to prison for child cruelty. We'll just have a tea instead. Don't worry about us.'

'I'm sorry,' said Sinéad, hotly. 'I'm sorry for not letting Rory have an ice cream. I'm sorry for trying to keep him safe and not allow processed food to invade his innocent infant body. When you have a child, then you can judge.'

Sinéad looked out to sea, upset, and Becca put her arm around her. 'I'm sorry,' she said, gently. 'I'd prefer tea anyway. Healthier.'

The three of us sat on the bench drinking tea, while Rory ate his banana.

'I can't believe you've done so much swimming,' said Becca to me. 'You are quickly developing the smug look of the sea swimmer. It's a fresh glow, mixed with inner peace, with a sprinkling of superiority complex.'

'It's the ultimate in being out of your comfort zone and just when you think you can't stand it a moment longer, it changes to this feeling of invincibility. It's addictive.'

'Well, the only thing that is addictive in my life,' said Becca, 'are biscuits. I just can't stop eating them lately.'

There was a sound of a bicycle bell and someone called my name. There, on a tandem, whizzing towards us, were Mum and Dad, both of them looking as though they were a little out of control as though neither knew who was in charge of the bike and who was the passenger.

'Are you okay?' I shouted, as they got closer and seemed to be picking up speed as the road fell away a little.

'We're fine!' Mum's voice clung to the breeze. 'It's your dad's idea... and I had to say yessssss!'

And they were gone, the two of them looking happier than I'd ever seen them and disappearing into the distance.

THE JONES FAMILY!

Me: Was that really you?

Dad: 'Twas.

Mum: My life flashed before my very eyes. Your dad wasn't the best at steering.

Dad: It needed adjusting.

Me: Is this how you now get around? Are you selling the car?

Mum: Someone dropped it in for your dad to fix.

Dad: We couldn't resist a spin.

Mum: I still feel wobbly.

Dad: We had to go for a drink afterwards.

Me: Had to?

Dad: For medicinal purposes.

Mum: But it was fun, wasn't it?

Dad: The best!

23

On the Friday morning of my second week on *The Daily Show*, I parked my car and there was a loud knock on my window as Angela's face appeared. 'You can't stay in there, you know!' she shouted in. 'We've got a show to make!'

We began walking into the office together.

'I've been thinking about the show,' she said. 'I thought that we could tweak the dynamic...'

'Which dynamic?'

'The one between you and David.'

'We have a *dynamic*?'

She laughed. 'There's *always* a dynamic,' she said. 'In every relationship. Even fake TV ones. But listen, I want to make the most of this time we have you, hence the dynamic tweaking.' We walked through the main doors, waving to Cathy on reception, and heading up the stairs to the production offices. 'You know I've been trying to introduce new things to the show and to be a bit braver in our content.'

We stopped in the corridor before entering the large open-plan office.

'David is amazing at what he does, light conversations. There is literally no one better than him on daytime TV. But I would like you to take the lead on some of our interviews. It's not that I want to denigrate his role because he's great at what he does. But I also think we need to widen the show's demographic. And...' – she glanced up and down the corridor – '...up until now we've been resolutely controversy-free. No more bland.' She laughed. 'It sounds so disloyal. I grew up on David and Barbara. I watched it every afternoon with my nanna, after school. She'd make the tea, I'd get out the chocolate digestives and we'd settle down to analyse absolutely everything about it... what Barbara was wearing, did David's ties symbolise anything... that kind of thing. My nanna was something of an armchair radical. In another age, she would have been an academic, writing books about gender and feminism and changing the world.' Angela shrugged. '*She's* who I think of every morning if I'm feeling scared.'

'Nanna power,' I said.

Angela laughed. 'That was actually her name,' she said. 'Mary-Rose Power. Nanna Power. We all need Nanna Power in our lives. And it doesn't matter what it is and where you get it from, but you need something bigger than yourself to inspire you to get out of bed, to keep on fighting, to make you braver than you thought you could be.' She smiled. 'Now, come on, we'll go in there and make the best show possible. Only with a slightly tweaked dynamic.'

***

At that morning's meeting, we sat around the large table, pens poised.

'So,' Angela said, 'happy Friday, everyone, and I am particularly excited to welcome the writer Penelope O'Brien on the show later. I've been back and forth with her PR for weeks now and they've decided to give us the chance of an interview. I really believe that this is a brand-new avenue of content for us.' She beamed at us. 'I've been a fan of her feminist dystopian fiction for years. In fact...' She gave a slightly nervous laugh. 'I actually wrote my dissertation in college about her. So, big fan. David and Cat... you've read her latest novel? The book has been optioned by Netflix and will be coming out next year as a huge series. It's really important that we are ahead of the curve, part of the zeitgeist. Did you enjoy the book?'

'I thought it was amazing,' I said. 'When the prisoners decided to escape and Helen, the main character,' I said, 'had to stay because the one person who knew where her child was was back in the prison... It was very emotional.'

'I agree,' said Ava. 'A very powerful book about the strength of women, the way that the patriarchy will use a maternal love against them...'

Angela was nodding. 'Yes, very strong...'

There was a clearing of his throat from David and he held up his hand. 'Well, if I may say, I didn't have a clue what was going on or who was who and what exactly the point of it all was.'

Angela nodded slowly. 'That's fine, David,' she said. 'I'd like to suggest that Cat takes the lead on this interview. You would be *there*, of course...' She tried to smile at him. 'But it would be Cat talking to Penelope... and maybe then you could exchange a few remarks on her time in Dublin, how she is finding the weather, has she tasted Guinness yet, the usual clichés.'

David blinked at her. 'You mean...?' He swallowed, looking hurt. 'You mean take a back seat?'

'Well, not exactly a back seat, more a passenger's seat...'

'But...'

'I'm just trying something new,' said Angela. 'Tweaking the dynamic, that's all.' She looked over at Tom for support.

'Maybe it will work, maybe it won't,' said Tom, evenly. 'Why don't you give it a chance?'

David nodded. 'Well, if you think so...' He managed a brave smile. 'But I'm just thinking about Middle Ireland again...'

'Middle Ireland are loving PJ Doyle,' said Angela. She glanced at me.

'You are right,' said David. 'I was wrong in my initial sentiments about him and I must be open to new things. Jennifer says I am getting set in my ways. I reminded her I was the one who was reading the new Sally Rooney from my lounger in Quinta do Lago and therefore am hardly set in my ways.' He sighed. 'But Jennifer, my dear, long-suffering, better and more beautiful half, is usually always right about everything. The two of us ventured forth to PJ's restaurant. Eye-watering prices, portions the size of my thumb, an indecipherable menu. But the food was divine. Which reminds me, to remind you, about my barbecue at Casa Fitz tomorrow.' David looked around. 'It's just a small event, a glass of vino, a steak or two...'

Angela shook her head. 'I can't, David, sorry, I already RSVP'd weeks ago, remember? My mother's birthday. Taking her and the nieces to Tayto Park for the day.'

'I'm going for lunch with some friends,' said Ava. 'Sorry, David.'

'Tom?'

'Of course, David,' said Tom. 'Sounds great. I'll be there.'

'And bring your lady friend... all welcome to Casa Fitz.'

Tom glanced at me. Was he going to bring Susie?

David turned to me. 'Cat? You weren't with us when Jennifer sent out the invitations, but we would be honoured if you could join us?'

What else could I say, except yes?

24

Penelope O'Brien was to be our last guest of the show and we chatted to a woman who made shoes for hamsters and a gardener who was attempting to grow the world's tallest beanstalk – 'Like Jack's,' David offered – and a fashion item on how socks and sandals were suddenly cool again.

'Now, after the break,' said David, 'we'll be talking to the...' – he peered closely at the autocue – 'great Penelope O'Brien...' He added a question mark to his inflection. 'She's the writer of all those...' He paused. '...Those *books* that some people seem to enjoy so much.'

Angela had prepped me thoroughly and we had decided on a shape to the discussion, a little on the current book, bring in her biggest seller and the one currently on the Irish school syllabus, talk about how she feels about the rights of women in her home state of Texas and then back to the current book. David could then ask a couple of jovial and general questions to end the show. I felt nervous. Until now, the only interviews we had done were feather-light. This was a lot of pressure on my shoulders. I wished Angela hadn't been so keen to tweak the dynamic.

'Back after these,' I said, straight down the camera, and I moved from the area of the studio where we'd been admiring the models in their sandals and socks to the yellow sofa.

'Two minutes,' said Angela, in our ear. 'Penelope is making her way on to set.'

'Here we are!' I looked up to see a young blonde PR woman bringing over a bespectacled woman, dressed in navy tunic and turquoise scarf. So this, I thought, was the great Penelope O'Brien, world-blazing feminist writer, destroying the patriarchy with every stroke of her keyboard.

'Penelope, this is the great David Fitzgerald...' said the younger woman, holding out her hand. 'Lovely to meet you.'

'Likewise,' said David. 'And who is this remarkably intelligent-looking woman?' He beamed at Penelope. 'I can feel the intellectual quotient in the room has just shot up. The average IQ is double what it was ten minutes earlier.' He held Penelope's hand in his. 'What an honour. To have the hand that wrote all those wonderful, groundbreaking books in mine. It's like the hand of God.'

I wondered what Penelope would do? Would she shake him off, annoyed at being patronised and sucked up to? But instead she laughed.

'Who is this old charmer?' she said. 'I'm taking him home with me. I need this kind of positivity in my life.'

When she was released from David, she turned to me.

'I'm Cat Jones,' I said, standing and shaking Penelope's hand. 'You are very welcome to Ireland, and to our show...'

'Delighted,' said Penelope, her hand small and cool in mine. 'So lovely to be here.'

In my ear, Angela counted us down. 'And back in ten... good luck both of you... and seven... six...'

While David brushed invisible fluff off the lapel of his linen jacket, I braced myself, staring down the camera.

'Three... two... one... and we're live. Camera two to Cat.'

'Welcome back to the show,' I said. 'And we are delighted to be joined by one of the most important and influential authors currently working and one of the most outspoken voices on the lived experiences of women. Referred to as one of the world's greatest feminist, dystopian authors, she currently has two books in the *New York Times* bestseller list, a new Netflix television series in the pipeline and is on school syllabuses the world over, including here in Ireland. Penelope O'Brien, thank you for joining us today.'

'You're so welcome.' There was a hint of a smile, but she gazed at me through her large glasses, ready for whatever question I was about to fire at her.

I swallowed hard. 'I wonder,' I began, 'if you believed that women's voices are finally being heard and if your books have contributed to...' – my mouth felt dry – 'to a movement where women believe...' I completely lost my train of thought and the more I grasped for it, the more my brain scrambled. But as I floundered, David seamlessly joined the conversation, immediately taking charge.

'Is it difficult to type?' he said. 'I find typing something of a trial. Everyone has to be so good at typing away, but I still cling to the old piece of paper and ballpoint pen.'

Penelope brightened. 'So do I,' she said. 'But I use a fountain pen. One my father gave me for my eighteenth... before he...' She stopped, lost in her own train of thought. David waited. 'Before he died,' she said. 'It was very sudden... Oh gawd, I've never talked about this before but...'

David reached over and gently touched her knee, nodding kindly. 'I lost mine early as well,' he said. 'I've been there.'

'Dad wasn't well... hadn't been for some time... and he... well, I always think he stayed longer than he should have done for me. It was Christmas and I'd come home from my first term in college...'

Tears were in her eyes, behind her glasses. 'And I was so full of life... It had been my birthday a couple of days before...'

'Sagittarius,' said David, nodding sagely.

'That's right,' she said.

'Me too,' he said. 'The highly sensitive, creative sign.'

She nodded, as though she was being heard for the first time in her life. 'And I arrived back, you know the whirl of youth, all the stories and everything I wanted to tell him. My mother too. And she said Dad's upstairs... Dad was never in bed... apart from when people should be in bed... and when I went into their bedroom, there he was.' She was tearful and David produced from his jacket pocket a crisp cotton handkerchief and handed it over. 'He was in his pyjamas and, do you know, I had never seen him in his night-clothes before. He was the kind of man who wouldn't leave his bedroom without being fully dressed. He looked so tiny. My big dad, small in bed.'

David touched her knee again. 'It's not easy...'

'No... no, it was a shock. And I was trying to process all this when he apologised for not getting up.' She dabbed at her eyes. '"Sorry, Pen," he said. Pen, that's what they called me. And then he gave me a small parcel from the nightstand. "For your eighteenth," he said. And it was... well, it was the pen I still use today. "A pen for my Pen," he said, and every time I write I think of him.' There was a moment of silence, before she smiled. 'I don't really tell that story.'

'It's an important memory,' said David.

'It is, it really is.' She seemed relieved, grateful even, to be given the opportunity to remember her dad. 'And now, if I close my eyes, I can see him, I can bring him back to me. Before, I was so traumatised, I think. He died that same night, my mother and I, holding his hand... but losing your father... well... I couldn't go back to college. I took the year off and I found a writer's group and that was it, really...' She smiled at David.

Meanwhile, I was riffling through my notes, looking for something to ask, but before I could think straight, David had another question.

'Your surname is O'Brien,' he said, 'so you *have* to be Irish… yes?'

Penelope nodded, smiling, looking more relaxed than she had earlier. 'I've traced it back. My great-great-grandfather left Skibbereen and arrived in New York, and he met my great-great-grandmother who was straight off the boat all the way from Ballyhaunis in County Mayo.'

'Wonderful, wonderful…' said David, eyes moist as though he was moved by these stories of emigration and heritage. 'You're home now…'

'Yes,' she said, her voice nearly cracking. 'I am.' She blinked at him as though she too was on that ship, sailing to America, leaving everything they had behind them, their future selves and life unknowable. 'I'm home.'

'And as you're one of us,' went on David, 'are you a fan of the black stuff? Guinness?'

'I am but I prefer whiskey.' She smiled. 'Irish whiskey has incredible depth of flavour. I buy a bottle of twelve-year-old malt every time I launch a book and raise a glass to my forefathers and mothers… especially foremothers because where would we be without our mothers?'

I tried desperately to think of a question about the book, but I was aware that Martin had moved into position ready to count us down to the ad break.

'So, the book,' I said, pathetically. 'What's it called?'

Penelope stared back at me. 'It's called… Oh my Lord, I've forgotten what it's called.'

My mind was blank as well. I hoped Angela would step in, but all I could hear was her saying, 'It's something to do with women…

something like... Oh God... where are my notes? Ten seconds to break.'

And then it came to me. *The Ages of Women*. Of course! I opened my mouth when David spoke.

'The book is called *The Ages Of Women*,' he said, smoothly. 'I could *not* put it down.' He gave me a nod as though to tell me not to worry, but I was still mortified.

Martin stepped forward to count the interview down. Five, he signalled, four...

'Well,' I said, defeated, 'I thought it was an excellent read.'

David faced the camera. 'Back after these.'

I had just witnessed a masterclass in interviewing by David. You didn't just ask questions, it was about being able to plug into something, find a connection, an instant rapport, and that was what he could do so easily. He and Penelope were still chatting away as the ad break rolled on. 'Are you around tomorrow?' he was saying. 'My partner, Jennifer, and I are having a little gathering. Barbecue?'

'Oh, I wish I could,' Penelope said, 'but it's back to London this evening.'

'And I was going to open the single malt just for you,' said David. 'Next time you're in Dublin. Okay? It's a date.'

Penelope smiled. 'I would love that.'

David, I realised, was brilliant. Presenting wasn't just a talent, it was an art.

As we were leaving the studio, he gave me a nod. 'Goodnight, Cat,' he said. 'See you at the barbecue.'

'Looking forward to it,' I said. 'And by the way, you were great, today. I was hopeless.'

'Oh, just doing my job,' he said. 'That's all. And you weren't hopeless. Far from it. George Clooney was once in town promoting some film or other and I kept forgetting his name and calling him Gerard – my brother's name. George thought he was in some hidden camera show. In the end, I tried to explain and ended up making it worse. I said that he reminded me of my brother, who'd spent two weeks in prison for holding up a hairdresser's with a plastic gun he'd bought in the toyshop.' He paused. 'And so, poor George was insulted that he reminded me of my jailbird brother.' He shook his head. 'I would wake up for months – years – after that, in a cold sweat. Nerves can make anyone say the wrong thing or even nothing.'

I nodded, grateful. 'Thank you.'

'That's the thing that producers don't get,' he said. 'They have no real idea of what we do. But now you know too, you'll do well.'

He turned to go.

'David,' I said. 'What happened to Gerard?'

'Oh, he went into politics,' he said, vaguely. 'He's the current Minister for Justice.'

'*That* Gerard Fitzgerald? I had no idea.'

'Mam half forgave him before she passed away,' said David. 'On her deathbed, poor old Gerard cried and said, it's been forty-five years, will you forgive me now? He gripped her hand, desperately. Gerard, she said. I can forgive, but I will never forget. And she died. Just like that. Mothers, the hardest people to impress and the most important.' He turned to walk away again, his linen jacket slung over his shoulder. 'Until we meet again, young Catríona!'

25

Tom caught up with me as I left the building. 'Great show,' he said.

'Because of David,' I replied. I felt awful after my floundering. Angela had put her faith in me, but I wasn't up to it. 'I was meant to take the lead on the interview. And I couldn't think of a single intelligent question. And David had to rescue me.'

'It's the way things go. Interviews become their own thing. You can plan all you like and then, on live television, they take their own shape and that's the joy... that's why we do it. And it was amazing. David is very skilful at talking to people, drawing them out. And the two of you are a great team.'

'We are?'

He nodded. 'Totally. There's an easiness between you. He and Barbara hated each other and so nothing really flowed. The two of you have chemistry. I am a believer in the old broadcast adage about bringing your humanity to the proceedings,' went on Tom. 'It's just a fancy way of saying, be real. React in real time. Be normal and respond as you would in normal life. Give people room to be themselves. And if you can't think of an intellectual question, ask a human one. Or lie about being the same star sign.'

'David's not *Sagittarius*?' Wow. He was even better than I thought he was.

'Of course not! His birthday's Paddy's Day, March the seventeenth. He'll do anything to connect with someone. And that's what makes him so good. You know what I would love for him is to give him his own show, just a really good, entertaining programme for older people. I've talked to him about it before, but he's not ready to leave *The Daily Show*.'

We stood in the car park, beside my car.

'Are you finding time to relax and wind down?' Tom asked.

'Sea swimming,' I said. 'I'm saying yes to everything lately... It's why I said yes to you, actually. Otherwise I don't think I would have done it, not with such short notice.'

'And is this yes thing something that people could take advantage of? Ask you to do things for them and you can't say no?'

'I think there's a clause in the small print that states that if it's unreasonable...'

'Or dangerous...'

'Well... my mother is contemplating a parachute jump, thanks to her best friend Lorraine. That is definitely unreasonable and dangerous.'

He laughed.

'Mum is petrified of heights. But typical Lorraine never thinks about that. She's just the kind of person who launches herself into things without thinking.'

'And out of aeroplanes.'

'Exactly.'

'My dad was the same,' Tom said. 'He lived life to the full. Honestly, he never stopped. Read every book that came into the library. Would get involved in anything in the village. He even entered a poetry competition once and came third. He bred different sheep, always trying out new ways of farming... he even went to Newfoundland because he'd always wondered what it was like.'

'And what was it like?'

'He and Mam came home and said it was just like Ireland. The food, the people, the landscape... everything. Except he didn't like the tea. First thing he did was send some teabags to their new friends in Newfoundland.' Tom rested his hand on the top of his car. 'At his eulogy, everyone said he couldn't have squeezed more out of life.' He smiled. 'What are you doing now?'

'Swimming,' I said. 'And then going home to listen to my lodger, Callum. I realise that part of my job as landlady is to listen to his problems. He is really making progress. He seems far less down than he was when he moved in.'

'Ah, so you are an unpaid counsellor... lucky Callum.'

'I don't really give advice, more sit there while he sorts things in his head,' I said. 'Last night he showed me texts from his ex-wife to see if I could tell if she still loved him.'

'And what did you conclude?'

'Well, I couldn't tell,' I said, 'but I didn't know whether to give him hope or to advise him to give up. So I said, he should just focus on himself.'

Tom nodded his head. 'Good advice. The only advice, really, wouldn't you say? We can only live our own lives and hope that they meet up with the right person.'

'I think so,' I said. 'I mean, you can often run into the wrong person...'

'Tell me about it...'

'Yeah, me too...' I grinned at him. 'But as soon as you realise they are Mr Wrong...'

'Or Ms Wrong...'

'Exactly,' I went on, 'then you need to get out of it as swiftly as possible and work out what lessons you can learn from the encounter.'

'Oh, to be so methodical in dating,' said Tom. 'You make it sound so easy.'

I laughed again. 'God no... I haven't a clue what I'm doing. I just don't mind listening to Callum...'

'You can tell me more about Callum tomorrow...' he said.

'Tomorrow?'

'The barbecue... You have to say yes or you would upset your mum's friend Lorraine by saying no. Or would a barbecue at Casa Fitz be considered too dangerous and unreasonable?'

I laughed. 'Well...'

Tom smiled at me for a moment. 'So...' he began, but there was a voice from the other end of the car park.

'Tom!' Susie was walking towards us.

'Well,' said Susie, 'look at you both.' She smiled at me and at Tom. 'You're on *Daily Show* duties, is it? Sometimes I feel like you are neglecting us on *Quiz Me*. Maybe it's because we're doing so well in the ratings, you don't feel you have to spend quite so much time with us?'

'Sorry, Susie,' said Tom. 'We were just talking about the show.'

'Saw it,' she said. 'Bits of it, anyway. David was fabulous. He turned what was going to be a boring interview into something brilliant.' She went and stood at the passenger door of Tom's car. 'My car's at home. Would you mind giving me a lift?'

Tom hesitated for a second. 'Of course not,' he said, opening his door. 'See you tomorrow, Cat.'

'Yes, see you,' said Susie, and slipped into the passenger seat of Tom's car, just as I heard her say, 'What's happening *tomorrow*?'

He beeped his horn goodbye as they drove away. What was

going on between them? And would Susie be coming to the barbecue? For a moment, I felt disappointed, as though I had wanted him all to myself.

26

The sea was at its sparkling best. Cool, rather than cold, like being bathed in diamonds and sunshine. *It's like a magic potion*, I thought, as I paddled around.

Nora was floating on her back, a few yards out from me, only her toes and nose were visible, poking through the surface. Dolores was far out, close to the buoy, her arms slicing through the water. Malachy was even further out, just a red-haired dot, as far as the sea broke, the waves with their white caps, and Margaret, after singing her hymn, sedately bobbed along, her yellow-flowered cap and dignified profile, cruising slowly along, like a Victorian matron. There was no sign of Brenda and after waiting for a while and texting on the group:

Are you coming?

We decided to press on with our swim without her.

'She'll be delayed,' said Nora. 'She'll be along shortly, no doubt.'

Ten minutes later, I was in the water, floating on my back, when

I heard a shout from the shore. There on the rocks, waving her arms and yelling something incomprehensible, was Brenda.

Margaret paddled towards me. 'What is she saying?'

'I've no idea.' I looked back at Brenda, who looked, from this distance, very upset. She kept yelling.

'We'd better go in,' said Margaret,

Nora was already swimming towards us, and beyond her Dolores and Malachy.

Brenda had stopped shouting and was pacing up and down, distress etched on to her face.

As soon as we reached the steps, she rushed towards us. 'He's taken Arthur!' She'd been crying, her hair, normally not a strand out of place, looked as though she'd been camping for a week, and she was wearing what looked like a pair of pyjamas.

'No!' said Margaret, pulling herself up to standing. 'I don't believe it.' She turned to Nora and Dolores and Malachy who were gaining on us. 'He's taken Arthur.'

'The fecker!' shouted Dolores.

Arthur was her dog, I remembered.

Soon, we were all standing on the rocks, around Brenda.

'I knew he was planning something,' Brenda was saying, 'but I never knew he'd stoop so low.'

'Who?' I said.

'My ex, Pete,' said Brenda. 'The postman! I ended it last year and I love my new life...'

'Freedom,' said Nora.

'Peace,' said Margaret.

'Exactly,' said Brenda. 'Just me and Arthur. He's seventeen, ancient little fella. Basically, my four-legged son. And Pete threatened to take him... I thought he would never stoop that low... but I came home earlier and Arthur wasn't sitting on the back of the sofa looking out of the window. Immediately, I thought he was dead. I mean, he doesn't have much time left... and I spent half an hour looking for his body. Including under the sofa...' Her hands, and voice, were shaking. 'And then I saw a footprint...'

'A large, man-sized footprint?'

'Pete's?' said Malachy.

'Has to be,' said Nora. 'No one else would steal an ancient, half-blind, arthritic, balding dog.'

'Or steal *any*thing,' said Margaret. 'Thou shalt not steal.'

'Nor covet thy neighbour's dog,' said Dolores.

'But I just might kill him,' said Brenda, her eyes shining with murderous rage. 'Thou shalt kill if thou has a very good reason. Arthur's heart is weak and he's off his food. He doesn't have much strength. This could hasten his demise. The poor little boy could die of fright.'

There was a small, stifled scream from Dolores as she clapped her hand over her mouth. Margaret steadied herself by holding on to the side of the benches. Nora had her hands over her mouth.

'We'd better go and get him,' said Malachy. 'Who's coming?'

'Me,' said Nora.

'Me,' said Dolores.

'And me,' said Margaret.

They all turned to me. 'Coming, Cat?' said Nora.

'Yes,' I said. 'Of course I'm coming!'

27

According to Brenda, Pete the postman had moved back in with his mother, in the cottages behind the village.

'He only moved in with her because he was going to be made homeless,' explained Brenda, as we walked purposefully from the Forty Foot, across the road and into the village. The six of us turned the corner. 'It's number six,' said Brenda, whispering.

The road was a small tree-lined square, with cottages around the edge and in the middle a space where children kicked balls and adults sat on benches chatting.

'But why would he take Arthur?' I said.

'Badness,' said Dolores. 'Some people are pure bad.'

'He's got a mean streak half a mile wide,' said Brenda. 'He'd do anything just to be mean. He'd finish the milk in the carton and leave it there, even though he'd know I'd be on my way home late, dying for a cup of tea. Or he'd throw something away. My Jilly Cooper collection. All of them. My Mozart CDs... and now little Arthur.'

'Should we go past the house and stay at the other end of the terrace?' said Malachy. 'Be ready for him.'

Brenda nodded. 'Good idea. You and Dolores stand guard if he goes to leave. Margaret and Nora, you stay here, be ready to call 999 if he comes this way. Cat, you come with me. He doesn't know you, so you're going to have to do the talking.'

'About what?'

'I don't know,' she said. 'You're the television presenter!' She pushed me ahead of her. How could I say no?

Brenda stood nervously behind a red Hyundai, her hands clasped almost in prayer position. Beyond her were Nora and Margaret, their thumbs held up hopefully to me.

I rang the bell. After a moment or two, someone was coming. My mind, just as it had when faced with Penelope O'Brien, went blank.

A man, answering the description of Pete, opened the door. He was one solid mass of muscle, his neck like that of a prize bull, his nostrils the size of egg cups, a bald head like polished mahogany, and both arms tattooed with badly drawn, shaky-hand pictures and indiscernible drawings.

Somehow, I managed to speak. 'Hello,' I said, smiling broadly. 'I'm your new neighbour from across the way.'

'Yeah...' He wasn't about to hang up the bunting or organise a welcome party.

'And... well, I have a dog and I was wondering if you had a dog and if it would like to be friends with my dog.' I smiled. 'I mean, I don't want to impose...'

'Wha...?'

'My dog is a very sociable animal,' I blustered on, 'and gets lonely if she doesn't have another dog to play with. She finds humans very boring.'

He was looking at me, porcine nose scrunched up, as though I was mad.

'*Do* you have a dog?' I said, brightly, feeling more confident about this role I was playing and getting into the swing.

He seemed to consider the matter and then he turned, leaving the door open. 'Wait there,' he muttered. In a moment, he returned with a small black and white dog, grey whiskers, and a rheumy look in its eyes. The poor thing looked scared and defeated as it lay in Pete's arms, limp and dejected. On its thin red leather collar hung a small disc – 'Arthur'.

'Oh! He's so cute! I just love dogs! May I?' I asked, sweetly, holding out my hands.

Pete, the tattooed dognapper, shrugged. 'If you want...'

I reached out and took Arthur into my arms and for a split second, as I held this warm, little parcel of dog, I wondered what my next move was going to be. And then, my body took over, and I turned on my feet and began running.

'I've got him! I've got him!'

In an instant, Brenda was beside me, and then, like two firefighters running towards danger, there was Nora and Margaret, making straight for Pete to head him off and keep him away from Brenda and Arthur.

Behind us, I heard the shouts of Dolores and Malachy as they were now heading towards Pete too. The four of them formed a little circle around Pete, and then, as he tried to run, Nora stuck out a foot and tripped him up.

Brenda and I kept going and when we reached the village, we gasped for breath. Brenda was crying as I gave her Arthur and she covered his small head with kisses.

'Mam's here, Arthur,' she was saying. 'Mam's here.'

'Where are the others?'

'I hope they are all right.' Brenda had Arthur pressed to her face.

And they were. Along the path, heading our way, were the rest of the Sandycove swimming tribe.

'We did it!' called Dolores, as they walked towards us. 'He just said "take the bloody dog then" and went back in.'

'I need a drink,' said Nora. 'Anyone want to join me?' She paused, glancing at Dolores. 'Or a coffee... Alison's?'

'It's grand, Nora,' said Dolores. 'I can be around drink... it's not the drink that makes me drunk, it's me drinking the drink...' She laughed. 'So, I'll be fine, don't you worry. And anyway, I'm old pals with Mick behind the bar. It would be nice to see him.'

We found a small space in the back of The Island and Malachy ordered a round at the bar.

'Just a lime and soda for me, Mal,' said Dolores.

'Small sherry,' said Margaret.

'Whiskey,' said Nora.

Brenda ordered a glass of white wine and I asked for a gin and tonic.

Malachy returned with a tray with our drinks and a glass of Guinness for himself. 'I can't stay long,' he said. 'Just a half for me. You know, Mam...'

'How is she?' I said, taking my drink from him. 'Thanks, Malachy.'

'Dementia is not easy,' he said. 'For anyone. Not the person themselves or their carer. Luckily, my work is very understanding.' He sat on the small stool facing us. 'But it's nice to have a drink from time to time. Mick pulls a good pint.'

'He does indeed,' said Dolores, picking up her lime and soda. 'You know, I will never, ever drink again. It was such a chaotic time in my life, I was constantly on edge. I really believe I am safe now, all that...' She searched for the right word. 'All that misplaced energy has just dissipated. It's a very nice feeling.' She held up her glass. 'Sláinte.'

'Sláinte,' we all said.

'Good on you, Dolores,' said Nora.

'Yes, you're a lesson to us all,' said Margaret.

Arthur was on Brenda's lap, gazing up at her, like a long-lost lover, with his lovely little face. 'Ah, Arthur,' she said. 'My little dote.'

'Tell me this,' said Dolores, 'and tell me no more, how did you ever end up with that man?'

'I can't understand women,' said Malachy. 'They always seem interested in the men who aren't worth their time of day.'

'It's a mystery that will never be solved, Mal,' said Nora.

'I wish I knew,' said Brenda. 'But it was a long time ago and I wasn't as sure of myself as I am now. He was my postman and he'd always knock and we'd have the chat and one day he asked me out for a drink. Within days, he'd moved in. Said he loved me, but it turned out he'd just been evicted by the one before me.'

'It's called being a cocklodger,' said Dolores.

'Indeed,' said Nora. 'They're no rare breed.'

'Suffice to say,' Brenda went on, 'that I eventually saw sense and got my life and house back. Except, he wasn't too happy about it and I should have changed the locks. Anyway, doing that first thing tomorrow...' She kissed the top of Arthur's head.

'We've all been there,' said Nora, 'a dalliance with an undeserving type. Me with Finty.'

'Me too,' I said, thinking of PJ.

'And me with too many to mention,' said Dolores.

'Well, I haven't,' said Margaret. 'I wouldn't allow any kind of that nonsense.'

'Well, then, you're lucky, Margs,' said Nora.

'When I lived in Cricklewood,' Dolores began, 'I had a succession of ne'er-do-wells.'

'I wouldn't mind meeting a ne'er-do-well,' said Malachy. 'A

female one. At this point, I would take on anyone. But who'd take on me?'

'A very lucky woman,' assured Nora. She held up her glass. 'All's well that ends well,' she said. 'Here's to Arthur and his safe return home.'

'And here's to making sure that no one is entangled by a ne'er-do-well ever again,' said Margaret, holding up her little glass. 'And that our Malachy finds himself someone nice.'

'To Malachy,' we all said, as Malachy blazed crimson, but he dutifully held up his pint glass.

'May we all find someone nice,' he said.

'Well, I have Arthur,' said Brenda. 'He's all I need.'

'By the way,' said Dolores. 'It's my twentieth anniversary of being sober today. Who would have thought I could have sat in a pub and not have been tempted?'

'It's very impressive,' said Nora.

'If only more of us had your strength of character,' said Margaret.

Dolores shrugged. 'I will never go back there, to that person I was, the place I was in. I've no fear now, at all. I can look at alcohol and not want a drop. I feel liberated. It's a wonderful thing.'

'Praise the Lord,' said Margaret.

'Praise *Dolores*,' said Nora. '*God* isn't the one going to all those AA meetings.'

'I don't pray to Him,' said Dolores. 'My higher power is Mother Nature. The sea. The trees, the sky, the birds.' She held up her hand. 'Mick,' she called over to the bar, 'same again, please, and why don't you join us for one?'

'Coming up, Dol,' he said. 'And I'll join you another time. Promise.'

And then it was Dolores's turn to go red.

THE FORTY FOOTERS!

Me: Sorry but won't be at the Forty Foot this evening. Going to work barbecue.

Margaret: We'll see you soon.

Me: I'll be back on Sunday.

Brenda: Say hi to David and tell him I promise to come next time.

Nora: Have a good time, Cat.

Dolores: Definitely have a good time. But not too good. If you know what I mean? 😉

Malachy: See you soon Cat.

Nora: How is your Mam, Mal?

Malachy: Doing fine, Nora.

Nora: I will be in with some tea for the two of you. Have some nice fish pie.

Margaret: I have tomatoes from the garden. Will drop them in.

Dolores: Your tomatoes are the best, Margaret.

Margaret: They are nothing to do with me, Dolores. God provides. We reap his harvest.

Dolores: Whatever you say. I still think you might have something to have done with them.

Me: How is Arthur?

Brenda: Fast asleep. Tucked up in his special blanket. Had chicken for his tea. His favourite.

Margaret: He's a good little boy, that one.

Brenda: He is indeed. Thanks again to you all. Arthur sends his love.

Nora: Liked your interview with Penelope O'Brien, Cat. Must buy her new book.

Margaret: I never miss *The Daily Show* now. I always have my cup of tea to coincide. A very illuminating and often amusing programme.

Nora: David did not get that sun tan from Dollymount Strand.

Malachy: I tape it and Mam and I watch it. Perfect television for her.

Brenda: Cat is brilliant, isn't she?

28

On Saturday, I was just about to leave to meet Becca and Sinéad for coffee in Alison's when Callum came into the hall, holding Loulou's hand. Loulou had her pink rucksack on her back. 'Loulou's going to come to the garage with Daddy, while he gets his car fixed.'

'It sounds boring though,' said Loulou.

'It's not,' said Callum. 'You get to see the mechanics at work. And there's a sweet shop nearby that we can go to...'

'But I don't want to go,' she said, firmly. 'Can I stay here on my own?'

Callum glanced at me as though he didn't know what to say to her. 'If you want to,' he said, slowly. 'But you might get lonely.'

'I won't,' she said. 'I'm always on my own, anyway. And I'm never lonely. Well, not all the time. Only sometimes.'

'Would you like to come with me?' I said, tentatively, not sure if I was treading on any toes but wanting to help. 'I'm meeting my friends Becca and Sinéad. And there's a toddler, Rory. We're just having a late breakfast?'

'Really?' She looked delighted. 'May I, Daddy?'

'If you really want to,' Callum said, looking a little deflated.

* * *

The two of us walked into the village, Loulou talking the whole way there.

'I hate socks,' she was saying. 'They always get holes in and my toes get stuck in the holes and it really hurts. It's like the sock is trying to cut off my toes.'

I laughed. 'I've been there.'

'Why doesn't someone invent socks which don't get holes in them? Why can't shoes come with socks attached and then you'd never need to wear socks? What is the point of them?'

'Warmth?' I suggested. 'I mean, today we don't need them because it's so sunny.'

'Yes, but...' She wasn't going to accept anything other than her determination to rid the world of socks. 'Which is your favourite meal?' she said, suddenly, changing the subject. 'Not *food*. A *meal*.'

'Breakfast,' I said, 'followed by afternoon snack.'

'Mine's brunch,' she said. 'And then afternoon snack, then morning snack and then evening snack. And *then* breakfast.'

'Snacking is definitively my favourite way to eat,' I agreed.

'Me too. Cutlery is just annoying. I think a meal is a snack if you don't have to use a knife and fork.'

We stood outside Alison's café. 'Ready to go in?'

Loulou nodded.

'Well, come on, and you can meet my friends.'

Becca and Sinéad were already at Alison's. Rory was sitting on Becca's lap.

'Quick,' said Sinéad, 'take a picture. Becca is holding a child.'

Becca kissed Rory on the top of his head. 'He seems to like it,' she said. 'I thought he would wriggle and try to get away, you know when dogs sense a hostile adult. But...'

'Maybe you are not as hostile as you pretend to be,' I said, making room for Loulou to push past and then sit down. The chatty Loulou of the walk was gone, and she was shy, sitting so close to me, we were touching.

'Who's this?' said Sinéad, smiling at her.

'Don't tell me you've had a daughter all these years, locked up in a secret room in your house?' Becca said and Loulou smiled shyly back.

'This is Loulou... Callum's... my lodger's daughter.'

'Ah,' said Becca, 'the mystery is solved. Loulou, you are very welcome this morning.'

'Thank you,' said Loulou, taking up one of Rory's crayons. 'May I?'

'Of course,' said Sinéad, pushing the paper towards her. 'Are you a good artist?'

Loulou shook her head. 'I like doing it. I'm just not very good at it. Miss Lally, my teacher, always says liking is the important part.'

'Very true,' agreed Becca. 'Which reminds me... do you think Birkenstocks are suitable for the Irish Television Awards? I like them, you see, and as Loulou has just said, the liking is the important part. I have to get my dress next week and the thought of wearing heels is horrifying. It's like being released from prison and you come out a reformed character. I am never going back there again.'

'What is wrong with you lately?' said Sinéad. 'You've changed.'

'I'm doing Cat's yes challenge,' Becca said. 'And once you say yes to one thing, other things follow. I said yes to not straightening my hair and I am beginning to like my curls. And yes to comfortable shoes. I just bloody love my new shoes.' She poked her foot up so we could all admire then. 'Don't look at my feet, though. Still haven't managed to get a pedicure. Too busy.'

Loulou was looking at her feet. 'Why would shoes *not* be comfortable? Who would wear uncomfortable shoes?'

'Exactly,' said Becca. 'Loulou here is a genius.'

Loulou beamed at the praise.

Alison came over to take our order. 'Ladies?'

'What about pancakes, Loulou?' I said. 'I know you like them. And hot chocolate with marshmallows? Okay with you?'

She nodded. 'Thank you, Cat.'

'Croissant for me,' said Becca.

'And for me,' I said.

We waited for Sinéad to order her sliced fruit, no honey, soy yogurt.

'Croissant, Sinéad?' said Becca, eyebrow arched.

'Yes, actually. And one for Rory as well.'

Becca and I stared at Sinéad, as Alison disappeared to the kitchen with our orders.

'Are you feeling all right?' Becca asked. 'Do you need a lie-down, a mental health break, an intervention?'

'I just really, really desperately need, want and desire a croissant,' said Sinéad. 'I think I will die if I don't have something nice in my life. I need joy and pleasure and indulgence and sometimes I wonder if I reintroduced dairy into my diet and fat and...'

'Germs?' suggested Becca.

'And perhaps germs,' continued Sinéad, 'then I might be happier. I might have E. coli or bacterial gastroenteritis, but I could be happy. I mean, I *am* happy. I am so blessed to have Rory and everything. Blessed to be a mother and to be on maternity leave... and I love being a mother and all that. Like, *really* love being a mother, more than anything.' But tears had sprung into her eyes. 'Being a mother makes me so... so... content... except... except...' She had now started crying. 'Except, I'm not happy. Not at all. I love Rory and I want to be the best mother I can be and keep him safe and well and all that... except this was the life I wanted and then I realise it's not quite the life I wanted and I don't know what to do.

Sorry, Rory. It's not you, it's me, but I am going slowly and steadily mad. And with Conor always around and Rory and I having to tiptoe and speak in whispers, I think I am going fecking doolally. And just once, if that's okay with you, Becca, I just really, *really* want to eat a croissant.' And she began to bawl as Loulou stared, fascinated. Rory carried on colouring his picture, oblivious to the emotional breakdown his mother was having.

We were interrupted by Alison, who put our orders in front of us. 'Enjoy, ladies,' she said, as Loulou stared in wonder at hers as though she was gazing upon the crown jewels.

'It looks amazing. Too nice to eat.' But she spooned some of the cream into her mouth, closing her eyes.

Sinéad had dived down to her handbag as soon as Alison arrived, searching for something. She reappeared, red-eyed, tears still forming, clutching a tissue.

Becca was still holding Rory and put her free arm around Sinéad. 'It's been really hard, hasn't it?'

Sinéad nodded. 'How can you be doing the thing you love most in the world, parenting your child and also not be enjoying it?' she said. 'I wake up feeling dreadful. But the thought of leaving him in some creche where I don't know how clean it is, or if they treat him well, or if they talk to him and help him develop... that's awful. And so I am stuck. Trying to do the right thing for my child, and yet not living for me.'

Becca and I nodded. I had my hand on hers, Loulou was spooning the cream into her mouth and listening intently.

'Can't you just find the world's best nursery?' I said. 'The cleanest, best creche ever?'

'They don't exist,' said Sinéad, sighing. 'They are all bacteria-ridden places.'

'Maybe you need to lower your standards?' said Becca. 'I mean... you might have to?

'I can't,' said Sinéad. 'The thought of it makes me feel all panicky inside.'

'But you've been the perfect mother for three years,' said Becca. 'You've done the hard work. He's a great kid. Happy, interesting. For a three-year-old, anyway.' She kissed Rory's head. 'And he has good taste in sweatshirts.'

Sinéad laughed. 'He's better dressed than me.' She looked at us. 'I know it's all down to me. But everything is down to me. *Everything*. And I'm exhausted.'

'You poor thing,' I said.

'I need to change,' Sinéad continued. 'I know that. I need to say yes to not trying to make everything perfect because...'

'...perfect doesn't exist,' Becca and I said together.

'Exactly,' said Sinéad.

'Miss Lally says that,' added Loulou. 'She says just do your best and your best is good enough.'

Sinéad laughed again. 'I couldn't have said it better myself, Loulou. I'm going to remember that and I am going to try to be less perfect. Because I think I'm driving myself mad. Poor Conor, I'm driving him mad. And all I do is complain about him, but I'm not exactly easy myself. He shouted at me yesterday because I dropped Rory's lunch all over the floor and the bowl went skittering across the floor and I shouted... okay, swore. Really loudly, and he was on a conference call. He came in, furious, and said it was hardly professional to have someone screaming in the background when he is talking a client through the delicate matter of tax evasion.'

'Can't you soundproof his room? Egg boxes? Aren't they what people use?' said Becca.

'What did you do?' I asked.

Sinéad shrugged. 'We just left the house for the afternoon and came back after 5 p.m. and at that point, he had made us both a gin and tonic and had his feet up. He was apologetic, but I was still furious with him. I couldn't let it go.'

'You need him back in the office,' said Becca. 'For the sake of your marriage.'

I was nodding in agreement. 'Tell him he either renews his rail-card and starts commuting every morning or it's divorce.'

'It will have to be divorce,' said Sinéad, sadly. 'I am not coping.'

There was a squeal from Rory as his croissant, which he'd been gnawing on, fell to the ground, and quickly, Sinéad picked it up and put it back on his plate.

'There you go, Rory.'

He put it straight into his mouth and we watched him chew on it, all of us, wide-eyed, wondering what would happen next? Would Sinéad rethink it and claw it out of his mouth or would this be a breakthrough? She remained still, her hands clenched.

'And breathe,' she said. 'And breathe. And don't think of the germs, and let go of perfection.'

'You're doing really well,' said Loulou, holding a forkful of pancake. 'We're all proud of you.'

Sinéad, Becca and I all laughed. 'And we're proud of you,' I said, as Loulou glowed with pride as she chewed on her breakfast.

29

Loulou and I called in to see Mum and Dad. I kept checking my phone to see if Callum had called or if he was back home. I only had two hours before David's barbecue. I wasn't sure what to wear. Jeans, perhaps. Sandals. Nice top. Or should I go silk dress? Or perhaps my long paisley skirt?

'I won't be around this evening,' I said to Loulou, as we waited for Mum to answer the door.

'Where will you be?'

'Just going to a party and it might be late.'

Loulou looked disappointed, just as Mum answered the door.

'Who's this?' she said, smiling at Loulou.

Loulou held out her hand. 'I'm Loulou,' she said, 'Cat's lodger's daughter.'

Mum laughed and Loulou looked confused because she didn't know what she'd said that was so amusing.

'That's exactly what she is,' I said. 'Thank you for introducing yourself so clearly.'

'Yes,' said Mum, who looked a bit guilty for laughing at Loulou, 'it's always helpful when people explain who they are. Well, I am Annie, Cat's mum.'

Loulou and I stepped inside and Loulou followed me through the hall.

'Sometimes,' Mum was saying, 'you could meet someone and can't remember their name or you only hear half of what they said and they don't bother introducing themselves. So it's very helpful when someone does.'

'My Nanna Pat is like that,' said Loulou, immediately comfortable with Mum, 'she only says half-sentences, Mum says. *I* can understand what she is saying because I just try to imagine the invisible bits of her words.'

'That's exactly it,' agreed Mum, 'so you work out what she is saying.'

When Loulou spotted Dad sitting at the kitchen table, she said, 'I'm Loulou, Cat's lodger's daughter,' and, again, Dad laughed.

'Well, I'm Cat's mother's husband,' he said. 'Or Cat's father, Johnny.' He stood up, nearly braining himself on the ceiling light which hung over the table, and held out his hand. 'Good to meet you, Loulou, Cat's lodger's daughter.'

'Good to meet you, Johnny, Cat's mother's husband.' And now Loulou laughed.

'I was just admiring your T-shirt, Loulou,' said Mum. 'Live Love Unicorns.'

'They are three very important things,' said Loulou, pulling it down at the bottom so we could all get a better look. 'Live. That's important. Love. Very important too. And Unicorns. Extremely and very important.'

Mum and Dad looked delighted at her. 'Wise words, Loulou,' said Dad.

'I would have a T-shirt which said Tea Biscuits Sleep,' said Mum.

Loulou nodded and then turned to Dad. 'What would yours be?'

'Well, Loulou,' said Dad. 'Perhaps it would be Lemon Drizzle Cake.' He looked over at Mum, an eyebrow raised. 'That's my favourite.'

'I *buy* a very good one,' said Mum to Loulou. 'From a bakery in the village. And do you know I used to tell people I made it myself.'

Loulou's eyes were wide. 'Why?'

'Because I was embarrassed that I wasn't a very good baker and that my sister was so good,' she said. 'Isn't that silly?'

Loulou nodded again. 'It doesn't matter if you are not good at something because you just have to find the thing you are good at. My teacher, Miss Lally, says everyone is good at something.'

'When is The Great Sandycove Bake-Off?' I said to Mum, sitting at the table next to Dad. Loulou came and sat next to me.

'Next Saturday,' Mum said. 'Would you like to come, Loulou?'

Loulou nodded.

'And,' went on Mum, 'I've been practising my own lemon drizzle cake. Maybe you would like to try some?' She opened the cake tin and placed it on the table while Dad stood and filled the kettle. 'By the way, Lorraine has bought us all a present. It's just over here...' She took out a small bag which was tucked behind the toaster. Then she brought out a smaller paper bag and handed it to me. '...And Loulou can have mine,' she said. 'Lorraine bought them from a market stall in Dún Laoghaire. I'll ask her to get another for me.'

Loulou sat for a moment, holding her paper bag, as though waiting for permission to open it.

'We'll go together, shall we?' I said. 'One, two...'

'Three,' we both said, and put our hands into the bags and both drew out silver necklaces. A delicate chain with silver twisted to make a word.

'What does it say?' I thought that it was my name for a moment. 'Yes,' I said. 'It says yes.'

'Yes is the world's most powerful word, I think,' said Mum. 'My friend Lorraine says yes to everything, and Cat and I are doing it for a while, aren't we, Cat? Once you start saying it, everything changes. You are just open to things. Conversations, experiences...'

'Happenstance,' added Dad. 'And you said yes to me, all those years ago, and if you hadn't, we wouldn't be here right now with our beautiful daughter and the lovely Loulou.'

'Exactly,' said Mum.

'Miss Lally always says that if someone said to jump off a cliff, would you?' said Loulou. 'But I think it depends on the cliff.'

'But you don't have to say yes if you think it might kill you,' I said, giving Mum a look. 'Like a *parachute jump*.'

Mum looked over at Dad quickly and then changed the subject. 'I am still recovering from Pilates on Thursday night. I spent most of yesterday lying flat on my back unable to move.'

Loulou was listening, fascinated.

'But,' went on Mum, 'at least I did it? Isn't that right, Loulou? It's better to give something a go than not bother at all?'

'Miss Lally says that as well,' she agreed.

'Well, it's good advice,' said Mum. 'And I've joined the Sandycove Women's Group and I'll be going on trips... there's one booked for two weeks' time to the Irish Writer's Centre to hear a talk on...' She smiled. 'You'll never believe what? On the work of Georgette Heyer. Now...' – she nodded at us – 'how's that for a coincidence?'

'You'll be able to ask your question,' I said.

'If I could remember what on earth it was,' said Mum, 'then I might.'

'But you have to,' said Loulou. 'You have to say yes to everything.'

'That's true,' Mum remarked. 'I'll remember you, Loulou, when

I feel all nervous about asking my question and I'll keep going because you reminded me.'

'I didn't know adults got nervous,' said Loulou. 'I thought it was just children.'

'Yes, Loulou,' said Dad, 'nerves never go away. I think grown-ups just learn how to hide them a bit better...'

'What are you nervous about?' asked Loulou.

'Oh... lots of things,' he said. 'Anything happening to Cat or Annie.'

Loulou turned to Mum. 'What are you nervous about?'

'New things,' said Mum. 'I was nervous going to the Pilates class the other day, thinking everyone would laugh at me because I can't touch my toes and my yoga mat is Cat's old one, which is a little battered.'

Loulou turned to me. 'And you?'

'I'm scared my mother will say yes to doing a parachute jump.' I gave Mum a look.

'Well...' Dad looked at Mum. 'We have made a decision. She's not going...'

'Good...' I began, just as Dad said: '...alone. We're *both* going to go.'

'Life is short,' said Mum.

'And we're in it together,' said Dad. 'After doing the tandem the other night, we thought we'd do more things together. And the couple who parachute together, stay together.'

'But you don't need to do a parachute jump to stay together, you *are* together,' I countered. They had both lost their minds. It had been worrying enough when it was just Mum, but now the two of them?

They smiled at each other. 'Well, we used to have fun,' said Mum. 'A lot of fun.'

Dad nodded. 'We motorbiked around Germany, years ago.'

'And we used to camp all over Europe,' added Mum. 'And go dancing and... I don't know... be spontaneous.'

'I once stood up at a festival in Spain and sang an Irish song,' said Dad.

'Did you?' I'd always thought of him as an introvert. I couldn't imagine him getting up on a stage.

'We've forgotten who we were. Who we are,' said Mum. 'Being on the tandem reminded us how much fun we used to have together. I haven't laughed so much in years.'

'And so we're *both* doing the jump,' concluded Dad. 'We're starting the training this week. We've only got a couple of weeks and then we'll be heading off.'

'And raising money for the hospice,' Mum reminded him.

'Yes, very important,' said Dad. 'But also reminding ourselves that life may be short, that we're going to get as much fun and adventure out of it as possible.'

'And out of our comfort zones,' said Mum.

It was hard enough to be out of *my* comfort zone, but I selfishly wanted my parents to stay very firmly in theirs. I didn't want them to have adventures which might likely lead to a shattered pelvis or death.

'But you might die,' I said. 'Or break every bone in your body. Smashed to smithereens.'

Dad looked quite energised at the thought. 'But it's about time I got out of the shed, don't you think?' he said. 'Live a little? We should all leave our sheds from time to time. Take a risk.'

I could tell by the look on their faces that their minds were made up.

'We're determined,' he said, saluting. 'Can't let Lorraine down. Or the hospice.'

'Definitely?'

Mum nodded. 'Definitely. Form filled in and sent off. It's for the hospice, so we can't say no. And anyway, we can't let Lorraine go up there alone. What if she has a panic attack like she did when we flew to Marbella for her sixtieth?'

'It wasn't a panic attack,' said Dad. 'It was because they told her that they wouldn't be serving alcohol on the flight.'

'Now,' said Mum, 'who fancies some of my *home-made* lemon drizzle cake? Tell me what you think? Loulou, I want your very honest opinion. Don't hold back.'

Mum's cake looked pretty good, covered in white icing. It didn't look as impressive as Sally-Anne's, but it had a charming, home-made quality.

Loulou took a bite, a thoughtful look on her face.

'Do you like it?' Mum asked.

Loulou smiled 'Yes,' she said, managing to hold both her 'yes' necklace and a forkful of cake. 'Definitely yes. It's the best I've ever had.'

30

When Loulou and I arrived home, thankfully Callum had returned. I showered and dried my hair and put on make-up, just nice, non-TV, natural make-up, and changed into my old silk summer dress and took a taxi to David's house. I wished I wasn't going. Making small talk with strangers was my very least favourite thing to do, and, apart from David, the only person I knew who was going was Tom, and whether he was with Susie or not, he'd probably be busy networking or whatever it was executives did. And if Susie *was* there, it was unlikely she would even want me to spend any time with them. I was going to be on my own, that awkward guest at a party who knows no one and hangs around in the corners until she can leave as early as possible.

I gave myself twenty minutes, from showing my face and saying hello to David to making some small talk with any other stray guests and then just slipping away home.

The sky was a rich blue, not a cloud or a wisp, the air heavy and warm. A perfect day. The taxi turned down a leafy lane. Large Range Rovers and sleek Mercedes had been parked on the grass verges. All around, women were climbing out of small sports cars or taxis dressed in off-the-shoulder maxi dresses and men in chinos and aviator shades. Thank God at the last moment I had changed out of my jeans and put on an old silk dress and my gold flat sandals. Above the gate, the curved wrought-iron letters stated 'Casa Fitz'.

The house itself was modern but was built to look like an old stately home – sandstone brick, large windows, long, wide steps leading from the cantilevered glass doors to the garden, which was like a large and beautiful park, a long, manicured lawn stretching like a green carpet, the size of a football field, curving its way to include rose bushes and flower beds and mature trees.

Around me waiters carried trays of drinks and canapés. I hesitated, wondering what to do first.

'Catríona!' It was David – looking like a runner-up in a 1980s Eurovision final, in white skinny jeans, pink espadrilles, mirror shades and a Breton T-shirt. His toupee matched his mood and seemed to have extra bounce in it, the glossy dark hair reflecting the sunlight like a disco ball.

Beside him was a tiny, pale-skinned woman, maybe fifty going on twenty-five, her hair luxuriantly layered, her eyes fringed with long, spidery lashes. Her T-shirt was slashed at the neck and her super-short white skirt revealed long, tanned legs.

'Ah! Catríona Jones! My current TV wife!' He laughed at his own joke. 'I traded Barbara in for a younger model! Meet my one and only Jennifer. Jennifer, Catríona Jones. And I know you wouldn't be caught dead viewing *The Daily Show*, Jennifer, but Cat is currently co-presenting with me.' He turned back to me. 'She doesn't ever watch it,' he said. 'Can you believe it?'

'David,' said Jennifer, shaking my hand and giving me an eye roll in David's direction, 'I have something which you might not know much about, but it's called a life. I am busy. I don't want to sit at home watching television. I hope he's being nice to you,' she said to me. 'He can be tiresome. And difficult.'

David seemed delighted by Jennifer's underwhelm. 'Difficult? *Moi*?' he said, with a laugh. 'I *have* to be difficult. It's in my contract. You can't be a star and not be difficult. Let Catríona be the judge. Am I difficult?'

'He's actually very easy,' I said to Jennifer.

'You see!' said David, giving me a wink.

'Well, I hope you don't take any nonsense,' said Jennifer.

'The only person who takes my nonsense is you, my dear,' said David to Jennifer. 'I don't know how you put up with me.'

'Now he's trying to make you feel sorry for him,' she said. 'Don't fall for it.'

'I'll try not to,' I replied, smiling. She was surprisingly nice and David was lucky to have her.

Two men on the lawn were practising sword fighting with branches, making the other guests move away from them so they didn't receive a twig in the eye.

'Who are they?' said David.

'Two of the Four Paddys,' said Jennifer.

'The Forp what?' said David.

'The Four Paddys… Good God… surely, you have *heard* of them?'

David shook his head. He lifted up his sunglasses to squint at the men, both dressed in too-tight suits and ties worn over a T-shirt.

'Their podcast is the most popular in the country,' said Jennifer, 'their TV show is up for loads of awards. Paddy O'Gara is up for Best Presenter at the ITAs… against *you*.'

David's glasses fell back over his eyes. 'Best if I avoid him, then. *Who* on earth invited him?'

'I did,' said Jennifer. 'I thought we should keep your enemies close.'

'Enemies!' laughed David. 'As if I care about awards.' He winked at me. 'I am above awards. Not interested in cattle markets and beauty pageants.'

'I'm going to circulate,' said Jennifer, 'and see what I can learn from Paddy O'Gara. Lovely to meet you,' she said to me. 'And remember, don't take any nonsense from this one here. He's not to be indulged. He's on a strict diet of sarcasm, cynicism and not being taken seriously. Adoration and love are strictly rationed on home turf.'

'I don't know where I would be without that woman,' said David as we watched her descend the steps, stopping to talk to guests along the way. 'She keeps me on my toes. I was born to a mother who thought the sun shone out of my proverbial. So I went through life trying to find a woman who would just love and adore me. And then, finally, last-chance saloon, I meet Jennifer, and she couldn't give a shite about who I am. She's more interested in her own life than mine. And I've got to tell you, Cat, it's very refreshing. My divorce from Mrs Fitzgerald Number Two came through last week, but I haven't told Jennifer yet... I don't know what she'd say to a proposal. She'd probably tell me to feck off. I can't say I was scared proposing the first two times. Jennifer might refuse me and laugh in my face. I probably won't ever find the right time.'

This vulnerable David was a very different David to the super-confident one I'd witnessed in work. I found myself smiling at him. 'You won't know until you try,' I said.

And then I spotted Tom. I'd rarely seen him in anything but his usual corporate look, but today he was wearing jeans and a pale linen checked shirt, sleeves rolled up, a glass of white wine in one hand. He looked younger than he usually did, though he seemed as apprehensive as I did when I had arrived. But then he spotted us and walked straight over, his hand outstretched towards David.

'What a wonderful party,' he said. 'Thank you for inviting me. Such a great gathering. And I met the lovely Jennifer and one of the

Four Paddys. Don't know which one.' Then he turned to me, smiling, and suddenly I felt strange inside, as though something had changed, the world had shifted. 'How are you?'

'Great,' I said, trying to smile back. But I was really attempting to work out what exactly I was feeling. I hadn't even the excuse of a drink yet. 'Have you been here long?'

'No, about fifteen minutes,' he said, still smiling, looking straight at me.

'This young lady needs a drink,' said David. 'What will you have?'

'I'll find it,' I said. 'Don't worry.'

'I'll bring her to the bar,' said Tom.

'And please help yourself to food,' David went on. 'There are a few roasted animals at the barbecue area... so you should find something you like. I'll go and mingle and I shall speak to you both later.' And, with a too-hard slap on Tom's back, David disappeared into the house.

Tom and I turned to each other and, for a moment, I couldn't work out what he was thinking.

'I have to leave this, somewhere,' I said to Tom, holding up my gift bag of wine. It seemed quite inadequate now, faced with the reality of the party.

'We could just crack it open and drink from the bottle?' Tom raised his eyebrows.

I laughed. 'Let me just leave it in the kitchen, and we can go and eat.'

And just like that, it seemed we were going to spend the party together.

31

There was a topiary hedge which was trimmed into a shape which looked like a man's head. 'Could that be... David?' I said.

'That's the ultimate in success,' replied Tom. We were sat on the steps just in front of the house. 'Your own hedge-head. Beats a Warhol print or a Lucian Freud portrait.' He smiled again. 'It's such a beautiful garden,' he went on. 'I have just a tiny balcony. I tried to grow my own potatoes this year, in a barrel...'

'How did they turn out?'

'I haven't harvested them... Is that the right word?'

'Picked?'

'Trust me, delusions of grandeur...' He smiled. 'Last time we had a drink together was in that pub of yours, the evening you agreed to do *The Daily Show*.'

'Seems like a long time ago.'

'Are you enjoying the show?'

I nodded. 'I think so,' I said. 'It's scary stuff doing live television...'

He shook his head. 'I wouldn't be able for it. Too anxious.'

'You? Anxious?'

He nodded. 'I used to play hurling for Galway minors. And every time we had a big match, I would just feel so ill. I couldn't eat, couldn't sleep. I'd just feel so awful. My parents would be so worried about me. I went for therapy... I was even hypnotised at one time. I think it was then I realised that maybe I wasn't cut out to be a professional hurler.' He shrugged. 'Or maybe I was just a rubbish player? Who knows?'

'And so you went into TV?'

He nodded. 'I worked for a production company after university. And then went to another company, and so on. I don't ever get nervous any more, just excited. It's easier when it's not you on display. And it's never boring because there is constant interaction with such interesting people, there's this creative energy and making programmes that people will watch. And then there are the ITAs soon.' He looked at me. 'I am hoping we will do well.'

He stood up briefly to take another two glasses of wine from another passing tray.

'So, tell me about you,' he said, sitting back down again and handing me my glass. 'What makes you happy?'

'Friends, family,' I said. 'Food.'

'That's everyone,' he smiled. 'Who doesn't like those things?'

'Depends on the friends, family and food,' I replied.

'But what is it that really excites you? Apart from live television?' He gave me a look.

'Swimming,' I said. 'I am loving it. It's really strange, but you are both freezing and warm when you come out and you get this feeling of... I don't know... incredible well-being.' I paused. 'It doesn't last, though, so you find yourself returning the next night. And we've started having a cup of tea after we come out.'

'Who's we? Your partner?'

I shook my head. 'It's a group of people. Friends, I suppose. Brenda in make-up. There's Nora, Margaret, Dolores and

Malachy... it's being part of a community, all of us so different. I love it.'

He nodded. 'Shall we go and find these roasted beasts or whatever there is?'

The barbecue had been set up in a lower part of the garden, in a large, square dip in the grass, surrounded on one side by a large bed of tall roses and on the other by a small copse of birch trees. Tom and I hovered in the queue at one of the upturned oil drums turned barbecue and helped ourselves to the salads, chicken kebabs, steaks and burgers.

Tom had taken a bottle of rosé from a cooler and, once we found a place on the grass, poured us a glass each. 'Cheers,' he said.

'Here's to television...' I said, raising my glass.

'And here's to swimming,' he said.

We ate and talked and drank the wine until the bottle was empty and then found another and started all over again.

'So how is the yes thing going?' asked Tom. 'Or have you given up and started saying no?'

'I'm still saying yes,' I replied, showing him my 'yes' necklace. 'My best friend, Becca, said yes to a pair of Birkenstocks at a clothes swap and she's now changing in front of our very eyes. She's even stopped straightening her hair.'

Tom laughed. 'Wow, who knew a pair of sandals would have such a powerful effect?'

'And my other friend, Sinéad, is obsessed with germs and bacteria, but she let her son, Rory, eat something off the floor this morning.'

I was tipsy, I realised, rambling on. I wondered was he bored and wanting to get away from me. But he looked as though he had no intention of going anywhere, stretching out, his hands under his head.

'I've been eating off the floor all my life and I am still alive,' he said. 'My cat has higher standards of hygiene than me. Pierre won't drink his water unless it's a clean bowl every day. And he wipes his feet on the mat every time he comes in from the garden.'

'He and Sinéad would get on well.' I refilled our glasses again.

And then I told him about Mum and Dad's parachute jump and how worried I was.

'Dad said he didn't want Mum to do it alone.'

'Ah. That's sweet.'

'Until they both die and leave me an orphan.' I felt a little light-headed, but incredibly happy, one of those moments in life when you can't remember a single problem you have, when everything just seems easy. And talking to Tom was so easy. I'd always thought he was nice, but now I felt we were *friends*.

'My parents were very happily married,' he said. 'Same sense of humour. They laughed a lot, but were always on the same page. I remember before Dad got ill and he and Mam were off on a holiday to Tenerife, but the dog died the day before they were leaving. Padraig, our old collie. So obviously, we were all distraught, including Dad who loved Padraig more than anyone.' Tom shook his head. 'He didn't go. He said he couldn't go off without giving Padraig the memorial. And Mam was totally with him. She said that she couldn't be married to someone who would just continue with their holiday.'

'How is your mam doing?'

'She's grand. She's in Oughterard, spends a lot of time in her garden and is in a walking group where they tackle a different mountain in Connemara every month. So far they are up to thirty-two.'

I picked up the bottle again and topped up our glasses. 'I was dreading the barbecue,' I said. 'But it's been really nice...'

'So was I,' he said. 'I thought you might bring someone.'

'Like who?'

'Oh, I don't know...' He looked vaguely away. 'I just thought I might be on my own, making small talk, chatting about work... not my favourite thing to do on a Saturday.'

'Are you seeing anyone?' I hoped I sounded casual and as we now seemed to be friends, maybe it wasn't too nosy. But I needed to know what was going on with him and Susie and why she behaved so proprietorial about him.

But he shook his head. 'Apart from my cat, Pierre, and my lovely cleaner, Mrs O'Donovan, who brings me apple tart every week, I'm on my own.'

'What about Susie?'

He frowned for a moment. 'Susie? What is it with all these rumours? We had a very brief fling years ago, before I even joined the station. We'd met at the ITAs, saw each other for a few months, but it wasn't right. At all. It was all such long time ago now I can barely remember it. She became a bit possessive. Which is fine, if you want to be *possessed*.' He smiled. 'She was really nice,' he ended, emphatically. 'But not for me. And she didn't make me laugh. Does that answer your question?'

I nodded. 'It does.' But it didn't completely answer my question and why Susie was so possessive over him. Could she really just be someone who didn't cope with rejection very well?

He smiled. 'So what about you? Who's this Callum?'

'He's my lodger. Nothing going on. Never. He just needed a place to stay for a while and I had to say...'

'Yes.'

'Exactly. Anyway, I like being single,' I went on. 'I was seeing someone, but he was far too controlling and not that nice...'

'That would put you off someone.' Tom was listening, intently. It was so nice to talk to a man who wanted to hear what you had to say.

'It did.'

'So you are saying no to relationships?'

'Well, no one has asked me out yet, so it hasn't come up.'

He laughed. 'I can see how this can be manipulated to your advantage. If no one asks, then you don't have to answer.'

I laughed. 'Something like that.'

'Why don't we have a wander around the garden?' he suggested, standing and reaching for my hand, pulling me up towards him. As soon as he touched me, I wanted him to pull me all the way into him. But I stopped myself and let go as soon as I was on my feet, my face red, my heart pounding. It was the alcohol, I told myself. I was being silly, and a little tipsy and the sun was too hot. And yet... something had happened.

We took two more glasses from a tray and sat down on a bench close to the rose garden, near the house. I slipped off my shoes and moved to one side so I was facing him, my feet tucked under me. Tom held up his glass to mine. 'Slainté.'

'Slainté.'

Around us, people were talking and there was even dancing on the terrace to a jazz quartet.

And then I felt his hand on my bare leg. His eyes met mine. His skin on mine.

I stopped breathing.

'Sorry,' he said.

'No, leave it there,' I said.

We were still staring at each other.

'I can't stop thinking about you,' he said.

'Really?' My mouth was dry.

He nodded. 'Yeah...'

His eyes were locked on mine. His hand on my leg. All I knew was that I wanted his hand to stay where it was. People were similarly tipsy, laughing and shouting. Some were starting to leave, kissing each other goodbye, calling for taxis. But Tom and I stayed staring at each other, his hand on my bare leg. I thought I was going to lose my mind.

'How are you getting home?' he said, casually.

'Taxi, I suppose.'

'Do you want me to call one for you?'

I nodded.

'Unless,' he said, 'you'd like to come home with me?'

'Yes,' I said.

THE FORTY FOOTERS!

Nora: Dolores?

Margaret: She hasn't seen any of our messages.

Brenda: Dolores, are you there?

32

The next morning, I woke in an empty double bed, a large black cat curled in a ball on the other side. The previous day – *and night* – came back to me. Oh God, what had we done? Lorraine's ridiculous 'yes' game had meant that I had now slept with my boss. Lorraine's problem was that she never knew there were things you just shouldn't say yes to, such as marrying a waiter you'd met on holiday after six weeks and sleeping with a man who had power over your career and that you would have to see on Monday morning in the corridors of your workplace.

The cat lifted its head and looked at me and then stood up and stepped gracefully like a feline ballerina towards my pillow, where it then lay down, its large body next to my head, and went to sleep again.

Where was Tom? Had he left? And if so, should I just leave? I had no idea what the protocol was. Would it be too awkward to appear in the kitchen and say goodbye? Maybe the best thing to do was shin down the drainpipe, run through Ringsend and flag down a taxi to get me home.

Then I heard a sound, a clatter of cutlery, the slide of a drawer, and then a voice quietly singing to himself.

Pierre lifted his head as the door was pushed open. And there was Tom, in shorts and a T-shirt, carrying a tray.

'Are you awake?'

'I think so,' I said.

'I made us tea and toast.'

'Thank you.' I tried to smile. I had woken up in my boss's house after drinking way too much wine. How incredibly embarrassing and unprofessional.

He put the tray down on the bed beside me. 'How are you feeling?'

'I don't know,' I said. 'How are *you* feeling?'

'Pretty good,' he said, with a laugh, handing me a mug.

I sat up in bed, dislodging Pierre.

Tom sat down on the edge of the bed. 'I hope you like toast and jam.'

'Of course.'

'I don't think I could sleep with someone who doesn't.'

'Nor could I,' I said. 'I used to go out with someone who didn't believe in toast. He said it wasn't a complete meal and that eating something on toast was lazy.'

'Who was this maniac?' Tom took a piece of toast and began eating. 'Was he that controlling one you mentioned?'

I nodded. 'He was just very serious about food.'

Pierre had resettled himself against me. 'He's never this friendly,' said Tom, drinking his tea. 'He must like you.'

'I like him too,' I said, scratching Pierre's head.

'He's meant to be a country cat,' Tom remarked. 'Some neighbours from home had this litter of kittens to be used as mouse catchers and rat hunters, but I fell for this big guy. And now Pierre is definitely a city slicker. Like myself these days. My dad would be a little bemused. He wouldn't have known what to do with himself in Dublin. Always said he needed fresh air and big skies.'

'I couldn't live inland,' I said. 'I need to see the horizon.'

'Well, you and Dad would have got on very well.' Tom took another slice of toast. 'He was the kind of man who took to people and things. You know the type? If he liked you, he really liked you. If he didn't, then he was still polite, but unenthusiastic. But he liked nearly everybody. Could see the good in them, even if other people couldn't.'

'It must have been hard to lose him.'

Tom nodded. 'Yeah... absolutely. It's been two years now... and of course it changes everything. It was a little destabilising. I remember in the weeks after, I kept having this dream that I was standing at the edge of a cliff and I was looking down this vast ravine, all the way down, and I was sort of teetering, like I was going to fall.' He looked at me. 'It was really terrifying. I would wake up and it would take ages for me to remind myself it was just a dream and I would think everything was okay, but then I would remember something was really wrong and that it was Dad. He was gone. I had to try to focus on getting into work and being all grown-up and in control when really I felt like a kid whose dad had just died.'

'I'm so sorry,' I said, scratching Pierre's head, who was now in a deep purring sleep.

'You learn to live with it,' he said. 'Or, rather, you get used to feeling like that. In the end, I would wake up and almost have a checklist – Dad's dead, go to work, eat, drink water, phone Mam. My brain took over, almost, to stop me from having that daily shock of remembering. And then I started running every evening and I joined the five-a-side for men who are over the hill...'

'Over the hill?' I raised an eyebrow and nodded towards his arms, which were muscular, bulging from under his T-shirt.

He laughed. 'It feels like that sometimes.'

'Over the hill is a state of mind,' I said. 'I swim with the most amazing group of women. And one man. But Nora, for example, would consider herself only getting going, she's still heading *up* the hill. Margaret wouldn't even understand that there is a hill, she's just living the best life she can. Dolores has been up and down the hill all her life and is just happy she's still around. Brenda – you know Brenda? Well, she's on her own hill of her own making, following no one's rules but her own.' I shrugged. 'I want to be just like them. I want to get to a place where I follow my own rules. Ageing, living, being the best I can be, for me.' We spent so much time living by rules we'd never made for ourselves, we rarely found the time to find out how we really wanted to live.

'What about the man in the group? What kind of hill is he on?'

'His own, I think,' I said. 'He's just a really good person.' I thought of Malachy and his dedication to his mam, and smiled. 'Would do anything for anyone.'

Tom stood up. 'Look...' he began, 'I know it could be awkward between us...'

Oh God. He wanted me to leave. *Of course* I should have left already, not stayed chatting. Nor should I have gone home with him. What had I been thinking? I was suddenly overcome with mortification. I had practically thrown myself at him, dragging him into the taxi after me. Shame, embarrassment flooded my body. How stupid of me. My big break in TV and I go and sleep with my boss. This month of saying yes had gone too far. If I was more like Lorraine, she would have enjoyed this part of the adventure. She probably would have got another marriage out of it. But this had gone too far.

Tom was looking at me strangely. 'Everything okay?'

Saying yes to a one-night stand with my boss had placed me in a very vulnerable position. I had ruined everything. If I hadn't been so foolish – and desperate – I would never have gone home with him. And, worse, the thought of him thinking that I wanted more, or that I would behave weirdly in work, or that it would be awkward between us, was horrifying. He'd been polite enough to make me breakfast. Best if I just acted cool and go.

'I'm going to go,' I said, standing up and finding my clothes. 'It's not going to be awkward...' I smiled at him. 'Don't worry...'

'I didn't mean that...'

'Thank you for a really... a really... nice time.'

'You're welcome.' He was looking at me, curiously. 'I had a nice time too...'

'Good, good...' I checked that my phone was in my bag, and almost broke into a run.

He walked me to the front door.

'How are you getting home? I'll drive you? It's Sunday, it's not easy to find a taxi. Buses practically don't exist on a weekend.'

'No, absolutely not,' I said, not making eye contact. 'I can make my own way home...'

'Are you sure?'

'Perfectly.' I gave him my TV smile.

'Okay... well, enjoy your swim.'

I had to wait forty-five minutes for a bus to Sandycove, standing in my silk dress and high heels, feeling foolish and stupid. I didn't know what to do, except chalk this one up to experience. First rule of adulthood: never sleep with your boss. Second rule: you don't have to say 'yes' to everything. However much you wanted to.

33

That evening, when I arrived at the Forty Foot, Brenda, Margaret and Nora were standing in a huddle, looking worried.

'Have you seen Dolores?' Margaret said, urgently, when she saw me.

I shook my head. 'Why?'

'You haven't seen her going in and out of The Island, have you?'

'The pub?' I said. 'No, why?'

'She didn't come swimming yesterday,' said Brenda.

'She's been spotted,' added Nora. 'Several times. Going in during the day. And then we all went in the other night. And, well, we're a little worried.'

'*More* than a little worried,' said Margaret.

'We think she might have relapsed,' explained Brenda.

'And we don't go in for gossip, obviously,' said Nora, 'but there's a few in the village who have seen her going into The Island over the weekend. In and out like a yo-yo, apparently. And there she was celebrating her twenty years on the wagon.'

'I thought she was doing so well,' I said.

'Idle hands are the devil's playthings,' said Margaret.

'Margaret,' said Nora, 'let's leave the devil out of this. Anyway, I thought I saw her this morning. I was cycling along Church Street and I saw someone with the same coat as Dolores, that billowing thing that makes her look like Lawrence of Arabia.'

'Her kaftan,' said Margaret.

'Well, then, exactly like Lawrence. I met him,' Nora went on, 'a couple of times. I was working in the national library and he was working on his memoirs or some such. Lovely man. Great actor.'

'Nora, are we talking about Lawrence of Arabia or the actor Peter O'Toole?' asked Margaret.

'Peter O'Toole, obviously,' replied Nora. 'I'm not that old! But can you stop getting away from the point? Dolores. She's *drinking* again.'

'Have you been to her house?' I asked.

They shook their heads.

'She always says she doesn't like visitors,' said Margaret.

'I've called her,' said Nora, 'but no answer.'

'Why don't we go now?' I suggested. 'Where does she live?'

'About five minutes away, on Bird Road,' said Margaret. 'Come on, let's go.'

* * *

The four of us stood outside Dolores' front door, feeling more than a little apprehensive.

'You knock,' said Nora to Margaret.

'No, you!' Margaret whispered back.

'I will,' said Brenda, rapping on the door. 'Dolores? It's us!' she called. 'Just wondering if you are okay.' She turned to us. 'I'm going to call through the letter box. Is that all right these days or is it officially trespassing?'

'How can it be trespassing,' said Nora, 'when you are not actually trespassing?'

'But my voice would be,' said Brenda. 'You never know what's new these days and what things you used to do without thinking that are now wrong.'

'I think it's still okay to call through the letter box,' I said. 'As long as you are not abusive. That's probably illegal.'

'Hear that?' said Nora. 'Just don't be abusive!'

'What on earth did you think I was going to say?' said Brenda, exasperated. She leaned down and poked open the letter box with both hands. 'Dolores?' she called in. 'It's us here, your swimming friends just wondering how you are.'

There was a sound, a shuffling of feet.

'She's coming!' said Brenda, standing up in a panic as we all bristled to attention. Would she even be able to open the door? Would we have to call the fire brigade to kick it down? But the latch was being turned and the door slowly opened. And there was Dolores, dressed in her kaftan, looking... not drunk at all. In fact, she looked remarkably healthy.

'Well, hello, hello,' she said. 'So you've found me at last!'

We glanced at each other. 'We haven't seen you for a few days,' began Nora.

'We wondered how you are,' said Brenda.

'We thought that maybe you were back on the not-so-holy water,' added Margaret.

'I'm grand,' replied Dolores. '*More* than grand.' She gave a throaty cackle. 'I've been a bit busy, that's all. Socialising with an old friend.'

Behind her, from the kitchen, walked Mick, the barman from The Island.

'The thing is,' went on Dolores, 'we've known each other for years...' She smiled at him. 'And we've discovered that we...'

'... Really *like* each other,' said Mick. 'And we want to spend time together.'

'I've been calling in to see him in The Island. Where we've been drinking *tea*.'

Mick nodded. 'I'm not a drinker either. I mean, I have the odd one, but I want to be with Dolores and mind her.'

'And I want to mind you,' said Dolores to him. 'It's nice to have someone to mind.'

'And love,' said Mick.

'And that as well,' she said. 'We've got a lot in common.'

Mick nodded. 'A lot,' he agreed. 'I've always fancied her,' he went on. 'But thought she was out of my league.'

Dolores tapped her head. 'I had to get this right first,' she said. 'Takes time. Now, would you all like to come in for a cup of tea?'

She hadn't even finished getting the words out before Nora was inside. 'Would love one,' she said. 'I'm gasping.'

We all sat around the kitchen table while Mick made the tea.

'She began coming into the pub for a cup of tea in the afternoon,' said Mick. 'And I'd give her an extra biscuit...'

'And I wondered if he liked me more than just liking me.'

'A biscuit can say many things a person can't,' said Mick.

'Indeed it can,' agreed Nora. 'Very wise words there, Mick.'

We chatted for ages around that little Formica table, listening to stories of love and hope until the sun began to slink off to another hemisphere and I thought of Tom and the night we'd spent and my heart ached. It wasn't our time, that much was true, but I wished it was. At least it was Dolores and Mick's time. At least they had found love.

34

'So how was it?' said Angela on Monday morning. 'How was the party of the century?'

We were in the meeting room, waiting for David and Tom. I felt nervous, thinking about how to behave today. Back, I supposed, to being professional around each other again and hoping it wasn't going to be too awkward. Life was complicated enough without getting involved with colleagues. Or worse, your boss. I must never be allowed to drink alcohol again. I should take a leaf out of Dolores' book.

'Fine,' I said, not wanting to go into any details, knowing that the only details on my mind were exactly the ones no one could ever know about.

'What's his house like?' said Ava. 'Is it all gold lions and life-size panthers and a kind of Safari-does-Drimnagh vibe?'

'Actually really nice,' I mumbled.

'So, what's Jennifer like?' urged Angela.

'Really nice,' I said again. 'She doesn't let him take himself too seriously.'

Angela and Ava were waiting for me to say more.

'The house is really grand,' I elaborated. 'Big house, amazing garden... not just amazing, but huge... and trees.... and steps... and...' All I could think about was Tom. Oh God. I had made an already stressful work situation more stressful. Talk about self-sabotage. The only way to deal with it was to just pretend it hadn't happened and move on. Why did I drink so much wine? What was *wrong* with me? 'And there were all these people there, dressed for a garden party...'

'I thought it was a barbecue?' said Angela.

'It was... that was just part of it,' I said. 'You queued up for your food and then wandered around. I... um... didn't stay long, just showed my face and left...' I smiled at them, hoping that would be the end of the questions.

'I wouldn't have minded that,' said Angela. 'Doesn't sound as intense as a small, intimate barbecue.'

'*I* would have minded it,' said Ava. 'Being in the sun, nightmare. Talking to people, horrific. Eating meat.'

'Did Tom bring Susie with him?' Angela asked.

'Susie Keane?' I asked, trying to look neutral. I felt my hands go suddenly clammy. 'I'm not sure. I didn't see her... but I wasn't there for all the party...'

'I was just wondering,' said Angela, 'because I heard that she was mad about him. Apparently, they had a fling years ago and she's been after him ever since. But what man would pass on Susie Keane?'

'I think she's boring,' said Ava. 'Tom's got better taste. Susie thinks the world revolves around her.'

'Yes,' said Angela, 'but all of our stars are like that. Have you *met* Barbara Brennan?'

They both laughed.

'It's just that they would make a very photogenic couple, wouldn't you think?' went on Angela. 'I think it would be nice for him to find someone. He's always going on about missing Galway and his family back home. He needs an anchor here in Dublin.'

'I think he's fine,' I said. 'He's never given the impression of being lonely. I think he plays football with friends sometimes...'

'Morning, morning...' Tom pushed open the door, letting David walk in first. 'So sorry I am late. Just caught up with an issue...' He slipped into his chair at the head of the table. 'Thank you for waiting...' Tom glanced around the room and gave me a quick smile and I looked away. I liked him, I realised. But he was obviously not interested in taking it further, otherwise he would have said something to me. I wondered if he hadn't been entirely truthful about Susie and that things were more complicated than he had let on. Memories of that night kept coming back to me. While he talked, I thought of his voice in my ear. When he took out his mobile phone, I looked at his hands. I thought of his body under his suit or how he had looked in his shorts the morning after.

'Morning all,' said David. 'Ah, Catríona, last time I saw you, you were necking white wine by the bottle.'

Everyone in the room laughed.

'I wasn't,' I said, hastily. 'I was very well behaved.' I hadn't been though. I was the opposite. I could still feel Tom's hand on my leg. But everyone was still chuckling, even Tom seemed amused.

'Ah no, David,' he said. 'That was me. And it was also me who organised the giant line dance on the lawn and then the singalong of "Sweet Caroline".' He caught my eye and gave me a nod as if to ask if I was okay.

I found my voice. 'The party was wonderful, David. Thank you.'

'Wasn't it just?' David agreed. 'Jennifer was happy with the way everything went. And that's the main thing. Happy Jennifer equals happy David. She pulled the caterers and florists all together. She's militant about parties... I couldn't have done it without her.'

Once the party talk was done, and the meeting began, I started to relax. Right. Chalk it up to experience. Note to self: do not drink alcohol. Do not sleep with one's boss. And do not linger in the morning like a desperado.

But afterwards, as we were walking out, Tom called my name.

I turned. There was no one else around. Angela and Ava had headed back to the office and David had gone in search of a cup of tea. Did Tom want to talk about Saturday? Was this the 'it's not you, it's me, let's not make things awkward in work' conversation?

'How are you getting on?' he said, smiling.

'Everything's fine,' I said. 'I'm halfway through my stint on the show. Still lots to learn.' PJ was back with us later that day and I was dreading it.

He smiled again. 'And did you see your friends?'

'Which friends?' I was confused.

'Your *swimming* friends... friend... whatever...'

'Oh yes, they're all fine.'

He looked at me strangely for a moment and I couldn't work out what was going on.

I wanted to tell him about Dolores and Mick and about the gang and how much I loved this group of people. 'They're keeping me sane. As is swimming...' I gave a strange, false laugh. I was wrong. It was going to be awkward between us. Tom carried on talking but he was different as well, the easy rapport that had existed was gone. Of course it had. You can't go back to as it was before. You can't pretend nothing happened, when it so definitely did. We needed time and space. A *lot* of time and space. Maybe moving-hemispheres time and space.

'I need something like that,' he said, with a similar laugh as mine. 'I mean, I have football, but it's not the same.'

'You have Pierre,' I said. 'Doesn't he keep you sane?'

'It's very grounding to have a cat,' he agreed, 'because they don't care about anything but themselves. I am but his humble servant.

Though I had to take him to the emergency vet yesterday evening...'

'Oh no!'

'He's getting old. Seems to be off his food...' He looked away briefly. 'Haven't a clue what's wrong with him.'

'What did the vet say?' We were both trying very hard to have a normal conversation but I kept having flashbacks to us in the taxi together and then us... oh God... stop thinking!

'To try him on different food,' said Tom. 'I paid one hundred and eighty euros to be told that!' He laughed again. 'I bought a tin of salmon and he ate some of it. Which was better than not eating any of it.' He looked at me and was about to say something else when we heard a voice call his name.

'Tom!' Susie was walking towards us, her eyes fixed on him, smiling. Was she constantly hiding, I wondered, waiting to see if the two of us ever had a conversation and then she would spring out? She, as always, looked amazing, in a long yellow tea dress, loosely unbuttoned, her skin lightly tanned, her blonde hair glinting and just falling over her shoulders. 'Tom, I need help with something.'

'What is it?'

'I can only talk about it... when there's no one else around,' she said, only then turning to be and bestowing the smile to me. 'So sorry. Private business. Just something that I need Tom for.' She stood in front of us, small, beautiful, smelling of something expensive. Some women were permanently camera-ready, I thought, feeling jealous. Whatever she and Tom had going on, it didn't involve me. Relationships were rarely cut and dried the moment you walked away – I should know. They could be messy. Maybe that was what was happening with Susie and Tom.

She waited for a moment until I took the hint. 'I'd better get back,' I said, 'see you both later.'

'Oh, wait,' she said, smiling her fake smile, 'how was the party?

You were going as well. That's the problem with presenting a show on a Saturday, you just can't make these things. No matter how much someone begs you to go.' She glanced at Tom. 'Sorry, darling. When the series is over, then we can go and do all these wonderful things.'

Tom looked embarrassed… or furious… I couldn't tell, but as I walked away, I heard him say, slightly sharply for him, 'So what's this about, Susie?'

'Oh, Tom,' she said, 'I just need help… there's…'

But I didn't hear any more.

35

For the finale of the show, David and I stood beside PJ.

'What delights do you have in store for us today?' said David, pleasantly.

'Duck confit,' replied PJ. 'A French classic. Thought I would show your viewers how to make something utterly delicious.'

I made sure I was standing on the far side of David, away from any forkfuls.

'What is confit exactly?' I asked.

'It's cooking something in fat,' said PJ. 'Entirely encasing the meat in lard...'

'Lard?' queried David. 'Oh, no... that doesn't sound very nice. Some of us have to mind our cholesterol levels...'

'But if people ate less processed shite,' said PJ, 'they wouldn't have high cholesterol or high blood pressure or blocked arteries. Don't blame the French classics.'

David was smiling, trying to inject some levity, to defuse PJ's deadly seriousness. 'Indeed, indeed, wise, if intemperate, words from Dr O'Malley....'

'I'm not a doctor,' said PJ. 'I'm a chef, but it doesn't mean I don't know what I'm talking about...'

'Move on,' said Angela, in our ears.

'Talk us through it,' I said. 'What are you doing exactly?'

Even David was slightly lost for words, the wind taken out of his presenting sails, as PJ explained his process. Both of us were unsure of how to treat PJ, he was so unpredictable – sometimes able to take a joke, other times prickly at the sign of any banter. I remembered him as being thin-skinned, unable to take a joke and the only thing he had been able to take was himself very seriously indeed. Finally, when the dish was presented to us, we both took tiny tastes.

'Magnificent,' pronounced David, glancing at me.

'Truly stupendous,' I agreed, not wanting to anger PJ any further. We had two minutes to the end of the show.

'It is,' said PJ, 'isn't it? The flavours, the textures... it's not something that ordinary people could make, it takes years of practice, learning from the best, but if people at home are inspired to ditch the ready meals, they could perhaps start eating properly.'

'Food for thought,' remarked David. 'Although, it has to be said, I am very partial to a macaroni and cheese from a certain well-known supermarket. Bang in the microwave, two minutes, and dinner is served.' The smile on his face began to fade as he realised that PJ was glaring at him. 'Not a patch on this magnificence, though, this work of art... this... perfection...'

'Ten seconds,' said Angela.

'And that's it from me and David,' I said, reading the autocue.

'And me,' interrupted PJ.

'She was getting to you,' said David.

'And from all our guests,' I added. 'Including the brilliant PJ Doyle. Until tomorrow... it's goodbye...'

'Goodbye,' said David, just as PJ started speaking.

'I can't work with you two being sarcastic...' was then broadcast to the nation, as the titles rolled.

'We weren't being sarcastic,' said David, 'were we, Cat? I never do sarcasm, lowest form of wit and all that. We are just trying to present television. It's not actually important, it's light fluff, candyfloss...' He smiled at PJ. 'And thank you for bringing in your duck comfy or whatever it was. And when I say it was incredible and out of this world and the best thing I have ever eaten, literally, in the world, forever amen, I am not being sarcastic. Oh no.' He smiled at PJ. 'I would never stoop that low.' And as he left, he gave me a wink.

'I have to go too,' I said. 'Debriefing meeting. See you, PJ.'

And I left him fuming, snorting through his nostrils, as the crew gathered to devour the duck.

* * *

Later, in the cool, calm sea, I swam a little away from the crowds, leaving real life back on land.

In the debrief meeting, David had turned to me. 'I've met a few men like him in my time. All mouth, nothing much going on in the trouser department.'

Angela had joined in. 'My nanna would have said the opposite, she would have called him Billy Big Bollocks.'

She and David exchanged a look. 'Is he worth it though?' asked David. 'I mean, some talent is worth the bullying... I once worked with one fella – naming no names – who once threw a chair at my co-presenter's head and then tried to trip me over. He was eventually brought to an internal inquiry for sexual harassment and was retired off. But he was tolerated because he was so good on-air. Magic, he was. One of the best. Just a horrible person.'

'And I worked with this man,' said Angela, 'again naming no names, who used to corner the younger girls and ask them to go on errands for him. Errands including massages and drinks in late-night bars. Most of the girls were too terrified of him to say anything because he also had a reputation for getting people fired for the slightest misdemeanor. He too was tolerated because he was too important to the station.'

'There are many of them,' said David. 'Too many. In television, talent is everything. The worst kind of people are allowed to carry on, just because they can do what so many can only dream of... presenting. It's an art, you see. And I'm not the best presenter in the world, but at least I am not a total arse.'

'What do you think?' said Angela to me.

'I don't know,' I said. 'I mean, he's not an abuser, he's not that bad... he's just difficult.'

And we left it like that. David had to rush off to a meeting and Angela had to make a phone call and nothing more was said.

Here, in the sea, the gentle undulations soothed and relaxed me and I floated, like a piece of driftwood, sun-bleached, sea-smoothed, the water clinging to me as though I was part of it and it was part of me. I felt as though I was a better version of me, not the *best* version, but I liked the person who was floating on the sea.

I paddled my way back towards shore, passing Brenda who had been swimming around the deep basin close to the rocks.

'That PJ is typical alpha male,' she said, doggy-paddling around me, her hair still perfect on top of her head. 'Reminds me of Pete.'

'The dog-napping postman?'

She sculled around me. 'The very same.'

'How is Arthur?'

'He's grand,' she said. 'I mean, he's as grand as a seventeen-year-old dog can be. Can't hop up and down on my bed like he used to when he was a young fella. I've had to make some kind of steps for him out of boxes and chairs so he can get up. And he's going deaf. The good thing is that his deafness may have mitigated the trauma of the dog-napping. He wasn't quite sure what was going on. And anyway, you got him back pretty quickly.' She smiled at me, and then paddled around in a complete circle. 'I did think of pressing charges, but how far would I go? I have considered revenge... but not quite sure what that would entail. The best revenge is living a good life, isn't it?'

'You mean just getting on with things?' I said.

'That's right. Not obsessing about the wrongs people have done you. Not worrying about justice and teaching someone a lesson. What did you learn from going out with the crazy chef?' Brenda said.

'That food is nice but that it's not *art*,' I said. 'And I learned that if someone exhausts you, by going on about things, then you don't have to listen to them.'

Brenda nodded. 'I learned with Pete that if someone wants to know where you are all the time, then it's probably a red flag,' she said. 'We survive, we prevail. We move on. Next adventure, please!'

After our swim, we sat in a group, half-dressed and half-damp, while Brenda poured out the tea.

My hair was wet and hanging down my back, my mascara was smudged and I sat with a towel wrapped around me. This was the very opposite of show business. There was nothing glamorous about sea swimming – even those in the expensive fleece blanket-coats didn't look glamorous, they just looked nice and warm. It was just about the simple life, and the pleasure of being immersed in nature.

Earlier, I had stopped off at Sally-Anne's bakery in the village and picked up one of her lemon drizzle cakes and when we were sitting with Margaret's mugs in our hand, I sliced the cake and handed it around.

'Delicious,' said Malachy.

'It's a family recipe,' I said.

'Well, it's superb,' said Margaret. 'So light and moist.'

'Your mother's?' said Nora.

'Sort of,' I said. And then explained. 'My mother has been buying it from Sally-Anne's and passing it off as her own, just so her sister didn't make her feel bad.'

'Quite right,' said Nora, through a mouthful of cake. 'I've never baked in my life. Bought cakes are much nicer.'

'I'll bring it every week, if you like,' I said. 'Now I know I can just buy my mum's famous lemon drizzle, I don't have to wait around for her to make it.'

'Useful too,' said Dolores, 'when she dies. You can still eat her cake.'

'Dolores!' Margaret was looking horrified. 'How could you say such a thing?'

'No, she's right,' I said, smiling at them both. 'It is incredibly useful.'

'Unless,' said Malachy, 'Sally-Anne should die and then no one will have cake.'

We all laughed again, except for Margaret, who shook her head at this heresy. 'Malachy,' she said, 'death is no laughing matter. It's only cake.'

'But very good cake,' said Malachy, reaching for another slice. 'May I?'

I passed him over another slice, balanced on a bit of the cardboard sleeve it had come in.

'Mam used to put cake in my lunch box every day,' he said. 'All the other boys would have crisps and chocolate and I'd have a slice of Mam's fruit cake.' He looked up at us. 'Wrapped in parchment. It was heavy and tasted of treacle and was too crumbly, but I loved it. And sometimes you'd get an almond stuck in the top of the slice and on those days I'd think it was going to be an extra-good day, and I'd look out for what that good thing was...'

We were all listening, intently. I'd never known Malachy to talk this much.

'And it could have been getting full marks on my maths test or the teacher saying something nice to me or the boys not making fun of me... that kind of thing.' He stopped. 'The almond days, I'd call them, and it was as though, when it was an almond day, I'd look for the good, and when it wasn't, I'd look for the bad. A small nut can change your entire perspective.' He stopped, blushing from his collar up.

'It really can,' agreed Margaret.

'How *is* your mam?' said Nora, gently.

Malachy played with his hands for a moment, his long, bony white fingers stretching and twisting around each other. 'Ah, you know... lucid moments, good times sometimes... but mainly... she's gone...'

We were silent for a moment and I noticed that Dolores patted him on the back while he returned to twisting his hands again.

'Tell her I'll be in tomorrow,' said Margaret. 'I have a nice rose from my garden that smells beautifully.'

'Thank you, Margaret,' said Malachy. 'She really responds to your visits.'

And then I remembered something. 'Sally-Anne does a fruit cake,' I said. 'With almonds on the top. I'll buy you one, you can see if it's as good as your mam's.'

'I doubt it will be,' said Nora. 'There's no cake as good as anyone's mam's.'

'Except my own mother's cake,' I said, and everyone laughed, including lovely Malachy.

The sun was still warm, there was heat in the rocks as we sat on the ground, our backs against the old stone seats, our legs stretched out in front of us, soaking up the last of the day's rays.

'If this is life,' said Nora, her eyes closed, her face glowing in the setting sun, 'then I'm not complaining.'

36

Becca, Sinéad and Rory met me after my swim. 'New York office again,' Sinéad said, as an explanation.

'I just need some fresh air,' said Becca. 'It's weird, because I never used to like fresh air. I used to prefer the confines of air-conditioned offices and sweaty pubs, now all I want is to be outside.'

The four of us began walking towards the pier.

'We even had a work meeting outdoors,' she went on. 'We sat on the grass and we had to go through our Television Awards final prep list and there's me, making a bloody daisy chain.'

'Were you wearing your Birkenstocks?' said Sinéad.

'I've just bought a neon pair,' replied Becca. 'I think I am in love with them. I wore them in the house with socks and Ryan did this double take. What. Are. You. Wearing? Comfort, I said. I'm wearing comfort. So I made him try them on, and he squeezed his massive feet in like an Ugly Sister, but even he, Mr Fashionisto, was very taken with them.'

The three of us sat on a bench beside the children's playground. Rory sat up in his pushchair. 'Has he eaten anything else off the floor?' I said to Sinéad.

'He has, actually,' she said. 'We're doing really well. It was broccoli.'

'That doesn't count,' said Becca. 'Broccoli is incapable of having any germs or bacteria. You've got to ramp it up a bit. Get him to eat a slice of toast that's been behind the sofa for a week or a yogurt that's been in the back of the fridge for the last year.'

Sinéad shuddered. 'We're not quite at that stage yet. I thought we were pushing a few boundaries with the broccoli.'

'Careful,' said Becca, 'you'll be giving him an ice cream next. With a flake.'

Rory perked up at the word ice cream, but Sinéad just gave Becca a look.

'Ice cream?' Rory said, hopefully.

'Apple slices,' she said, smiling at him. 'Your favourite.' She took out a small lunch box inside which were dried apples. 'Here we go.'

Becca caught my eye and made a face, but she was spotted by Sinéad.

'Do you know how hard it is to digest ice cream? Our stomachs are not evolved to adequately digest cow's milk or—'

'Trans fats,' said Becca. 'So you've said. And I am not saying give him ice cream *instead* of the broccoli, I am just saying an *occasional* one.'

Sinéad was silent for a moment. She reached out and brushed Rory's hair out of his eyes. 'Go and play in the playground,' she said. 'Mummy will stay here with Auntie Cat and Auntie Becca.'

We watched as Rory ran over to the slide and began clambering up to the top.

'I love him so much,' she said. 'It's crazy. I loved him from the first moment I knew I was pregnant, it's mad. You just love them. And you know them, it's so hard to explain, but you sense them, the person they are, even before they are born.'

'Sorry, Sinéad,' Becca began to say, but Sinéad held up her hand to speak.

'I know I'm over the top and ridiculous. I know I fuss too much and I am obsessive. Conor wiped Rory's mouth with a tea towel which had been on the floor and I shouted at him. And the other day, his mum gave Rory a bit of apple pie and cream and I had to tell her about the cow's milk evolution thing and she was looking at me as though I was mad. Which...' She stopped. 'I am. I feel absolutely fecking mad, a sort of crazed intensity. Rory still sleeps with us, in the bed. Conor now sleeps on the single bed in the spare room. And he's tried to talk about it, says isn't it time that Rory sleeps in his own room... but what if something happens? It's like everything could go wrong and I am the only one trying to stop it.'

'It won't,' I said.

'But it could!' She turned to face me. 'It could. Because it has.'

'What do you mean?'

'I miscarried.' Keeping her voice steady was an effort. 'A year before I got pregnant with Rory... and I had no idea that it could be so painful. I had no idea that you could love someone you never met and would never meet. I didn't even know if the baby was a boy or a girl... but it was my baby. And I lost it. And that's what they mean when they say baby loss... it's *such* a loss. You are *so* lost.' Her eyes filled with tears.

Becca took one hand and I took the other.

'Why didn't you tell us?' I said, softly.

'I couldn't find the words. And I was hoping that I could move on and forget about it, just get pregnant again and it would all be over. Except, it turns out you *can* get pregnant again, have a baby, but you don't forget the one you lost. Nothing erases that. It's just part of you.'

Becca and I nodded.

'When I was pregnant with Rory, I clung on to him even *before* he was born. And now, it's so hard to let him go... there's so much *danger* out there. And I didn't tell anyone about it because no one really wants to hear it, everyone just wants happy news when it comes to babies.'

'We would have...'

'I was kind of lost for months,' Sinéad went on. 'It wasn't as though the baby existed... not really. Conor had to go away with work and he felt bad leaving, but I think he was quite relieved to go, to get away from me. I don't think he understood quite how grief-stricken I was...' She stopped. 'I cried for hours that week. I would go into the bathroom at work and cry. I would cry on the bus home, behind my sunglasses. And the evenings would just be me, crying. I was really annoyed when Conor came home...' She gave a slight laugh. 'It meant I couldn't cry any more and I had to just get on with things. Or at least pretend. Maybe it was a good thing.'

'I wish you had told us,' said Becca. 'We could have cried with you. And I would have made it all about me, by crying the most and the loudest.'

Sinéad laughed. 'I know you would have. And it might have been the perfect distraction. Except, I didn't want to be distracted. I just wanted to focus on the moment, this overwhelming grief. Like part of me had been ripped away.' She shrugged. 'I wouldn't have ever thought that was what a miscarriage was like, as though this was a real person... rather than just a collection of cells.'

'But they were your collection of cells,' I said. 'It was your baby.'

'My baby in waiting,' she replied. 'Except... it couldn't wait.' She swallowed. 'I can talk about it now, but back then I couldn't even get the words out. And then I got pregnant with Rory and... well, I felt I just had to get on with it. Poor Conor. He told me he felt as though he wasn't important to me any more, that I didn't love him, and how can you prove you do love someone when you never show it? I was just crazy. Still am.'

'It makes total sense,' said Becca. 'I'd be crazy too.'

'So would I,' I said. 'And Conor understands.'

'I am not sure he does.' She sighed. 'It's been intense. It really has. And it's why I think I am so obsessive. And why I feel so guilty even complaining about anything.'

Rory ran back towards us. 'Did you see me on the slide?' he said, coming and sitting between Sinéad and Becca.

'We did,' said Sinéad. 'You were brilliant.' She reached over and kissed Rory's head. 'I love you,' she said. 'And you love Mummy, don't you?'

Rory looked up at her and smiled. 'I always love Mummy,' he said.

Sinéad turned to us and smiled. 'He's magical.'

'He really is,' said Becca, making Sinéad and I glance at each other.

'You've changed your tune, Becca,' I said. 'You like children now?'

'I've always liked Rory,' she said. 'I make an exception for him. But talking of magic, I was feeling a bit ropey for some reason and somehow wandered into the book shop on Dawson Street and found myself in the witches section...'

'They have a *witches* section?' I said.

'Oh yes,' replied Becca. 'It's all the rage now. Once they burned us at the stake, now they are flogging us books. But anyway, I bought a *Handbook For The Modern Irish Witch* and there are all sorts of spells in there. Including' – she gave a significant nod – 'a happiness one. I didn't think it would do any harm so I've been and bought all the ingredients.'

'Most people just buy chocolate to make them happy,' Sinéad said.

'Eye of newt and toe of frog?' I suggested.

'Wool of bat and tongue of dog?' said Sinéad. We'd all done

Macbeth in school.

'Kind of,' said Becca. 'Dried sage which I have to burn, olive oil to rub on my stomach. And I bought really expensive extra virgin olive oil made by a wizened, ancient farmer in the Tuscan hills. Cost a fortune. And I have to light a candle, so I have just bought a gorgeous Jo Malone one. The whole thing cost me a hundred and fifty euros.'

'Happiness does not come cheap,' I said.

'And I'm pretty sure olive oil wasn't used in Salem,' said Sinéad.

'Yes, but I'm a modern witch,' replied Becca. 'This is what we do.'

Becca was softening, I thought. Before, she was the kind of person who hated astrology, thought anything woo-woo was nonsense and once refused to take part in an I Ching reading because she said it was nonsense. And now she was buying books of *spells*.

'What's happening to you, Becca?' I said. 'Natural hair, Birkenstocks... spells?'

'I am on a quest for happiness,' she said. 'Work is stressful and I just want something more. There was a time when nothing was more important than work, I loved nothing more than a meeting or a presentation or a pitch. But now I just want to be happier and more comfortable. Is that too much to ask for?'

'No,' said Sinéad, 'I think you are right. I think that sometimes we can be focused on one thing – me on Rory, you on work, Cat on being single... we forget that we need a little bit of everything.'

'I am focused on being *single*?' I said, put out.

'Oh God, yes,' said Becca. 'You never stop saying that you are so glad to be on your own, that life is so much easier without a man in your life, that after PJ you are delighted just to be alone.'

'I literally have never said any of those things,' I argued, but they looked at each other and laughed.

'I'll do you a spell to meet someone,' said Becca. 'Someone nice, non-toxic, agreeable, kind... okay?'

'Maybe...' I didn't tell them I'd already met someone like that but it hadn't worked out.

'Is there a spell for fertility?' said Sinéad, reaching over and giving Rory another apple slice. 'Can you do it for me? A baby brother or sister for Rory.'

Becca nodded. 'And I'll do a love one for Cat, whether she likes it or not.'

'There's no need,' I said. 'I don't want you wasting your Jo Malone candle on my love life.'

'Not a waste at all,' said Becca. 'Us witches love being useful.'

Rory had dropped his apple slice and the four of us all looked at it on the pavement.

Becca began counting. 'One... two... Five second rule, Sinéad...'

'But the pavement!' Sinéad was in agony.

'Four... five...'

And then, in a blur of motion, she bent down, picked up the apple slice and gave it to Rory. 'Oh God! How germy is it?' Sinéad watched Rory, who was oblivious to the drama, as he munched away.

'His immune system will be improved...' said Becca.

'But it's so gross...' Sinéad was tortured but managed to remain still, eyes on Rory.

'More,' he said, smiling at Sinéad.

'Of course, sweetheart,' she said, handing over another one.

'Right,' said Becca, 'so it's fertility for Sinéad, general happiness for me, and love for Cat. Or would you rather a career one? Or there's an inner poise and confidence one?'

I laughed. 'No, just love.' And, yes, I realised I was ready to fall in love again. There had to be someone *else* out there who would induce the same feelings as Tom had?

37

Back at home, Callum was sitting in the living room, in the semi-dark. I'd become used to seeing him, bathed in the glow of the giant TV, but this time it was off.

'Everything okay?'

'Yeah, grand, you know...' he said.

'What's wrong?' I went closer and sat on the edge of the armchair beside him.

'Nothing... nothing...' And then he looked up at me. 'I think... I think Denise is seeing someone else. She's moved on.' His face crumpled. 'I didn't really think about it. I wasn't prepared. But I dropped in to see her and she said she was off on a date on Saturday when Loulou is with me. I said, who? And she said none of my business. Which it isn't...'

'I'm sorry, Callum.'

'Yeah, I know. And there's nothing I can do. She'll probably go out with some amazing man with a proper job, who goes to the office and has meetings and makes himself a proper packed lunch every day and does the *Irish Times* crossword on the commute... and goes to the gym and drinks water and always knows who he votes for and is never in the polling booth just looking at a long list of names...'

'You can be like that man... know who to vote for. Just read up on it. Or watch the news before an election. Or go to the gym or drink water.'

'There's probably more to being an amazing man than just those,' he said, which was the wisest thing I'd heard him say. 'It's just that I love her. And I let her down, and I know I lost her a long time ago, but it's only now that I realise it.'

'But... maybe it's not too late,' I encouraged. 'What changes have you made that might change her mind? Have you done anything about finding your purpose? A job?'

'I lost confidence a while ago,' he said. 'Not getting the acting jobs. Being crap at everything else I tried to do. And Loulou isn't that bothered about being with me. She said she had the best day of her life when she went with you.'

'We just went for something to eat and a walk,' I said. 'And we popped in to see my mum. It was very ordinary. And she loves you. Maybe she's just finding it hard to know how to be with everyone?'

He nodded. 'I don't blame her. I'm finding it hard to be with me right now.' He tried to laugh. 'But it's as though I don't know how to do ordinary things, like normal people.'

'You can,' I said, 'just try it. Go with the flow.'

'There's a flow?' He looked astounded. 'How did I not know about this flow? How do I find the flow?'

I laughed. 'The flow is just there, you just go with it.'

'I was thinking...' His voice dropped to a whisper. 'I was thinking of therapy.'

'Good idea. And what else do you want to do? If you could do anything, what would you do?'

'I'd like my own wine shop,' he said, immediately. 'A good selection of wines, a small counter where you can have a glass of something, a few nibbles. A bit of Miles Davis on the stereo. But... how do people make these things happen?'

'Step by step,' I said. 'Make your plan.'

'Oh God, plans! They are everywhere.'

'Well, you need retail experience. You need to do a business course. A wine course... you need to find a job to pay the bills and pay for your plan...'

'How do you even know any of this?'

I shrugged. 'Alison's café in the village is hiring.'

Callum was sitting upright now, looking much brighter. 'So this is what people do? Thank you, Cat,' he said, standing up. 'I'm going to research everything. And also I want to tell Denise that she deserves to find someone amazing... and I am happy for her. I have to be happy for her, don't I? Because otherwise it's selfish of me. Right... first thing text Denise and tell her I can take Loulou whenever she wants, to give her a break during the week and also early on Saturday so she has time to get ready for her date. Also research college courses and to Alison's in the morning to look for a job.' He gave a determined nod. 'If you love someone set them free. Who said that?'

'I can't remember.'

'Bob Marley,' he said. 'I think. Either him or Jesus. Right, time to knuckle down to some work.'

* * *

Becca called in tears. 'I'm so stressed,' she said. 'The ITAs are on Friday week, there is so much to be done, I can't even think straight... There is a problem with the sound guys... one of them has come down with food poisoning. The golden carpet is delayed at customs, the ice sculptor has given the job to his assistant, who I don't think has ever done one before, and the catering staff at the hotel say that there is a shortage of prawns. You can't have canapés without bloody prawns!' She started to cry.

'Becca,' I said, 'everything is going to be fine. You've been running your company for fifteen years now...'

'Thirteen,' she said, in a small voice. 'So not that long.'

'It is so a long time. You know what you're doing. You must have organised thousands of events.'

'But this is the biggest thing we've ever done,' she said. 'I'm just not feeling like myself. I feel weird, like I'm ill or something, but I'm not ill. I'm fine.'

'Of course you'll be okay,' I said. 'You always are.'

'Am I?' she said. 'I just don't know lately. I really don't.'

THE GIRLS!

Sinéad: Does anyone fancy a night out?

Becca: As in out-out or just out?

Becca: Because I am getting bored of walking the seafront.

Becca: And I think I must have early-onset perimenopause. Or at the very least ennui. They used to have ennui, didn't they? Those Victorians. Well, I have it.

Sinéad: Out-out.

Becca: Out-out would help in curing my ennui.

Me: Where?

Becca: I have an idea! There's a supper club in Dún Laoghaire? Could be good? It's raising money for charity. Run by this local woman, in her mother's garden. Meant to be lovely. Great food. Really nice atmosphere.

Me: Sounds good.

Becca: Hard to get tickets though. I will see what I can do. Sinéad?

Sinéad: When is it?

Becca: Saturday night.

Sinéad: Tomorrow?????!!!

Becca: I thought you wanted to go out-out.

Sinéad: But it's short notice. I thought next month or something.

Becca: It's tomorrow or never. My ennui is hanging in the balance.

Sinéad: Okay. I was going to work up to leaving Rory. But… it will be good for me.

Me: It will.

Becca: So, will I buy the tickets?

Sinéad: Do it!

38

'So, PJ will be doing a vegan menu today,' Angela announced in the Friday meeting.

It was the end of my third week on the show and I looked up. Tom saw my reaction.

'Everything okay, Cat?'

'Yes, fine, it's just I thought PJ was very much a... a meaty chef.'

'We suggested it to him,' said Angela. 'The rise of veganism is something we want to reflect... we're not just a nation of Irish stew or black pudding.'

'We're not?' David looked confused. 'Those would be my two favourite meals.'

'Just widening the focus,' said Angela. 'We have many vegan viewers. And we should *all* be eating less meat.'

'I am not convinced that a meal is a meal without meat,' said David. 'I don't think any repast can call itself by that name if—'

'An animal hasn't died?' Ava rolled her eyes. 'Sorry, David, but get with the programme...'

'I am,' he said. 'I *am* the programme.'

'Meat is murder, plants are power.'

'Thank you, Ava,' he said, stiffly. 'I will bear it in mind.'

* * *

I didn't see David for the rest of the day until he was sitting on the sofa when I joined him on set, already doing his facial exercises.

'Hello, David,' I said. 'How's it going?'

'Very well, Cat,' he replied. 'I've been giving what Ava said earlier some thought. I've decided to turn vegetarian... we must keep with the times, must we not?'

Angela spoke in our ear. 'Okay, you two? Ready in three minutes.'

There was a hand on my shoulder. 'Boo!'

David and I both screamed, and turned to see PJ behind us, laughing.

'You two are so uptight,' he said. 'Chillax, would you? You are both so wound up, as though TV is so difficult. I've found it so easy. I think once you work in a professional kitchen, then you understand what pressure and perfectionism is.'

David didn't say anything for a moment. 'We're just focused on staying calm, regulating our adrenaline...'

PJ laughed again. 'Oh right,' he said, sarcastically, 'regulating your adrenaline. Very important.' And then he spotted David's book, which was behind the sofa cushion. '*The New Vegan*! Don't tell me you're one as well, David. I had you down as a meat eater... they've *made* me make vegan food today... and I tell you it's not what I call a meal. It's just a collection of side dishes...'

'We must get with the programme,' said David, giving me a quick look. 'We must stay abreast of the times. Meat is murder. Plants are power.'

'Oh God,' said PJ, 'so they have got you as well. It's like the zombification of the men of Ireland. Who is going to fall under the woke spell next?'

Angela spoke again in our ears. 'Thirty seconds to live... all ready? Places, please.'

'PJ, please,' said David, sharply. 'You'll have to go to the kitchen.'

'Ten... nine...' Angela began counting down.

David and I powered through the show, laughing, bantering, interviewing, and eventually it was time for the cooking slot. During the last ad break, we made our way over. PJ was standing behind the stove and didn't even look at us. It was as though he no longer could keep up his pretence of charm. Perhaps being tasked with making a vegan meal had tipped him over the edge.

'Welcome back to *The Daily Show*,' said David, looking down the camera. 'Now we have a treat today... a magnificent menu of meat-free marvels...'

PJ stood between us and I could sense his hackles rising, his body tense, like a pit bull who has just spotted his Rottweiler nemesis.

'I'm a big fan of meat-free meals,' went on David. 'My old pal Paul McCartney and I spent many hours discussing the terrible things that go on in some of those farms... not the good farms, obviously... Cat, you must know a bit about it from your time on that faming programme?'

'A little,' I said, cautiously, trying to remember to smile.

PJ turned to me. 'Are you a vegan?'

'Sometimes,' I said, 'I mean...'

'SOMETIMES?'

I laughed, trying to keep it light, but my eye was fixated on the vein which throbbed in PJ's temple. 'I mean, I don't always eat meat. In fact, I rarely eat it... I just can't call myself a vegan... yet.'

PJ sneered. He seemed to have forgotten that he was on camera and that his charmless offensive was being broadcast to the nation.

'I'm really looking forward to seeing what you have for us today,' said David. 'Maybe you could talk us through it?'

PJ held his gaze for a moment too long, before pointing at his dishes with little enthusiasm. 'So this is a nut roast,' he said, 'with a tomato coulis... and this is a mushroom stroganoff... and this... is a vegetable tart.'

'Make it sound a little more appetising, will you?' David said, with a laugh. 'You'll have everyone back on the ham sandwiches and the breakfast rolls, with rashers, black pudding and extra sausages.'

PJ glared at him. 'It's hard to make it sound appetising. I've been *forced* to make this kind of food. You know, I wasn't even allowed to use milk or cream?'

'Obviously not,' said David, who was now Ireland's self-styled vegan champion. 'Dairy is from cows...'

PJ leaned forward and, before David could move away, he ruffled David's hair, dislodging the toupee. When David looked up again, it was hanging slightly over one eye and, as he moved, the toupee slid straight off his head and onto the floor.

In the control room, we could hear Angela directing the cameras away from a close-up. 'Camera two,' she ordered. 'Camera two! Oh, Jesus Christ! Camera two!'

David fell to the ground to retrieve his wig.

'So, PJ,' I said, overly brightly, 'tell us why have you chosen these vegan recipes?'

PJ flung the tea towel which had been on his shoulder onto the worktop. 'It's no good. I can't do it. I shouldn't be made to make rabbit food and pretend that I think that it's fit for human consumption.'

'Careful,' said Angela, quietly. 'We may have to go to an early close.'

David had now found his hairpiece and had it back on his head, very slightly askew, his TV smile in place. 'I'm sure whatever you make will be delicious,' he said.

Stay calm, I told myself. *Pretend you are in the sea, floating on your back, feeling the gentle lap of the water around you.* I breathed in, just as I did when I was in the sea, the tension leaving my body.

'Maybe you would finish the dish so we can taste it?' I smiled.

'Atta girl,' said Angela in my ear.

PJ stared at me for a second or two and then, just as I thought he was going to walk off set, he turned around and took out the tart from the oven and placed it in front of us. 'There you go,' he said, cutting a slice and plating it up, along with the green salad, and then drizzled the dressing on top. 'Vegan bloody tart.'

'More intemperate language,' said David, smiling smoothly into the camera. 'Apologies to those at home.'

I took a minuscule bite, hoping that we would get to the end of the show without another outburst.

Reading my mind, Angela said in my ear, 'Two minutes, you're doing great.'

'Delicious,' I said. 'David, what do you think?'

'Gorgeous,' agreed David. 'All that's needed is some salt, and then it would be really... really quite tasty.' He looked around for the salt, just as PJ's hand reached forward for another hair ruffle, but David ducked away just in time.

'Camera one,' said Angela. 'Get away from PJ. And David. Close on Cat.'

'And that's it for another week from *The Daily Show*,' I said, my smile actually hurting me now. 'Have a wonderful weekend, whatever you are up to, and we'll see you on Monday afternoon. Goodbye!'

Martin signalled that we were off-air and there was a collective exhalation from everyone on the studio floor.

PJ untied his apron. 'I've had enough of telly,' he said. 'It's boring.'

'PJ,' said David, politely, 'it's not good manners to touch another man's hair. And I would be grateful if you would respect my wishes.'

'If you actually had hair,' PJ retorted, 'then I wouldn't touch it.' He walked off the set.

'Says the bald man,' said David, to PJ's retreating form. 'Wearing one of these is like wearing any costume. Like your chef's whites. So, please. Hands off.'

The crew had gathered around to demolish PJ's tart. 'Iss good,' said Dmitri, his mouth full. 'Iss very good.'

Martin's mouth was even fuller as he managed a thumbs up and even Ava looked impressed.

'Not bad,' she said. 'I mean, my mam can do a better vegetable tart, but this is a close second.'

Angela scooted up to me, just as David walked off in the other direction. 'Oh my God,' she said, shaking her head as though she'd just survived a multi-car pile-up on the motorway. 'Oh my God. I can't believe he touched David! Chaos. Total and utter chaos. But not in a good way. In an awful way.' She looked at me. 'My plans to reduce the testosterone levels on this show don't seem to be working. It's like the patriarchy is fighting back. It's time for Betty to come back. Or find some other new cooking sensation.'

* * *

After the show, I sat in my dressing room when there was a knock on the door and Tom poked his head around.

'Just seeing how you are?' He looked concerned.

'Fine, thanks. You?' I hadn't seen much of him during the week and luckily I wasn't getting any flashbacks to that Saturday night.

Well, not as many. With any luck, we'd be able to move beyond it and all awkwardness would be gone.

'Well, *I'm* fine,' he said. 'I mean I wasn't just on live television dealing with a madman. I don't know how you kept your cool...'

'I don't think I did,' I said. 'I think I stopped breathing at one point.'

He stepped inside and perched on the small plastic chair. 'You couldn't make it up,' he said, shaking his head. 'David holding on to his hair.'

'Poor David,' I said. 'His wig...'

Tom started laughing now. 'I know I shouldn't. I know it's awful... but... his face! The poor man...'

'I know.'

I could see Tom trying to control his face and look serious.

'It's just...' he began. 'I mean... it's just... when he was lying on the ground, feeling around for the wig, all I could think about was Richard the Third. We did it for Leaving Cert. My kingdom...' And now he really started laughing. 'My kingdom for a wig...'

And then I began to laugh.

Tom wiped away a tear. 'Oh God, we shouldn't be laughing. Please don't tell anyone, will you?'

'Promise,' I said.

'I'm *meant* to be respectable and grown-up...'

'You are,' I said, smiling. 'Most of the time.'

'Poor David,' said Tom. 'Why is he going to such lengths to look younger? He's a good-looking man, fabulous career. Very well paid. Lovely partner. And yet... he is seeking youthfulness...'

'I know,' I said. 'It is sad. He's got it all.'

'When I'm that age, I hope I am happy. No regrets.' He smiled at me. 'By the way... the controlling, food-obsessed maniac you mentioned... it wasn't PJ, was it?'

I nodded. 'Unfortunately.'

'I thought there was something going on when he touched you that time. And his entitled behaviour... I just had a bad feeling about him then.' He shook his head. 'And I thought you had higher standards.'

'So did I.' I gave him a look, making him laugh suddenly.

'But why's he so angry?'

'I left him in a restaurant in Bilbao and he's never forgiven me.'

'What a fool.' Tom shook his head. He was looking at me with that strange expression on his face. 'How's the swimming...?' he said finally.

'Fine...' I replied. 'I'm going tonight...' I wished I could ask him to come with us. He'd enjoy it, or I hoped he would. And it was the perfect antidote to all this craziness.

He opened his mouth to say something and then closed it again.

THE JONES FAMILY!

Mum: Are you coming to the Great Sandycove Bake-Off? It's at 11 a.m. Tomorrow. At Our Lady's Hall.

Me: Wouldn't miss it. Becca and Sinéad said they would pop in too. Did you make your cake?

Mum: It's the best I could do.

Me: But at least it's yours.

Mum: No more subterfuge.

Me: Still can't believe you did that.

Mum: Stop! I am ashamed.

Me: I forgive you! See you at the bake-off.

Dad: I don't mind. We had years of delicious cake. Happy to be deluded if it means quality cake.

THE GIRLS!

Becca: Got the tickets for the supper club.

Me: Great.

Becca: Starts at 8 p.m. We could meet in The Island at 7 p.m.?

Sinéad: See you then. And at Bake-Off. We will call in and buy something.

Becca: Love cake.

Me: Who doesn't?

Becca: Psychopaths mainly. See you both later.

39

Malachy missed that evening's swim and it was when we were changed and ready to go our separate ways again, the WhatsApp group beeped.

Margaret checked her phone. 'It's Malachy,' she said. 'His mother's had a fall...' She looked up at us all. 'The poor thingeen.' She read on and gasped. 'She's in hospital and is in a bad way.' Tears filled Margaret's eyes. 'I am going to go and sit with him,' she said, her voice choked. 'Make sure he has someone beside him.'

'He's a sweet boy,' said Nora. 'His mam is his whole world...'

Suddenly, everyone was on their feet making a plan. It was decided that I would drive Margaret and Nora to the hospital, Brenda and Dolores would go home and wait by the phone, just in case anything else was needed.

At the hospital, I stopped the car just in front of the main entrance, and Margaret and Nora began to get out.

'Are you sure you don't want me to come in?' I said.

Nora poked her head in through the open passenger window. 'There's no need. We won't overwhelm the poor lad, just see what we can do and then we'll go home.'

'I can come and collect you?'

'No, you need your sleep,' said Margaret. 'You've been working all week. We're both retired, so don't have that worry.' She stood for a moment and began humming. 'Pardon for sin... and a peace that endureth... thine own dear presence to cheer and to guide. Strength for today and hope for tomorrow, blessings all mine, with ten thousand beside...'

Nora, small, her long grey plait hanging down her back, Margaret, tall, her hair cut short, walked determinedly into the hospital.

All Friday evening, I kept an eye on my phone, worried about Malachy's mam, worried about Malachy, and wishing that Nora and Margaret would send a message. It was strange to be so invested and to care so much about a person I'd never met. But I felt part of this group, their concerns were my concerns, and these were my community, my tribe. We were all in it together.

Eventually, at 11.45 p.m., a text.

She's been seen. Finally. Off the trolley and is now on a ward. Very comfortable. Had a cup of tea and slice of toast and old neighbour in next bed. Malachy delighted she recognised her. Malachy driving us home now. Will send updates when we have them. Nora.

* * *

The Forty Footers WhatsApp group was busy the following morning with the latest updates from hospital. I read the messages over my Saturday morning breakfast. There was a text from Nora on the group.

No news yet. She's still on a trolley. Hopefully will get a bed in a ward soon.

I could see Margaret was typing, but then a message came in from Dolores.

I'll go around to Malachy's and put some milk in the fridge.

And then Margaret wrote:

I'll bring some soup to the hospital, Mal. I'm just quickly helping out at the Sandycove Bake-Off.

Brenda joined in.

Love to you and your Mam. Call me if you need anything. At all.

And then Malachy wrote:

Thanks for all your help. And yes, Margaret, soup would be much appreciated. I can be round later to put up that bookshelf for you.

Nora wrote next.

Will you be in for a swim, Mal?

He replied:

Wouldn't miss it. See you all later.

I wrote:

Let me know if I can do anything. See you all in the sea.

Callum and Loulou came into the kitchen.

'Morning, Loulou,' I said.

She came over and put her arms around me. 'Happy Saturday, Cat. Miss Lally says you should say that rather than good morning, because you want people to be happy not just good.'

'I like it,' I said. 'Happy Saturday, Loulou.'

'Happy Saturday.'

Callum made himself a cup of tea and poured Loulou a glass of apple juice. He sat down across from me. 'Loulou's mum is busy today,' he said. 'Going out for a drink tonight, so we are giving her space to get ready. Hair done, nails... and whatever else she needs.' He smiled at me. 'She's going to look beautiful, isn't she, Loulou?'

Loulou nodded. 'She's bought a new dress,' she said. 'Sequins on it. She said I could have it when I'm older.'

'That sounds lovely.'

'And we're celebrating the fact that Daddy has got himself a job.' Callum beamed. 'I'm starting at Alison's café on Monday. I'm going to call down today and Alison is going to show me where everything is.' He turned to Loulou. 'Would you like to come with me?'

She nodded and then glanced at me. 'But Cat's going to the bake-off,' she said, pulling out her 'yes' necklace from under her T-shirt. 'I said I would go.'

'That's right,' I said. 'But it doesn't matter if you don't come. Mum won't mind. And I will let you know how we get on.'

'But I said yes,' she insisted, holding out the necklace again.

'I don't mind,' said Callum. 'What you want is what matters. And anyway, it gives me a chance to complete my application.' He reached over to the table. 'Business Studies at Dún Laoghaire college. Two years, full-time. Starts the end of September. And one day I hope to have my own wine shop.' He reached over and kissed Loulou's head. 'What do you think about your old dad's plan? Is it a good one?'

Loulou pulled a face. 'Why can't you open a *nice* shop? A *chocolate* shop.'

'But I'll have a little space where people can have some cheese and bread. Or a slice of cake and a cup of coffee. But also wine. Lots of good wine. Arranged because of type, same kind of taste, that kind of thing. Don't you think that's a good idea, instead of arranging according to country?'

'Genius,' I said.

'Will you have cheese strings?' said Loulou. 'They are my favourite cheese, but Mummy won't let me have them. Says they aren't cheese, but why are they called cheese then?'

Callum nodded. 'I will have cheese strings,' he said. 'Just for you. And tonight, because Cat is going out, and it's just going to be the two of us, I thought that nice pizza we like, watch *Quiz Me I'm Irish* and then play some cards. I thought I'd introduce you to the wonders of gin rummy.'

'Gin!' Loulou looked shocked. 'Mummy—' she began.

'It's a card game,' said Callum. 'We'll have orange squash. Okay with you?'

She held up her necklace. 'Yes,' she said.

* * *

Our Lady's Hall in Sandycove was ablaze with colour. It had been adorned with bunting, balloons, and a large hand-painted sign – 'The Great Sandycove Bake-Off Here Today!' – was propped up against the main door.

'Do we eat the cakes?' said Loulou. 'Do we all judge them?'

'I think they leave that to the professionals,' I said. 'But whatever happens, we have to buy Mum's cake. Even if it's the worst cake there.'

'Why can't she bake?' asked Loulou. 'I thought all old people could bake.'

'Well, Mum isn't old,' I said. 'Not technically. But she's just been too busy to learn how to make cakes before. She was a nurse. But when she retired...'

'You said she wasn't old. Retired people are old.'

'Well... she's not *old*-old,' I said. 'Just older than you. But she's trying out new things...' I held up my matching necklace. 'And her friend Lorraine challenged her to enter a cake competition.'

'Miss Lally says that we are allowed to say no, if we want to. She says that we are in control of our bodies.'

'Miss Lally is right,' I said. 'But I think Mum wouldn't do anything she really didn't want to do.' Like a parachute jump, I thought, hoping that Mum and Dad would see sense and pull out while there was still time. The summer had slipped by so fast and this time next week would mark the end of *The Daily Show* run and I'd be back in my old life. Except... I wasn't sure I wanted to go back to my old life. I wanted to keep going forwards, and saying yes to things. Being uncomfortable was something you got used to, and it soon became bearable and then normal. Like being in the sea. Horrible, then okay, and then actually quite nice, leading to euphoria at your achievement. I didn't want to live safely any more. I wanted to be out there. Maybe not to the extent that Lorraine was out there, but I wanted to be out there all the same.

Loulou held my hand as we walked into the hall. At the far end, on a long row of tables were around thirty cakes – all different sizes, some brilliantly decorated, some simply presented. Mum was standing with Lorraine at the side of the room. Lorraine was wearing a lime-green off-the-shoulder ruffled top, with matching trousers with ruffles at the ankles. Her eyeshadow was a matching green. Every part of Lorraine's life was 'out there', even her wardrobe.

Loulou hugged Mum. 'We've come to see your cake. We're here to support your efforts,' she said, making Mum laugh.

Lorraine barely glanced down at Loulou. I didn't introduce them because Lorraine claimed she suffered from 'child-blindness' and couldn't see children until they were well out of puberty. I think I may have had my first conversation with her when I was about nineteen.

'Where's your cake?' I said to Mum.

'In the middle,' she replied. 'In between Greta's *apfelkuchen* and Mary O'Brien's chocolate Guinness cake. Lorraine's Victoria sponge is on the end.'

'I can't believe Petula O'Connor has made Victoria sponge as well,' said Lorraine. 'I met her in SuperValu and she said she was making blueberry loaf, but then she turns up with *her* Victoria sponge and pretends she can't remember me telling her. She's never forgiven me for the incident at the carol service last year. It wasn't my fault that I was given the lead voice in "Gaudete". What was I going to say? No?' She turned to me. 'Now, you are coming to the aerodrome to see us doing our jump, aren't you? We need someone to drive us there and back because I don't know if our legs or nerves will be up for the driving. Our instructor, Wing Commander Kettle...'

'Wing Commander *Kettle*?'

'Wing Commander Charlie Kettle. Tall, shoulders like the Cliffs of Moher, tiny moustache... Anyway, he says don't even *think* about driving. You can't use the pedals when you've just flown through the air from 10,000 feet. Your body will be like jelly. I said to him my body was already jelly just looking into his ice-blue eyes.'

Mum laughed, but Lorraine was deadly serious.

'Yes, of course I'll drive you.' I was going to have to witness the broken bodies of both my parents.

I spotted Sinéad, Rory and Becca coming in through the door, just as Margaret from the Forty Footers tapped a microphone.

'Testing, testing…' she said, and cleared her throat. 'Thank you for coming, ladies, gentlemen, boys and girls. And welcome to the fifth Great Sandycove Bake-Off. We have been tasting all morning and we have come up with our prizes. Each person will go home with a cake from Sally-Anne's plus a twenty-euro voucher for James' Deli.' She smiled at us, and then, when she spotted me, gave a small wave. 'One of my sea swimming tribe over there,' she said. 'Now, back to the competition. Right…' She put on her glasses. 'Best decoration goes to Maureen Dempsey for her "Sandycove Au Soleil" design. Beautiful, Maureen.'

We clapped Maureen as she marched up to Margaret and accepted her prize.

Finally, we got to the last prize. Loulou and I crossed our fingers. Loulou, clutching her yes necklace, closed her eyes tightly, her lips moving, as though saying a prayer.

'And our final prize… is for most improved baker…'

Loulou and I dared to hope.

'She told us she wasn't much of a baker and that she's not a huge fan of cake and that she is more into her kettlebells class than baking…'

Loulou and I looked at each other. This did not sound like Mum.

'In fact, this person said that she only entered the competition as a joke. And the award for most improved baker goes to Lorraine Daly!'

We clapped, even though I had to nudge Loulou to make sure she joined in, as Lorraine made her way to the front of the room, taking the microphone from Margaret. Mum, of course, was clapping harder than anyone.

'I just want to say thank you to everyone for supporting me in my baking endeavours,' Lorraine said. 'And to Noel, my first ex-husband, who once claimed I had zero culinary skills. Bet you're sorry now, aren't you, Noel? Don't worry, he's not here. He's probably still in the pub, where I left him back in 1994. But, most of all, I want to thank my friend Annie, my best friend of...' she coughed '... years. Always by my side, which she will be when we do our parachute jump, all in aid of the hospice. Anyone who wants to sponsor us, just grab me today.'

Loulou and I went to join Becca, Sinéad and Rory.

'Everyone on for the supper club?' said Becca. 'Sorry we can't bring you, Loulou, but maybe next time.'

'Yes' signalled Loulou's necklace.

'We got the three last tickets,' said Becca. 'A cancellation. It's going to be amazing.'

'I don't think I can come tonight,' said Sinéad. 'I'm too tired.'

'You have to,' said Becca. 'It's all arranged.'

'But, like, so incredibly tired...' insisted Sinéad. 'Rory was up at 5 a.m. Bouncing around. Look, hold off on that fertility spell, will you?' she said to Becca. 'I don't think I can handle another one.'

'Too late,' said Becca. 'I did it last night. Burned sage, said the words, stared into my Jo Malone. Ryan said the house smelled like the Beauty Hall of Brown Thomas, which is possibly the only time he's ever noticed anything about our house.'

'Why don't we look after Rory for you while you go and have a nap?' I said to Sinéad. 'And then you'll be ready for tonight. What about two hours?'

'I can't,' said Sinéad. 'What if—'

'Let him go,' said Becca. 'Just let him go.'

'It's just that...' Sinéad looked uncertain.

'You've never left him with *anyone*, have you?' said Becca.

Sinéad shook her head.

'It might explain why you are so tired,' I said.

'Go home,' said Becca. 'We are two responsible people.' She looked down at Loulou. 'Well, one responsible child and two irresponsible adults.'

'I'm not sure,' said Sinéad.

'You will have to trust us. Just say yes,' I said.

'Ohhh...' Sinéad looked agonised. 'Okay then,' she said, 'yes.'

40

I was in charge of pushing Rory's buggy along the seafront, Loulou held Rory's hand and walked beside him, Becca on the other side.

'This is the most grown-up thing we have ever done,' said Becca. 'Not just being trusted with one child. But two!' She reached over and poked Loulou, who giggled.

'Be careful, Becca,' she said. 'I might run into the middle of the road and be knocked down. Splat. And then no one would ever allow you near a child again.'

'Probably a good thing, Loulou,' said Becca. 'I am truly awful with children. They all hate me and start crying. Good job I am never going to inflict myself as a mother on anyone.'

Loulou laughed again. 'Your baby might ask to go to a foster home, like Tracy Beaker.'

Now Becca laughed. 'And it would be right to do so!'

We wound our way along the path, the sky blue, the yachts scudding across the bay, like toy boats.

'Can I have a go now?' Becca said, trying to take the handles of the pushchair from me. 'You said I could.'

'Go on then.'

Becca began pushing Rory in a wild zigzag across the pavement, making him squeal with delight.

'So, you've started your spells,' I said, when she'd zigzagged back to us.

Rory began to get out of the pushchair.

'I want to walk now,' he said.

'Okay,' said Becca, 'just keep hold of Auntie Becca's hand.'

Rory grabbed on and stayed beside her.

'Are you a witch?' Loulou looked up at Becca.

Becca nodded. 'Yes, I'm a fully unqualified modern witch,' she explained. 'I've been reading this book all about spells. I'm doing a fertility one for Sinéad, because she wants a baby brother or sister for Rory. Happiness for me and love for Cat.'

Loulou looked up at me. 'Love?'

I nodded. 'I wouldn't mind some,' I said. 'But as Becca is fully unqualified, I don't expect the spell to work.'

'What about Dad?' said Loulou. 'He wouldn't mind some too.'

I shook my head. 'Not your dad, Loulou. He's lovely, but we're better as friends.'

'But you're not friends. He's your lodger.'

'Yes... well... I don't think it would work.'

'I hope I don't do the spell wrong,' said Becca. 'You know, make you love the wrong person. You wake up and find yourself incredibly in love with... I don't know...'

'A dog,' said Loulou.

'Or a banana?' I suggested.

'Exactly,' said Becca. 'I had better be very careful.'

'Will you do one for me?' said Loulou. 'Make my mum happy? She's tired and grumpy and she needs something nice to happen.'

'Consider it done,' said Becca. 'I'll add her to my list.'

The four of us stood outside Teddy's, the old ice cream shop.

'Right,' said Becca. 'Who wants one?'

Loulou stuck up her hand.

'Cat?'

'We can't,' I said. 'Rory.'

The three of us looked at Rory.

'But she'll never know,' said Becca.

'I know, but we will. Can you live with a guilty conscience?'

'Yes... but I know you can't. And it's a bad example to set in front of Loulou.'

'What?' said Loulou. 'What's going on?'

'Rory isn't allowed ice cream,' I explained. 'Not healthy. And so... we can't eat one in front of him.'

Rory was listening to every word with great interest. 'I can,' he said. 'I can have ice cream.'

Becca and I looked at each other, both agonised. And then, 'No,' I said. 'We can't.'

'Not when we're both trying to be responsible,' said Becca. 'Look, Rory, I tell you what, I'll do another witch's spell. Just for you. A spell that makes your mummy say yes to an ice cream one day very soon. Is that a deal?'

'Yay!' shouted Rory, punching a tiny fist into the air.

'Until then,' I said, 'let's see if there are any of those apple slices.' I found a large bag of dried apples and handed one to Rory.

'Give us one,' said Becca. 'Let's try these monstrosities.' She popped it into her mouth and chewed. 'Not bad. Not bad at all. Like apple crossed with cotton wool.'

The four of us sat against the wall looking out to the sea, Rory and Loulou in the middle, eating our apple slices.

'I am going to bring you swimming one of these days, Loulou,' I said. 'In the sea.'

'Cat's a *sea swimmer*, don't you know!' said Becca, making herself laugh. 'Hasn't she *told* you?'

Loulou giggled. 'She has, actually. Many times.' She slipped her hand into mine to show she was only joking.

'How do you know someone is a sea swimmer…' said Becca. 'They'll tell you!'

Loulou laughed all the more and even Rory joined in.

'Come on,' said Becca. 'Pass over the apple slices. May as well finish the packet.'

Loulou rested her head on my shoulder, her hand still in mine.

One day, I thought, I would like a child just like her.

41

Sinéad was waiting for us in The Island when we arrived, sitting in the courtyard, under the shade of a large fern. Becca and I had dropped Rory back earlier and Conor had opened the door. 'She's asleep,' he'd whispered, taking the pushchair from us.

'Tell her we need her full of beans for this evening,' said Becca. 'She needs to be up and at it for 7 p.m.'

And Sinéad did look very well rested and full of beans, a glass of wilted mint leaves and melted ice cubes in front of her. 'This mojito is going down too quickly,' she said. 'It's like riding a bike. You never forget.'

'Forget what?' I asked, hugging her and sitting down beside her.

'Me, life, the taste of alcohol, being able to walk around without worrying about Rory... now I've got myself two babysitters.'

'Three,' I said. 'Loulou took it all very seriously.'

'Well, then,' said Becca, nodding towards the half-drunk mojito. 'You need another one of those. We may as well get plastered.'

'Wouldn't a mojito affect your abilities as a witch?' I said, as Becca tried to grab Mick's attention so she could order.

'Not at all,' said Becca, confidently. 'In fact, I am reliably informed in the *Handbook For The Modern Irish Witch* that alcohol vastly improves one's powers. I checked before I left the house, specifically. Interestingly, alcohol dissolves the psychic barrier between you and the spirit world...'

'I bet it does,' said Sinéad.

'Mick,' called Becca. 'Three of your delicious mojitos, please!' She turned back to us. 'The good thing about being a witch is that it's like a secret identity. No one knows that I am a witch, able to cast spells and communicate with an alternative universe.'

Sinéad and I burst out laughing. 'You're right,' said Sinéad. 'No one knows. Not even you.'

'Ah, come on,' said Becca. 'I really want to be a witch. Allow me this one chance to be interesting and mysterious. And you may scoff now, but wait until I try out a few spells and make things happen, then you'll be asking me to wave my wand.'

We laughed again.

'Poor Ryan,' said Becca. 'He was looking at me with a really concerned look on his face as I was reading my handbook earlier. He said he didn't realise I was into airy-fairy nonsense and I said it wasn't fairies, it was witches. I think he thinks he's lost me. I just don't know what's happening to me. I think it's Cat's fault. She started with the yes thing, and next I was doing yoga and then not straightening my hair... and now I'm a witch.'

'They all seem very transient fads,' said Sinéad. 'Somehow I don't think you'll be a witch for much longer.'

'Ryan tried to talk to me this evening,' Becca went on. 'I think he was trying to end things.' She shrugged. 'He kept opening and closing his mouth, this worried expression in his eyes. I said I had to go and get ready. I will have to face that in the morning. But first I drink!'

'He might not be,' said Sinéad. 'Wasn't your spell for happiness?'

'Maybe it was happiness for him? And he'd be happier without me. I feel kind of mad lately,' admitted Becca. 'Slightly disorientated, and not quite myself.' She shook her head. 'It's weird. Maybe I'm ill?'

'I felt like that when I was pregnant with Rory,' said Sinéad. 'I looked the same, everybody treated me the same, but I was different. I kept wondering why everyone didn't see it. Conor told me that sometimes he wakes up and for a moment he forgets he's married with a baby and he's just about to roll over to sleep again and then he hears Rory... and he says in that moment, he wishes he could just be left alone to sleep.' She shook her head. 'Imagine if I said such a thing?'

Mick placed three brimming glasses of mojitos on the table. 'Thank you, ladies,' he said. 'Enjoy your drinks. Sip them slowly, mind you, because they don't come cheap.'

'We will, Mick,' I said. 'We'll make sure to make them last.'

Becca held up her glass. 'Here's to us, the three of us, with babies, without babies, together, forever.'

'Together, forever,' Sinéad and I echoed.

42

Slightly tipsily, we found our way to the supper club, which was a short walk away in a garden at the back of one of the big houses on the old, beautiful Victorian squares.

'So what is this place again?' I asked Becca.

'It's just run by a group of friends,' said Becca. 'I think it's only on for the summer. I've heard amazing things about it. Just down here...'

We turned into a small, grass-lined lane at the end of one of the terraces where hollyhocks swayed at the edges, and then through a wooden door, under an archway of honeysuckle and jasmine and into a private garden. Lights had been strung up, a jazz band played in one corner. People stood in groups, beside some apple trees, chatting, holding cocktails. It was beautiful.

'It's like a secret garden,' said Sinéad. 'I love it.'

'And so far from the pretentiousness of some restaurants,' said Becca.

'Exactly,' I said, glad to be away from everything, and with my two best friends. 'It's absolutely gorgeous here.' It was like standing in the middle of a fairyland, as though you had been transported somewhere far removed from ordinary life. Being outside in the warmth of the evening, the sky darkening, the lights twinkling, the air scented with jasmine and honeysuckle, there was a feeling that normal rules didn't apply and that anything could happen.

'Come on,' said Becca. 'Let's go and get ourselves one of those cocktails.'

Just as we held our glasses, I glanced across the garden and saw a group of three men, talking and laughing together. It took a moment to realise that I was staring at Tom. My whole body was suddenly electrified. Every part of me was suddenly on fire, it was like his hands were touching me again, the way his hand had been on my calf that time at the barbecue.

He was looking straight at me, not smiling. He was wearing shorts and a faded navy T-shirt and he looked even more handsome so casually dressed. The last time I'd seen him in shorts was the morning he brought me breakfast in bed.

Tom raised his hand and I managed to wave in return. Becca and Sinéad immediately swivelled around.

'Who's that?' said Sinéad.

'Tom Doherty,' I said. 'Head of Entertainment. Oversees *The Daily Show* and other things.' I could barely get the words out, my mouth was so dry.

They both stared over again.

'Wow,' said Becca. 'I never knew Irish men could look like that. Tall, sexy...'

'Rory can stay home alone, I'm going to work with Cat,' said Sinéad.

I pretended to laugh. But really I was desperately trying to compose myself.

'Oh God, he's coming over,' said Becca. 'Do I look all right?'

'Jesus Christ alive,' said Sinéad. 'It's like if Disney did Irish men.'

'Shut up!' I hissed.

'Look casual,' said Becca. 'I *knew* I should have worn more make-up.'

'Guys, please,' I tried again, managing to turn and smile. *Be cool*, I told myself. Be more like Susie Keane, a self-possessed modern woman.

Becca already had her hand out. 'Hello, I'm Becca,' she said. 'Apparently, you're a colleague of Cat's? It's always nice to meet people Cat works with. Cat told us *all* about you.'

'I haven't,' I said, quickly. 'I haven't mentioned you.'

'I don't know which is worse,' said Tom, 'being mentioned or not mentioned at all.'

Becca laughed. 'I have no idea why she hasn't.' She gave me a side-eye as though she guessed my silence on this handsome man had a deeper meaning.

'And this is Sinéad,' said Becca. 'Mother to the cutest toddler in Ireland.'

'I kind of thought that I might be more than that,' said Sinéad, shaking Tom's hand. 'But obviously not. Wow, good grip.'

'I hate a limp one,' said Becca.

'So do I,' agreed Sinéad. 'My father used to say don't judge a man by what he says, but how he shakes your hand... but... then Dad wasn't the best judge of character. Two of his accountants ended up embezzling money and poor old Dad is far away from the sunny retirement he'd set his heart on.'

If we hadn't had a raft of mojitos which had gone straight to our heads then we might have stood a chance of being a little more impressive, but Tom seemed amused by the two of them.

'Handshakes are greatly overrated,' he said. 'I judge people on the company they keep. Or how good they are with a hurley.' He glanced at me and there was a look on his face that I couldn't quite work out. 'Why don't you sit with us?' Tom went on. 'We could eat together? I'm with two of my friends from five-a-side.'

I was about to politely decline, when Becca elbowed herself in closer. 'We would love to,' she said. 'Wouldn't we, girls?'

And so we did. The three of us sat on either side of a trestle table, Becca, Sinéad and me on one side, Tom and his friends, Barry and Jim, on the other. We laughed throughout the whole evening, at one point Becca insisted on demonstrating how Sinéad used to dance in nightclubs, and then Sinéad had to show how Becca used to. 'She thought she could do the robot,' explained Sinéad. 'In her head, she was half-woman, half-machine. In real life, she looked like she was having some kind of allergic reaction.'

Later on, as Barry and Jim and Becca and Sinéad were deep in conversation about who was better, Blur or Oasis, it was just Tom and me.

'So, it's your last week,' he said.

'I know.'

'We'll miss you. Angela and Ava, particularly.'

'I'll miss them,' I said. 'But looking forward to going back to *Farming Weekly*.'

'You don't sound as if you've enjoyed it,' he said.

'I need time to let it all settle,' I said, trying to laugh. 'I'm still in the middle of it all.'

'Well, next week is the Irish Television Awards. Hopefully, you are coming...'

'I'm not sure yet,' I said.

He nodded, as though not wanting to pursue the matter. He didn't care if I was going to be there or not. And that was okay, I told myself. We would politely say goodbye next week and that would be it.

'Look,' he said, 'I just want to say... just to clear the air... well, I've been trying to say this for a while and I know it's been a bit weird between us and... well...'

I'd never known Tom to be lost for words, his usual suave,

smooth, confident persona was gone. 'I don't make a habit of sleeping with colleagues. Ever. It's never a good idea...' He stopped. 'Except when...'

He was about to say more when Becca pulled at my sleeve. 'Time to go,' she said, grabbing my arm. 'Sinéad's not feeling well.' I looked back at Tom and he gave me a half-smile. Becca linked arms with Barry and Jim, Sinéad was on the other end. 'Come on, Cat,' she called. 'Tom,' ordered Becca, 'grab hold of Cat before she falls over!'

I felt Tom's arm wrap around me. And then, as we walked to the main road, for a moment, Tom's hand found my own and we squeezed each other's hand. And then that was it. He waved for a taxi.

'Thanks, Tom,' called Becca, as she crawled in.

'Love you, Tom, Barry and Jim!' shouted Sinéad, from the open window. 'Thanks for an amazing night!'

I scrambled into the taxi after the girls and off we sped.

43

On Sunday evening, the Forty Footers met for our swim – minus Malachy, who was at the hospital with his mam.

'She's going to be in at least a week,' said Nora, as we swam around.

'Nursing home is the next step,' said Margaret, bobbing beside us.

'That's a ferocious difficult decision to make,' said Brenda in the water beside me. 'I remember when Mam had to go. I was at the end of my tether. Tried everything. Home help. Day care. Moving in with her. And then, I had to face the inevitable. But she was safe, if she fell, there was always someone there.'

Dolores paddled up. 'The state of some places,' she remarked.

'Some of them are like prisons,' said Margaret.

'And some are filthy,' said Brenda. 'But Honeysuckle Lodge is lovely. They have quizzes. And their own choir. And a book club. And it's only down the road.'

'It would be perfect for Malachy's mam,' said Margaret.

'Nice and close,' said Brenda.

When we were drying ourselves, Dolores began singing quietly to herself, 'You make me feel so young...'

'Happy, Dolores?' said Brenda.

'Quite content, thank you, Brenda,' said Dolores, still humming.

'So how is everything going with Mick?' asked Margaret, giving me a wink.

'Making her feel young again,' said Nora. 'She looks like a new woman.'

'Well, she's got herself a new man,' said Brenda.

Dolores laughed and continued to sing.

'Any tips for those of us who wouldn't mind feeling young again, Dolores?' said Brenda.

'I thought you were only as young as the man you feel,' quipped Nora, 'and I think Mick's older than you, isn't he?'

We all laughed, including Dolores.

'It's not age,' she said. 'It's *experience* that counts.' She grinned at us.

Margaret took out the cups and held each one, while Brenda filled them and handed them out.

'What are we raising a cup to?' asked Nora.

'Malachy's mam,' I said.

'To Malachy's mam,' everyone echoed.

'And to Mother Nature,' Dolores said. 'There's no higher power. And that's why I swim every day. In the sea, you feel Her at Her most visceral and raw...'

Brenda nodded. 'It's quite the feeling. Especially during the storms. Do you remember Storm Cedric? None of us would go in, except for Dolores here. Fearless.'

Dolores was still smiling. 'It was like meeting your god. Or goddess.'

'Definitely goddess,' said Nora.

'The tea is great, Margaret,' said Dolores. 'There's nothing like a cup of tea. Wouldn't ever go back to the way I was. I'll always be an alcoholic, but every day is a new day.'

'Halleluia,' said Margaret.

Dolores was bathed in a pool of light, her kaftan tucked around her. She looked like a goddess of love. Hope for tomorrow, I thought. That's all we need: hope for tomorrow.

As I walked down from the Forty Foot, towards the village, my hair wet and half towel dried, my nose peeling from having caught the sun, I hadn't even bothered changing and just had my towel wrapped around me. I was deep in thought, thinking everything through, from what Malachy had been saying about his mam, about Dolores and her constant and brave struggle and just how much I liked everyone. It was as though I had found another side to life, one I didn't even know existed, like finding a life extension, a secret room that I was exploring.

'Cat?'

I looked up. Walking towards me was Tom, and beside him was an older woman, dressed in a yellow sundress, a white cotton cardigan.

He waved and I walked over towards them. 'I didn't know you'd be here,' he said, taking off his sunglasses and peering down at me. 'I mean, I know you swim here but what a coincidence...' He gave a laugh. 'I'm just giving Mam a tour of Dublin. She's up for the night to go to the AGM of the Women Farmers of Ireland.'

I turned to his mother, smiling, wishing I wasn't just wearing a towel, and that my hair didn't look like a rat's nest and that I wasn't sunburned. 'Hello, Mrs Doherty,' I said. 'Welcome to Dublin...'

She took my hand. 'I am here under duress,' she said, giving me a good shake and looking straight into my eyes. 'If only my son didn't live here and I was forced to come and see if he's looking after himself, I would never come to Dublin.'

'But you've got the AGM tomorrow,' said Tom. 'No one is forcing you to be its president.'

His mother gave me a wink. 'I've got to keep myself out of trouble somehow, don't I? Can't be twiddling the old thumbs back at home, waiting for a telegram from my one and only son.'

'Mam, you've never twiddled your thumbs in your life and I text you every day.'

'But Mary Joyce's son phones her every morning. And he's in America,' said Mrs Doherty. 'He's going to bed and she's getting up.' She gave me a wink again. 'Now, isn't that a good son?'

Tom shook his head. 'Mickey Joyce was always a strange one,' he said. 'Do you remember he still sucked his thumb when he was a teenager...'

'Better than twiddling them anyhow,' said Mrs Doherty.

I laughed and she laughed too.

'So, your dutiful son is giving you the grand tour?' I said.

'Oh, yes,' she said. 'We've been all over. And then we came to the seaside for an ice cream. And very nice it was too. And I see you are one of those sea swimmers? Not too cold for you?'

'It's definitely too cold for me,' I said. 'But the point is you have to tell as many people as possible that you are a sea swimmer. And everyone has to look impressed and tell me how brilliant I am. It's the only reason I do it.'

They both laughed.

'Cat's also a presenter on *The Daily Show*,' Tom said to his mother. 'She's standing in for Barbara Brennan.' Mrs Doherty looked blankly at him and Tom turned to me. 'Mam doesn't watch television. She thinks it's as bad a vice as smoking and voting Fianna Fáil. She only reads.'

His mother nodded. 'I do admit that Tom felt very neglected as a child when we were the only family for miles around who didn't have a television. He asked for one every birthday and Christmas.

Even saved his communion money to buy one. But I remained firm. Books, I said, you can go and read books. Much better for you.'

'Is it any wonder I went into television production?' said Tom, laughing. 'It was the only way I could rebel.'

'But I am sure you are very good at what you do,' went on Mrs Doherty, 'you have a look about you that I can tell makes you good on television.'

'And I'm a sea swimmer,' I said. 'You forgot to mention that.'

She laughed again. 'I did!' she said. 'How could I forget the most important thing about you?'

'Where are you going now?' said Tom.

'Home,' I said. 'Shower. See how my lodger is. Feed myself. What are you two up to?'

'I think Tom said he'd bring me for fish and chips,' said Mrs Doherty.

'You can join us if you like,' said Tom.

'I'm not dressed properly,' I said. 'And I have to go home.' Tom had had to ask me, out of politeness. Of course they wouldn't want a half-dressed banshee floating after them while they ate their fish and chips. 'But thank you. And lovely to meet you, Mrs Doherty.' I shook her hand again.

'And you too, Cat,' she said. 'And call me Nuala. Everyone does.' She smiled at me. 'Make sure you tell everyone you swim, now, won't you?'

'I will!'

I walked back to my car, giving them a wave and the last I saw was them walking up towards the Forty Foot. As I drove home, I thought how nice it was to see someone being so kind to his mother. As obviously he should be. But still. They had a lovely relationship. I glanced at myself in the mirror and almost screamed in shock. But what did it matter? What had happened between Tom and me was becoming a distant memory. And soon, when my stand-in stint was over, I wouldn't see him again.

44

My last week on *The Daily Show* flew by and on Wednesday I came home from swimming to find Callum in the hall, his bag packed.

'Denise has asked me if I want to give it another go,' he said, his eyes shining. 'I've said yes.'

'Of course you've said yes,' I said, hugging him. 'That's wonderful news.'

'I'm scared though,' he admitted, 'what if it goes wrong again? What if I am the same? What happens if she throws me out again?'

'But you've got your plan, now, haven't you?' I said. 'One step at a time. Believe in yourself.'

He nodded. 'I hope I can do it. Be the person Denise fell in love with. Be good enough for her.'

'You are,' I said. 'But are you good enough for you? Do it for yourself. Make *yourself* proud. You've already done so much, you're working and all the other changes...'

'Working at Alison's is going great,' he said. 'It's been good for my head. To be part of a team. Have colleagues again. Have a laugh. Look after customers. Being on my own all day was making me even more depressed. I think I've stopped the spiral.'

'And your course,' I said. 'You're enrolled?'

'Starting in four weeks,' he said. 'Probably be the oldest one there.'

'Age is just a number.' I hugged him again and he picked up his bag.

'I've left you the television,' he said. 'I was watching too much of it before. I'm going to be too busy to sit in front of it again.'

I didn't want it either. 'What about giving it to Honeysuckle Lodge nursing home?' I suggested.

I helped him load it into the car, along with his other things – Steve the plant was balanced on the front seat – and handed him an envelope. I'd saved all the money he'd given me for rent over the past four weeks.

'Take this and put it towards your college supplies or buy something nice for Denise and Loulou.'

He teared up and, for a moment, refused to take it.

'Please?' I said. 'I'd really like it if you did.'

He didn't say another word, as though if he tried to say something, he might start to cry. 'Thanks, Cat,' he croaked, and then shut the car door and drove off.

The following morning, my penultimate day on *The Daily Show*, Tom caught up with me in the corridor. 'I wondered if I could have a word, please?' He smiled. I hadn't seen much of him that week. He'd missed all our meetings because he was in, according to Angela, 'intense contract renegotiations with the talent'.

'They must mean you, David,' said Ava.

'I don't get involved,' said David. 'Leave the dirty work to my agent. By the way, I won't be around for tomorrow's meeting as I have a very important medical appointment. I'll be back in time for the show.'

I followed Tom along the corridor, past the paintings by Irish artists, the photographs of various programme teams triumphantly and a little boozily holding up awards at ceremonies and a large poster for tomorrow's Irish Television Awards, and into his office.

'Take a seat,' he said, sitting across from me. He smiled. 'How's your last week going?'

'Grand,' I said. 'You know... getting there...'

'Have you enjoyed it? The whole experience? I'm trying to work it out from your facial expression. You don't give much away...'

Oh, I do, I thought. Especially after too much wine. Never again, though.

'It's been a whirlwind...' I said.

'A good whirlwind?'

'Once I'm on the other side of my therapy sessions, I'll let you know.'

He laughed. 'Well, we all think you have done remarkably well. I am fully aware that being parachuted on to *The Daily Show*, with the myriad trials, tribulations and personalities that such a programme has, was a challenge – one you more than ably conquered. You handled some very tricky situations very well. You've shown a light touch, you ask intelligent questions and... you look good. I mean...' He became slightly flustered, but then recovered himself. 'You know, on-screen. It works. *You* work. So thank you.' He paused, as though about to say something. 'You've been brilliant.'

'Thanks.' I wondered if that was it and was just about to stand, when Tom began speaking again.

'I'm currently talking about David and Barbara's contract renewal.' He pulled a face. 'It's not easy. They have the same Rottweiler agent. It would be easier to negotiate with the Mafia. I was hoping you might like to stay on,' said Tom. 'Obviously, I am still negotiating contracts and I have some ideas to move our talent around. Barbara is due back after the show's two-week break starting on Monday, but we...' He paused. 'Well, we don't want to lose you. *I* don't want to lose you.'

'What are you suggesting?' I was ready to return to *Farming Weekly*, to my old team. But I'd thought a lot about the last month, and Lorraine's yes scheme. It had been remarkable. Without it, I wouldn't have gone swimming and met my lovely tribe, or taken on *The Daily Show* and met the gang here. Everything I had said yes to had opened up a million more avenues, like a kaleidoscope. I was excited about what else could be next.

'If you say yes to being on *The Daily Show*,' Tom continued, 'then I will tell Barbara that we won't be renewing her contract. I have something else in mind for David. So it would just be you.'

'You mean I would take Barbara's place?'

He nodded. 'I haven't spoken to her yet. I'm just trying to get my ducks in a row.'

I didn't need to think about it. 'No,' I said. 'I could never take Barbara's place. It wouldn't be fair.'

He looked at me. 'It's a massive opportunity. It's a year's contract on *The Daily Show*. I know so many brilliant and talented people who would like the job. But we want you...'

I shook my head. 'It's not fair on Barbara. I think it's best if I just go back to my old job. I've already rung Mike, my producer, and told him I'd be there on Monday.'

'Won't you think about it?'

'I've just spent a month saying yes to everything,' I said. 'I need time to think about a few things. I can't go through life just saying yes indiscriminately.'

'You feel a bit rushed...'

'A little, yes.'

Tom nodded. 'That's what this business is,' he said. 'A bit full on.'

'A bit?'

He laughed. 'Okay, then, a lot.' He paused. 'So you need a break? Space? Peace? Time to think?'

'Exactly. Next time I say yes, it will be because it's the right decision.' I stood up and held out my hand. 'It's been great working with you.'

He shook my hand. 'It's been a pleasure.' He smiled. 'Will you be at the awards tomorrow night? Angela and Ava are coming,' he went on. 'And David, of course. Entertainment has three tables booked, my PA will be sending cars to collect everyone. She has all the details, I think there is a budget for hair and make-up. We'd like you to be there,' he said. 'You're still part of the team. For now. Anyway.'

Maybe it was better just to slip away? 'I'm not sure,' I said.

'Have you got something else on?'

'Swimming.' I smiled at him. 'How's your mam? Did she enjoy her trip to Dublin?'

He laughed. 'Hated every second. At one point, she said she couldn't breathe the air was so thick with smog. And she kept pretending she couldn't understand people. I saw her off on the train and she never looked happier in her life.'

I laughed.

'She always says that, though,' he went on, 'but there's always some flimsy excuse that brings her up. Always manages to get a bit of shopping done, buy some cakes in Bewley's and go to that second-hand bookshop she loves.'

'And to see you...'

'Yes, she likes to check up on me... make sure I am eating and still remembering that there is a life outside TV. She left a pile of books for me, with a note: "read these, your eyes are too square".'

I laughed again. 'She's brilliant. I love her.'

He nodded. 'She's a great mam, that's for sure.'

We looked at each other and for a moment an awkward silence fell. 'Well,' I said, finally, 'I'd better get on and read my briefs for today. See you later, Tom.'

'See you, Cat,' he said.

As I walked back along the corridor, I considered all that had happened. I had really liked Tom, but it was all a bit messy, with work and contracts and jobs and one-night stands. My mortification and embarrassment still burned. In another life, things might have worked out for us, but in this one, it was time to move on and get back out there and see what else life had in store for me.

LORRAINE!

Me: Just to say thank you for making me say 'yes' for a month.

Lorraine: I know. I'm always right. When will you just listen to me on everything.

Me: SO much has happened! It's been amazing.

Lorraine: All good things?

Me: Not necessarily. But mainly. How is the parachute jump training going?

Lorraine: Superb. Am thinking of going for my advanced training after this jump. I've been told I have what it takes.

Me: I don't doubt it.

THE JONES FAMILY!

Dad: We were at the aerodrome today for parachute training. We were practising landing.
Mum: Land, fold, roll...
Dad: I thought it was roll, fold and land?
Me: Dad, you're not going to survive this. Are you sure it's a good idea??
Mum: Lorraine has taken a fancy to our instructor. She's now reading a book about the SAS parachute regiment that he recommended.
Dad: Another wedding before the end of the year. Mark my words.
Mum: Good luck with today's show, Cat! We love you!
Dad: Yes, we most certainly do.

45

On set, just a few minutes before going live for my penultimate show, David took his place on the sofa beside me. He had been at his medical appointment and for some reason he was wearing sunglasses.

'David... do you...? Is everything all right?' I motioned to the eye area.

'Conjunctivitis,' he said, quickly. 'I'll have to present the show like this. It's fine, plenty of people appear on television wearing sunglasses.'

'Do they?' I couldn't think of one example.

'Of course. Don Johnson in *Miami Vice*... If he can do it, so can I.' He paused. 'And anyway, it's the ITAs tomorrow. I really need to win and show everyone I am at the top of my game.'

Angela's voice in our earpieces: 'Please, David, we need to see your eyes.'

David carried on reading his briefing notes, as though he hadn't heard her.

'David, *please*. We can explain the hay fever...'

Hay fever? He'd told me it was conjunctivitis.

'People will understand,' she went on, but David was fiddling with his cuffs and clearing this throat. 'David,' she sounded weary, 'you look ridiculous.'

He snapped to attention. 'Ridiculous?' he said, into the air. 'Do you think Don Johnson looks ridiculous. Arnold Schwarzenegger? Bono?'

'Well, yes, I do,' said Angela bravely, but obviously desperate not to begin the show with a presenter in dark glasses, 'if they were to wear sunglasses *inside*. You've got fifteen seconds before we're live. What are you going to do?'

'Leave them on.'

And that was it. Martin stood forward, Dmitri was in position, the camera focused on the first to-camera opening, and David had won the battle of the sunglasses.

Not a single guest, throughout the whole show, said anything. Everyone, in that typically Irish way, pretended there was nothing unusual about a man wearing sunglasses indoors. Except for one person.

It was ten minutes before the end of the show and I began my introduction to our last item. 'And now we have a very special guest, and one very brave guest. Adam Parker is only five years old and was in the house with his mam, when she fainted. Adam called 999 and stayed on the line and even performed CPR... and we are delighted to have Adam and his mam, Sarah, on the show today...' I turned to Adam and Sarah. 'You're very welcome to *The Daily Show*... Sarah, why don't we begin with you... it was just a normal day...'

Sarah told her story about being at home with Adam when she started feeling unwell. All the time his mother was talking, Adam was staring at David.

'So, Adam,' I said, 'what gave you the idea to call 999?'

Adam didn't answer, just continued staring at David.

'Apparently, you like watching programmes about hospitals.' I tried again to get his attention. 'Is that right?'

Adam still didn't speak, just stared at David, open-mouthed.

Eventually, he spoke. 'Is he alive?' he said, pointing at David.

'Yes, yes,' said Sarah, embarrassed, pulling down Adam's arm. 'So, yes, Adam loves a programme called *Operation Hospital* which is about a children's ward—'

'He doesn't look alive,' said Adam. 'He hasn't moved.'

In my ear, Angela – with a note of panic in her voice – said, 'Give him a nudge. Quick.'

I turned to face David, only to see him fall like a tree trunk on top of me, his sunglasses dislodging and revealing two incredibly bruised eye sockets as though he'd been in a round with Tyson Fury.

'JESUS CHRIST!' shouted Sarah as Angela screamed in my ear.

Meanwhile, Martin had leaped forward, looking bewildered.

I blinked into the camera. 'Thank you all for watching,' I shouted hysterically. 'Back tomorrow!'

The only person with any semblance of calm was Adam. 'Do I need to phone another ambulance?'

* * *

We all stood outside the television building to see David being wheeled off to hospital.

'Don't worry,' said the ambulance driver, cheerfully. 'We'll look after him. He'll be back on-screen before you know it. My mother's a big fan. Thinks he's sex on legs. He keeps them all going in the care home.'

Poor David was wrapped in a blanket which was tucked up to his chin. 'Don't let this get out,' he rasped, as he was lifted in to the back of the ambulance. 'Don't let anyone know... It was just a little bit of Botox!' The driver shut the door.

We stood watching the ambulance take off at breakneck haste over the speed bumps.

'David just technically died on television,' said Ava, turning to us all. 'I mean, I know we could always improve our ratings, but he didn't need to *die* to do so. That's taking the cause too far.'

'What on earth happened to him?' I said.

Angela shook her head. 'I don't know, but the ambulance driver said his heart stopped for eight seconds. If Adam hadn't noticed he was dead, he might actually be properly, *really*, unresuscitatedly dead.'

Tom came up to us, putting away his mobile phone. 'I was just talking to Jennifer,' he said. 'Apparently, David went to see his "doctor"...' – Tom made quotation marks in the air – 'and he had a "quickie eye-lift", whatever that is. Apparently, his heart stopped twice already since he came home and then Jennifer found him slumped on the toilet. Each time, his heart started again with the aid of caffeine and a *very* hard slap on the back. But he's obviously better off in hospital.'

'With proper doctors,' I said.

'Jennifer is on her way now,' Tom said. 'They'd had a huge row, apparently, about him trying to look younger.'

'But he looks amazing,' said Angela. 'I mean, I'm forty-nine and *look* seventy-three.' She rolled her eyes. 'Fecking menopause.'

'Right,' said Tom, 'I'm going to follow the ambulance and make sure David isn't alone until Jennifer gets there. And we'll just have to do tomorrow's show without him.' He looked at me. 'Is that okay with you, Cat?'

I nodded. 'Of course.'

46

After my swim, I checked my phone to see if there was any news about David.

'There she is,' I heard Becca say. 'Come on, can you get Rory over the rocks?'

'It's an all-terrain buggy,' said Sinéad, confidently. 'So I doubt there will be any trouble.'

'Ahoy!' shouted Becca, as they walked over. 'Isn't that what they say to swimmers?'

'I thought we were meeting by the pier?'

'We were early,' said Sinéad. 'I had to get out of the house. Poor Rory won't settle this evening and Conor has a meeting with someone in the States.'

Rory was wide awake, looking around him with his big blue eyes. 'Going swimming, Mummy?' he said.

Sinéad shook her head. 'No, darling. Not ever.' She smiled sweetly at him. 'Mummy doesn't swim, does she? Mummy wouldn't be caught dead in a swimsuit in public getting into the freezing sea and being attacked by jellyfish.'

I stood in front of them, dry-ish and dressed-ish. 'Come on,' I said, wriggling into my hoodie, 'let's walk along the seafront.'

The whole of Sandycove had the same idea on this beautiful evening, the sky streaked with orange, the seagulls flying overhead, and the yachts way out in the bay. We took up our space on the pavement along with the dog owners, the power-walkers, the young and old lovers and a few parents, just like Sinéad, who were all hoping a blast of sea air would knock out their wide-awake offspring.

We found a bench looking out to sea and sat in a row, Rory on Sinéad's lap.

'Give me a go?' said Becca, reaching for Rory and lifting him from Sinéad's arms. 'Here, sweetheart,' she said, kissing his head. He snuggled into her and Becca gave us both a look. 'See. He loves me. And I love him.'

'I confronted Conor,' said Sinéad. 'Told him that he either goes back to the office or he leaves the house. Forever. We can't do the office-in-a-shed thing because our garden is the size of a postage stamp. But he says he's got social anxiety after the pandemic and the thought of being back in the office is freaking him out. I think that maybe it's time I made some changes. For me. And for Rory. And so I have an announcement... drum roll...'

Becca and I began tapping away on our laps and Rory joined in.

'So, after nearly three years of maternity leave, of three years of spending all my time with the best boy in the world, I've decided that it's time for me to go back to work part-time. Rory's ready. I'm ready and I'm going to find a really nice creche.' She smiled at him. 'He's growing up so fast and I think he's going to be okay. And, you'll be pleased to know, Becca, I've stopped anti-baccing everything. And Rory's still alive. We even ate something off the floor which had been there for longer than five seconds. I can't keep him wrapped in cotton wool forever. Soon, he'll be able to have an ice cream and other unhealthy things.'

Becca and I glanced at each other.

'Congratulations,' I said. 'Balance in all things – your parenting life, your work life...'

'And your sanity might be saved,' said Becca. 'Talking of which. Mine is hanging by a thread. As you know, tomorrow night is the ITAs. Are you both coming? I was looking at the table plan and Entertainment at ITV has taken three tables, hosted by the lovely Tom Doherty, our *friend...*' She winked at Sinéad. 'And Susie Keane is coming...'

'I love her,' said Sinéad. 'She always looks amazing. I bet she doesn't eat mainly biscuits throughout the day.'

'I doubt it too,' I said.

'Are they an item?' Becca said to me. 'Only I got a call to the office and one of the girls said it was Susie checking on the table plan. Wanted to be put next to Tom. We said we couldn't confirm anything at the moment. And I thought he seemed to like you. A lot.'

'Me too,' said Sinéad. 'There was chemistry.'

And then we heard a voice behind us. 'Sinéad!'

Loping across the road, dressed in tracksuit bottoms and a faded T-shirt, dodging the bikes and the trikes and the dogs on leads, was Conor. 'The meeting is finished!'

Sinéad stood up, looking confused. 'I thought it was going to last another hour.'

'No, we wrapped up really quickly. I told them about you...'

'You told your clients about me?'

Conor was standing on the other side of the bench. 'Yes, I told them we had a three-year-old and that I have been working from home and... well, losing my rag...'

'I've been losing my rag too,' said Sinéad.

'Yes, I said that...' said Conor.

'Thanks,' said Sinéad.

'But it's true,' said Conor. 'And anyway, I told them how much I loved you and how much I loved our son and that without you I have nothing, and that you are everything to me. *Everything*. And that you make me laugh, and that you are sweet and intelligent and the most wonderful and impressive person I have ever met.'

Sinéad was looking at him, a smile dawning on her face. 'Conor,' she said. 'How embarrassing.'

'It's not,' he said. 'It's true. And I said that I was finding it hard to go back to the main office and my client said he also had social anxiety. And what about an office pod? And I said our garden is the size of—'

'A postage stamp,' said Becca and I.

'Yes,' said Conor. 'And then he said that he and *his* wife were on the brink of divorce. And he found this office pod thing and I googled it and they have them in Sandycove. Individual offices, your own workstations, proper coffee... I've just been down there, and there was this lovely woman on the desk and she says they are open until 10 p.m. every day and they have a vacancy.'

'So...?' said Sinéad.

'So, I'm booked in. I've taken one for a month, just to see. Tomorrow, you won't see me all day.'

Sinéad looked slightly overwhelmed. 'I won't *see* you?'

He shook his head. 'Not for hours and hours and hours. A proper day.'

'That is the best news ever,' said Sinéad. 'The thought of not seeing you is wonderful.'

'The thought of not seeing you too is wonderful,' said Conor, grinning.

'Your voice won't be echoing around the house,' she went on.

'The sound of your clippy feet won't be shattering my nerve endings,' said Conor.

'That smell of damp dog won't be lingering in the air when you've just vacated a room,' added Sinéad.

'And I'll be able to make myself a coffee without someone shouting after me to put the teaspoon in the dishwasher.'

They grinned at each other. 'It's wonderful!'

'It's brilliant!'

'I'm still going to go back to the office, though,' she said. 'Three days a week. Drink coffee, talk to humans, use my brain again.'

'And not watch *The Daily Show*?' I said, in mock horror.

'Catch-up,' she and Becca said together, but then, behind us, in one leap, Conor exhibited an athleticism that I didn't think even he knew he possessed because in a moment he was teetering on the back of the bench, one leg in the air, arms waving to keep him balanced, his face pure awe, and then he jumped down and toppled onto Sinéad and they both fell to the ground.

'Daddy,' said Rory, pointing with his chubby hand. 'Daddy has broken Mummy!'

'Mummy's fine,' shouted Sinéad, wriggling from beneath the hulking form of Conor. 'Good news, Rory, your parents won't be getting a divorce after all!'

* * *

After Sinéad, Conor and Rory had disappeared into the sunset together, Becca and I walked back to the village. Still no text from Tom about David and I was starting to get worried. What if he'd died?

'You know I'm on the coil,' Becca suddenly began. 'Have been for the last fifteen years...'

'Not really,' I said, 'but go on.'

'You *do* know,' she said. 'Remember? I told you about the incident when they couldn't get the old one out and the new one in, and the nurse took out a secret bottle of whiskey that she told me I was not to tell anyone about and only then it worked...'

'Of course. How could I forget yet another story of medical negligence and misadventure?'

'Well...' she went on, 'I have this feeling... that...' She stopped in the street, her face had drained of colour. 'I think... I don't know... I mean, I can't be, but I suppose I can be... it does happen... but I need to be sure. Because I can't sleep...'

'What is it?' I said.

'You know the spells I was doing? I was to do a fertility spell on Sinéad? And love for you and happiness for me... Well, I think I got them mixed up.'

'What do you mean?'

'I think I did the happiness for Sinéad – and it worked. I never realised I had such powers. And I've done the fertility one on me...'

'You're pregnant?'

Her eyes were so wide that she looked haunted. 'Maybe. I suppose it's possible, but I just don't believe it. I really don't. I mean, how could I be? I have to destroy that witch book,' she said. 'What if it fell into the wrong hands?'

I laughed. 'First of all, *if* you are pregnant, then you would have got pregnant before you bought the book. And, secondly, witches' spells don't work...'

She nodded. 'I know... I don't know what's got into me lately.' She held up a spiral of her hair. 'I haven't had hair like this since I was fifteen and discovered straighteners. My shoes are ugly and incredibly comfortable. I have been feeling ill every morning and then buying a *pain au chocolat* on my way to work.'

'And you think you're *pregnant*?'

She nodded. 'Will you do the test with me?'

* * *

Back at mine, I waited downstairs while Becca disappeared to the loo in my house, and then we stood, staring at the thing.

Finally, the alarm went off and I held up the instructions with the diagram and Becca looked at the test.

'Two lines,' she said. 'But they are faint. What does two faint lines mean?'

I studied the diagram and looked at her.

Her face fell. 'Look again,' she urged. 'Remember, they are faint. See what it says about faint lines.'

I looked again. 'Becca...' I began.

'Oh God.'

'It's happening,' I said.

'It can't be.'

'It is.'

Her hands were shaking as she put down the test. 'I need whiskey,' she said. 'Immediately. I've gone into shock.'

'You can't have whiskey,' I said.

'I can't have *whiskey*?' She looked as if she was about to cry. 'Oh God, this means no blue cheese. No shellfish. No nice things.'

'For nine months.'

'Nine months,' she repeated, shaking her head. 'Oh my God. Oh my God. OH MY GOD! I don't want to have a baby. But I'm having one. I am having a bloody baby!' And then she began to smile. 'I don't believe it! I really don't... This is the most exciting and wonderful thing that has ever happened to me.'

'I thought you didn't like babies?'

'So did I,' she said, her eyes gleaming with excitement. 'But that was before I was presented with my own! I love it already. And if it's a girl, I am going to call it Mabel.'

'And what about Ryan?'

'I hate the name Ryan!'

'No, what about telling him?'

'I'd better go home,' she said. 'Face the music. All I know is that I want Mabel. Or Marvin. Or whatever it is.'

I dropped her home and my phone beeped. A text from Tom.

David doing well. Will live to negotiate another contract!

And I turned my car around and drove straight to hospital.

47

I knocked on the door of the private room in the expensive wing of St Vincent's Hospital. It was all beige and cream, with fake potted plants and patients wandering around in silk dressing gowns and expensive slippers.

'Come in.' David sounded frail.

'It's me, David,' I said, stepping inside the room.

Jennifer, sitting on the chair beside the bed, reading *Hello!* magazine, looked up and smiled.

David didn't look much better since I'd last seen him, laid out on the stretcher, being wheeled up the gurney of the ambulance. His skin was still grey under his fake tan. He was wearing burgundy silk pyjamas but his teeth glowed in the UV lamp above the door.

'I just bought you a few things.' I handed him the paper bag.

'Well, that,' he said, 'is remarkably kind.' David was peering through the paper bag. 'Oh, Red Bull. Thank God. And crisps. And...'

There was a loud tut from Jennifer. 'David,' she said sharply. 'You can't drink that stuff, you know that! You have to stay *off* the caffeine. It might have got your heart going again, but you're also on medication.'

I felt awful for bringing him a drink that was obviously so bad for him, however much he loved it.

David sank back into the hospital pillows, defeated. 'Everyone drinks it though.'

'Not seventy-somethings,' said Jennifer, rolling her eyes. 'Think of your heart.'

'But I'm only...' he began, and then stopped, as though the game was up. 'Look, I'm not fifty-nine,' he said to me. 'I'm seventy-three. In the old days, men my age would have been pottering around the golf course, shuffling along the streets, waiting for the Grim Reaper. Not any longer. We're vibrant, fit, able to work, but this industry is so ageist. I didn't want to be shunted off to a nursing home for bewildered former broadcasters, wandering the corridors of the TV centre, trying to force people to talk to me. I wanted to be on-screen, where I was born to be, bathing in the hot lights of television. I am only truly alive when the red light is on.' He reached over and took Jennifer's hand. 'Actually, that's a lie. I am only truly alive when I have this woman by my side.'

Jennifer rolled her eyes again. 'What *am* I going to do with you?'

'I thought you were going to go off with one of the Four Paddys,' said David.

Jennifer shook her head. 'No thank you very much. They wouldn't be able to hold much of a conversation and their personal hygiene wouldn't be as good as yours. I like a man who smells as though he showers at least once a day and wears nice aftershave. However *old* he is.' She smiled at him.

David looked pleased. 'I'm very lucky,' he said. 'Very lucky indeed.' He looked back at me. 'I know I should have waited until the show was on a break, but my doctor had a cancellation. And if you knew how hard it is to get Botox from the best in this town, then you would have gone for it as well.'

Jennifer shook her head at me.

'Anyway,' David went on, 'Tom was in earlier with a plan. I am going to do a big double-page spread in the *Sunday Independent* this week, explaining everything. Tom says it's my renaissance, my coming out as a new champion for the older man. He says I'm an attractive, well-dressed gent, one with, if you don't mind me saying, not an immoderate amount of sex appeal.'

Jennifer rolled her eyes. 'Sex appeal. This is the man who likes an early night, pyjamas on.'

'My pyjamas are silk,' said David. 'My mother always said a man must be a gentleman in the bedroom.'

'That's not what she meant,' said Jennifer.

David looked confused for a moment.

'Anyway,' said Jennifer, 'David is usually asleep before he's finished his crossword. I have to finish it for him.'

David nodded sadly. 'I am wholly representative of my age group. Which is Tom's big idea. He's helping with my rebranding. And he's going to give me a new show, called *David Exclamation Mark*.'

'*David Exclamation Mark*?' I said.

Jennifer held up *Hello!* 'The exclamation mark is silent,' she said. 'Like David should be now. He needs to rest.' She took his hand and patted it. 'What are we going to do with you? What am *I* to do with you?'

He shrugged. 'Throw me on the rubbish heap of life?'

Jennifer laughed. 'Now you're milking it,' she said.

As I stood to leave, David clutched at the sleeve of my cardigan. 'Thank you, Cat, for being a wonderful co-presenter. I hope Tom has offered you something very nice indeed.'

'I'm going back to *Farming Weekly*,' I said.

David shuddered. 'Please don't,' he said. 'I can't bear to think of you there, out in the cold and rain, talking to people in mud-splattered clothes about blight, badgers and botulism.'

'I thought it was botulism you injected into your eyes, David,' said Jennifer, handing me the paper bag with the Red Bull in it. 'He doesn't need it,' she said. 'You take it.'

But David, with his tanned and bony hand, like that of E.T., reached out. 'You never know when I might need it,' he said, sliding the bag under his pillow. 'Everything in moderation. I promise.' He looked up at me. 'You'll have to present on your own tomorrow.'

'It won't be the same without you,' I said.

'I think you'll do okay,' he said. 'We'll be watching. Go and show them what you can do. Break a leg.'

* * *

Before I left the hospital, I took the lift to the top floor, to St Theresa's Ward, far from the glossy private wing where David was. This was a very ordinary, slightly run-down, disinfectant-smelling ward. Two rows of beds on either side, visitors and patients talking quietly to each other. At the far end, I spotted Malachy, sitting beside the bed of his mam, holding her hand. She was propped up on the pillows, wearing a pale yellow cardigan over a floral nightdress.

They looked up as I stepped, as quietly as I could, towards them. 'I thought I would just see how you both were,' I said. 'I was visiting someone else on the third floor.'

Malachy smiled. 'That's very kind of you, Cat,' he said. 'Mam, this is Cat, she's joined us at the Forty Foot. Remember? The Forty Foot? You used to bring me down there when I was little? Swimming? Dad used to love it there, didn't he? Remember?'

His mam looked blankly at him.

'Good evening, Mrs Murphy,' I said, putting one of my hands over hers. 'I hope you're nice and comfortable?'

'We're not bad, are we, Mam?' said Malachy. 'The nurses are top-class and the food… well, it's surprisingly nice.' He turned to his mam. 'Not a patch on your dinners, but there's a very nice nurse who is making sure I get an extra portion.' He smiled at me. 'We're just waiting to see what the doctors say in the morning. They're trying to find a place for her in a really lovely home. Honeysuckle Lodge. Do you know it? It's behind the church in Sandycove. Really nice, by all accounts. Lots to do there, isn't there, Mam? Didn't they say there was music and there's a bridge club… Not that you're into that, are you?' He looked at me. 'They're ringing around tonight to see if there's a room available.' He looked unbearably sad for a moment and then, as though putting on a mask, turned again to his mam. 'You can bring in all your favourite things. Blankets, photographs… we'll have to have that good one of Dad, the one where you always said he looked like Jimmy Stewart. And… what else?'

His mam just stared into space.

'Mrs Murphy,' I said, taking out another carrier bag, 'I've bought you some cake, from Sally-Anne's in the village. Fruit cake with almonds on top. She gave me six slices, so you can have some now and more tomorrow.' I turned to Malachy. 'I asked her for the ones with as many almonds as possible.' I unwrapped the paper and laid the cake, in its papery plate, on Mrs Murphy's lap. 'Malachy said you were the queen of fruit cake,' I went on.

She looked down at her lap, blinking at it, as though curious. 'Spider cake,' she said calmly. 'Is it made with spiders?'

'No, Mam,' said Malachy, 'dried fruit.'

Mrs Murphy looked up at me and then stared at my face. 'I've seen you,' she said. 'I've seen you…'

'Mam, you've never met Cat before,' said Malachy, shrugging apologetically at me.

'No, I've seen you, with Davy Fitz.'

'Yes,' I nodded. 'With Davy Fitz.'

'You came round to tea...'

'That's right. Tea... and cake.'

'Tea and spider cake,' she said. 'With almonds on top.'

'Maybe tomorrow,' said Malachy, 'is going to be an almond day? What do you think, Mam?'

Her eyes were blank as though she'd retreated again.

'Every day could be an almond day,' went on Malachy. 'You've just got to see the almonds.'

'How are we all doing?' Behind us stood a very nice-looking nurse. 'Mrs Murphy? All well?'

'Thank you, Jess,' said Malachy, blushing suddenly. 'Mam's doing well, aren't you, Mam?'

Jess smiled back at Malachy. 'I'm finishing my shift now,' she said. 'I just thought I'd say goodbye and that I'd see you tomorrow.'

'Oh right...' Malachy hesitated. 'I could...'

Jess was nodding. 'You could walk me to my car? Oh yes, that would be lovely.'

Malachy stood up. 'Be back in a few minutes, Mam,' he said, suddenly smiling. 'I won't be long. Don't want Jess finding her way out to the car park all alone, do we?'

Today, I thought, was definitely one of Malachy's almond days.

THE GIRLS!

Me: HOW ARE YOU?

Becca: Strangely calm. Ridiculously excited. Overwhelmed. Happy. Now, trying to focus on the last-minute arrangements for the ITAs. Anything could go wrong and I wouldn't care.

Me: Have you told Ryan?

Becca: Not yet. Trying to find the right time. You are coming to the awards, aren't you? I can put your name on the door. Sinéad and Conor are coming.

Me: Not sure. Will let you know.

Becca: Thanks for everything. I don't know what I'd do without you.

Me: Me too.

Becca: And you are coming. I want you there! Xxx

48

When I arrived in work the next morning, for my final day on *The Daily Show*, there was a huge bunch of flowers on my desk. 'They're from all of us,' said Angela, 'just to say thank you and we'll miss you.'

Ava hovered behind her. 'You've been a marked improvement on the other two,' she said. 'But they'll probably be back, reinvigorated after their time off, ready to annoy us and the nation again.'

'We've all got two weeks off and then back on-air,' said Angela. 'But something's happening. I can tell it is. David's agent has just tweeted about very exciting moves for David and Barbara. But Tom isn't saying anything. Has he spoken to you?'

'I'm going back to *Farming Weekly*,' I said. 'That's all I know.' I didn't like to mention *David!* Just in case I wasn't meant to know.

'We'll miss you.' Angela smiled at me. 'It's been lovely having you.'

'I'll miss you too,' I said. 'But I've learned a lot and I can't believe it's only been four weeks. Come on. Let's go and have our last meeting.'

My phone beeped in my bag. A message on Forty Footers from Margaret.

Malachy and his mam are on way to Honeysuckle Lodge. Found room for her. Good news.

I quickly texted back.

Great. I'll drop in later.

Nora was already typing.

Tell Malachy I have a kettle and small fridge for the room. Tabitha says she will drop them in later.

Dolores was typing just as Brenda joined in.

I thought I could call in over the weekend and do the ladies' hair and bit of make-up. Nails and whatnot. Could do it weekly? Love to Malachy. Give him a big hug from me. Can't call in today as have award ceremony tonight and will be on duty from late afternoon. Won't be swimming either xxx

Dolores finished her message.

Come swimming tonight, Malachy. You need it.

And then Malachy responded.

See you at the Forty Foot at 6 p.m. Thanks all.

Tom caught up with Angela, Ava and me, carrying coffee for all of us. A paper bag was balanced on top and held on with his chin. 'Decent coffee,' he said, as we pushed open the door of the conference room and sat ourselves around the table, 'in honour of Cat's last meeting.' He placed a cup in front of each of us. 'And cakes. We can't let Cat go without a celebration.'

'Coffee *and* cake?' said Ava. 'Talk about pushing the boat out. Who left you in charge of the petty cash?'

'Talking of which,' said Tom, 'I've already put a lot of money behind the bar for the awards this evening.'

Angela interrupted him. 'And will you be bringing a certain gorgeous woman as your date?'

Tom looked surprised. 'Who?' he said. 'Are you talking about my cleaning lady, Mrs O'Donovan? Because she says she's too busy.'

'I actually meant the one and only Susie Keane,' said Angela. 'Just wondering if you are going to corroborate my source?'

Tom shook his head. 'It's an amazing thing, office gossip. It is based on absolutely no truth at all.' He quickly glanced at me.

'So, it's true then, is it?' said Angela, grinning at me and Ava.

'Angela,' said Tom, 'I keep my private life very private, as you know.'

'Which is why I'm asking,' said Angela. 'I just think that it's best to tell us just in case we say the wrong thing.'

'Well, if I have any news,' said Tom, 'you'll be the first to know.'

'That confirms it,' said Angela. 'You're an item.'

'Angela, please...' Tom seemed flustered and looked at me. 'Still not coming?'

I shook my head. 'I need to do a few things...'

'Like what?' said Angela. 'What's more important than having a glass of champagne with me and Ava?'

'Nothing,' said Ava, 'that's what.'

'Well...' I began.

'You've *got* to come tonight,' said Angela. 'I've got my sparkly gold suit all ready to go.'

'And *I've* ironed my Robert Smith T-shirt,' said Ava.

'I think I am just going to go swimming at the Forty Foot,' I said. 'It's kind of my therapy now... can't miss a session.' I smiled at them. 'Anyway...' I said, changing the subject, 'I really hope David gets best presenter.'

'Well...' Tom looked at Angela. 'He's up against stiff competition, including one of the Four Paddys – God knows which one. Also Dingo O'Bingo and Valentine O'Malley... Valentine isn't going to get it, but Paddy or Dingo are in for a shout.'

'David's going to be devastated,' said Angela. 'I was hoping that winning would make him feel better about everything. I know he's a dose, but he's *our* dose. I rang him this morning and spoke to Jennifer. She says he'll be in hospital for another few days at least. Whatever his doctor gave him...'

'Some kind of black tar botulism,' said Tom. 'The doctors have been trying to syringe it out of his face. He was looking far from his linen-suited best when I was in the hospital with him yesterday.'

'He should just embrace ageing,' said Ava. 'That's what my mam does. She's gone full hag and says she's never been happier. She hasn't brushed her hair in five years, just keeps it really short. She talks to the birds and eats as much chocolate as she wants. She genuinely has never looked better.'

'Sounds bliss,' said Angela, enviously.

'Imagine,' I said, 'just letting everything go...'

The sea gave you that feeling, though. When I was in the water, moving with the waves, hair streaming, face half-submerged in the cold, salty water, it was utter freedom from everything... *every* single thing, until there was just you, a tiny body in a giant ocean, a speck in this great primordial soup we call existence.

'Right,' said Angela. 'Let's get on with the day. So, PJ Doyle will be joining us again... unfortunately, he was booked before the incident. He promised us it was a one-off and that he will behave himself.' She shrugged. 'The problem is the audience love him. Our ratings are up thirty-five per cent this last month and I think we can put it down to a combination of Cat and edgier items such as PJ.'

'I'm not sure about him,' said Tom. 'At all. I thought he was unpleasant last time. Messing with David's hair.' He glanced at me. 'I don't want to subject Cat to him.'

'It's not ideal.' Angela turned to me. 'It's your decision, Cat. What do you want? Do you want PJ on the show today?'

Absolutely not, I thought. But how could I make a fuss? Wouldn't that make me a diva? It was my last show. How bad could it be?'

'Yes,' I said. 'It will be fine.'

* * *

It was just me on the sofa, staring at the cameras, Angela's voice in my ear. 'Okay?' she said. 'Coming to you in ten... nine...' I was on my own, no one to interact with. I missed David. He never missed a cue, was never short for anything to say and was never anything but utterly energised by that little red light.

I wondered if he was feeling any better. He'd probably have to watch the awards from his hospital bed and I could just imagine how angry he would be if someone else won.

'And three... two... one... we're live...' Angela's voice made me start.

'Good afternoon!' I began, reading the autocue. 'And welcome to *The Daily Show*... Now, you will remember on yesterday's show that David became unwell and, thankfully, I am so glad to report that he is very much recovered. Just taking a little rest and relaxation, his feet up and he's watching us now. Hello, David, get well soon...'

I got through the show, interviewing a woman who'd given up her career as a chartered accountant to become a unicycling, juggling street performer and a woman who believed she could talk to ghosts. As a solo presenter, the show had gone better than I could have imagined. At last, I was on the home straight... just the cooking segment with PJ before it was the final goodbye to *The Daily Show*.

During the ad break, I walked over to position myself at the kitchen area. I smiled. 'What are we cooking today, PJ? Something smells pretty good...'

'Pretty good?' he said. 'That's a distinctly underwhelming response. I would say that it smells incredible, that's what I would say. Garlic, fresh herbs, the sautéing of alliums in olive oil... Not the kind of cooking my mother did, that's for sure.'

I peered into the saucepan. 'Hollandaise?'

He nodded. 'Deceptively difficult to get right.'

'What's the secret?'

'A light touch, the right amount of butter ratio. Knowing the exact moment to take it off the heat. Here.' He dipped a spoon into the sauce. 'Taste it.'

It wasn't the usual flour-heavy, clumpy sauce that was oh-so normal to us mere mortals. 'Amazing,' I admitted.

He nodded. 'I know.' And then he turned to the oven and took out a piece of white fish that was wrapped in foil. 'Hake,' he said. 'Freshly caught this morning, baked with butter... but my own home-made butter. And you can't overcook it, or undercook it. Ten seconds either side and it's ruined.'

'How is it now?'

He nodded. 'Perfect. But I'll put another one in, just in case your preamble takes too long.' He raised an eyebrow.

'I'll keep it short,' I said.

Angela was in my ear. 'Thirty seconds.'

'Do you miss my cooking?' he said, trying to flirt. 'Or at least *anything* about me?'

I ignored him, checked my notes, cleared my throat.

'There must be *something*,' he persisted.

'Ten seconds,' said Angela.

'Come on...' PJ put his arm around my waist. 'My cooking... my conversation... my... *coq...*' – he paused, staring at me – '*au vin...*?'

'We're live,' said Angela.

'And you're very welcome back to the show,' I said, smiling down the camera. 'And as it's Friday,' I went on, 'you might want to do a little bit of cooking this weekend. Our guest chef, PJ Doyle, is here to show us something we could all try... What are you making today, PJ?'

'Lightly buttered hake,' he said, smiling charmingly as though he hadn't just grabbed me. 'Sweet leeks and a lovely white sauce...'

In my ear, Angela said, in a serious voice, 'Are you *okay*?'

PJ was still smiling. 'I love cooking for people,' he was saying. 'You know, for people you love.' He looked into the camera. 'It's a shame when people don't appreciate you.'

I laughed nervously. 'Who wouldn't appreciate a man who can cook?'

PJ laughed. 'Well, *you* didn't... Here...' He picked up a large forkful of the hake, added a jangle of leeks and a scoop of sauce and thrust it at my face. He laughed as I felt the sauce smear over my chin and cheek. 'Sorry, Cat... oops!'

I looked around to try to find a tea towel, but all I could see was the damp cloth used for wiping down the surfaces. But PJ picked it up first and wiped my face.

'I thought he was meant to be behaving himself,' said Angela. 'We're sending on Una as a distraction. He's a madman.'

Next moment, Una, the juggling unicyclist from earlier in the show, pedalled on to the set.

'Would you like some fish?' PJ called to her.

'No thank you,' she called, cycling past, her clubs circling in the air above her.

'Ten seconds,' said Angela. 'Just get ready to say your goodbyes.' Martin had moved forward to count us down to the end of the show. 'Seven... six... five...'

'And that's it from *The Daily Show*,' I said. 'Thanks to all our guests... PJ Doyle, Una the Unicyclist and everyone else... We're taking a break for a couple of weeks and then *The Daily Show* will return! Thanks for having me...'

My heart was beating hard, my head was reeling. I steadied myself on the counter in front of me. Keeping cool on-air was extremely difficult, it was more than acting, you had the weight of the entire production on your shoulders, everyone relying on you not to be anything but utterly in control. But it was all over. We were off-air and the crew all broke into applause.

'Thank you, everyone,' I said, feeling a little emotional. My month on *The Daily Show* had come to an end. Brenda appeared, the girls from wardrobe, Martin, Dmitri, Ava. Angela was opening up a bottle of champagne.

There was a tap on my shoulder. Tom. 'Are you okay?'

I nodded.

'Sure?'

'I'm grand.' I was. Embarrassed, humiliated, I supposed, but ultimately grand.

'That was practically an assault...'

'It doesn't matter... and it wasn't really an assault... I just need to block him from my life again.'

'But you should never have been put in that situation...'

Now it was PJ who was tapping me on the shoulder, he then moved in between me and Tom. 'We should go for a drink,' he said, smiling again. 'There's no reason why two old friends can't go for a drink together, is there?' He turned to Tom. 'We used to go out with each other,' he said. 'Did you know that?'

Tom looked at him. 'I think it might be better if you left. And I don't like you touching my presenters, feeding them, trying to be in control. Not here. Not in my studio. Stick to cooking and charging those exorbitant prices.'

PJ gaped at Tom. 'But I was only trying to be nice,' he said. 'Just trying to talk to Cat.'

Tom shook his head. 'It's best if you don't...' he said, firmly.

PJ opened his mouth to speak again and then decided against it. He turned around and walked out, his tea towel still on his shoulder.

'Drinks in my office, everyone,' said Tom. 'To raise a glass to Cat? And then we can go to the ITAs? It's a shame David won't be able to make it...'

This month of saying 'yes' was over. It had been more stressful, more challenging than I could have imagined. But what I had gained was immeasurable. I was braver, more resilient and ready for my next adventure. So instead of going upstairs to be with them all, I went straight to my dressing room, scooping up my cards and flowers, my bag and jacket, and left the building. The thought of stretching out my body in that cold water, my breathing slowing down, my brain stopping whirring...

To the sea, I thought, to lose my mind and find my soul.

49

The Forty Footers – minus Brenda – were all changed and ready to get in when I arrived, slightly breathless. The sun was beginning to set, bathing the world in a golden cloak of evening sunshine. The rocks under my feet hot from baking in the summer sun all day, the air calm and the sea so still it was like a vast mirror, shimmering and glinting. The Forty Foot was packed with people and the tribe had been pushed to one small corner of the changing area.

Margaret was just pulling on her swimming cap, Nora was replaiting her hair, Dolores was sitting in the sun, her face to the sky, eyes closed, Mick was beside her, looking very content. And Malachy was standing a little to one side, as though unsure of what to do.

'How's your mam?' I asked him.

'She is doing well,' he said, nodding as though trying to convince himself. 'Place is nice, the staff seem kind. And we've decorated her room with some of her bits and pieces...'

'Ornaments,' said Dolores. 'Pictures... a lovely one of Malachy when he was knee-high to a leprechaun.'

'We had no idea he was so chubby,' said Nora.

'A cherubim,' said Margaret.

'And in a sailor suit,' said Dolores. 'Like a royal baby.'

'Mam was given that by this woman she used to work with,' Malachy said. 'She'd never buy that normally. But she did say I didn't look like her baby that day. She always said it was as though she'd borrowed a much posher baby for the day of the photograph.' He smiled. 'She always put me in nice clothes, though. Everything was ironed. I hope they iron her clothes in Honeysuckle Lodge.'

'Ah, they will of course,' said Dolores. 'The place is only beautiful. My friend Pauline is one of the nurses. It's a lovely place, a real home from home. And she says they have great craic all the time, there's always something going on.'

I sat on one of the benches, next to Nora.

'We thought that maybe you weren't coming,' said Margaret. 'Isn't there an awards thing tonight?'

'I'm not going,' I said.

'Not going?' said Nora. 'I thought it was a big deal. Tabitha and Red, my son-in-law, said they'd be watching it. You should go. Have some fun.'

'I wouldn't mind having something to go to,' said Margaret. 'You know, you run out of big events as you get older.'

'Me too,' said Dolores. 'Mick was only saying the other day that he and I should get ourselves dressed up and go out for a meal sometime. Weren't you, Mick? Step up from fish and chips.'

'That's where we differ,' said Nora. 'I'd rather have my right arm amputated than have to go to an event. The very idea of having to dress a certain way, talk to boring people... I'm not a small-talk kind of person. I only do big talk.'

'I like the people going, though,' I said. 'My colleagues Ava and Angela... and I still like getting dressed up. It might have been fun...' Except Tom would be there with Susie and there was no way I wanted to make it awkward. Best to just leave it.

One by one, we stepped into the sea, Margaret singing her hymn – '*hope for tomorrow*' – just ahead of me, and then it was my turn, my body cutting through the water, pushing out through the people, paddling further out to sea until I felt the water get colder. I swam along the coast and then drifted on my back for a while.

The others were already changing again and I could see Margaret drying herself with a towel and Dolores swishing her robe around herself in a queenly manner, stopping when she saw Mick making his way towards them, across the rocks, smiling, his hand in the air. And there was Malachy talking to Nora, her making him laugh.

I was so glad I had found them, I thought, and this. Something simple, something free, something for everyone.

Out to sea was the red bobbing buoy. I'd never made it that far, even after a month of daily swims. But this evening, I felt braver than ever, and I reached my arms overhead, and pulled myself towards it. Stroke by stroke, arm over arm, I kept going, the voices from the Forty Foot getting fainter, the silence of the sea, deep water beneath me, pushing through any of my fears, until my hands touched it, the orange rope anchoring it to the seabed draped in green seaweed. Now, that wasn't too bad, I thought, as I held on to the buoy, for a moment, looking back to shore. Everything looks insurmountable before you start doing it. The thing was just to start doing something. Say yes to life.

I began my swim back in, leaving the buoy behind. Now I'd done it once, I'd do it the next time.

I swam back to the rocks and pulled myself up onto dry land, and as Margaret handed out the mugs of tea, 'To what or to whom are we drinking this evening?' said Nora.

'To Malachy's mam,' said Margaret, 'and everyone in Honeysuckle Lodge.'

We held up our cups and stood around Malachy. 'Thank you,'

he said. 'I'll tell Mam when I see her in the morning.' And then he stopped, his cup held mid-air. 'She won't be there when I get home,' he said. 'For the first time in my life, Mam will be gone.'

Margaret put her arm around him. 'She'll still be everywhere,' she said. 'Just let her spirit find you...'

'She's not dead yet, Dolores!' said Nora. 'Jesus! She's only up the road in Honeysuckle Lodge. No, Malachy,' she said, turning to him, 'she won't be there and it will be lonely, but you can sleep properly tonight knowing that she's in a safe place and, in the morning, someone will be there to have breakfast with her...'

'And Brenda's going in to do their hair and make-up,' reminded Margaret.

'And I thought I could drop in some bottles of ginger ale and some crisps,' said Mick. 'You know, like, from the pub. They could have them as a treat tomorrow afternoon.'

'That's a lovely idea, Mick,' said Nora, as Dolores nodded proudly.

Malachy looked beyond us, his face lighting up. Walking towards us, her arm raised in a wave, was the nurse from the hospital. 'It's Jess,' he said. 'A friend of mine. She said she'd come down after her shift. I started my new job today... team leader... so it's all change...'

He raised his hand to her. Margaret, Nora and Dolores all nodded at each other, trying not to show too much interest and not to embarrass Malachy.

I checked my phone where there was a text from Becca.

Please please please please please please come! The place looks amazing. Would love you to see the hotel. You can just be with me all night if you don't want to be with the TV crowd. Can't believe what happened earlier.

Sinéad texted.

I'm getting ready now. See you there?

And then one from Tom

Ticket is on the door. Would love to see you. If you can tear yourself away from the sea. PS would REALLY love to see you xx

I put my phone away, trying to listen to the chat of the Forty Footers, and drink my tea. Except... I thought of Tom, taking out my phone and looking at his text again. Why was he so keen to see me?

'I'd better go,' I said, suddenly, standing up, and not really saying goodbye, as I broke into a run on my way back to my car. I think the wheels actually screeched as I sped away from the sea, away from my swimming tribe and on my way to my other life.

* * *

Back at home, after my shower, I took out my old, faithful black dress which was tight and had feathers around the hem, and my 'yes' necklace. My hair still damp, I drove straight to the TV studio. Brenda was in the make-up room with three other stylists and make-up artists and a trail of women in different stages of awards readiness.

'You made it!' Brenda called over the sound of the hairdryers. 'Michael there will do your hair and then come to me for make-up. Michael, will you do Cat next?'

Michael patted his chair and I sat down and he began to blow-dry my hair and then Brenda started on my make-up.

'I'll keep it natural,' she said, dabbing and daubing at me.

I told her about swimming out to the buoy.

'It's remarkable what we're all capable of,' she said. 'It's only when you look back, do you see what you've achieved. And I hope you are all right after this afternoon,' she went on. 'I mean, why would they let that awful PJ on again after the wig attack? That's the problem with producers. All they care about is ratings. Tom is furious.'

Eventually, she declared me ready.

'Not bad,' she said, smiling. 'Time to go to the ball, Cinders... Now, off you go, they'll be arriving by now.'

THE GIRLS!

Me: I'm coming!

Sinéad: Yay!

Becca: Yay too! Talk later. Just a bit busy.

Sinéad: What are you wearing? I haven't worn anything glam in years.

Becca: My black dress.

Sinéad: Good idea. I have my red one. Gold shoes. Done. Rory is being looked after by his granny. See you later xxx

50

The Hotel Oscar Wilde was on one of Dublin's most beautiful squares, in the heart of the Georgian Quarter. On two sides of the square were terraces of the famous houses dating back from the late 1700s, with curved fanlights above the wide, brightly coloured doors which were once residences of the upper classes but were now mainly offices. On one end was the National Gallery and the houses of parliament and at the other end was the hotel.

Tonight, the whole street outside the hotel was strung with lights, as though a field of stars was balanced overhead. The place was in chaos, with taxis pulling up, discharging ball-gowned and tuxedoed guests, before pulling away. Hotel staff in top hats waved traffic on as the glamorous and the good of Irish TV made their way towards the golden carpet, which spilled out of the wide door of the hotel and on to the street, past a bank of photographers who were yelling at the stars to stop and pose just for them.

All of the Four Paddys were dressed in identical tuxedos and I spotted Dingo O'Bingo giving peace signs for fans' selfies, and everywhere there were actors from the soap operas and news presenters. And then, bathed in the lights of the flashbulbs, in sunglasses, a pink linen suit, sleeves – of course – pushed up, and sockless, was David.

'Feeling much better, thank you,' I heard him call out to the bank of photographers and showbiz journalists. 'Yes, exhaustion, working too hard! Much rested now! Thank you... thank you... thank you... thank you... I know! I do look good for my age... Ponds Cold Cream is my secret and good genes... Yes, thank you... give her my number and tell your granny to call me!' He was enjoying himself. And then he spotted me. 'Catríona!' he called out. 'Come and stand with me for a moment.' There were flashes from the cameras. 'The dream team,' David was saying. And then in my ear, he said, 'Thanks for the Red Bull. It was like a shot of adrenaline! I am being powered solely by caffeine. Jennifer is furious, but I said to her I was not missing tonight. I could be dead tomorrow! Literally!' He blew a kiss to someone beyond us, at the door of the hotel, and there was Jennifer, dressed fabulously in a tiny black sequinned dress, glaring at him. 'She's refusing to pose with me,' he said. 'Still angry that I am not in hospital, but if you can't defy your doctor's orders, what can you do? It's the rebellion of the septuagenarian.' He laughed wildly again, his whitewashed teeth flashing, as he posed in different shapes. 'I hear you're leaving the show,' he went on. 'I would have thought you would have been angling for the job full-time.'

'I don't have your charisma or your talent for live television,' I said.

For a moment, a look of genuine pleasure bloomed on his taut face and tears formed in his eyes, behind his sunglasses. 'Thank you, Cat,' he said. 'But I have to say that I've been very impressed with you. You have a charm that is totally natural. Likeability, I call it. The rest of us fake it. Some of us fake it very well. But you just have it.' He squeezed my arm.

'Thank you, David,' I said.

I walked into the hotel, stopping briefly to chat to Jennifer. 'I know I signed up for this,' she said. 'But he really is incorrigible. All my other friends are married to estate agents and bankers. And I chose Davy Fitz.' She shook her head. 'But then my friends are all bored out of their brains. Their partners don't do anything but play golf and go on and on about house prices.'

In the foyer, Becca was shouting orders into her mobile phone. She waved, excitedly, when she saw me, and rushed over, clipboard in hand. 'You came! Oh, thank God!' She hugged me tightly. 'You look magnificent. Like a film star. You are glowing. Must be all that bathing in sea water.'

'How are you?'

'All my bourgeois dreams come true!' she said. 'I'm a bit worried because of the amount of mojitos I drank the other night, but Ryan's booked me in for a scan first thing Monday morning and I think it's such early days that Mabel or Marvin will be okay.'

We hugged each other, dancing up and down. 'That's brilliant,' I said. 'I'm so glad.'

'Sinéad's just over there, with Conor and Ryan, she's already had a couple of cosmopolitans and is now on the Pornstar Martinis.'

Sinéad came over and hugged me hello. 'Oh my God,' she said, slurrily, 'this is the mosssst glamorous thing I've ever been to. I just saw Valentine O'Malley and Ssssusie Keane looking beautiful. Everything and everyone is just ssssso nice. And it's so good to be out of the house. Conor's mum is minding Rory. She almost cried with happiness when I asked her. And Conor's booked us into Kelly's hotel for the weekend tomorrow, just the three of us. Conor says we are only allowed to go if we have dinner all alone and I'm to have a massage and a facial.' She smiled at us and she looked immediately just like the old Sinéad, the one she used to be, before she was so worried about everything. But then she teared up. 'Rory,' she said. 'I missss him.' But then, just as quickly as the tears arrived, they dried up and she smiled. 'But I also love this. Being with my favourite people and a small drink or two.'

'Or fifteen,' said Becca. 'You're basically a lost cause.' She smiled. 'Drink up, because tonight is your night, Cinderella. You deserve it.'

Conor and Ryan were drinking pints and in deep conversation.

'And Sinéad...' went on Becca. 'I have some news.'

'What kind of news?' said Sinéad, suspiciously.

'Ryan,' called Becca, 'come and tell Sinéad.'

At the bar, Ryan gave her a nod and walked over smiling. 'Well,' he said to Sinéad, slipping his arm around Becca, 'we're having a baby.'

For a moment, Sinéad was silent, her mouth opening and closing, her face a kaleidoscope of confusion, puzzlement and then, finally, joy.... then she flung her arms around Becca. 'This is wonderful,' she said, and then paused. '*Is* it wonderful?'

Becca was nodding. 'I wanted to tell you in person. But yes, it's wonderful and I'm really, *really* happy about it. I think I got my spells mixed up. You happiness, me fertility...'

'It was something of a shock,' said Ryan. 'A good shock.'

'I thought Ryan was going to leave me...' said Becca.

'Never,' he replied.

'But from the moment I saw I was pregnant, I just knew I wanted it...' Becca shrugged. 'I mean, I was looking forward to a glass of champagne at the ITAs tonight. But all I can think about is Mabel...'

'Mabel?' said Sinéad.

'Or Marvin,' said Becca. 'We haven't decided yet.' Her mobile rang. 'Tell him that ice sculpture is meant to be like that!' she shouted. 'I'll be over now.' She turned to me. 'The ice sculpture was meant to be a microphone but has melted into something disturbingly phallic. Stay there. I'll be right back, okay?' She went one way, while Conor and Ryan drifted to the bar again, to resume their conversation. 'So,' I heard Ryan say, 'you're bringing Rory swimming... how soon could I do that with ours...?'

Next, I was tapped on the shoulder by Angela and Ava, both with glasses of champagne in their hands. 'And we thought you weren't coming!' Angela gave me a bear hug. 'It's great to see you.'

'This is my friend Sinéad. Sinéad, Angela and Ava, the brains behind *The Daily Show*.'

'That's us,' said Ava. 'The people who bring you daily dross.'

'Apart from the wonderful Cat,' said Angela. 'Who I must say made the whole show wonderful.'

'Thanks. Angela,' I said. 'And by the way, great suit...'

'Too gold?' she said. 'Ava said I looked like an Oscar statuette.'

'I just don't believe gold is a colour,' said Ava. 'Now, *black* on the other hand...' Ava was wearing a slightly elevated version of her Curehead daywear. Her black tights were ripped, her black puffball skirt was paired with a black T-shirt with Mrs Robert Smith scrawled in red across the chest.

'Can you believe that David made it to the awards?' said Angela. 'He's our very own Lazarus.'

'If Lazarus had amazing teeth, which I doubt very much,' said Ava.

And then I heard a voice. 'Well, if it isn't *The Daily Show* dream team.' Tom, dressed immaculately in black tie, was standing behind me, smiling. 'It wouldn't have been the same without you, not after the last month we've had.'

Ava and Angela shook their heads. 'It's felt like a year,' said Ava. 'In a good way.'

'So...?' Tom was still looking at me. 'What persuaded you...?'

'Nothing really,' I said, thinking of his text.

'We're going to get some of those nibbles,' said Angela, and she and Ava drifted off, arm in arm.

'Get me ssssome!' yelled Sinéad to their retreating forms, but Tom was looking straight at me. Last time he'd looked at me like that was when he took my mug of tea out of my hand when we were in bed and... oh God.

'You look...' he began, and then stopped.

'Beautiful,' said Sinéad. 'We both look beautttifullll? Am I right? Thass what you were going to say, yes?'

Tom laughed. 'Yes... but I didn't know if it was appropriate.'

'Iss allways appropret,' said Sinéad. 'Now, I need anozzer drink. Anozzer Martini... be righttt back... where's Conor...?'

Tom smiled. 'Glad she's having a good time,' he said. 'But you do... you do look absolutely beautiful... I just wanted to say that... and... well...' He opened his mouth, about to speak again.

'Tom Doherty! Would you ever go and get a girl a glass of champagne!' Standing behind him, wearing a pale blue strapless fishtail dress, her hair piled on her head and looking ravishing, was Susie Keane. 'I need topping up!' She shook her head at me. 'This man is very hard to pin down, have you noticed... *Katie*?'

'I don't know...' I said.

'It's Cat,' said Tom, but Susie wasn't listening. Instead, she gripped his arm, possessively, turning away from me.

'The awards are about to start. We have to go in,' she said. 'You can find me a glass of champagne once we're sitting down.'

Tom turned to me. 'We can make room for you on the Entertainment table? We can always squeeze in another chair.'

'There isn't room,' said Susie, quickly. 'Come on. We need to go... and anyway, we can't just *budge up*. This isn't a music festival!' Her hand was gripping his elbow with the same force of a mother trying to remove her toddler from soft-play.

Tom looked at me again. 'Come on... Ava and Angela will be disappointed if you don't...'

I shook my head, aware of the laser focus of Susie. 'It's fine,' I said, 'I'm going to sit with everyone at the back.'

Susie dragged at Tom's arm again. 'Come on! Really, Tom!' she said, on the verge, I thought, of stamping her foot.

And then Tom removed her hand from his arm. 'I'll come in a moment, Susie,' he said, firmly.

Susie tilted her head to one side, and breathed out through her nostrils heavily. Her face, now furious and petulant, had lost some of its attractiveness. She opened her mouth to say something and then closed it again before turning on her heel and marching in to the ballroom.

Tom turned back to me. 'You sure?'

I nodded. 'Sure.'

As Tom left, Sinéad reappeared with a tray of Martinis. 'One for you, one for Conor and one for me,' she said. 'Ryan's not drinking in solidarity with Becca. Can you believe they're having a *baby*?'

'I'm having a meltdown, that's what I'm having,' said Becca, slipping in beside us. 'As is the bloody ice sculpture. We had to blow-dry it so it looks less like a penis. By the way, how good does Tom look in that suit? Like fecking James Bond. Now, come on, let's go and find some seats.'

At the back of the room, we found two sofas and sat down. Conor and Ryan were still in deep conversation about babies. 'So,' I heard Ryan say, 'during labour, what exactly are you meant to be doing?'

'Just repeating how amazing your partner is, how you could never do it,' said Conor. 'Just repeat that she's incredible.'

'Got it,' said Ryan.

'Now we can finally relax,' Becca said. 'I've done all I can. If there's any problems, they can phone me. Let the awards begin!'

Sinéad promptly put her head back and fell soundly asleep.

The lights in the room dimmed, but the stage was lit up as Phonsie O'Sullivan, one of the country's best-known comedians, walked on.

'Good evening, *cailíní agus buachaillí!* And to everyone watching at home, remember to have a drink every time an award winner says all they've ever wanted to do was to make people happy...'

51

Bathed in a pool of light, just in front of the stage, were the three Entertainment tables. Tom was in side profile, looking up at the stage, Susie was on one side, laughing at Phonsie's routine, and on Tom's other side was David – still in sunglasses – looking as though he was flagging somewhat, as though the caffeine was wearing off. Jennifer was sitting on David's left, scrolling through her phone, already bored.

'And now,' said Phonsie, 'time for Best Talk Show... please welcome Valentine O'Malley to present the award.'

We watched as Valentine hobbled on to the stage and read out the nominees. He opened the envelope, read the contents and squinted into the crowd. 'Well, thank feck for that,' he said. 'The award for Best Talk goes to *Dingo O'Bingo's Lingo...*'

I turned to Becca. 'We didn't win,' I said.

'That Dingo is an idiot,' she said. 'And he comes across as so nice on television.'

We watched as Dingo bounced on to stage, his comedy over-sized tie flapping as he dashed towards Valentine, arms outstretched. Angela and Ava clapped politely as David sank further into his seat.

'So,' whispered Becca to me, as Sinéad lolled beside us, 'do you think David will get Best Presenter?'

'I hope so,' I said. 'He deserves it.' None of the others in the category had his experience, his longevity, even his talent. But to many in the industry, he was a bit of a has-been, a relic of the golden age of television in the internet age.

Phonsie stepped forward, 'And now, to announce Best Male Presenter,' he said, 'is the sizzling quizzling mistress herself, Ms Susie Keane!'

I gripped Becca's hand tightly. Susie walked on stage, smiling, looking beautiful. 'I love all the nominees... they are all personal friends, and before I open the envelope I would just like to say good luck to you all, and please, guys,' she winked, 'don't hold it against me if you don't win. I'll see you all in the bar later...' As she held up the envelope, at the table below the stage, David stiffened to attention. 'And the winner of Best Male Presenter is... Paddy O'Grady! Of the Four Paddys! Come on up here, Paddy! I told you you'd win, didn't I?'

Paddy ran up on to the stage punching the air and tripped on the last step, landing in a heap at Susie's feet, to whoops from the audience, before staggering to his feet with the aid of Phonsie.

'Poor David,' said Becca, as we both strained to see.

Everyone else in the audience was listening and laughing along to Paddy's speech, but David had slumped in his chair, as though defeated at his very own Agincourt. Tom placed a hand on his arm, consoling him.

'I can't stand the Four Paddys,' said Becca. 'It's all shouting and football and talking about tractors. And now, they are probably going to fall out because one of them has won an award.'

'Then, it'll be the Three Paddys,' I said.

'And then the Two Paddys until it's just the One Paddy.'

David's sunglasses were crooked now, his lovely suit looked as though he'd slept in it and, like an ageing dog, his wig had lost its bounce. I wished there was something I could do to help.

Becca was flagging as well. 'I'm ready to go home,' she said, 'but we'll have to wait until the end, I suppose.'

'It can't be long now,' I said, as Sinéad's head lolled onto my shoulder. But I couldn't help thinking about David, this once great performer had been felled by the events of the last week. And these stupid awards hadn't helped matters, but he needed to just get through it, not fall, wounded, on this broadcasting battlefield.

Becca and I drank another lime and soda, teared up through the In Memoriam section, did Wordle on Becca's phone during an indulgent performance of modern dance and then, finally, we were on the home straight.

'I'm going to buy us some more drinks,' I said to Becca. 'Won't be long.'

I also ordered a Red Bull, and after leaving our drinks with Becca, picked my way through the tables, in the dark, towards the front of the room and placed the can in front of David. He looked every day of his seventy-three years. Susie was back in her seat and glaring over at me. 'David,' I said, 'drink this. Just to give you a little energy.' I looked at Jennifer. 'Is that okay?'

She nodded. 'Oh, thank God,' she said. 'That's exactly what he needs. Just a couple of sips and then he'll be fine. It worked wonders for him last time. Everything in moderation, right?'

She tried to put the can in David's hand, but Tom took it from her and then, like a parent feeding a baby, brought the can to David's lips. 'Just a little sip,' I heard him say, as I quickly returned to Becca.

Back in my seat, I watched David slowly come to life again, as though he was being refuelled.

Conversely, Becca was flagging even more. 'I've had enough of the awards,' she said. 'I've been working on these for ten whole months and all I want is to go home.' She smiled at me. 'They have been good though, haven't they?'

'It's been brilliant,' I said, my arm through hers. 'You've done an amazing job.'

'And now,' said Pat Coyle, one of the main news presenters, 'we have our Legend Award. It's a chance to show our appreciation to someone in the industry who has shown great longevity, someone who has brought style, sometimes chaos but always entertainment to our screens. It brings me great pleasure to award this year's Legend Award to the one, the only, Davy Fitz himself, Mr David Fitzgerald!'

The audience suddenly shot up out of their seats, clapping and cheering wildly. David remained seated, looking around, as though stunned, and Tom leaned down to say something in his ear and then began pulling him to his feet. David's face suddenly lit up as Tom gave him a push up to the stage and, after a kiss from Jennifer, he made his way, past the back-slappers and the high-fivers, dodging the hair-rufflers, grasping outstretched hands, stopping to hug Angela and finally making it to the podium.

He removed his sunglasses and, with the bruising much diminished, he had tears rolling down his face.

'I don't know what to say,' he began. 'It's such a surprise. I am honoured. Taken aback, if I may be honest. There was a time this year when I thought I was done. I was getting tired, the old bones had begun creaking. I would wake in the middle of the night and wonder if it wasn't over for me. Show business is a cruel mistress, it loves you deeply and adores you greatly. Until one day, you realise it has tired of you. And it's all gone, all that love, all that adoration. But I stand here today thinking of two women... one who started me on this journey, my dear, departed mam. And...' – he peered out into the audience – 'Jennifer, my partner, the person who talked me down from quitting earlier this year, who convinced me I was still worth something. Thank you for sticking with me. I hope the last few years haven't been too eventful and I hope you stick around a few years more. My mam taught singing and dance in the local hall in Drimnagh. She started me off on a life in show business and Mam believed in me, every step of the way. "David," she used to say, "not everyone is going to love you, but you don't worry about them. Worry about the ones who do." And sometimes...' His eyes looked heavenwards. 'Sometimes I forget those words. Sorry, Mam. I thank all of you for believing in me and perhaps, I dare to hope, that some of you here tonight love me.'

The audience cheered and stamped their feet as hard as possible. Even Ava looked as though she was about to cry.

'And I wish for one more thing,' he went on, using his hand to peer out to the crowd. 'Jennifer is out there somewhere. And she is yet to make an honest man out of me. And you know? I'd like to continue this journey with Jennifer, as my wife. Jennifer, will you marry me?'

A spotlight raced around the room until it landed on Jennifer who had her face in her hands. Someone ran over with a microphone.

'David, for God's sake!' she said, getting to her feet. 'I can't believe you've done this!'

'I have,' he said, smiling. 'I have. I am terrible, I really am!'

'Yes,' she said. 'Go on then, yes!'

And David, surprisingly athletic for his seventy-three years, jumped off the stage and ran over to her.

That was it from the night, we thought, and we found our bags and checked to see that Sinéad was still breathing. She was actually lightly snoring. Conor and Ryan were also asleep. But then Bryony Murphy from *Fair City* came on stage.

'And our last award this evening is the Rising Star Award...'

'Rising Star?' I said.

'She's been around for the last few years, but it's only been in the last four weeks she has shown her true talents...'

I looked at Becca.

'As we all know, live television is the hardest job in entertainment, yet our winner has performed foot yoga, learned how to unicycle and interviewed a motley crew of guests, and always with a calm good humour. Our Rising Star is Cat Jones!'

Becca looked at me, and I looked at Becca. 'What?' we both mouthed at each other.

'Come on, Cat!' said Bryony. 'Where are you?'

Everybody in the room turned around, as the spotlight again searched for me.

Becca pushed me forward, really hard, and I found myself, in a daze, trying to make my way to the stage, past tables of drunken media personalities, who clapped me all the way. All Four Paddys slapped me on the back.

Angela ran over and grabbed me. 'You deserve this!' she said. 'You've been amazing!'

After she released me, I was grabbed by Tom, who hugged me tightly. 'It's brilliant,' he was saying. 'You're amazing.'

Bryony came and took me by the hand. 'You deserve this, Cat,' she said, in my ear. 'All those toxic men we all have to deal with. Especially that *awful* PJ Doyle.'

I stood, holding the award, and stared out at the audience.

'I don't know what to say, except I've had a great summer,' I began. 'Working on *The Daily Show* has been an amazing experience. I've learned so much from the legend – now *officially* a legend – David Fitzgerald. To the brilliant team, everyone from Martin and Dmitri, to our wonderful researcher Ava, the world's greatest producer Angela and to Head of Entertainment Tom Doherty. And of course the brilliant Brenda Mulcahy in make-up and all the girls in wardrobe.' I was aware that the whole of the Entertainment table were on their feet. 'And most of all, I'd like to give a shout-out to my best friends, Becca and Sinéad, to my mum and dad who may be watching at home and a special mention to my sea swimming friends and to Mrs Murphy and all the other residents at Honeysuckle Lodge.' Something possessed me to hold up the award in victory – an act which haunted me for weeks afterwards. 'Thank you!'

But what I really wanted to say was how pleased I was that I had said yes to Tom that evening in The Island. My whole life seemed so incredibly different than it had four short weeks ago. It wasn't about saying yes to everything, or even no to everything, it was simply about being open to life and not being afraid. Saying yes was about being available to opportunity, to chance, to new adventures.

* * *

'I don't belieeeve it!' Becca shrieked, once we were reunited in the foyer, and suddenly there was a rush of people.

Angela was next and squeezed me so hard I stopped breathing. 'Amazing! Amazing!'

Ava gave me a thumbs up. 'Cool,' she said.

David looked thrilled. 'Well, it was quite a night for *The Daily Show*,' he said. 'We both came out with awards.'

And then there was Mike, my old producer. 'Congratulations!' he said, hugging me 'Taught you everything I know. Love it when a protégée does well.'

Becca still had her arm through mine when Ryan dropped to one knee in front of her. 'Oh God, Ryan's having a heart attack!' said Becca. 'I knew I shouldn't have done that spell on you...'

'Which spell...?' said Sinéad.

'To make him slow down and stop being so busy...'

But Ryan seemed completely fine and was now holding out his hand, which had a Haribo ring on it, and smiling up at Becca. 'Will you marry me?' he said.

'Oh God,' said Becca. 'Really? You're actually doing this?'

Ryan nodded. 'Yes, I am actually doing it and if you would hurry up and give me an answer, then I can stand up again.'

She smiled at him. 'Yes,' she said. 'Yes, I will marry you, Ryan. Only, can we get married somewhere unconventional? We don't want to be complete sell-outs. Somewhere like Donnybrook Bus Depot or the recycling treatment centre at Ballymount?'

'Anything for you,' said Ryan, standing up and kissing her. 'Whatever my beautiful Becca and my marvellous Marvin or Mabel desires.'

We only had a few moments to hug them both and dance around a bit before there was a tap on my shoulder.

Tom.

'It's fantastic,' he was saying. 'What a brilliant surprise. None of us knew about it. How are you feeling?'

'I don't know,' I said. 'I mean, aren't you the one who said awards don't matter...'

'Until you win one,' he laughed. 'Anyway, I talk bollocks most of the time, so don't take anything I say too seriously. I'm just pleased for you.'

'I'm pleased for David, as well,' I said.

'Thank God he won,' Tom said. 'That Red Bull was a genius move. How did you know it would help him? I was so worried about him. I was ready to call 999 again.'

'I just thought he needed another boost.'

We looked over at David, who was back to his effervescent TV-self, shaking hands, laughing, back-slapping, making jokes, the life and soul of the party.

'I just spoke to Jennifer,' said Tom, 'she's getting him on a green-juice diet and off the caffeine from Monday. But even she thought it was a good idea...'

'For one night only.'

'For one night only,' he repeated, looking straight at me. 'Sometimes the one-night-only occasions are the best.'

'Sometimes,' I said, swallowing hard. Was he referring to *us*?

'Except sometimes, they are so good, you want more,' he said.

'Yes...' I croaked, still looking up at him. 'Where's...?' I began. 'Where's...?'

'Who?'

'Susie? It's none of my business anyway.'

'I told you there was nothing between us,' he said. 'But what about that man you swim with?'

'Which man?'

'The man you ran off to be with?'

'Who?' I tried to think who on earth could he mean. '*Malachy*?' I nearly laughed.

'Is that his name? Yes, then him. Your swimmer. The man who is so *good* to everyone, you said. You couldn't wait to get away from me that day. I was ready to suggest we go for a walk and go for some lunch but you were like Sonia O'Sullivan trying to get away.'

'I left because I thought you were trying to get rid of me. The tea and toast was your polite way of saying goodbye.'

'It was my way of saying please stay, actually.' He looked at me.

'And I was so embarrassed because I had thrown myself at you...'

'Au contraire,' he said. 'It was me who threw himself at you. I hadn't met anyone like you in... well, ever. And then, just when I was trying to get you out of my mind and tell myself you were obviously not interested and far more into the swimmer man...'

I laughed. 'Malachy.'

'My rival Malachy,' he said, 'well, I went out with my friends, trying to forget about you and then I see you at the supper club and I fell for you all over again. And then it was game over, really, I was just so into you. I just couldn't stop thinking about you and even dragged my poor mother out to Sandycove, just in case we bumped into you...' He paused. 'I didn't actually *expect* to see you, I just needed to be near where you were... at that point I was going slightly mad. Mam knew something was up and when I saw her off at the train the following evening, she kissed me goodbye and said that I was a star worth catching and that she hoped I had found mine, just as she found Dad.' He looked at me. 'I thought I was going to start crying in Heuston Station, in front of everyone, but I just managed to wave her off and pretend she hadn't said anything. But...' He paused and took my hand. 'The thing is I haven't been able to get you out of my mind. And the thought of not seeing you on Monday is killing me. So, no, not Susie. Never Susie.' He paused. 'Just you.'

And then I saw Susie, on the other side of the foyer, snogging one of the Four Paddys – the one, I think, who had just won the award. Susie, I knew, was going to be fine.

'I think you're pretty wonderful,' Tom said, 'if I'm honest. And I don't care any more. I have to tell you and if I never see you again, then at least you know. Full disclosure. Cards on the table. Heart open. Ready. Waiting.' He cleared his throat. 'Well, just that, really.'

But we were smiling at each other. Me gazing up at him, him down at me. His hand still holding mine.

'In fact,' he went on, 'I think you're magnificent. Properly magnificent. As in heroically so. Look,' he said, 'I like you. A lot. I would like to spend more time with you, away from television, away from all this...'

I nodded. 'I feel the same way. Exactly the same way. The thought of not seeing you again is horrible.' And then I had an idea. 'The sea?' I said. 'Would you like to come swimming with me? Tomorrow?'

He nodded. 'I'd do anything with you...'

We didn't kiss then, however much I wanted to, however close his mouth was to mine, but we did later, when we got back to mine and we went to bed and stayed there until Sunday evening when we went for our first swim together.

THE GIRLS!

Sinéad: AMAZING night. Thank you!!! Bit of a headache this morning (under-exaggeration). Conor has brought Rory swimming. Currently planning work wardrobe. Jackets still fit. How are you both?

Becca: I feel incredible! Slept very well! Relieved it's all over, happy that nothing went wrong.

Sinéad: It was fabulous. Everyone had so much fun, and Conor's mother watched it live on TV and said it looked brilliant. Very glamorous. Enjoy your lazy mornings while they last. Still in shock about the BIG ANNOUNCEMENT! So happy for you!

Becca: I am still in shock as well. Ryan very calm and chilled! He's gone out to buy some baby books.

Sinéad: You can have all of mine. And baby clothes. Will drop them round.

Becca: That would be great 😊 🩶 thank you xx

Sinéad: Any word from Cat?

Becca: Last seen going off in a taxi with Tom Doherty… looking pretty pleased with herself. So was he. The two of them couldn't stop smiling.

Sinéad: We'll never see her again, will we?

Becca: Bye, Cat! Thanks for everything!

Sinéad: Cat, when you read this, you have to tell us EVERYTHING!

Becca: And he has our seal of approval!

Sinéad: Although, we are rubbish judges of character. We liked PJ!!!???

Becca: I didn't.

Sinéad: You did!

Me: I'm here! Can't talk now. Bit busy. Will text later. Love you girls!

Sinéad: Love you, Cat! Love you, Becca!

Becca: Love you two. By the way, will you be godmothers to Mabel? Or Marvin?

Sinéad: I will speak on behalf of the two of us. We would be honoured! LOVE YOU BOTH xxx

52

A week later, on a cloud-free, end-of-August morning, Tom and I drove Mum, Dad and Lorraine to the Bray Aerodrome. Tom and I stood nearby while the hospice fundraisers put on their boiler suits, strapped on their parachutes and were about to board a tiny, rickety-looking plane.

Lorraine, dressed in a lime-green boiler suit, seemed to behave as though she had done a thousand jumps before, taking on a certain leadership role, checking everyone's harnesses. I was relieved to see a huge man with a tiny moustache went round rechecking them. I assumed this was Wing Commander Kettle.

We watched as Lorraine laid a hand on his arm. 'Now, you promise me, the parachute is going to open, isn't it, Wing Commander?' she said, fluttering those heavily mascaraed eyelashes which had been men's downfall for at least the last half a century. 'Or you'll have to grab on to me.' She laughed gaily.

'I think,' Wing Commander Kettle said, moustache twitching, 'you'll find I'm at your service.'

Dad gave us a look. 'Husband number five right there,' he said, quietly, but Lorraine was laughing a little too hard to hear him. 'Mark my words.'

I hugged Mum and Dad goodbye. 'Thanks for being great parents,' I said. 'I've really enjoyed knowing you.'

'We will see you both in precisely thirty minutes,' said Dad. 'Every limb intact. And money raised for the hospice. And then we're all going for lunch. Okay?' He looked over at Tom. 'What do you say, Tom? Think I'm going to do it?'

'I don't doubt it.' Tom slipped his hand into mine. 'We'll be here to sweep up the pieces if you don't.'

Dad laughed. 'Oh, ye of little faith.'

I felt Tom squeeze my hand and I squeezed back. Since the evening of the ITAs, we'd spent the whole week together, in and out of each other's houses, swimming in the sea, even beach cleaning with the Flotsam Army and piecing together the jigsaw of each other's lives – 'so after college... and then... so, you went travelling when?', that kind of thing – and trying to see if we could make a jigsaw with his pieces of life and mine. And so far, the picture was coming along nicely. Yes, *of course* I could do life *alone*, but I thought I just may have met someone who made it even better.

I hadn't expected to be falling in love and I felt that perhaps now I understood it a little better. Love came from the inside out, from deep within and then wrapped you up within it. A bit, I thought, like the sea.

Across the hangar, Lorraine was looking a little ashen for the first time that day.

'Don't worry,' Mum said to her. 'We're in this together.'

'I suppose,' said Lorraine, in a slightly trembling voice, 'what goes up, must come down. I just can't wait to be having a gin and tonic at the end of it all.'

'Just imagine you're a bird,' said Wing Commander Kettle.

'What kind of bird?' Lorraine said.

'Well,' said Dad, 'as long as it isn't a dodo, we'll be grand.'

And then they were gone. Out of the door of the terminal and on to the little bus which brought them to the plane which looked smaller and more decrepit than planes should. Tom and I watched as they chugged higher and higher into the sky. And then it seemed to hover in the air. We squinted, shielding our eyes as tiny ants appeared, one by one. Two of which, we knew, were Mum and Dad.

It was one of the strangest feelings in the world to see your parents suddenly so small, so incredibly vulnerable, so out of their comfort zones. I craned my neck. *Please let them be okay*, I thought. I kept my eyes fixed on the dots in the sky. One figure seemed to be plummeting to earth, like a rocket going the wrong way. 'That's Dad,' I said. 'I'm sure of it.' I clutched Tom's hands.

And then the plummeting Dad was suddenly caught on a current of air and was whisked and whirled around and up, his arms and legs outstretched. And then he caught the hand of one of the other dots and they held on. Mum and Dad were holding hands in the sky. They were my heroes. Always had been. I could swear I could see them smiling.

The parachutes of the others opened one by one, but Mum and Dad were still whirling and floating high above everyone else. And then, they let go of each other. They landed two fields away, Dad first, his body folding in two and then immediately submerged. And then Mum fell to earth in a cloud of parachute. And then nothing...

I ceased to breathe. Clutching Tom's hand tightly, I strained my eyes, waiting for a sign of life. *Please be okay*. A life with my parents played in my mind: birthdays, Christmases, Dad in his shed, Mum giving me my grandmother's bracelet, the two of us with tears in our eyes. *Please be okay*.

And then a wriggle and, a moment later, out and up staggered Dad, and from under her parachute out crawled Mum. Tom and I watched as they then began to stumble towards one another and fall into each other's arms. They looked as though they were laughing.

'When I'm that age,' said Tom, looking straight into my eyes, 'I want to be like them. I want *us* to be just like that.'

* * *

At lunch, Mum and Dad were euphoric, both of them talking over each other, excitedly telling their tale of heading up into the clouds and then jumping out. 'It's amazing what can happen when you say yes,' said Mum.

I nodded. I'd already come to that realisation.

'Maybe,' said Dad, 'Lorraine isn't as hare-brained as I previously thought. I take it all back.'

Tom seemed to really like them and when we dropped them home, Mum whispered to me as we changed seats, 'I love him. One of those good men. Like your father.'

When Tom had gone home quickly to feed Pierre and get his swimming trunks, I called Becca.

'What about a swim? You and Ryan? Forty Foot? In an hour?'

'In the *sea*?'

'Of course in the sea! And then an ice cream. Just say yes.'

'Yes,' she said, and then I heard her shouting, 'Ryan! Grab your togs! We're going swimming. It will be good for the baby!'

I called Sinéad next. 'Would you and Rory like to come swimming in the Forty Foot? Now?'

'The sea?' she said. 'No. Never.'

'Go on,' I said. 'Get Conor to come too.'

'He's right beside me,' she said. 'He'll say no, too. Conor, would you like to go for a swim? In the sea? What? No, come on, please don't make me? It's not a fun family activity! It's too cold!' And then she laughed. 'Yes, I do remember. No, I haven't forgotten.' She came back to me. 'Conor is reminding me that we used to swim every day that first summer we met. He wants to bring back the tradition.' She laughed again. 'So, yes, we'll be there.'

I was just about to leave when the doorbell rang. Callum and Loulou were standing there, Loulou with her pink rucksack on her back.

'We've just come to say hello,' said Callum, smiling brightly. 'We were on our way back from the park and we thought we'd just drop in. They've got this amazing zip line which we both went on, didn't we, Loulou?'

She nodded, gazing up at me.

'That sounds fun,' I said, 'would you like to come in? I have some apple juice...'

'We can't,' said Callum, smiling. 'Denise is making chilli and... well, we don't want to be late.'

'Well, that sounds nice.' I smiled at Loulou. 'Better than pizza.'

Loulou nodded again. 'Daddy says we'll all still be friends,' she said.

'Of course we will be,' I said. 'Always.'

She looked a little upset. 'But I liked having two houses. It felt like going on holiday every week.'

'But this way you get to have both your mum and your dad,' I said to her. '*All* the time. Isn't that perfect?'

'We're going swimming tomorrow,' said Loulou. 'Just Daddy and me.'

Callum nodded. 'There's a family fun swim at the pool and there's a slide and I think there are inflatables.'

Loulou smiled. 'And Daddy brings me to his café and gives me extra cream on my hot chocolate.'

'She's my best helper,' said Callum. 'Wipes down the tables, sweeps up the crumbs. Don't you?'

She nodded. 'I would like my own café one day. Miss Lally says it is important to have dreams. Without dreams, she says, life is very boring.'

'We'd better go,' said Callum, and I hugged him goodbye and then I turned to face Loulou. 'Now, remember, you know where I am,' I began, when suddenly I felt something push against me, as though I'd been tackled by a tiny rugby player. Loulou's arms were around my waist as she clung on, eyes scrunched shut. 'Oh Loulou...' I stroked her hair and leaned down and kissed the top of her head.

'I won't ever see you again,' she said. She was crying.

'You will see me,' I said. 'Whenever you want. We can go to the cinema or you could come and watch films with me. I'd love to see more *Tracy Beaker*. Would you like that?' I kneeled down and hugged her back, just as hard.

'I liked you being my friend,' she said.

'I liked it too,' I said. 'But it's brilliant that so many people love you. You're a very lovable girl.'

She nodded again, being brave, and then picked up her rucksack and pulled out a book. 'It's my copy of *Tracy Beaker*,' she said. 'I thought that because you liked the television programme you might like to read the book.'

'I will start it tonight,' I promised, still kneeling down, and taking it. 'And I will make sure I get it back to you.'

'I don't mind if you lose it,' she said, 'or it gets ruined because I would prefer you to enjoy it and for something to happen to it than not read it because you were afraid of ruining it.'

I looked at her. 'Loulou,' I said, 'I think you might have said one of the wisest things I've ever heard. Life is for living, like books are for reading. And if on the way, you get a bit battered, then at least you've lived.'

She nodded thoughtfully. 'Like Tracy Beaker. Nothing stopped her.'

'No, nothing will ever stop her. Just like you.'

Loulou took out her 'yes' necklace and held it up to me. 'I say yes,' she said. 'To everything now. Just like you.'

I dug my necklace out and showed it to her. 'Yes,' I said. 'Let's keep saying yes.'

She smiled then, her arms around my neck and I felt her mouth kiss the side of my hair.

'By the way,' Callum said, as I got to my feet again, 'the TV went down very well in Honeysuckle Lodge. They were all stuck watching a tiny old thing, now they have surround sound, high definition.'

'All the better to watch David!' I said.

They walked off together, hand in hand, and Callum glanced back and gave me a smile. 'Thanks,' he said and lifted his hand in a wave.

'Good luck,' I called. 'Both of you!'

* * *

The sea was glorious. The Forty Footers were already there getting changed. Brenda was most interested to see Tom. 'I thought you weren't the sea swimming type,' she said to him. 'And I don't recognise you in shorts.'

'I do have another life away from the office, Brenda,' he said. 'My hinterland is wide and varied.'

'Good to know,' she said. 'We all need a hinterland. Mine is a hintersea.'

I introduced him to the rest of the gang, including Mick, who wouldn't get in but was there to 'look after the things'.

'How's your mam?' I asked Malachy.

'Grand,' he said. 'Brenda was in all day doing all their hair and nails. And the men as well.'

'We didn't leave anyone behind,' said Brenda. 'Luckily, I had help. Nora and Lorraine were on nail-painting duty and Dolores, turns out, is a dab hand at the old blow-dry.'

'I used to do my mam's and her friends for a few pounds back in the day,' said Dolores. 'I'd put their hair in rollers on a Saturday afternoon, they'd give me a fiver and I'd go off to the pub.' She shrugged. 'And that's how it all began.'

When Sinéad, Conor and Rory arrived, followed by Becca and Ryan, we all waded into the water. Seeing the looks on Becca and Sinéad's faces reminded me how far I'd come when it came to cold water. Ryan and Conor threw themselves in off the furthest rock, but Sinéad and Becca, squealing and holding my hands, tiptoed down the steps until eventually they dunked their shoulders under. Rory watched, fascinated, from the benches.

Tom and I swam out to the old red buoy and for a moment we paddled around. He turned over onto his back, his toes poking up. 'I need to persuade you to do more TV. You've won that award now, you've proven you can do live television, you can handle chaos. I want to change the afternoon. Barbara has really lost interest. She called me on Friday afternoon saying she needed another week off... but...' – he flipped over again – 'a little bird, aka Barbara's agent, has told me she's moving to Mallorca to open a bar. She's just holding out for a nice little payout.'

'Are you going to give it to her?'

He nodded. 'She deserves it,' he said. 'Forty years' loyal service.' His hand caught hold of mine. 'Look, I don't usually hold meetings in the sea, but I really want you to do it. And I've just heard that I've been promoted, so I won't be so hands-on. Which might make it less awkward between us. Angela and Ava want to work with you again. What about your own show? At lunchtime – cooking, chat, consumer stuff. *Lunch With Cat* or something.'

I stopped paddling for a moment and let my body drift with the gentle current. I should say no, I thought. I should just go back to *Farming Weekly* where it wasn't live, where if things went wrong you could make them right again. What if I was terrible? What if no one watched it? But then I thought of Mum and Dad falling out of an aeroplane. I thought of David refusing to give in, and of Sinéad and her determination to keep going after her miscarriage and Becca who found another way of living. If it went wrong, it went wrong. And it didn't matter. If I was going to fail, I may as well fail big.

'Yes,' I said. 'Yes...'

Tom smiled and moved towards me, and there, in the sea, he kissed me... just long enough for me to feel that life couldn't get any better and long enough for me to remember the huge changes that can come about by saying a tiny word. Yes. Yes meant life. Yes meant being open to everything. And the only way to live was to take risks and put yourself out there. Because that was where the fun and adventure was. Whatever happened, I knew I was ready.

BIG MOVES ON THE SMALL SCREEN

FAB NEW OPPORTUNITIES FOR IRELAND'S TOP TV TALENT

By Shazza Keegan – chief showbiz editor

Irish TV's autumn schedule was revealed today, with some significant changes to some of the country's favourite shows, meaning some of our stars will be busier than ever!!! Held at Dublin's swankiest eatery, Chez Peej, I caught up with some of our fave TV peeps to hear all the goss from TV land.

Legendary presenter David Fitzgerald – Davy Fitz to his legions of fans!!!! – made the whole country weep when he announced he will be leaving The Daily Show, after twenty-seven mega years. However, sob no more, as Davy will be fronting his own eponymous daytime chat show called David! When asked about the exclamation mark, David said, 'My mother said I was always destined to stand out and punctuation does just that.'

On leaving The Daily Show, he added, 'It's not a goodbye, just an adieu to my bosom pals there and bonjour to my new friends at David! We have a great set which will be like welcoming everyone into my own home. Not my actual home, of course!!! But an approximation, only not quite as grand. I will be "shooting the breeze", as they say, with old and new friends, and bringing some of the Davy Fitz glamour to the nation.'

David is busy planning his wedding to gorge long-time girlfriend, Jennifer. 'I don't know how she puts up with me, I really don't,' he said. 'We're hoping my old pal Lulu will be on hand to officiate and wise old sage Ronan Keating will be flying in to sing "Life Is A Rollercoaster". And once we're back from our honeymoon, I will be ready to focus on David! The audience will be my own generation – the silver foxes and vixens – and we'll show that we're all still ready to rock and indeed roll!!!'

Barb's new life

More changes in tellyland include the retirement of David's long-time Daily Show co-host Barbara Brennan, who is moving to Mallorca to run an Irish-themed pub. 'It's a big change for me,' Barbara said. 'But one I will relish. After my accident, I took time to re-evaluate my life and work out what exactly is important to me. Television is a superfluous activity and I believe it's time to go and do something with meaning. At Barb's Bar, we look forward to welcoming the Irish on holiday, except, naturally, those with tattoos and criminal records.' See you in Santa Ponsa, Barb!!!!

Cooking up a storm

Sexy chef, PJ Doyle, hosted the launch and told me he's bored of being on TV. 'It's a dying medium,' he said. 'My passion remains in the restaurant.' Nothing to do with the fact that he is rumoured to be persona non grata in tellyland after throwing a few hissy fits on and off the screen? We've all heard about wiggate, where Davy Fitz's hairpiece was dislodged by PJ. But the fiery chef told me that all was well. 'I am just not that into it,' he said. 'The TV guys lined up some new ideas for shows but none of them were as interesting to me as cooking in my restaurant.'

Whatever, PJ! We believe you!!!!

The Cat who got the cream

Rising star, Cat Jones, also fresh from success at the ITAs, has been tasked with a new, female-focused show, Cat's Lunch. 'I'm looking forward to bringing stories from women to television screens,' she said. 'I learned so much from working with David over the summer and I hope I can bring some of what I have gleaned to my new role.'

Cat is bringing some of the Daily Show team with her, including top TV researcher Ava Smyth. 'We hope we will have the right balance of fun and serious topics, as though you are sitting down with close friends.'

Sounds fab, Cat, crack open the Prosecco!!!!!

Movers and shakers

More big news as Paddy O'Gara has announced he is moving on from The Four Paddys, after his recent Irish Television Award. Paddy admitted saying goodbye to the other Paddys has been hard. 'The lads have been like brothers to me. That is, if you were allowed to have the same name as your brothers, which, as far as I know, is illegal. But it's time to move on with Susie by my side.'

Susie Keane – in case you haven't been keeping up with all the showbiz goss!!!! – is his new girlfriend, the über-gorgeous star of the nation's fave Saturday night show Quiz Me I'm Irish.

'We're taking it slowly,' said Susie, 'but we're excited about our new adventure, Kiss Me I'm Irish, where wannabe romantics have to kiss a stranger to see if sparks fly. Just like me and Paddy.'

Galway's finest

Another big TV move is that of top exec Tom Doherty, who is moving to an even bigger job – that of Head of Television. 'I'm sad to leave Entertainment, but my focus will now be on the whole of the station. As well, of course, as watching Galway win the All-Ireland this year!' You can take a man out of Galway, but you can't wrestle him out of his jersey!!! Am I right?!!

And rumour has it that handsome Tom is courting the gorgeous Cat Jones after they were seen at Bray Aerodrome holding hands. 'We're very happy,' said Tom. 'Cat's a huge talent and I know that the new Head of Entertainment, Angela Browne, will look after her, as she will look after all my stars and shows.'

Special place

Tom and Cat have also been spotted in the sea at Sandycove's famous bathing place, the Forty Foot, and having a post-dip glass of wine with a tribe of swimmers. 'The sea saved my sanity,' said Cat. 'I don't know what I would have done without it. It's an ocean of peace out there.' Looks like Cat has found her special place on and off the screen!!!

EPILOGUE

EIGHT MONTHS LATER…

It was the end of April when we drove to Dublin port to wave Mum and Dad off on their big voyage through France and the full length of Spain, to Morocco, and back through Spain, and down through Italy and then… they hadn't planned the next leg of the journey, but all they knew was that it was going to take as long as it took. The last time I'd seen them this excited was just after the parachute jump.

They had bought a camper van at Christmas and Dad had spent the last few months tweaking the engine, twiddling the knobs, or whatever he had to do to make it roadworthy. And the day had finally come when they were departing on their big adventure, the van piled high with essentials for the trip.

'I think I have enough teabags to last the year,' said Mum. 'Is 1,250 enough?'

'I'll send some,' I said. 'If you run out, send me an SOS.'

Tom had been helping Dad peel and stick the 'IRL' sticker for the back of the van. 'Just in case there are other Irish on the roads,' Dad said. 'They can give us a toot.' He turned to Tom. 'When are you two coming out to stay with us again?'

'When you get to that campsite in Biarritz,' said Tom. 'In July...' He gave me that smile of his which always melted me from the inside out. 'On your way back from Spain...'

'Lorraine and the Wing Commander are insisting we stay with them, in their apartment in Malaga,' said Mum. 'Lorraine says it will be too hot in the van. She's going to take time off from the estate agency so she can show us around. She sold three apartments last week. All to Irish people fed up with the Irish weather. And we'll be able to still watch you on your show every day. Lorraine says she watches *Cat's Lunch* without fail. Siesta time, you see.'

The cars in the long line began to move towards the ferry. 'We'd better go,' said Dad. 'And don't you have the christening to go to?'

'It's tomorrow,' said Mum.

'Naming ceremony, actually,' I said. 'Mabel Catríona Sinéad Egan-Walsh.'

'That's quite the name,' said Mum.

'Which is why it needs a whole ceremony,' I said, smiling at her, just as I noticed tears welling up in her eyes.

'I hate saying goodbye,' she said.

'But it's not goodbye,' I said, stoically. 'We'll see you soon.'

'I'll miss you,' she said. 'And you, Tom. Both of you. And give my love to your mother, Tom. Tell her thank you for the books. They'll keep us going for months. And we're looking forward to seeing her in Nice, in September, when she's there with her French group. It was such a coincidence that she was going. And you two could come as well? We could make it a family thing?'

I nodded. 'Why not? Sounds lovely.' Since Tom and I had been together, we had spent many weekends in Galway, staying with his mother, helping on the farm, going for long walks over fields together, hearing his stories of growing up and falling in love with his home place, just as he had fallen in love with mine.

'Look after her, Tom,' said Mum, before hugging me. 'I love you.'

'I love you too.' I wiped away a tear. 'Say hi to Lorraine.'

'And give Mabel Maggie a kiss from me. And little Rory.'

'Sinéad has promised him ice cream,' I said. 'He says his favourite is a 99, but Conor says he needs to try a choc ice. His mind is going to be blown.'

Mum laughed. 'I am so glad,' she said. 'He's a lovely boy. And did I tell you I saw little Loulou the other day? She was running through the supermarket and I heard this voice shout my name.'

'She just won a creative writing competition,' I said. 'I met her and Callum. Won first prize for her story called "The Hot Press of Doom".'

'Sounds a winner to me,' said Mum.

'Wait... I almost forgot.' I reached behind and unclasped my necklace. 'Remember this? The "yes" necklace. You wear it and remind yourself the power of "yes".' I wound it round Mum's neck and fastened it at the back. 'There,' I said. 'To bring you luck.'

Mum turned to me. 'We'd better go...'

'If you don't, you'll regret it. And we'll talk every day,' I promised.

We waved them off as the engine rattled to life and the van joined the long queue of cars ready to board the ferry to Cherbourg.

'You okay?' said Tom, his arm around me.

I nodded. 'I'm more than okay.' I smiled at him. 'I'm amazing. Tom,' I said, 'you know we are going swimming later...'

'Of course,' he replied.

'What would you like to do until then? It's Saturday afternoon and isn't a certain team playing in Croke Park today?'

'Galway semi-final,' he said. 'We could go home and watch it? And then go swimming?'

'Or...' –I reached into my bag – 'we could just drive to Croke Park and see the match live? I managed to get two tickets...'

'Really?' He turned to me, grinning. 'Seriously? The whole of Galway are going. There's not a single ticket left to be had. Even I couldn't get one, and I rang every contact I had. How did you get it?'

'Oh, friends in high places,' I said. 'David Fitzgerald was given two VIP tickets and he passed them on to me. He's giving a TED Talk today, the title is *Ageing Brilliantly – How to do it without needles or nonsense, embracing experience and inner wisdom*. Something like that anyway.'

Tom laughed. 'Cat Jones,' he said. 'Did anyone ever tell you how magnificent you are?'

'Takes one to know one,' I said, and reached over and kissed him. 'Come on, let's go and see Galway win!'

And we did. And *they* were magnificent, trouncing Mayo and leading the whole stadium in a rendition of 'The Fields of Athenry'.

* * *

Later, at the Forty Foot, at sunset, the sea cold, the April air chilly, just as Margaret was handing out the cups for our tea and I was busy handing around slices of Sally-Anne's lemon drizzle cake, Tom stood up.

'Ladies, gentlemen...' He nodded over to Mick and to Malachy. 'I hope you don't mind me interrupting...'

Everyone looked up, intrigued.

'Just that...' Tom turned to me. 'I wonder would you, Cat, contemplate or consider or even do me the honour of giving the idea of marrying me a second thought? Life with you is always fun, continuously joyful... and I am just so happy when I am with you... even if it does involve swimming in subarctic waters...'

The Forty Footers were leaning forward, listening, nudging

each other excitedly. Margaret squeezed the hand of Jess, Malachy's girlfriend – who always joined us whenever she wasn't on some nineteen-hour shift. Dolores and Mick gave each other a quick kiss and even Nora, whom I would have thought was above such nonsense, looked delighted.

Brenda, who had the aged Arthur in a wicker basket at her feet, gave me a wink. 'Taught the two of them everything they know,' she said.

'Yes,' I said to Tom. 'Of course I will. Yes.' It was the easiest 'yes' I ever had to give, and as the waves crashed against the rocks behind us and the Forty Footers all clapped and cheered, and Dolores whistled, we kissed. My favourite person, my special place and my tribe. Yes was definitely my favourite word.

ACKNOWLEDGMENTS

Thank you...

As always to my fabulous agent, Ger Nichol, who is always so kind and thoughtful, and cheering me on...

To the dynamic and brilliant Boldwood team, especially Caroline, Amanda, Nia, Jenna and Ross Dickinson...

To my own tribe of lovely friends...

To my dad, for reading my books – and in memory of our wonderful bookshop...

And most of all, as always, to my amazing Ruby who makes the world and *my* little world a far better place.

MORE FROM SIÂN O'GORMAN

We hope you enjoyed reading *The Sandycove Sunset Swimmers*. If you did, please leave a review.

If you'd like to gift a copy, this book is also available as an ebook, large print, hardback, digital audio download and audiobook CD.

Sign up to Siân O'Gorman's mailing list for news, competitions and updates on future books.

https://bit.ly/SianOGormannewsletter

Explore more heartwarming, emotional Irish stories from Siân O'Gorman...

ABOUT THE AUTHOR

Siân O'Gorman was born in Galway on the West Coast of Ireland, grew up in the lovely city of Cardiff, and has found her way back to Ireland and now lives on the east of the country, in the village of Dalkey, just along the coast from Dublin. She works as a radio producer for RTE.

Follow Siân on social media:

facebook.com/sian.ogorman.7
twitter.com/msogorman
instagram.com/msogorman
bookbub.com/authors/sian-o-gorman

Milton Keynes UK
Ingram Content Group UK Ltd.
UKHW041254140524
442697UK00032B/517